LINE OF SUCCESSION

William Tyree

This book is a work of fiction. Names, characters, places and incidents are products of the author's imagination or are used fictitiously. Any semblance to actual events, locations, names or persons living or dead is entirely coincidental.

Published in the United States by Massive Publishing.
MassivePublishing.net
ISBN: 9780615302317
Library of Congress Control Number: 2009905688

Keywords: Thriller, Political Thriller, Water Rights, World Water Shortage, Wars over Water, Blake Carver Books, Fiction, Espionage, Action Thriller, Military Thriller, Suspense, Spy Novel, Terrorism, Terror Attacks, Counter-Terrorism, CIA, NSA, CENTCOM, Intelligence, Political Assassination, Capitol Hill, White House, Special Forces, Security Contractor, Military Coup, Iran, Syria, Israel, Middle East, Washington D.C., Line of Presidential Succession, United States, USA

Story by William Tyree. Edited by Matthew Hoffman and Michelle Dalton Tyree. Proofed by Jacqueline Doucette. Cover design by Brion Sausser. Author photo by Jon White.

PART I

"The Pentagon's reliance on outside contractors ...amounts to a second, private, army, larger than the United States military force, and one whose roles and missions and even casualties among its work force have largely been hidden from public view."

The New York Times

Fort Bragg, North Carolina
Thursday, August 18, 2:25 a.m.

The steady cadence of cricket chirping echoed throughout the enlisted men's barracks. Private Matt Doheny roused from sleep, his sheets sweat-soaked, the balls of his feet stinging from a 10-mile march through North Carolina hill country. He checked his watch and fell back asleep until the cricket's looping high-decibel strain resumed. The racket was coming from under the bunk bed he shared with Private Walker. The jumbo-size insects at Fort Bragg beat anything the Boston native had ever seen. From his perch on the top bunk, Doheny turned and shined his penlight over the side of the bed. Sweat trickled off his nose and onto Private Walker's outstretched arm. Walker didn't wake. The cricket flitted into the shadows.

Doheny grabbed his can of spray insecticide, a recent acquisition that had prompted the other soldiers to dub him "Private Orkin," and descended stealthily down the bunk bed ladder. He stretched his beanpole physique flat on the concrete floor and, holding the insecticide at the ready, shined the light under the bed frame. Nothing. Seconds later, the chirping resumed on the other side of the room.

A kneecap bored into Doheny's back. A hand slipped over his lips before he could scream. "Easy there, bug man," a voice whispered into his ear. Doheny recognized the hoarse drawl of his unit's Commanding

Officer, Lieutenant James Flynn. "Dressed and outside in sixty seconds."

The CO uncoiled and exited the room as quietly as he had entered it. Doheny scrambled into his khaki utility uniform and canvas boots and emerged into the sticky mosquito-swarmed night 34 seconds later.

Flynn stood some distance away, scowling, with his hands on his hips. The creases of his forest-green trousers were impeccably starched. Doheny ran to him and stopped at attention, saluting, his eyes fixed on an imaginary point across the darkened Army base. It was important not to make eye contact with Flynn. Especially when you were in trouble.

"I'm not even goin' to ask why you were half-naked on the floor next to Private Walker's bunk," the Lieutenant growled. "Anyone out of their bunk after lights out will work. That is the policy. Are you familiar with the policy?"

"Sir, yes sir!" Doheny bleated, though he was tempted to explain about the cricket.

"Hold out your hand, Private." Doheny held his right hand out, his palm facing the tiny sliver of moon overhead. Lieutenant Flynn pressed two keys into it. Doheny closed his hand into a fist but continued to stare straight ahead as Flynn drummed his orders into him: "The first key operates the motor pool gate. The second key operates Humvee OU-505. You will go directly to the motor pool and drive the Humvee out past the checkpoint until you are off base. Then you will stop the vehicle. Four minutes from now, a phone will ring. You will open the glove compartment. You will see the phone. You will answer it. You will listen to the next set of instructions. Got it?"

"Sir, yes sir," Doheny repeated, although in his anxiety he was afraid that he had not absorbed all the Lieutenant's directives. And he was downright petrified at the prospect of leaving base without an official travel authorization, but he wasn't about to ask the Lieutenant for one now.

Lieutenant Flynn stormed away without another word. Doheny sprinted to the motor pool. As the boots rubbed against his blisters, he realized that he had neglected to put on socks.

He found the open-air, forest-green Humvee easily, put it in gear and drove it past the checkpoint, where the gate was already raised for him. As he drove past, he noticed that the Humvee's rear end sat low on its shocks. There was something heavy in the back.

The headlights were suddenly thick with mosquitoes. Doheny stepped on the gas and raced through the swarm, hoping to avoid adding to the two dozen chigger welts he had already picked up in this insect-infested swamp of a state.

Once off base, Doheny did not stop the vehicle as Flynn had requested. But sure enough, the phone rang, just as the Lieutenant had said it would. Doheny pulled off to the side of the road, opened the glove compartment and found the disposable handset. He answered. "Reset your GPS," Lieutenant Flynn told him without preamble. "Head south for exactly twenty-two-point-six miles."

Doheny felt compelled to give his exact location. "Right now I'm about –"

"I know where you are!" Flynn shouted. "When the GPS odometer reads twenty-two-point-six miles, you should see FR 66B. Take this road north for exactly one mile. Then park and shut off the engine. Leave the vehicle lights on. Do not leave the vehicle for any reason. Do not make any other calls. Await further instructions."

The conversation ended abruptly. Private Doheny put the Humvee into gear. He drove off into the night as the wind cooled his closely cropped scalp and the gnats filled his teeth and the headlights attracted moths by the thousands.

Just two weeks out of basic training, Doheny had been sent to Fort Bragg to train with the 192nd Ordnance Unit, where he would learn to disarm or remove unexploded missiles, shells and improvised explosive devices. His unit had just eight more weeks of training before they would be deployed. Rumor was that they were headed to the Indonesian islands where the U.S. was battling Islamic revolutionaries that were slowly but surely taking over the local governments. Apparently the militants had taken to shelling the schools and universities in an attempt to keep little girls – and anyone else, for that matter – from getting a decent education. It wasn't hard for Doheny to envision his arms being blown off while attempting to remove an unexploded shell from some Indonesian schoolyard.

Meanwhile, he knew that at this moment his friends from Boston Bayside High School were down on Cape Cod enjoying a last blast of summer before going their separate ways for college. His girlfriend, an average student who had somehow lucked into George

Mason University, was probably with them too. Doheny had never imagined himself the odd man out of higher education. He blamed himself. He had pretty much slacked off his entire junior year, pretending to study in his upstairs bedroom, while actually spending all night every night playing video games. Come senior year, his grades were so bad that not even his safety schools out West would have him. By mid-June, four years in the Army and a $15,000 signing bonus had sounded better than local community college.

He swerved to avoid a trio of deer grazing on the highway's shoulder, slammed on the brakes and skidded on some gravel. He put the Humvee in park to catch his breath. The cell phone was blinking on the floorboards, having skidded off the passenger seat. He bent down to retrieve it and held it for a moment. Doheny was suddenly forlorn, gripped with a potent, undeniable urge to call his girlfriend back home. It was a no-brainer that the Lieutenant would find out later and punish him for it. But hearing her voice, the way she baby-talked him, would be worth it.

He dialed twice. When she did not answer the second time, he left a rambling, whining message that he regretted instantly. He put the vehicle in gear and continued on his mission.

In a few minutes the odometer read exactly 22.6 miles. Just as Lieutenant Flynn had predicted, he saw the tiny sign for FR 66B. Doheny motored over the cratered, muddy forest road for exactly one mile, where there was a clearing and a cattle pond. He shut off the engine and sat with the headlights on and the insects swarming about his head. His thoughts drifted back to the cricket in the barracks. He wished he had simply let it sing.

Doheny's vision flickered and then flashed white as a single .50 caliber rifle shot vaporized his brain stem. He was clinically dead before his forehead came to rest against the steering wheel.

Moments later, a Polaris off-roader came from the tree line, driven by a pale man with a pockmarked face and a clean-shaven head. He wore night-vision goggles and a black track suit and carried the .50 caliber rifle on a strap across his shoulders. His name was Chris Abrams.

The little four-wheel vehicle towed a lightweight trailer that jounced over rocks and mud as it sidled up alongside the Humvee. Chris Abrams leapt out of the Polaris and secured the area, his movements downright sprightly for a six-foot-six 34-year-old who'd been living with HIV for ten years. He put the rifle down, picked up a tiny video camera, and began recording as he briefly inspected Doheny's body. He set the still-running camera on the hood as he pulled his night-vision goggles off, revealing a pair of red-rimmed, hazel eyes with dilated pupils. He unwrapped a protein bar and shoved it into his mouth, chewing as he transferred the cargo – twenty shoulder-mounted Stinger missiles weighing thirty-six pounds each – into the trailer.

When Abrams was done, he covered the trailer, then placed C4 explosive under the Humvee's gas tank and set the timer for twelve minutes. Although he had eaten two full dinners totaling 3,000 calories, and had additional snacks, he was still ravenous. He opened a package of beef jerky and devoured it as he drove the back roads to the transfer point. By the time the explosion lit up the night sky, the Stinger missiles were safely aboard a TV repair truck en route to a warehouse in Frederick County, Maryland. There, Abrams would be able to snatch a couple hours' sleep and a hearty breakfast before meeting his crew for the next leg of the mission.

THREE DAYS LATER

Washington D.C.
Sunday, 4:45 a.m.

Blake Carver watched his prisoner, United States Army Lieutenant James Flynn, through a two-way mirror. Flynn knelt, blindfolded, with his hands cuffed behind him. His uniform lay in a heap in the corner, and the officer's fluorescent-lit skin had taken on a slight bluish hue.

"I want a lawyer," Flynn repeated in a raspy voice that crackled over the observation room's monitors. "I know you can hear me. I got my rights."

This was good. Flynn was about to cross an important psychological milestone. He was about to lose control of his emotions for the first time in twenty two hours of captivity. Carver had not been an interrogator by trade at the CIA, but he had logged more than 300 hours in rooms just like this in six countries. He had learned some things about breaking points and how to achieve them. Now he waited patiently, watching Flynn from behind the reflective mirror. Ten seconds later, the Lieutenant suddenly began screaming at the top of his lungs. "Where am I? Where am I? What day is it? Talk to me!"

It was Sunday morning, before dawn. Agent Carver was holding Flynn in the basement of Field House DC310, a two-level 1850s brownstone on a leafy Georgetown residential street. The National Security

Agency had acquired the home seven years earlier to spy on the Central African Republic Embassy, which had been located in a decaying mansion across the street. The upstairs bedrooms were outfitted with observation posts with night vision scopes and directional microphones that could penetrate twelve inches of solid concrete at up to one hundred yards. The field house's communication hardware had been completely replaced with equipment dedicated to NSA's private Ethernet. Though the original surveillance operation had produced nothing of value, the home had been retained by the White House as an urban outpost of sorts, where sensitive investigations could operate at a safe distance from the prying eyes of the Defense Department brass.

The home's ground floor was an elaborate façade for the fictional couple in residence, Ethan and Melissa Danforth. Carver had employed several aliases during his 16-year intelligence career, and he had been using Ethan Danforth for only a few weeks. The mythical Danforth had an MBA from George Washington University and an office on K Street, where he and his wife ran a small consulting firm called FutureK. The firm had verifiable clients – all dummy businesses – and a young receptionist named Madison who did not ask too many questions.

Brochures for European cycling vacations were magnetized to the fridge. Magazines were scattered on the coffee table. Bottles of limited production cabernet sat in a starter wine rack, and a digital picture frame on a bookshelf cycled slideshows of Carver and his partner,

Agent Meagan O'Keefe, with aspiring politicos at black-tie events.

Like Lieutenant Flynn, Agent Carver had not slept in more than a day. He went to the ancient sink basin in the corner of the room where there was a black and white photograph of the home's previous residents – or perhaps their grandparents – standing where he was now, filleting freshly caught trout.

He turned on the cold tap and splashed water onto his chiseled features. He squeezed anti-redness drops into each of his green eyes. The drops stung. He blinked the artificial tears away and looked into the mirror. His face was still tan despite having spent so much time in basements, surveillance posts and windowless offices during the past several weeks. Carver made a point to get out and run at least once a day, no matter how hot and sticky it was outside. A little sun on his face did wonders for his attitude.

A gray hair had sprouted on his otherwise black sideburns. He plucked it out, but neither the pain nor the cold water was enough to fight his drowsiness. He loosened his black necktie, popped in a piece of sugarless gum and dropped his lean 185-pound frame to the floor to rip off ten quick pushups. Screw caffeine. To hell with ginseng. Blood to the brain was all he needed.

He heard the row house's squeaky back door, followed by two sets of footsteps on the floorboards above him. Carver reached for his SIG 9mm and levered a round into the chamber. It was probably just O'Keefe, but Carver took no chances. He was, after all, operating blind – the building's security and surveillance systems were offline. Due to another round of crippling budget cuts, field house DC310 was on a 30-day waitlist for standard repairs.

Carver recognized Agent O'Keefe's clip-clop gait on the hardwood and put his weapon away. They had been partners for almost two months now, and he already knew O'Keefe inside and out, down to the tiny mole on her slightly crooked right index finger, her left-leaning voting record and the way her allergy to watermelon made her lips go numb for an hour after eating it.

O'Keefe did the perfunctory secret knock – more of a cheesy joke between her and Carver than insurance against accidentally blowing each other's brains out – and entered with the White House Chief of Staff, Julian Speers, behind her. Their clothes were soaked and they were tracking mud.

"Working late again?" Carver said to his fictitious better half. "Dinner's getting cold, honey."

Carver helped O'Keefe with her coat. The roots of her shoulder-length strawberry-blonde hair were matted against her head and the drizzle had spotted her black-framed eyeglasses. Carver pulled a hanky from his suit jacket and offered it to her.

At 26, with an M.S. in applied mathematics from MIT and a bachelor's degree in Middle Eastern languages, O'Keefe was more than a decade younger than the 39-year-old Carver. Like many at the agency, she was a numbers geek originally hired to work in cryptology. And like every NSA employee, field work was officially outside her job description. Recruited specifically to conduct counter-terrorism surveillance and interpret intercepted transmissions, she had never received combat training, nor had she been formally issued a gun. The target practice she put in after hours, as well as the matching SIG 9mm she wore in a holster around her left ankle, was at Carver's insistence. He needed to know his partner could back him up in a jam.

Speers had dark circles under his doughy eyes and he was sucking on a grape-flavored lollipop. "Thanks for the wakeup call," the Chief of Staff snapped, rubbing his hands through his damp, overgrown haircut. He'd missed two buttons on his white oxford shirt and his dress socks were different shades of black. Then he spotted Flynn through the observation glass. "What the hell?" he hissed, pushing past Carver to get a look at the naked prisoner. He'd seen that face on TV. He pulled the lollipop from his mouth. "Tell me that's not the missing officer they're showing on CNN every fifteen minutes."

Flynn was indeed the missing officer. The previous evening, Carver and O'Keefe had snatched him in the Fort Bragg Officer's Club parking lot. They had sedated him, thrown him into the trunk of their sedan and driven him back to the field house for questioning. It had been by far the most violent event of Agent O'Keefe's young career. For Agent Carver, who had been with the CIA for several years before his sudden transfer, it was just another day at the office.

"Don't worry," Carver said. "Once the Army finds out what he's done, they won't even want him back."

Speers' cheeks flushed crimson. "You're not CIA anymore," he snarled. "How am I supposed to explain this?"

Carver and Speers had first met in the Chief's Eisenhower Building office some two months earlier, on the morning of June 17th. Within three minutes, Speers had effectively ended Agent Carver's illustrious career at the CIA.

It had not been the homecoming that Carver was expecting. For the past several weeks, he had been in pursuit of an ex-Pakistani intelligence agent that had entered the U.S. on a student visa. The man suddenly left his chemistry program at the University of Mississippi mid-semester and fled the state.

The agency spotted him near El Paso, abruptly lost him, and then picked up the trail again near Laughlin, where the Pakistani spent two nights in a motel with an American-born Allied Jihad sympathizer. By that time, Carver had also arrived in Nevada, but he wasn't in a position to make an arrest. The Pakistani had committed no crime, and he still had time to return to the university before he could be legally deported.

The Pakistani and the sympathizer settled into a trailer park near Creech Air Force base about 35 miles north of Las Vegas. They lived off baked beans, white bread and five-a-day prayers. They spent the rest of the time hitting every 12-step program in the northern Las Vegas suburbs.

It didn't take long for Carver to surmise what the pair was doing there. Creech was home to America's unmanned aircraft program, where hundreds of Air Force pilots reported to virtual cockpits to fly Predator drones around the clock, attacking militants in the field with nearly supernatural weaponry in theatres as far away as Afghanistan. The war had been on for years. But unlike their counterparts deployed overseas, they would then return to the air-conditioned safety of their families and living rooms.

At least most of them did. Although the battles took place far from the threat of enemy fire, the pilots' power and responsibilities were nearly God-like. Pinned-down units in the field relied on them to spot enemy ambushes miles above the earth and destroy hostile militants in pitch-black darkness. Villagers planting roadside bombs had to be snuffed out while in the act. Attacks on remote bases had to be repelled with unforgiving vengeance. And there were the inevitable civilian casualties. Mothers, out of their minds with grief, trying to find a child's right arm in a pile of rubble. All of it caught on camera in high-definition. All of it available for replay.

It didn't take long before a drone pilot with shattered nerves wandered into an AA meeting in a North Las Vegas church basement. As the 32-year-old Captain stood, introduced himself and began sharing the horrors of his occupation, the sympathizer sat in the corner, studying the prey that had suddenly flown into his web.

By 2 a.m., the pilot was gagged and bound in a van on his way to Mexico. The Pakistani planned to torture the pilot and extract information that might help insurgents in the Afpak mountains evade the deadly drone attacks. When he was no longer useful, they would toss his body in a ditch and cover him with calcium oxide powder so that the bloodhounds would never find him.

But Agent Carver, who, like the Pakistani, had never in his life had a drink, had also been present at the AA meeting. Now he was in a chopper high over the desert. It had taken a great deal of trust in his team to allow the pilot to be abducted. He had to allow the operation to play out a little longer. If there were other Jihadists in the area, Carver wanted to know about them.

Near Barstow, the Pakistani decided that the risk in smuggling the pilot into Mexico was too great. He called an audible and broke into an abandoned warehouse to begin the interrogation. Carver's team moved in. Within the hour, the Pakistani and the sympathizer were on their way to a classified detention center halfway across the world, and the pilot was on his way to a hospital to be treated for shock.

Carver's team celebrated with a night on the town in Sin City that tested their immune system for days to come.

Not Carver. He didn't like to party. Instead, he rewarded himself with eight hours of uninterrupted sleep in a quiet Ramada Inn outside the city. The next evening he hitched a redeye aboard a cargo plane bound for Langley AFB. It was there on the tarmac that he was met by a pair of uniformed Secret Service officers, sent by Speers to bring him to the White House.

Twenty-five minutes later he entered the Eisenhower Building, adjacent to the West Wing, where

Speers sat behind a massive mahogany desk. The Secret Service agent shut the office door behind Carver and stood outside in the hallway.

Speers stood, leaned across the desktop and shook Carver's hand.

"The great Agent Carver," he said. "It's a pleasure."

"I guess news travels fast."

Speers sat and rubbed his Van Dyke goatee. "News?"

"The operation in Nevada," Carver said. "I assumed that's why you called me here."

Speers gestured for Carver to sit. Carver did, but not before angling his chair toward the corner. He never sat with his back to a door.

Speers seemed amused. "So you think you're here to get a medal? Is that it?"

The glow of victory that had surrounded Agent Carver suddenly evaporated. He folded himself into the low-slung chair and scanned the Chief's desktop for a clue as to the purpose of the visit. The desk was bare except for a small computer, some empty candy wrappers near the desk phone and two manila folders.

"I apologize," Speers said. "I only get briefed on the big ops."

Jackass, Carver thought. As if the abduction of a drone pilot on American soil wasn't huge. He crossed his legs and felt a bead of sweat forming on his brow. The air conditioners in the ancient building were no match for the hundred-degree weather outside.

"We're going to be joined by someone from NSA momentarily," Speers said.

"May I ask why?"

"You've both been chosen for a special assignment."

Carver didn't like the sound of this. He had been in the CIA long enough to know that the White House communicated its needs directly to the agency directors. They didn't just go pulling in field operatives fresh off a mission without going through the chain of command.

"You'll need to sign some paperwork." Speers opened a manila folder containing some documents bearing the Presidential letterhead. He plucked one of the docs from the pile and pushed it across the desk. Carver scanned the first paragraph. It was a letter of resignation from the CIA.

Carver found himself suddenly out of breath. "You want me to resign?"

"What I want is what the President wants."

"What exactly is it that the President wants? Does he want me in the Secret Service? The DIA? *What?*"

Speers sighed. He opened his desk drawer, pulled out a purple lollipop, and offered it to Carver, who refused the candy.

The intercom buzzed. Speers pressed the button and grunted into it. A pleasant voice chirped back on the other side. "Meagan O'Keefe from NSA is here to see you."

"Send her in."

O'Keefe entered, wearing a navy suit that flattered her bust. She looked as bewildered as Carver felt. He stood, reached for her hand and shook it firmly. "Blake Carver, CIA."

"Meagan O'Keefe. NSA."

The Chief of Staff did not stand. He smiled and motioned for O'Keefe to sit in the remaining chair. He opened the second folder on his desk and presented it to her. The form on top contained her letter of resignation from the National Security Agency. She let out a small gasp.

"There, there," Speers said. "Neither of you should be upset. This is a kind of promotion."

"A kind of promotion or an *actual* promotion?" O'Keefe said.

"Well, you'll work for me, which means the White House. But not officially. Officially speaking, you'll be on your own."

Now Speers scratched his overgrown beard and peered at Lieutenant Flynn through the observation glass. "The investigation was supposed to focus on Ulysses," Speers said.

He referred to Ulysses USA, a private security contractor that, by the DOD's own estimates, now made up a full third of the U.S. military presence around the world. Ulysses had been founded by a former Blackwater exec during the second Iraq war. In addition to the Department of Defense, Ulysses counted several multinational corporations as clients. Ulysses USA stock – its ticker symbol was UUSA – was trading at $119 per share.

But Ulysses had become a problem for the President. The company had slowly earned a nasty rep as indiscriminate mercenaries that killed not only for

U.S. interests, but for those of the company's shareholders.

"The investigation *is* focusing on Ulysses," Carver insisted. "Lieutenant Flynn here's been double-dipping."

Speers turned. "Explain."

"In addition to his government salary, the Lieutenant received three payments from Ulysses via various fronts in the past eight months. All deposited to accounts in the Caymans."

"Start from the top. How'd you even find this guy?"

O'Keefe slipped on her black wire-framed glasses and leaned against a metal tool cabinet. "We started working up personas on likely arms smugglers several weeks ago. We decided to look for any government employees between a G-5 and a G-12 that had paid cash for new luxury vehicles in the past year. We got four thousand matches. We filtered those results by military personnel. That dropped it to about a thousand suspects. Then we narrowed it to those with access to specific weaponry that had been reported missing or stolen in the past year. There were just two matches."

Speers smiled at the ex-NSA cryptographer. "I knew we hired you for a reason."

"But wait," Carver quipped, "You still haven't heard the punch line."

"Three days ago," O'Keefe went on, "Private Matt Doheny died in an explosion about 20 miles from Fort Bragg, where Lieutenant Flynn had significant access to military weaponry. It's listed as a suicide, but here's something that wasn't in the DOD report: Doheny was transporting twenty Stinger missiles."

Speers rolled his eyes. "That's all been documented. The Stingers were resupplies for the Indonesia campaign. Maybe you geniuses never thought of this, but our Army can't kill bad guys unless grunts like Private Doheny haul weapons from point A to point B."

Carver cut in: "Without filing a standard transport authorization form? In the middle of the night? The Lieutenant here sent Private Doheny off-base in a Humvee loaded with Stingers, and he made damn sure they never got to our units in Indonesia."

"Prove it."

O'Keefe picked up a transcript of a voicemail dated three days earlier and handed it to Speers. "That's the transcription of the voicemail Doheny left his ex-girlfriend that night," O'Keefe explained.

She gave Speers a moment to process the transcript, which mentioned Lieutenant Flynn by name. Then she handed him the forensics report. "I had forensics go over the blast area again and again. No trace of any of the unique composites used in a Stinger missile."

"Meaning the Stingers are still out there somewhere," Carver added.

Speers looked through the glass at Lieutenant Flynn. "So you're telling me Lieutenant Flynn has been selling arms to Ulysses?"

O'Keefe shook her head. "We're saying the Lieutenant directed an unauthorized weapons transport.

We have no hard evidence that he was preparing to sell them."

"Yet," Carver added.

"Stay out of this," Speers said. He turned back to O'Keefe. "What are the chances that Flynn's buyer isn't Ulysses? Could he be planning to use the weapons?"

O'Keefe bit her bottom lip. She wasn't used to having bureaucrats breathing down her neck before she had even analyzed all the data. "We don't know his intentions yet."

Speers' imagination was already running wild. This brought up an entirely new set of issues. "Could you shoot down a commercial airliner with one of those Stingers?"

"Why stop at one?" Carver cut in. "They're missing twenty from Fort Bragg alone."

The Chief's eyebrows furrowed with worry. "What now?" Speers had made no secret of the fact that he was unqualified to direct this investigation, a point he himself had made repeatedly in several self-deprecating conversations with President Hatch. But the unpopular President had enemies right in his own cabinet, and many more in the Pentagon. It came down to a matter of trust, and there was no one the President trusted more than Speers. The investigation was his, whether he liked it or not.

Carver sat down and folded his hands. What he was about to suggest was the real reason he'd woken Speers up. "Look," he said, "maybe at NSA you'd continue to build a case for weeks or months on end. But at the Company, we'd assume that the clock was ticking on something big, and we'd pull out all the stops."

"You mean torture," Speers said with disgust.

"Not technically," Carver said, referring to the Supreme Court's rather loose definitions of the myriad ways to inflict suffering on a human being. Although President Hatch had scored a victory for the left by putting a stop to water boarding, there was still a lot of wiggle room in the Court's interpretation of prisoners' rights.

"I can't support it."

"Imagine that a week from now, one of those Stingers is used against an airliner," Carver said. "Two hundred people die, including children. Would you be able to forgive yourself for not doing everything in your power to stop it?"

Speers crunched the lollipop with his back molars and pulled out the stick. "You've made your point."

"So?"

"I won't rule it out. But first I'd like the satisfaction of talking to Lieutenant Flynn."

"You?" Carver said.

"Yes."

"You can't risk the exposure. If he recognizes your voice…"

"He won't."

Carver wasn't the only experienced interrogator in the room. Before joining then-Governor Hatch's staff as General Counsel, Speers had worked as a district attorney. He grew famous in Virginia after his line of questioning prompted a key mob witness to urinate in his pants in federal court.

Carver pulled a tiny ear microphone out of his pocket and placed it in Speers' right ear. "You're the boss in there," he said, "but I'm going to be talking to you."

The Chief of Staff entered the ten-by-eight-foot soundproof cell. He approached Flynn apprehensively, like a toddler working up the courage to sit on Santa's lap. The last time Speers had been this close to a naked man was in his high school P.E. class, and the stench of Lieutenant Flynn's body odor – twenty hours of nervous perspiration and indigestion – hit hard.

In the observation room, O'Keefe sat down to watch the spectacle through the two-way mirror, resting her feet on a two-drawer file cabinet. Carver sat beside her, talking into the microphone, his voice crackling in Speers' ear: "Get closer," he urged. "He might bite, but he's not poisonous."

"Who's there?" the blindfolded Lieutenant Flynn rasped. Speers knew better than to answer fully. It was important that the President have full immunity. So far, he hadn't even disclosed the details of the ongoing investigation to the President so that the Chief Executive could never be held personally responsible for the team's actions.

"I'm a federal attorney," Speers told the soldier. It wasn't the whole truth, but it also wasn't a lie. Speers hadn't practiced law in years, but he was still technically a member of the Virginia State Bar.

Flynn's pectorals quaked as he trembled. "You gotta help me," he begged. "They can't hold me like this. I've got a wife and kids."

"Lieutenant Flynn," Speers said with sudden empathy in his voice, "I've had the misfortune of witnessing the darker side of intelligence operations. You don't look like someone who could survive it."

Flynn mumbled through quivering lips.

Speers went on: "I'll have to fight to even get permission to notify your family that you're in custody. A battle that I'll probably lose, by the way. From the looks of you, we should start with getting a doctor to make a house call, just to make sure you're okay, maybe dispense something for the nerves. If I can talk them into letting you sleep, I can see about contacting your family. But I can't convince these guys to give an inch unless we have something to offer." Speers could practically see the cogs in Flynn's brain smoking. "Now gimmie something I can sell."

The Lieutenant swallowed hard. "Rapture Run."

"Rapture Run?" Speers repeated. "Sounds like a death metal band."

"Forget it," Flynn said. "Forget I said it."

Carver spoke into Speers' ear microphone. "Stay on that," he said. "That key phrase has been floating around the intel database for a few months, but we can't get any context. Ask him where he heard it."

"Come on," Speers told the Lieutenant. "Tell me what Rapture Run is, or where you heard it, and I'll go back in and fight like hell for you. Promise."

Flynn's next utterance came up like a blast of vomit: "SECDEF Jackson."

SECDEF was military jargon for the Secretary of Defense. "Jackson?" Speers said. "As in Defense Secretary Dexter P. Jackson?"

"You heard me," Flynn said. "There was a supply order for Rapture Run with his signature. Worth billions."

"And what is Rapture Run?"

Flynn shook his head. "I dunno. Has something to do with USOC. Something they're building. Really skunkworks stuff. I'm not sure what."

"USOC?"

Flynn laughed. "Ulysses Strike Operations Command."

"And USOC does what?"

"Covert assassinations. Now help me, dammit!"

A smile broke across Speers' face. Over the past year, Secretary Jackson had become a hostile force within the President's cabinet, but the President didn't have the political capital to oust someone so popular with the Pentagon. "Thank you, Lieutenant. You did well. I'll see what I can do."

Speers rejoined Carver and O'Keefe in the observation room. The Chief was jumping out of his skin with excitement. "The Lieutenant just implicated a sitting cabinet secretary," he gloated. He used his sleeve to wipe the sweat from his face. He turned to Carver. "We've gotta wake the President."

Monroe, West Virginia
5:30 a.m.

The first hints of sunrise rose over Monroe Gatlin Raceway. Tiny shards of glass and metal, crushed into the asphalt by so many local hot-rods, shimmered like a hundred thousand tiny emeralds. The grandstands had long been sold off and weeds had sprouted on the sun-cracked drag strip. Faruq Ahmed, needing a private avenue to practice his mission several weeks ago, had gained access with nothing more than a bolt cutter.

Now the 29-year-old Yemeni got out of the Ford F-450 commercial-grade truck and knelt toward the eastern sky. Even at this early hour, his face felt the heat of the rising sun. The ribbed tank top he wore was soaked with perspiration. He prayed silently for several minutes, rocking back and forth on his knees. Then he got back into the vehicle to focus on the matter at hand. This was his final opportunity to practice. Later today, he would do the real thing.

He laid the loaded Smith & Wesson .38 revolver in his lap. A Koran rested in the glove compartment. It was important that his practice conditions simulate the real thing. Accordingly, the truck bed was full of oversized tires that weighed about seven hundred pounds collectively, or about the same as the combination of ammonium nitrate and explosive putty that he would replace them with.

He clutched a small stopwatch close to his chest, took a deep breath, and then clicked it.

Twenty-four seconds elapsed before he laid the stopwatch next to him and stepped on the gas. The super-duty rig wasn't exactly race-worthy, especially since Ahmed had let some of the air out of the driver-side wheels. But the V-8 under the hood managed to get up to 45 mph by the time he was halfway down the quarter-mile drag strip.

He drove toward a four-foot-high construction barricade at the opposite end of the strip. Next to it was a homemade ramp that he had fashioned out of concrete. At the last moment, he jerked the steering wheel sharply to the left with his left hand, while simultaneously working the parking brake. On cue, the truck began to "ski" – balance on the partially deflated driver-side wheels only – on the ramp just as his passenger-side wheels lifted high enough to clear the barricade. Releasing the parking brake, he tilted the steering wheel slightly to the right and was back on four wheels again.

He skidded to a stop and drummed the wheel happily. It was the twelfth time in a row he'd managed to clear the barricade. He was ready.

Ahmed's smile faded as he spotted the police patrol car entering the gates with its roof lights swirling red and blue. He clutched his firearm in his lap, switching off the safety. He had to carry out his mission in less than five hours. Nothing could stop that.

The officer was alone. He parked several feet away and got out, a barrel-chested man with a mustache as thick as a caterpillar and a sidearm so big and heavy that his pants hung dangerously low on his hips.

"That's some drivin'," the officer said, looking up at Ahmed in the jacked-up rig. Ahmed smiled at the small-town officer, who could not see the gun in his lap. Ahmed knew he was lucky to be in a rural place where the police were inexperienced. In any big city, the officer would have kept his distance and demanded that he step out of the vehicle.

"You some kind of stunt man?" the officer asked.

"Yes," Ahmed said, smiling as he looked down. It was half-true. He had arrived in a cargo container from Yemen via Hamburg three months earlier. His contact had met him at the Port of Long Beach and driven him to Burbank, where he was treated for dehydration, given a studio apartment, a fake California driver's license and enrollment in a local stunt driving school. After the stunt driving program was over, he was immediately offered a job as an extra in an Arab exploitation film during which he would have had to drive a sports car down a staircase into a crowd of people. The irony of the situation amused him, but he had no time to indulge himself. He was already due in West Virginia to prepare for his mission.

"We don't get too many stunt drivers," the officer said, looking at the ramps that Ahmed had set up for practice. "Well, that explains the props."

"Is there a problem, officer?"

"You're on private property. I'll need to see driver's license and registration."

"Yes sir." Ahmed pretended to look in his wallet. He glanced at his watch. He reckoned that the act of subduing the officer, tying him up and transporting him home would take at least an extra two hours of his time, maybe more. It wasn't worth it. He couldn't risk the mission. There were others to consider. The timing was critical.

He made his choice.

"Here you are," Ahmed said. He drew his .38 and fired a round into the officer's chest. The officer fell to the ground. Ahmed fired two more shots into the officer's ample gut to make sure he was dead.

He got out of the truck and lifted the officer by the shoulders toward the rear of the patrol car. He popped the trunk and, with some difficulty, lifted the dead weight up high enough to roll him in. He started the car and drove it into a dense field of high grass and young poplar trees at the end of the strip until it was completely obscured by the greenery.

He scratched his arms as he made his way out of the field. By the time he reached the truck, a rash had discolored his wrists, hands and forearms. He cursed the officer and climbed back into the truck. He had to get to a pharmacy. His mission would begin in less than five hours.

The White House
6:50 a.m.

This wasn't Blake Carver's first meeting in the Oval Office, yet it seemed as if every drop of moisture in his mouth had evaporated. His stomach had quivered less during joint-op missions with Green Berets in Afghanistan. The awe-factor Carver felt had little to do with President Isaac S. Hatch, the unpopular Chief Executive who sat on the couch opposite him in a white monogrammed robe and slippers, or Julian Speers, who sat beside him. It was what the office represented. It was the great ones who had sat there before them. FDR. JFK. Elvis.

The President thumbed through the 40-page brief that Speers had put the finishing touches on only minutes before. The paper in the President's hands was still warm from the printer.

Carver and Speers had come directly from Field House DC310, where O'Keefe still remained with Lieutenant Flynn. They wore yesterday's suits and a piece of sugarless gum had substituted for a toothbrush. All Carver's days seemed to be like this. It was the reason he kept his black hair clipped to a quarter-inch on the sides and an inch on top. It always looked the same no matter how long he had been up or what part of the world he had flown in from. Whenever his job allowed him to be in Washington, he went to this young barber on Adams Morgan who shaped it with a straight razor.

Mary Chung, the President's longtime personal assistant, entered with three cappuccinos on a tray. The President took a cup and continued to skim the document. Speers also helped himself. He took a moment to inhale the aroma of the ultra-potent brew that the White House barista had invented for the always-wired President. Carver politely declined.

"You've gotta be the only person in Washington who's never set foot in Starbucks," Speers said. "And you've been awake, what, thirty hours?"

"Never touch the stuff," Carver said of caffeine. He had been raised Mormon in a predominantly LDS town in rural northern Arizona. He'd long since quit the LDS Church, but the religion's edicts of clean living still agreed with him. The nature of Carver's work kept him from living a saintly life, but he still treated his body like a temple. To this day, he'd never touched alcohol.

"So what's your vice?" Speers pressed him. "Ginseng? Sugar?"

"Exercise," Carver explained. "Blood to the brain." He eyed Speers' pot belly, accentuated by the wide floral tie that draped over it. "You should try it sometime."

Speers wiped cappuccino foam off his goatee. "You really expect me to believe that you've never had caffeine."

"Okay, once," Carver admitted. "In '06. I was in Columbia."

"Columbia?" Speers said. "I didn't see that in your CIA file."

"By design, no doubt. Anyhow, my leg got caught in a rodent trap made of sharpened bamboo."

"Who kills a rat with bamboo?"

"Wal-Mart hasn't yet made it to the Columbian countryside, Chief. And this thing was really bad news. By the time I put on the tourniquet and could think about getting the hell out of there, I'd lost a lot of blood. I came across a coffee plantation and decided, for energy's sake, to eat some beans straight from a tree."

"See? Caffeine saved your life."

"No. It almost killed me. I had the runs so bad I barely made it back to Bogotá."

The President finished scanning Speers' report and set the document down beside him on the couch. "This is a heckuva brief," he said, folding his reading glasses and shoving them into his robe pocket. "Not quite brief enough, though. Paraphrase for me."

Speers leaned forward. "We think there's sufficient cause for a public investigation into DOD's oversight of Ulysses USA."

"Public?" the President said. "No, no, no. First I need to know definitively whether Ulysses USA is up to any hanky panky."

"With all due respect, sir," Speers said, "we started with that. We're not saying that Ulysses isn't the end buyer for the missing weaponry. We don't know that for sure yet. But we're saying that the trail seems to begin within the Pentagon. Or your own Cabinet, sir."

This wasn't the answer that the President wanted to hear. He had created a monster in Ulysses USA, and he was looking for a way to kill it. Ulysses' growth had coincided with a major downturn in U.S. military recruiting that had left America far short of the troops it needed to fulfill the President's commitments at home and abroad. Having run on a platform of change – principally a change from the previous administration's devotion to an open-ended assault on Islamic radicalism – he had, after two terror attacks on American soil, ended up entangling American forces in more foreign conflicts than ever.

If the Pew Research polls were to be believed, President Hatch's foreign quagmires had now made him the most unpopular President since Richard Nixon. With so little mandate, a military draft was not a feasible option. He didn't have enough support in Congress, to say nothing of the military itself, which prided itself as an all-volunteer organization. Even suggesting it would have been political suicide. Facing a significantly downsized military, the Joint Chiefs had proposed outsourcing some of the fighting to Ulysses USA.

President Hatch had been a businessman long before taking up politics, and the concept of outsourcing a governmental role to a more cost-effective private-sector company was, in principal, an appealing way to bolster the Virginia Democrat's pro-business reputation. It was also hard to argue with the economics. Training a volunteer army with taxpayer money – and paying out VA benefits for as long as they lived – had simply gotten too expensive. It was pricey on the recruiting end, too. After the quagmires in Indonesia and Afpak, even the grunts in the infantry were demanding $15,000 signing bonuses.

The President thumbed through the report again and leaned forward. "This is a helluva accusation. You have proof?"

"I wouldn't say proof per se," Speers said, "but we think that a small group of officers is supervising it, and that someone high up in DOD is the puppet master." He looked at Carver. "Tell him."

"Mister President," Carver said, speaking softly. "It's possible that Defense Secretary Jackson may be connected to this."

"Dex Jackson?" the President said. Now he understood the Chief's reference to his own Cabinet. "You think it's Dex getting rich off this?" It occurred to Speers that he had never heard the President refer to Secretary Jackson by his first name. These days, with the cabinet's all-too-public sniping, it was easy to forget that he and the President had once been friends. Jackson was also the sole Republican in the President's cabinet, a move that had bought him a little bipartisan support in Congress.

"We've got a witness," Speers said. "He said Secretary Jackson authorized a weapons delivery to someplace called Rapture Run."

"Rapture what?" the President said.

"NSA has been monitoring what they believe may be terrorist-related cells in both Syria and the U.S. The codename Rapture Run has come up before. We just don't have context."

The President shook his head and stood up. "If you're still trying to decode context, why are you wasting my time?"

Speers cut in. "Sir, we can't rule out the possibility of a domestic terrorist attack using U.S. weaponry."

"Julian, you used that word again. *Possibility*. It's all very loosey goosey."

"I'm requesting an executive order to raid Secretary Jackson's office so that I can get you better data."

The President frowned. As much as he secretly longed to nail Dex Jackson to a cross, he didn't have the political capital to do it right now. "Julian, I asked you to investigate a pattern of weapons smuggling that would help me weaken Ulysses. Now you're accusing Dex of either arms dealing or arming terrorists. There's a big difference. I can't go into this willy nilly."

"Sir," Speers pleaded, "I may not be able to hold off the reporter much longer." In June, a *New York Times* reporter had called Speers asking for commentary on an in-progress story claiming that the DOD had given Ulysses preferential access to government contracts, access to classified intelligence and non-secured loans of government-owned weaponry, which they were in turn selling to America's enemies. Speers had been able to use his strings at the *Times* to temporarily squash it. He had until after Labor Day. Then the story would run, with or without the White House's approval.

"Tell you what," the President said. "I'd like to meet this witness of yours. If it feels right, I'll give you what you want."

The door opened. Mary Chung popped her head in. "Mister President," she said, "Secretary Hudson's here for your meeting. Shall I have her wait?"

"No. Go ahead and show her in."

The President turned to Carver. "I want you in the Security Council meeting today. Sit in the back and keep your mouth shut."

Heads turned as Treasury Secretary Eva Hudson entered wearing a grey power suit and designer flats. Practical shoes were important in a city like Washington. Parking was a pain in the ass, even if you had your own driver. It was better to walk.

"Gentlemen," she said as she flashed a flawless smile that looked even whiter against her new spray-on tan.

"You're looking awfully tan for a politico," Speers quipped.

"Thank you, Chief." Eva picked at a coffee stain on Speers' lapel as she passed. He could smell the molding putty she used to give her long brunette hair body and bounce. He wanted to touch it.

Agent Carver wasn't immune to Eva's charms either. He turned at the office exit to check out Secretary Hudson's Pilates-toned rear end. The move didn't escape the President, who wagged his finger at Carver as he shut the door.

Carver and Speers hustled through the West Wing. Speers struggled to keep up with Agent Carver's pace. "Quick bite before the NSC meeting?" Speers offered. "Bet you've never had the Executive Omelet."

"I only eat egg whites." They headed down the stairs. "Was it just me, or was Eva's tan a little orange?"

"No, it was bronze."

"You think she's got any tan lines?"

"Funny."

"I should ask the President."

Speers didn't like the tone of the remark. "Don't believe the rumors."

"Rumors are a threat to national security," Carver said. "So if Eva Hudson, the hottest woman in politics, is intimately involved with the leader of the free world, I need to know about it." Carver referred to the latest issue of *Vanity Fair,* in which Eva had taken the top honors in an article titled "World's Sexiest Feds."

Whispers of an intimate relationship between Eva and the nation's first widower President had plagued them for years. Carver knew that Hudson had started working for the president twelve years earlier, as his Assistant Chief of Staff, when he was Governor of Virginia. During the term, Hudson's husband died in a tragic car wreck. A month later, then-Governor Hatch's wife was struck with a rare, aggressive bone cancer that ended her life within weeks. That was when the whispers started. Staffers went on record that the two spent an inappropriate amount of alone time together soon after the tragedies. Eva was then suddenly promoted to State Congressional Liaison, and then the next year, Lieutenant Governor. She didn't stay in the role long. The International Monetary Fund came knocking, and Eva, sick of the gossip and southern politics, jumped at the chance to join the IMF as Assistant Director. But two years later, after the election, she couldn't refuse President Hatch when he asked her to join his cabinet.

Sweat ran down Speers' forehead. "You okay?" Carver asked him.

"Forget for a second what I said in there What if the President's right? What if it's the wrong time to stir up trouble at the Defense Department?"

"That's crazy talk."

"You've seen his approval rating among the military."

"Please. Most of those guys voted GOP anyhow. And besides, the President's a second-termer. Nothing to lose."

"Any head of state will tell you," Speers warned Carver, "you don't wanna piss off the guys with the guns." Speers had long believed that if Thailand could have seventeen military coups in the past sixty years, and a superpower like Russia could have two in the past twenty years, it could happen anywhere. While most Americans worried about whether a few Arabs had weapons of mass destruction, it was the President's enemies at home that kept Speers from sleeping at night.

They came to the kitchen, where the President's security detail chief, Special Agent Hector Rios, was eating a five-egg omelet. Rios had been in the Secret Service for twelve years and spent the past six with President Hatch's team. Even before the six-foot-ten Rios stood to shake Carver's hand, Carver recognized the former NFL linebacker.

"Jacksonville Jaguars," Carver said, grinning, revealing a full set of semi-straight, but perfectly white, teeth. "The first Latino middle linebacker to ever be drafted in the first round."

Rios grinned and extended his oversized paw for a handshake. "I'm impressed," he said. "Intel guys are usually into the fringe sports. Mixed martial arts, roller derby. You know."

"I've been known to take in the odd roller derby match myself. So whatever happened to you? How'd you become a Fed?"

"Same answer to both questions. *Osama.*"

"What? Osama bin Laden killed your football career?"

"Different Osama. In my second year training camp, this defensive tackle named Osama Sinclair busted my left knee. He was just some poor guy from Miami trying to make the squad, but he ruined me. Couldn't get his name out of my head. Osama. Osama. Osama. I was in the hospital having fantasies about what I was gonna do to this guy when I got out. Next day was 9/11. Osama Bin Laden was all over the news gloating about what he'd done to America. Maybe it was the pain pills, but I had a dream – super vivid, I mean – that I was going to devote my life to protecting America. Next day, I called up the Army and asked about joining. They were real skeptical about the knee injury. Then I called up a guy I went to high school with that joined the Secret Service. Hadn't talked to him in years. Turned out to be a Jaguars fan. Said his kid had my trading card. And here I am."

*

The President loosened the belt on his robe, revealing the 28-inch waistline that his Presidential opponent had famously suggested was "out of step with mainstream America." The President moved in for a kiss, but Eva turned her head. She hated the awkwardness of Oval Office meetings. The President had assured her that he'd had all the customary microphones and cameras removed, but she knew the Secret Service often backfilled his feeble attempts at privacy.

She checked her watch. "This better be good," she said. "We've got a Security Council meeting in ten minutes and I still have to pack." They had planned a secret getaway to Martha's Vineyard, going so far as to have the President's body double rent an estate on nearby Cape Cod to throw off the paparazzi.

The President sat on the couch and motioned for Eva to sit opposite him. He put his palms together, as if to pray, and leaned forward, speaking as delicately as he could: "It's about the weekend."

He had hardly said anything, but Eva could tell where he was going with this. It was the downside of being the President's lover. "No need to explain," she said coolly, although she'd been looking forward to the trip for two months. "It's just business."

"The Iranian Ambassador's asking for an urgent meeting at Camp David."

Eva's brown eyes got wide. The President had made international headlines by extending an olive branch to Iran during his first term and opening up diplomatic relations for the first time since the 1970s. But the presence of an embassy in D.C. had done little to cool tensions. "I trust you're going to run this by the Security Council," she said.

"I can't. Half the council's against me."

"Work with me, Isaac. I'm in the half that's on your side."

"The Iranian hardliners are making threats again."

"So? Talk of wiping Israel off the map is an annual political rite for the clerics, nothing more."

"This isn't business as usual. Sixteen MIGs broke Israeli airspace last week. Looked a heckuva lot like a dry run for an attack. CIA says Iran's reserve armor brigades have been called up too. And there's this." He took a handheld computer from the desk and handed it to Eva. She looked at the satellite image depicting a number of official-looking state cars surrounding some sort of industrial complex. "That was taken near the Caspian Sea just a few days ago."

"Is that an Egyptian flag on that SUV?"

"Sure is, and that's just the tip of the iceberg. There are bigwigs from Jordan, Saudi Arabia, the UAE and Syria there too."

"What are they selling? Nukes?"

"Water."

"Water?"

"That complex in the photo is a desalination plant. It's a long story. I can fill you in up at Camp David this weekend."

Camp David. The suggestion that she would join him there was stunning, even for the President, who in his second term had too often thrown caution to the wind. "Oh, the GOP would love that," Eva quipped, giving the President room to play it off as a joke.

His face was as serious as it had ever been. "Eva, we're both widowers. We're doing nothing wrong. Maybe we should just – "

"Stop. We've been over this. MSNBC did that Web poll, remember? When they caught us going to dinner together?"

"Hardly scientific."

Eva was insistent. "Nobody wants the Commander-in-Chief dating a cabinet member. The fact that we're both widowers doesn't change anything. It just looks bad."

"I'm your boss. I could order you to come to Camp David to discuss the Iranian trade embargo."

"And that would be sexual harassment." Eva stood and picked up her Louis Vuitton attaché.

"I'm not joking."

"You've always been bold," she said. "I've loved you for that. Don't be reckless."

"You can always change your mind," he said.

"I won't."

As Eva left, Mary Chung took the opportunity to poke her head in the door. She was holding a freshly pressed suit. "Excuse me, Mister President," she said. "The Security Council is waiting."

White House Cabinet Room
7:30 a.m.

Defense Secretary Dexter P. Jackson arrived for the National Security Council meeting in uncharacteristically casual dress for himself on a Sunday morning, let alone Washington – chinos, boat shoes and an untucked white oxford shirt. Nearly the entire Congress and White House staff had already left town for the summer recess. Dex's bags were packed and his wife was standing by to pick him up as soon as the NSC meeting was over. In less than three hours he would be trolling for marlin in Chesapeake Bay.

Although his name was inscribed on a brass nameplate on his Cabinet chair, he could have found it blindfolded. Like everything in status-oriented Washington, the chairs around the long mahogany table that President Nixon had gifted to the White House were arranged in hierarchical order. The Defense Secretary's chair was next to the President's high-backed version. Chairs assigned to the Vice President and secretaries of State and Treasury were the next-closest, arranged in the order that the cabinet posts were first created beginning in the late 1700s. Likewise, the Homeland Security chair – vacant today, since President Hatch had recently fired the agency's Director – was situated at the far end of the table.

Dex stared out the French doors at the Rose Garden as the rest of the Council members filed in. There would be several additional vacant chairs today, since the Vice President was already on vacation, two of the four Joint Chiefs were abroad and the President's National Security Advisor was at an off-site meeting.

Speers sat in the back against the wall, chugging an energy drink. At the President's request, Agent Carver sat beside him, leaving O'Keefe to baby-sit Lieutenant Flynn in Georgetown.

This was Carver's first NSC meeting. He turned to Speers. "Is there an agenda, Chief?"

"There are two agendas," Speers whispered. "The President's and the Joint Chiefs'. The President's objective is to get NSC meetings over with as fast as possible, since he'd rather bypass General Wainewright and the Joint Chiefs altogether and keep expanding his executive powers. The Joint Chiefs' agenda – and Dex Jackson's, for that matter – is to bring up as many explosive items as possible within an hour, so that they can publicly say they've attempted to work with the President and won't take the blame for anything that goes wrong. It'll also make for gripping reading after they retire and fish for seven-figure book deals."

Carver shook his head. "Our tax dollars at work."

Secretary of Defense Dexter Jackson checked his watch. As usual, the President and Eva were late. Dex leaned over the table, his caramel face widened in a grin. "A hundred bucks says that Eva comes in about sixty seconds before the POTUS again," he said, using the acronym common in military circles for President of the United States.

General Wainewright looked up from the emails his assistant printed out for him each morning. "Too easy."

"Okay. You want odds? The President walks in right after Eva, and he's still tucking his shirt in."

"You're on," Wainewright said. "And make it two hundred."

Wainewright, a four-star General and the Chairman of the Joint Chiefs of Staff, pulled two hundred-dollar bills out of his wallet. The 58-year-old war horse was simultaneously muscular and overweight. He bench-pressed his weight every morning in his neighborhood gym. He also ate a piece of chocolate cake with brandy at bedtime every night. It all showed.

"Is the AC on?" Wainewright said. He wiped the sweat from his brow. There was nothing wrong with the temperature in the air conditioned room. These were the dog days of summer, yet Wainewright insisted on wearing a dress uniform made heavier by the decorations pinned to it. In addition to the four silver stars on each of his shoulders, General Wainewright wore the Bronze Star, the Army Commendation Medal, the Army Service Ribbon, an Air Assault Badge, the Combat Action Badge, the Distinguished Service Medal and the Legion of Merit.

Eva entered and bid them all good morning. Just as Dex Jackson had predicted, President Hatch arrived some sixty seconds after Eva's entrance, and he was indeed tucking his shirt in. Wainewright reached across the table and slid the two hundred dollars into Dex's waiting hand.

The cabinet secretaries stood out of courtesy until the President sat down. The Joint Chiefs no longer bothered.

"Appreciate you all giving up your Sunday morning," President Hatch began. "It's August. Congress is already in recess and Number Two's already on his way back home. Let's make this a quickie. Dex, whadda ya got?"

"NSA is monitoring several suspected terrorists cells. There's an unusually large amount of chatter, but nothing we can move on." Dex's crow's feet flexed with each utterance. "I recommend we go to Code Orange during the recess."

The President, who had made no secret of regarding Jackson as the politico who cried wolf, shrugged. "But you said yesterday you have no hard data. Nothing specific."

"I hear CIA has something. But frankly, without a Homeland Security chief to facilitate intel coordination between agencies, cooperation hasn't been that great. I'm left to speculate."

"Fine. Put some Guard units at the ports. And be quiet about it."

Wainewright cut in. "What Guard units? I don't know how many different ways I can say this, Mister President, but even my reserves are on their fifth tour overseas. Our only option is to ask Ulysses what it would cost to get some coverage there."

It was Eva's turn to push her agenda. "I don't know if you've looked at the defense budget lately, but I think we're into Ulysses for about all we can afford. Frankly, I think the level at which we're outsourcing our security is getting out of hand."

"All due respect," Dex cut in, "Ulysses is hardly the problem. We've had two domestic bombings in the past year, and our Army is in three war zones. That's not counting covert ops. I'd like to reiterate my proposal to begin strategic pullouts from several of our bases. We need help here at home."

The previous year, a young Islamic fundamentalist had exploded a Chevy Trailblazer on Santa Monica's 3rd Street Promenade on a sunny Saturday afternoon, killing 170 people. The scene repeated itself in Seattle's historic Fish Market, killing another 75. In both cases, the Allied Jihad – an extremist network borne out of the ashes of Al Qaeda – claimed responsibility. The Allied Jihad demanded that the U.S. close American bases in the Middle East, stop supporting Israel and "Zionist" organizations worldwide and cease military and intelligence operations in several predominantly Islamic countries.

In response to the terror attacks, Dex had recommended pulling back U.S. troops – or at least pretending to – while covert Ulysses units systematically located terrorist leaders and eliminated them at various global hotspots. The basis for reasoning was his firm belief that terrorist organizations could not be defeated through conventional warfare.

President Hatch had disagreed vehemently. He wanted to make a statement. Within eight hours of the second bombing, he ordered the Pentagon to immediately invade several Indonesian islands where Allied Jihad cells had taken control from the central government. Ten months later, American forces continued to fight a fierce insurgency that had spread to more islands. Indonesia was the new Iraq.

Now General Wainewright took the opportunity to drive the issue home. "Dex is right," he said. "We're just threadbare here at home. The Allied Jihad's whupping us in Afpack. They're whupping us in Indonesia. We've got twice as many combat-ready forces in the vicinity of Israel and Lebanon than we do stateside. We should start by pulling out of all those areas."

"Hold it," Eva clucked. They had been over and over this. Wainewright's repeated insistence that Israel go it alone was enough to convince her that he was an anti-Semite. "Iran will be in Israel so fast," she said, "it'll make the holocaust look like a warm-up round."

General Wainewright glared at her. "Madam Treasury Secretary, I suggest you stick to counting nickels and dimes."

"If the Pentagon hadn't misappropriated eight billion dollars last year," Eva struck back, referencing an accounting nightmare reported by the Washington Post, "I might have a few dimes to count."

The President tapped his pen against his drinking glass. The room quieted. "I've trimmed the Council size before," he cautioned, "and I'm prepared to go smaller until we find a group that works harmoniously together. None of you have tenure."

"Yes, Mister President," Speers and Carver said in unison from the back of the room. Nobody else responded.

"I expect everyone to bring cool heads after Labor Day. You are dismissed."

The Council wasted no time gathering their things.

"Wait," Eva asked in a voice loud enough for the entire room to hear her. "Was there anything to discuss on Iran?"

The President shot her a glare that was both wicked and intimate. "No," he said. "We're done for the day." Eva grabbed her attaché and left without another word.

The scarcely perceptible moment didn't escape Agent Carver, who elbowed Speers in the ribs.

Carver's cell phone buzzed as the room adjourned. It was O'Keefe. She began spewing something about Lieutenant Flynn. "Slow down," Carver said, retreating to a corner of the room.

"Flynn's dead," she said, only slightly slower.

"Dead? How can he be dead?"

"I went out to pick up breakfast, and when I came back...They came in through the upstairs window. I was only gone fifteen minutes, so they must've been watching the place."

Carver wasn't entirely surprised. Ever since the home's alarm system had gone unrepaired, Carver had been warning his superiors that something like this could happen. You couldn't keep a field house a secret forever, and you certainly couldn't keep one safe without minimum security measures.

"He was garroted," O'Keefe continued. "Looks like they used the sleeve of his own uniform. I'll get the lab out here to confirm it."

"Don't you dare," Carver said. He had handled situations like this at CIA. It was better to cut a few corners and contain the damage. "If anyone finds

Lieutenant Flynn, or finds out that we were holding him, this could blow up in our face and go all the way up the chain."

"I'm not sure what you want me to do."

Carver didn't respond. He couldn't risk anyone linking this to Julian Speers or the President. He was going to have to dump the body. But he didn't want to get into that now. He had to make sure he got all the facts while O'Keefe's mind was still fresh. "Just tell me everything you see."

As he listened to O'Keefe describe the crime scene in greater detail, the main question in Carver's mind was who could possibly know that they were even holding Lieutenant Flynn. Only Speers knew about Flynn's detainment, and Carver trusted him completely. It was evident from his meeting this morning that even the President didn't know the details of the operation's day-to-day activities. "I got a callback from my contact at MobiKomm," O'Keefe added. "Are you sitting down? Flynn put in sixteen calls to Congressman Bailey in the past week. And they were more than just crank calls. The calls lasted nearly two minutes on average, so clearly there was some conversation taking place."

"Bailey? As in Speaker of the House Bailey?" Bailey was an unabashedly redneck five-term Republican Congressman from West Virginia.

"One and the same."

Carver hung up, pulled Speers aside, and explained the situation. The Chief of Staff dashed out into the hallway, racing after the President. "Mister President," Speers said as he caught up with him, "Wait. There's been a development."

The President didn't stop to look at Speers. "Not now, Chief." Speers wasn't about to take no for an answer. He ran alongside the President like a spaniel chasing a truck. "Sir, please. It's urgent."

Exasperated, the President finally stopped and ducked into Mary Chung's office. The 68-year-old grandmother of eight was eating a lox and bagel sandwich as she typed at blistering speed. "I need a moment," the President said, which was a long-understood code that meant he was taking over the room and wanted her to leave. Mary rose and scrambled out of her own office to give him privacy. The President leveled his gaze at Speers. "So where's the fire, Chief?"

"The witness we told you about. He's been murdered. Right under our nose."

"Whoa, whoa, whoa," the President said. "By who?"

"I don't know."

"Julian, I need evidence. Find another witness."

"Sir, the deceased had been talking to Congressman Bailey."

The President's eyebrows shot up. "You can prove that?"

"Not the way we're going about this. It'll never hold up in court. We need an executive order to legitimatize the investigation."

"I will not look like an ass on the Hill. Speaker Bailey, like everybody else, is on vacation. He's probably back in West Virginia playing horseshoes and eating barbecue, which is probably what you should be doing."

"I could –"

"Julian, you need some perspective. I'm ordering you to get your ass on a plane out of D.C. You are not to return to your office for at least three days. Do you understand?"

Speers understood. But he disagreed. He didn't think that anyone in the White House should be going anywhere during wartime, and especially with predators right in their own government. But he realized he had pushed the limits of his freedom. As the vacant chairs in the Cabinet room illustrated, President Hatch had no trouble terminating long-term relationships once he felt they weren't serving his interests. Speers had no choice but to agree. "Yes, Mister President."

Speers stood pondering his options as the Commander-in-Chief exited down the hallway. Mary re-entered her office and put her hand on Speers' shoulder. The two had first been colleagues at the Governor's mansion in Virginia eight years earlier. "Need to talk about it?"

"Nah. I'll be okay."

"The President just asked me to help with your travel arrangements. He said not to take no for an answer."

"Okay, Mary. I won't argue with you. Please get me on the next flight to Charleston, West Virginia."

Mary squinted on him. "Who in their right mind vacations in West Virginia in August?"

Pennsylvania Avenue
8:15 a.m.

Corporal Hammond drove Wainewright's black armored BMW SUV in silence up Pennsylvania Avenue. Hammond was a pencil-thin 21-year-old who hailed from Bakersfield, California, spent his vacations cruising bathhouses in West Hollywood, and had ambitions of one day leveraging his experience in the Pentagon to negotiate a hefty salary as an analyst at Ulysses USA.

He had learned early on in his post at the Chairman's Pentagon offices not to speak until the General spoke to him first. This rule was especially important after National Security meetings at the White House. Wainewright was always especially tense before and after these meetings. Hammond glanced at his boss in the rear view mirror. Sure enough, his left eyelid twitched. It always did when he was upset.

"Fact," General Wainewright said without preamble, "thirty-six states will face severe water shortages in the next ten years." In private moments, the General tended to say odd things out of the blue. Corporal Hammond had still not gotten used to it.

"I didn't know that, sir," Hammond replied. He had learned never to offer his own views on any subject the General threw his way. Wainewright was easily upset.

"You're from California," Wainewright continued. "Your state is using way more than its share of the world's clean drinking water. And who do you think pays for that?"

"I wouldn't know, sir."

"The rest of us! And the President's doing nothing about it."

Hammond looked into the rear view mirror. The whites of his boss' eyes were pink and his pupils looked as sharp as pencil points. He prayed that the General's phone might ring.

"Are you religious?" Wainewright said without segue.

"Yes sir," Corporal Hammond said. "My parents brought me up Presbyterian."

"Do your parents love Israel? Do they believe in defending it?"

"They visited the Holy Land when I was fifteen," Hammond said hesitantly. "It was a dream trip for them, sir."

Wainewright leaned forward and spoke to the back of Hammond's head. "Pop quiz: what was the root cause of the Six-Day war between between Israel and Syria?"

"I don't believe we covered that in school, sir."

"Take a wild-ass guess."

"Anti-Semetism, sir?

"Water rights."

"Good to know, sir."

"Most people would say the war was started by Syrian terrorist attacks. But what was the root cause of that terrorism? Israel was diverting water from the River Jordan to the Sea of Galilee. People were afraid they were going to die of thirst, Corporal. "

"Very interesting, sir."

"Fact: The United States pays Egypt and Israel billions of dollars in foreign aid each year not to fight each other."

"I didn't know that, sir."

"We call it peacekeeping. You have any idea what kind of water-conserving technology we could make if we weren't paying the Middle East not to self-destruct?"

"Not a clue, sir."

"Fact: There are certain powerful evangelical groups that support Israel not because they embrace or even tolerate Judaism, but because they believe the Biblical prophecies stating that Jews have to be in certain settlements for the End of Days."

Hammond thought they had been discussing water rights. Now he had no idea what the common thread of this conversation was about. He chose to remain silent.

The General sighed and said, "You understand what I mean by the End of Days?"

"No sir. I mean not exactly, sir."

Wainewright laughed darkly. "Fact: The creation of Israel was an evangelical wet dream. Luke 21:20-33. Look it up. Jews will be judged and subsequently wiped out, just as the Christians will be judged and ascend to heaven to sit at the right hand of God. In order for the prophecies in the Bible to be fulfilled, Israel must continue to exist."

The Corporal was still a small town boy at heart. He hadn't met anyone in the military that was so openly critical of the Church. He tried to remain polite. "Thank you for the information, sir."

"Shut up." Wainewright pulled an open bottle of sparkling water from his drink holder, took a long sip and looked out the window. "Pull over in front of the park. We're taking a meeting."

Hammond merged into the right lane and pulled into a curbside spot in front of James Monroe Park, a sliver of green space where local yuppies took their dogs to poop on the grass. "Is this good, sir?"

"Put up the divider."

Thank God. Corporal Hammond pressed the divider button. A layer of tinted soundproof glass rose between the front and back seat. He caught movement in his peripheral vision and saw a man in an oversized black button-down shirt and sunglasses approach the car from the passenger side. The man, who seemed to have trouble walking, hobbled toward the BMW's rear passenger door and tapped a gold-tipped cane on the glass.

*

Jeff Taylor's Stanford MBA had done little to prepare him for his job as a Blackwater executive during the American occupation in Iraq. He escaped three ambushes during his first months in the country. In his sixth month, an IED detonated under his SUV, killing two of his colleagues and vaporizing his own legs above the knee. Taylor spent the next three months enduring various surgeries, then a few more learning how to walk with his new artificial legs.

By the time he was ready to go back to work, Blackwater had been banned from Iraq for indiscriminate use of force. It was bad timing for everyone involved. The American military was ramping back up in Afghanistan and could no longer maintain their troop levels in Iraq. The Iraqi infrastructure was growing steadily, but the government was still in no position to take up the slack that Blackwater had provided.

But while the rest of the world saw disaster, Taylor saw nothing but opportunity. He saw the private security industry as a veritable gold rush, an ancient industry that was still in a pubescent stage. His time in Blackwater had given him invaluable ties in the Pentagon that he had kept strong. He also had kept in touch with many of the company's laid-off employees. He began working the phones, calling his network of B-School grads, pitching the investment opportunities that could be made from the treasure trove of available government contracts. During the first round of fundraising for his Ulysses USA, he garnered $350 million in venture capital. Ulysses USA was born.

These days, Taylor had few complaints. Ulysses USA had taken in 9 billion dollars during the previous fiscal year. Given the President's voracious interventionist foreign policy, and the precipitous drop in volunteer military recruiting, Ulysses was still poised for growth. His primary challenge was dealing with the meddling and impossible personal demands of his biggest advocate, General Wainewright.

Taylor climbed into the SUV and sat next to the General. As usual, Wainewright spoke to Taylor without ever looking him in the face. "Appreciate you coming."

"I don't see why we couldn't meet in Chantilly," Taylor grumbled. Ulysses had recently completed its new corporate headquarters in Chantilly, Virginia. The campus included a private residence for Taylor and hydrogen-powered vehicles that whisked the disabled CEO anywhere he wanted to go in the sprawling complex.

Wainewright bristled. He had personally signed twelve billion dollars in new government contracts over to Ulysses in the past year, and had given the company access to some of the finest weaponry the United States military had in its possession. He realized that Taylor's injuries handicapped him a little, but he didn't see why taking a trip into the Capitol every once in a while was such a big deal.

"Your errand boy came to the Pentagon yesterday," Wainewright said. "He assured me my facility is ready to go. I wanted to hear it from you."

"That errand boy is the 60-year-old COO of my Engineering division," Taylor pointed out. "And like the man said, the facility is ready."

"Good. I'll be needing it today."

Taylor's skin turned a little paler. "Today?"

"I trust that won't be a problem."

"It's just that…that kind of facility is really built for the unexpected."

Wainewright measured his response. "Our intelligence has picked up on something. This is purely classified, you understand."

"I won't breathe a word, General." Taylor was clearly startled. "Is there anything you can tell me personally? Should I stay away from airports? Shopping malls?"

Wainewright ignored the question. "I'm also going to need those forces you promised me." The General was referring to an order for three full battalions of elite Ulysses soldiers that would answer directly to him. "Put the control operations team on alert. That means bags packed, ready to go at a moment's notice. The other units we discussed shouldn't stray too far from home either."

Taylor laughed nervously. "General, I've always been able to come up with what you need at the drop of a hat, but this is –"

"Are you happy with your stock price?" Wainewright said. He waited for Taylor to nod his head submissively. Then he began again: "Then know your place. All I have to do is speculate on a few of your government contracts. Just a little slip of the tongue, and Ulysses stock plummets by fifty percent or better."

The CEO's face lost more color. "There's no need for threats," he said. "We want the same things. You'll get what you've asked for."

"Next item. One of your senior field operatives works for me now."

"Who? I haven't been notified of any key staff changes."

"That will become clear to you shortly. All you need to know is that he's going to stay on your books and continue to enjoy his salary. I trust that'll be all right with you."

Taylor was hardly in a position to refuse. Although Ulysses had a growing revenue stream in private corporate contracts, losing the Pentagon's business now would be fatal. They had spent heavily this year on R & D, infrastructure and recruiting. Property taxes on the Chantilly compound alone would be nearly nine hundred million dollars a year. The bulk of their business plan was built around growth of Pentagon contracts, and leveraging that growth for global market share. Without the Pentagon's continued revenue, the security giant would be woefully overextended. They would have to lay off most of the soldiers they had spent so much to train.

Wainewright extended his hand and shook Taylor's. "Forget it. Thanks for coming into the city." With that, Taylor opened the door, steadied his cane on the ground, and hobbled back to the stretch limousine waiting for him on the other side of the park.

Georgetown
9:20 a.m.

Carver returned to Field House DC310 rolling two pieces of luggage behind him. It was the high-end stuff – industrial-grade locks, dent-proof, leak-proof – that he would never be able to afford on his government salary. It wasn't, however, beyond the means of his alias, Ethan Danforth. Sometimes being a spy had its perks. Too bad the luggage wasn't packed for an island vacation.

He drew his gun discreetly before unlocking the door. It wasn't likely that the perpetrators would return to the scene of the murder, but he would take no chances. He popped inside and cleared the ground floor rooms first, then the upstairs, where he found the point of entry – one of the rear upstairs windows had been broken, the too-thin window bars clipped with some sort of bolt-cutter. An aluminum ladder was still extended from the back lawn. Damn. If the agency couldn't afford to secure field houses, they should be condemned.

Carver went back downstairs, stopping for a moment to appreciate the photos that had been digitally created by the agency graphic arts department. Despite Carver and O'Keefe having never appeared together in public, or even taken a single photo together, the agency had inserted them as a couple at several black-tie affairs. They were dancing. Talking with "friends." Holding champagne glasses. Another set had them at a wedding among a big family that Carver wished was his own. He had to admit that he and O'Keefe looked good together in their alternate universe. It was too bad that the field house had been compromised. All these pics would have to be destroyed. He was going to miss them.

In the basement he found Lieutenant Flynn's body on the floor in the same position O'Keefe had described to him on the phone. The sleeve of Flynn's uniform was still twisted around his neck. Carver pulled it away and noted that the bruises around the neck were consistent with O'Keefe's assessment. Flynn had been garroted.

He shook his head. The crime scene was bound to be full of DNA samples. If only he could get the lab out here, as O'Keefe had suggested. But that was impossible now. He had to clean this mess up so that the clandestine investigation wouldn't be discovered. He had to protect the President. And Julian. Definitely Julian. The Chief had no idea what kind of trouble he had let loose with his investigation.

He opened the luggage and pulled out rubber gloves, sheets of plastic, a chemical suit, cleaning equipment and an electric buzz saw with spare blades. He tested the blade's sharpness against the fleshy part of his palm. Then he plugged it into an outlet near the basement sink.

The chemical suit was made of lightweight nylon, the type used by pest control professionals or arborists, not bio-engineers. He pulled it on and followed with the gloves. Then he stacked several antique milk crates next to the sink, taking care to ensure that the height was equivalent. Finally, he covered the area in plastic sheets – walls, floor and ceiling. He checked his watch. It had been eighteen minutes since he had entered the house. He had to hurry. He was supposed to meet O'Keefe at Lee Federal Penitentiary shortly.

He grabbed Flynn by the ankles and began dragging him across the basement. It never failed. The officer was much heavier dead than alive. What about those twelve grams the body was supposed to lose after death? It felt more like twelve tons were added.

With some trying, he managed to get Flynn's torso up on the milk crates. The Lieutenant's stiff legs were now extended over the sink.

As Carver turned on the tap, he gazed up at the black and white photo of the home's prior inhabitants filleting trout at the very sink where he was about to dismember Flynn. A chuckle escaped his lips.

"Sorry," he said as he picked up the saw. "I mean no disrespect."

Yeager Airport Charleston, West Virginia 10:40 a.m.

Speers drove out of the airport rental car lot in a white economy car, still wearing the gray suit he'd questioned Lieutenant Flynn in before sunup. He got onto the freeway and spoke slowly to the car's navigation system: "Local search. Monroe. West Virginia. Holy Grace Baptist Church."

The nav chewed on the request for a moment before it started barking out orders. "Turn left in twenty feet…Merge right onto I-79…Straight ahead for one mile…"

He had napped for the entire 73-minute duration of the flight, and yet he was still groggy enough to have trouble following the nav system's directions. He managed to merge onto I-79 toward Monroe before his phone rang.

It was Mrs. Tenningclaus, his 71-year-old neighbor. "Good morning, Misses Tenningclaus," Speers answered. "How are you?"

"Julian dear," Mrs. Tenningclaus began, "My sister in Phoenix broke her hip."

"Sorry to hear that. Is she okay?"

"I just said she broke her hip. I'm headed to Arizona to see her right now. Would you be a prince and look in on the cats?"

Mrs. Tenningclaus lived all alone in the big brownstone across from Speers' building, and the fact that Speers was the White House Chief of Staff – one of the most important jobs in the free world – did not dissuade her from calling on him often for trivial errands or cat sitting. Like Speers, she didn't have any other family in town. Speers didn't mind. Mrs. Tenningclaus reminded Speers of his late mother, who had passed from heart disease during the President's first term. Plus, he was often rewarded with Ms. Tenningclaus' homemade blueberry scones and strawberry jam. He loved the look on her face when he told her it was the best damn jam in D.C.

"Consider it done," Speers told her just as his call waiting flashed. He bid Ms. Tenningclaus good luck and switched to the other line, where Carver began complaining immediately.

"I've been trying to get through for an hour," Carver said.

"Just got off the plane," Speers explained. "On my way to see Congressman Bailey now."

"Hold it. You're not actually going to come right out and ask him about Lieutenant Flynn, are you?"

"You know your problem, Carver? You're a cynic. You assume everyone's dirty. There may be a perfectly good reason that Lieutenant Flynn called the Speaker of the House."

Carver couldn't believe his ears. "Oh, like what? Are they both members of the Capitol City Men's Chorus?"

"Think about it. The Lieutenant had obviously networked way above his pay grade. Doesn't happen by accident. Maybe he was being blackmailed. Bailey's the

Chairman of the House Intelligence Committee. Maybe the Lieutenant was reaching out for support."

"You've got a vivid imagination," Carver said. "I guess that's why you're in the Executive Branch."

The rental car's nav system cut in: "Exit in one quarter-mile."

"Listen," Carver said. "The reason I called. The Lieutenant never existed, okay? You never saw him. We never talked to anyone about him. Got it?"

Speers was quiet for a moment. "If you say so. You'll tell me what happened at some point, right?"

"No, Julian."

"I'm the Chief of Staff. Don't forget that. I could order you to tell me."

"For your own sake, no. Now go have a nice chat with the Congressman."

Lee Federal Correctional Facility
Lee, Virginia

Carver passed through the metal detector and gathered his watch, phone, SIG, ammo, money clip and belt from a plastic bucket. This was his first time in a federal prison. A tall, portly guard stood behind him, grinning as he watched Carver struggle to slip back into his black oxfords.

"Might help if you untied the shoelaces," the guard cracked.

"Shut it," Carver said.

Meagan O'Keefe came through next, pulling on her brown penny loafers. The humidity from last night's rain had shortened her long strawberry-blond curls to tight, shoulder-length coils.

"I raced the whole way here," O'Keefe said, a little out of breath. She wiped her sweaty hands on her pantsuit. "Suicide job threw himself in front of the Blue Line."

The guard motioned for them to follow him down the hallway.

"Death by subway," Carver pondered. "Not a bad way to go. Quick. A sure thing."

O'Keefe scrunched up her face. "Messy. Gimmie pills any day."

"No. Too painful. Not decisive enough."

"Exactly my point. It's that moment just as you decide to do it when you wish you hadn't. Or at least that's what they say."

Carver smiled. "I enjoy our banter."

The guard led them past several cells with bored-looking inmates in orange jumpsuits.

"Who's the convict?" O'Keefe said.

"Nico Gold," Carver said with dread. "Serving twenty years for grand larceny. He wrote a program that lifted small, nearly undetectable sums out of millions of foreign bank accounts."

"Sounds like a hacker. You said we needed a linguist."

"Hacking's just a lucrative sideline. Languages are his passion. That program he wrote? It worked in twelve languages, including Russian, Hebrew, Hungarian and Arabic. He cracked the World Bank and the IMF."

"Maybe he can fix my credit score."

The guard opened a second set of gates and led them to a white door with a four-by-four inch opening. The guard filled it first with his puffy eyes, then with his mouth. "Visitors," he said directly into it.

He unlocked the door and turned to Carver. "Nico's not dangerous. I'll be down the hall. Just yell."

They entered the windowless room that was illuminated only by a skylight and closed the door behind them. Nico Gold sat at the plain plywood table in a short-sleeve orange jumpsuit. He was pale and lean with clear-framed eyeglasses, just as he'd appeared in his mug shot five years ago, but he had added tattoos to both forearms that said simply, "EVA." He closed the book he was reading and placed it on the table before him.

"Carver and O'Keefe," Carver said by way of introduction. He had gotten used to saying *CIA* after his name. Now he was a man without an agency. "Federal agents."

O'Keefe eyed the title of Nico's book. "Conversational Cornish?"

"Cornish is a Celtic language," Nico explained. His voice dripped with condescension.

"It's also a dead language."

"What else am I gonna do, pump iron?"

Carver opened his briefcase and pulled out a folder marked CLASSIFIED. He threw it on the table in front of Nico. The prisoner opened it and began pouring over the scramble of letters and phonetic characters.

Nico's mouth twisted into a smirk. "Oh," he said with cynical delight. "You're coming to *me* with a problem?"

"Coded transmissions," Carver explained. "Our geeks got past the encryption phase, but the code is something else."

Nico looked for only a moment more, then rose from the table and walked to the door. He put his mouth to the tiny opening near the top of the door and yelled "Guard!"

O'Keefe was flabbergasted. "What're you doing? This meeting isn't over."

Nico turned to her. "You're not the first spooks to come in here looking for help. If you're serious, put an offer in writing and submit it through my attorney."

Carver reached into his briefcase once more, whipped out a pre-written negotiated deal. He handed it to Nico. "Official enough for you? It's signed by a federal judge."

Nico scanned the document, shrugged. "What else ya got?"

"Full disclosure," Carver went on, "There's no time for negotiations. We think we have a major terrorist threat on our hands."

Nico looked the agents over, sensing leverage. O'Keefe stood with her arms across her chest, biting her lip to the point of drawing blood. Nico smiled, clearly delighted. "Y'know, the Russians have a saying: Smart wolves don't chase deer. They just wait by the river."

Carver had expected this, and he was ready with the carrot. "Help us catch these guys and I'll cut your sentence in half."

"Uh-uh. Come back to the river when you're thirsty."

Carver heard footsteps and saw the guard's eyes fill the door window once again. He turned to Nico. "You want high stakes? Fine. You break the code before anyone gets hurt and I'll get you a Presidential pardon. Anything less and we double your sentence."

The guard spoke through the opening in the door. "Everything okay here?" he said.

Nico turned to the door and smiled. "Ask the concierge to send down my things. I'll be checking out today."

Carver and O'Keefe took some air outside the prison's main office as Nico was processed for release into their custody. Carver took a pack of mint-flavored gum from his pocket and offered her a piece. "Sugarless," he said.

"Figures." O'Keefe smiled and took a piece. She had long given up on coaxing the nutritionally pious Agent Carver to try so much as a donut. "Have you ever even had a cavity?"

"Nope."

She stepped closer to him. Close enough so he could smell her peppermint shampoo. Carver felt a chill on his neck. It always happened when O'Keefe invaded his personal space.

"So," she said. "Losing any sleep over this?"

It had been a long time since he had been with a woman. Even longer since he had been in a relationship. He had allowed his work to completely devour him. It was nearly impossible to get close to anyone with a normal life with his schedule. And unlike many of his colleagues, he had absolutely no taste for one night stands or hookers. O'Keefe was the first woman he had felt a connection to since coming back from Afpak, and it had taken a mountain of willpower to keep the relationship professional. He had gone down that slippery slope with her once, and barely escaped with the professional relationship intact.

He stepped back slightly. "Losing sleep over what?"

"The investigation. Someone died on our watch, and you did God knows what to clean it up. I'm wondering if that bothers you at all."

"No," Carver said. "Not in the slightest. We don't even know Lieutenant Flynn's motivation for doing what he did, but at the very least, he assisted in the killing of a soldier under his direct command, and coordinated weapons that got into the wrong hands, putting hundreds more in danger."

She shook her head. "He was still a human being. Not a piece of garbage."

"Look," Carver said with an edge that took her off guard. "If you feel you can't perform up to your potential on this case because of your political beliefs..."

She scowled. "Don't give me that. You know my work ethic. I'm asking your personal opinion."

"My personal opinion doesn't count."

"I'm asking as a friend."

"Tell me why it matters."

"Because I've got a right to know who I'm working with."

Carver grinned. "Good answer. Okay then. I think the President is generally well-meaning. But he's also a narcissist with lousy taste in friends. Starting these wars was a bad idea, and outsourcing the fighting is even worse. If we get half a chance, I'll gladly feed any of these Ulysses execs head-first into a wood chipper."

Monroe, West Virginia
10:57 a.m.

Faruq Ahmed sat parallel parked in his Ford F-450 on Main Street. Exactly one quarter-mile in the distance, at the end of the street, he could see the clock tower at Holy Grace Baptist Church. It was nearly show time.

As had become his habit during practice runs at Gatlin Raceway, he sat clutching a stopwatch. The .38 rested on his lap. The Koran lay on the seat next to him. Ammonium nitrate filled the truck bed, which was covered with a leather snap-down bed cover. Last night he had completed the final step – removing the front driver airbags and replacing them with a concentration of C-4 that had been molded to fit the airbag cavities.

He was proudest of this development. In the past, too many suicide vehicles had failed to detonate upon impact. For this reason, the latest Allied Jihad manual had instructed its jihadists to install a hot button on the steering wheel, which the driver would manually trigger a split-second before impact. Ahmed found this unacceptable. For one, it would leave too much to chance. God forbid he should crash on his way to the target, be knocked unconscious, captured and drugged for information. Also, he could be sure that if he could take the Ford into the church's front doors, he would be assured complete destruction and maximum casualties. Pre-crash detonation would leave too many wounded. That had been the beauty of 9/11, Ahmed, thought. The New York City hospitals had waited hours for the wounded to arrive. But there were no wounded. Only dead.

Ahmed had wired the front-impact crash sensors directly to the C-4, leaving nothing to chance. As a secondary precaution, he had doused the ammonium nitrate in gasoline.

He watched each passing car closely. It was already 10:58. The service was to start at 11:00. Congressman Bailey had a reputation for being on time.

Less than a minute later, the black sedan with Washington D.C. plates finally passed him. The windows were tinted too darkly to see inside, but he was sure this was the car. He clicked the stopwatch and started the truck engine, patiently watching as the seconds ticked by.

Finally he put the truck into gear. "May Allah's will be done," he said.

*

Julian Speers' rental car navigation system barked its final directive: *"Drive straight ahead one half-mile."* He drove slowly. There was little that amused him more than reading signage in the deep South. Biblical dogma was infused with everything from commerce to politics. A church: *JESUS WANTS OUT OF THE UNITED NATIONS*. An appliance store: *ALL DISHWASHERS 50% OFF! REVELATIONS 11:18 - NOW THE TIME HAS*

COME FOR THE DEAD TO BE JUDGED. GET YOUR KENMORE TODAY!

He could see the Holy Grace Baptist clock tower in the distance. It was there, he was told, that Congressman Bailey would be attending the 11:00 a.m. service today. Speers' plan was to slip in late, sit in the back, and approach Bailey afterwards.

How to approach Bailey was another matter. Speers' objective was to find out why the most powerful man in Congress would make time to speak directly with a simple army Lieutenant. The way he saw it, Bailey was unlikely to spill his guts. That was okay by Speers. All he wanted was an indicator. If Bailey denied talking to Lieutenant Flynn altogether, or pretended not to know who he was, then Bailey was likely in cahoots with him. If he admitted to knowing Bailey, then Speers would fact-check whatever he said.

"One quarter-mile to destination," the nav system said.

Suddenly a Ford F-450 pulled out from the curb, nearly broadsiding him.

"Asshole!" Speers shouted out the open car window, but the truck barreled ahead, running the red light and picking up speed as it went through the small-town intersection. "So much for Sunday drivers."

Holy Grace sat at the end of the small but bustling retail district, forming the T at the end of Main Street. From its pulpit, the Reverend Jimmy Swaggart himself had once stood denouncing rock and roll as the devil's music. The deacon opened the sanctuary doors, releasing the organist's sweeping call to worship as the last of the flock trickled in. He saw the heat fumes rising from the asphalt and felt the sweat trickle down his sideburns, into the collar of his white starched shirt.

Congressman Bill Bailey's black sedan pulled up to the space reserved for the church's most generous donor. The deacon grinned, knowing how pleased the reverend would be to know that the congressman was in services today.

"Hey Dale," Congressman Bailey yelled when he stepped out of the car. "How's your shoulder?"

"It's a-talkin' to me, Mister Speaker," the deacon shouted back. He had once called him Bill, decades ago, when Bailey was a mere junior congressman who still ran a machine shop in his spare time. Now he had risen to be Speaker of the House, just two steps from the Presidency. A man that powerful couldn't just go by Bill.

He helped the Speaker's wife, Gladys Bailey, up the steps and handed her a program. "Any luck wettin' a line?" he said as they stepped inside.

"The bass are slow. The heat, I reckon. We might try crawdads."

They never heard the Ford F-450 coming.

*

Faruq Ahmed accelerated to 65 mph. In a move he had practiced time and again in the preceding weeks, he jerked the steering wheel to the right at the last possible moment and sent the truck skiing up the church's wheelchair ramp, passenger-side wheels clearing the front steps. The truck went briefly airborne and sailed through the church's double front doors.

*

Speers felt the church blast in his rental car from five blocks away. His windshield filled with white light and the car bounced on its shocks. A cloud-like expanse of black smoke billowed before him.

He stepped out of the car. A piece of insulation hit him in the forehead. It felt more like a brick than a four-ounce piece of cauterized foam.

"C'mere," someone said. A liver-spotted hand gripped his bicep. Speers touched his own forehead and felt blood. The next thing he knew, he was standing in a storefront doorway next to an elderly man in a white suit. Chunks of smoking debris fell around them.

"That's my church," the man said. "That's my church."

Speers' face fell even further. "That's Holy Grace? Congressman Bailey's..."

"Yessir. The Speaker hisself. I saw his car pass by just a minute ago."

As Speers ran back toward the rental car, he held a newspaper over his head to shield himself from the ensuing particle rain. Once back inside, he switched on the windshield wipers to clear the ash from his view. He flipped a U-Turn and drove back down Main Street, honking as he drove through the fast-gathering crowd.

Shaw Air Force Base, South Carolina 11:02 a.m.

Major Cleveland Dobbs was halfway through his shift at CENTAF, the nerve center for the Eastern U.S strategic air defense. The burly, mustachioed officer sat at his terminal at the top of the CENTAF command room, an amphitheatre-shaped room about the size of a movie theatre. It was here that Dobbs supervised eighteen air traffic controllers who in turn coordinated over a hundred coastal fighter patrols in a single shift. Since 9/11, fighter aircraft were constantly in proximity to every major U.S. airport. Keeping them clear of mid-air collisions in the increasingly crowded skies was a tough job. Dobbs spent most of his day actively monitoring the work of his rather green staff. At a cost of between thirty and fifty million dollars per aircraft, there was no room for error.

His headset crackled as the Secret Service special agent aboard Marine One – the President's personal helicopter – hailed him. "CENTAF, this is Dynasty requesting a flight plan." For security reasons, it was protocol for the duty officer to manage Marine One and Air Force One personally. Marine One departure flight times were strictly classified; they happened unannounced, and flight plans were randomly generated by CENTAF on the fly. Helicopters, even the latest VH-71 Kestrels that Marine One flew, were simply too easy to shoot down to risk any security leaks.

"Copy that, Dynasty," Dobbs replied over his headset. "Verify destination."

"Red Zone," the Secret Service agent said, giving the current destination codename for Camp David, the longtime Presidential retreat in Frederick County, Maryland. The flight between the White House and Camp David was a short one, and there were eight randomized flight paths varying between nineteen and twenty-six minutes in duration. The algorithm by which the CENTAF computers determined the route was a mystery, even to Major Dobbs. He had simply been trained to log into the Marine One application, list "Red Zone" as the destination, and click a button marked "GENERATE." The computer would chew on it for less than one-tenth of a second and display the route to Dobbs.

The codename appeared on his screen. "The flight plan is Slasher," Dobbs said. "Slasher."

"Copy that CENTAF," came Marine One's reply. The pilots had each of the routes committed to memory. No written or electronic flight plans existed.

Flight plan Slasher took Marine One due north, where it would be joined in mid-air by three identical VH-71 Kestrels all bearing the Marine One paint and insignia. These helicopters were decoys. The choppers flew in a pattern that was similar to cards shuffling in and out of a deck. From the ground, it was virtually impossible to tell which chopper carried the President.

Precisely one minute later, Dobbs tracked a pair of F-35s launched out of Langley to enforce the six-mile no-fly radius that was enforced around Camp David when the POTUS was in residence. A former combat chopper pilot himself, Dobbs viewed this as critical, since there were typically dozens of civilian aircraft that unwittingly penetrated Camp David airspace each year. From the moment the escorts joined the group, it would be only minutes before the entire group cleared the I-495 beltway and flew at low altitude over the rolling hills of Maryland.

The route now set, Major Dobbs removed his headset and looked over his crew. He frowned at the less than bumper crop of controllers. Most of these recruits had been in less than a year. Some were trainees that had no business here. All the experienced controllers were either on duty overseas or aboard aircraft carriers and AWACS planes. Still others had left to work for Ulysses. CENTAF was stretched thin, just like everyone else in the military.

Dobbs' red phone rang. He knew immediately from the urgent voice on the other end that this wasn't a drill. He listened wordlessly, hung up, and turned to the room of controllers.

"Car bomb in Monroe, West Virginia," he barked. The controllers stared back at Dobbs blankly, unsure what a car bomb had to do with airspace security. "Assume threat level red," Dobbs said. "Keep the first shift patrols up," he said, referring to the fighter planes that, since 9/11, had been timed with the early a.m. wave of passenger jets rolling out of Regan National Airport, Dulles, BWI, Boston Logan, Newark, JFK and LaGuardia. The idea was to have a critical mass of fighter jets on the east coast in case of attack. They were prepared, if necessary, to intercept hijacked planes at the times of heaviest traffic. "Scramble the second crew to fill the gaps."

The controllers got on the radio and began notifying their patrols. Dobbs put on his headset and radioed the news to Marine One, advising them to pick up their airspeed and watch their altitude.

Frederick County, Maryland
11:07 a.m.

The forest was dead silent save for a very distant rumble of road noise that appeared only as gusts of breeze blew from the southwest. Chris Abrams and his four-man USOC crew were positioned roughly twenty yards apart, high in the canopies of beetle-ravaged hickory trees. The men had backpacked into the Maryland woods the night before, dressed as average weekend warriors looking for a trout stream and a place to camp. But in actuality their packs contained cordless drills, tree stands typically marketed to deer hunters, climbing spikes, MREs and, most importantly, shoulder-fired Stinger missiles. At an awkward five-foot long and thirty-six pounds each, the missiles were carried in hard shell fly rod cases that had been substantially enlarged and elongated for the mission.

Abrams listened intently for the sound of rotors. At a quarter past the hour, flight plan Slasher was due to bring the President's helicopter directly overhead. With five shooters and four helicopters, Abrams had eliminated the need to identify Marine One from its decoys. They would simply destroy all of them.

At six-foot-six, Abrams was easily the crew's tallest member. And as his sleeveless vest revealed, he also appeared to be the most ripped. But in actuality, Abrams wasn't as healthy as he appeared. His body fat was perilously low, and in addition to adjusting the medication that kept the HIV virus in check, his doctor had just put him on a ten thousand calories-per-day diet

– as much as some Olympic athletes. He was one of the few 34-year-old men in America for whom dessert was a necessity.

A Carolina Wren landed in the tree next to Abrams and launched into a loud, looping melody. Abrams shook his head and rubbed his shaved scalp. A reasonably quiet forest was essential to the mission. The rust-bellied, notoriously high-decibel wrens had pumped out a bumper crop this year all over the Southeastern U.S., and Abrams had brought a pump-action air pistol specifically for this reason. He pulled it out for the sixth time this morning, pumped it several times, leveraged it at the wren's white eye stripe and fired a pellet deftly into it. The songbird tumbled from the tree, gasping and fluttering on its way to rest in a heap of feathers beside the others that Abrams had killed that morning.

At exactly 11:10 a.m., Abrams pulled out a cocktail of HIV and metabolism-slowing medicine. He swallowed the four pills without water and pulled out a protein packet, knowing it might be at least two hours before he would have time to eat again. He was already thinking about his next meal. He wanted to celebrate. He wanted short ribs from Rocklands Barbecue over on Wisconsin Avenue, where the smoke coming off the grill was so powerful that you would smell like barbecue for two days. It was the best barbecue in D.C. The best anywhere.

But Rocklands was off-limits now. Earlier in the year, Abrams had eaten there every time he went to the city to meet his Pentagon contacts. The last time, the server had surprised him by asking to put Abrams' picture on the wall. He said that the staff had taken to calling Abrams "Trip," short for "Triplicate," because he always ordered and ate three courses. But Abrams didn't let them take his picture. He wouldn't even tell them his name. He just took his three bags and got the hell out of there. After that, he never visited anyplace more than once, no matter how good the food was.

Now the faint mechanical humming – like a thousand far-away bees – registered in Abrams' eardrums, growing louder by the second. To Abrams' trained ear, it was the unmistakable sound of four VH-71 Kestrel helicopters flying in formation. They were slightly ahead of schedule. He stuffed the granola bar in his pocket and readied himself.

"I hear rotors," Abrams said in Muskogee into the Bluetooth on his lapel. He repeated the phrase to make sure there were no misunderstandings. His four-man crew each knew only about fifteen hundred words of Muskogee, and he was far from fluent himself.

While these woods were typically unbearably thick with foliage in summer, this area had been chosen specifically for its thin canopies, the result of a beetle blight the year earlier that had killed off about half the area's hickories. Abrams had been assured that Marine One would fly directly overhead. They were just outside the six-mile no-fly zone, so they were unlikely to be spotted by patrolling F-35s.

Abrams listened closely, timing the growing decibel level of the rotors with his watch. "They're coming too fast," he said in broken Muskogee. He and his men had trained in these very woods during two previous Presidential fly-overs. During those sessions, the President's airborne convoy had flown 120 mph at most. He could only assume that some other part of the operation, which he had been in the dark of, had tipped Marine One off.

The rotor sound grew loud enough for all five men to hear it. Timing would be critical. Given the choppers' low altitude and relatively high speed, they would have a second or less for the Stinger to lock onto its target, emit its distinctive high-pitched buzz, and pull the trigger. Plus, they would have to fire at roughly the same time, ensuring that all four VH-71s were destroyed. There would be no opportunity for second chances. Should one missile strike a target too early, the other heat-seeking Stingers could converge on the exploded target, or worse, the real Marine One could release its anti-SAM countermeasures and escape amidst the mid-air fracas.

He stashed his air pistol, pulled out his field scope and watched as his men took the Stingers out of their five-foot long tubes, rose on their tree stands, placed the Stingers on their right shoulders, and pointed them skyward. Abrams' was like all the others, except for one detail – he had a tiny camera mounted on his scope.

"Get ready boys," Abrams growled in Muskogee. "Here they come."

Aboard Marine One
11:07 a.m.

"This is Santa Monica and Seattle all over again!" President Hatch complained into his skyphone. He had just learned of the bombing in Monroe. Dressed in a tweed blazer and dark denim jeans – Camp David attire was decidedly informal – the President sat aboard Marine One en route to meet the Iranian Ambassador. They were accompanied by three identical VH-71 Kestrels flying in an inverted V formation. To minimize their exposure, the pilots were maxing out at 190 mph and flying so low that they practically skimmed the tops of the power lines.

The unlucky bureaucrat on the receiving end of the President's rant was Homeland Security Deputy Director Devon Davis. Davis was on vacation in Fort Lauderdale, and had only learned of the incident seconds before the President himself. Davis' boss had been fired after the Seattle car bombing earlier in the year, and Davis was the Acting Director until a replacement was found.

"Mister President," Deputy Director Davis said as he tried to get off the phone, "I'll call you as soon as I have details."

"You've got a helluva nerve. Don't you dare cut it short on me at a time like this."

"Sorry, Mister President. It's just that –"

"Any intel pointing to Iranian involvement in this?"

"Not that I know of, sir. Do you have reason to believe they did? "

"Let's just say the timing is odd," the President replied, thinking of the sudden, out-of-nowhere request by the Iranian Ambassador. So far, Eva was the only cabinet member whom he'd alerted about the meeting with the Iranians, and he sure as hell wasn't going to explain it to the very green Davis now. He hung up and looked out the window as Marine One banked at high speed.

His phone rang again. It was Julian Speers. "Congressman Bailey is dead," Speers blurted out. "He was killed in the blast."

The President was stunned. "I just got off the phone with Homeland Security. They've got nothing on that."

"I was there!" Speers shouted so loudly that the President had to pull the phone away from his ear. "I'm ninety-eight percent sure. The explosion was so big. Nothing could've survived that." President Hatch got a breathless earful as Speers confessed that he had disobeyed the order to take a vacation, and had instead gone down to Monroe this very morning to talk to Congressman Bailey.

"God Almighty, Julian. Don't go rogue on me. I need you."

"I'm sorry. I can explain."

"Never mind. Where are you now?"

"Headed back to the airport. Sir, I don't want to sound paranoid, but maybe we should operate from Site R." Site R was codename for Raven Rock, the not-so-secret, but still virtually impenetrable emergency bunker in Maryland.

"Negative. Meet me at Camp David."

"I'd like to check with Agent Rios on that. I'd like to get his opinion about heading to Site R."

The President signed off tersely, privately fearing Speers was right as usual. He knew that if he had followed his Chief of Staff's advice more often, the administration would probably be in better shape. His main problem with Julian was that he made decisions from a position of fear. But as the President was learning, the world had devolved into a state where fear-based problem-solving was often the best approach.

He looked out the window and saw the green Maryland hills below blurring past. He turned to the Secret Service agent sitting in the seat beside him, and wished the man was Eva. She would know how to approach the meeting.

"Incoming!" the pilot suddenly shouted over the cabin radio. Deafening missile warning alarms sounded. Marine One jerked wildly left. The President grasped for something to hold onto.

A brilliant white flash blinded him temporarily. One of the decoy choppers had been hit. The President watched as the Marine One clone flying next to them jerked right to evade a SAM.

Time slowed as the President watched the adjacent Kestrel's rotors slice into Marine One's aft, sending the treetop-level craft spinning downward through the hillside vegetation. A vision of his late wife was suddenly thrust upon him. She was sickly and cross. He tried hard to summon an image of her face in the good times, before the cancer. A laugh. A smile. He couldn't. His thoughts turned to that gray winter day in Northern Virginia at Sovereign Hills Cemetery. Eva had been there, standing on the other side of the casket with the others from his Gubernatorial staff. He remembered the pre-inscribed, double-wide headstone.

Jan Tolle Hatch
Loving Mother
Born: 1960
Died: 2009

Isaac Samuel Hatch
Governor of Virginia
Born: 1961
Died:

The idea that they would someday be interred side-by-side had comforted his wife in the days before they passed. But Hatch had never been at peace with it. The pre-inscribed headstone seemed to beckon death.

A wave of compressed air knocked Marine One sideways. Kevlar air bags deployed in a protective cocoon around him. He was completely insulated as the smoldering chopper jounced manically through several poplar trees to the ground.

The President blacked out as he hung upside down by his safety belts. The air bags shrank magically away. The luxury helicopter cabin the President had known was reduced to a series of highly protective roll bars, not unlike the sand rails he had raced as a boy. The roll cage was in a patch of underbrush, and there was no sign of the Secret Service agent who had sat next to him, the pilots or any other part of Marine One.

Smoke wafted through the roll cage along with the scent of burning fuel and fiberglass. The smell brought him awake. The President blinked. Sharp pain bolted through his neck and shoulders, but he could move. He was alive.

It took several seconds for the President to realize that he had survived a deliberate attack. The Ambassador had set him up. There was little question about that.

He imagined a group of young Iranians, or other extremists from the Allied Jihad, perhaps in the U.S. on student visas, searching for him in the woods. He needed to get as far away from the wreckage as possible.

He pawed at the release button on his safety belt. It was jammed. He reached into his tweed blazer and found a pen. He pushed the tip out and tried using it to trip a bit of exposed spring in the belt buckle. Nothing worked.

Two quick bursts of gunfire echoed through the forest. The President smiled as he recognized the sound of an American-made M4 Carbine.

During his first term, members of the Secret Service's uniformed Emergency Response Team had taught him basic survival tactics in the unlikely event that he was caught without protection in a hostile environment. He had forgotten most of it by now, but one thing that had stuck with him was the difference between the sound of American-made M4s versus the developing world's weapon of choice, the AK-47. "If you hear an AK," he remembered one of the ERTs telling him, "run like hell or go into deep hiding if you can. If you hear M4s, stay put. Help is nearby."

He expected the gunfire was from Ulysses' Camp David unit, and that they were already hunting down the assailants. Last year, when the need for highly skilled special ops soldiers had broken out in the Central African Republic, General Wainewright had informed him that none were available. The last remaining Special Forces group that was not deployed was Marine Security Company, Camp David, a unit in which each solider was hand-picked from infantry, then sent through a rigorous program of psychological and physical tests to qualify for Marine Security Training in Chesapeake, Virginia. Wainewright told him that since there had never been an incident at Camp David, apart from accidental civilian aircraft fly-overs, MSC-CD's skills were being wasted there. He suggested that the unit be deployed to the combat zone, while Camp David security should be left to a joint effort between senior Ulysses USA employees and the Secret Service. The President had agreed, and he was anticipating seeing members of that highly paid Ulysses unit any moment now.

He hung helplessly from his safety belts for another minute, his ears attuned to a crackling forest fire that seemed to be getting closer. Finally, he heard rustling and footsteps. He remained perfectly still except for the heaving of his lungs.

Then, he heard conversation – two men, somewhere behind him. They were speaking a language that was nothing like any foreign tongue he'd ever heard before. He held his breath and pulled his limbs close to his body, as if to make himself smaller, less visible.

A pair of American-made hiking boots stepped directly in front of the roll cage. The upside down President strained his neck to see Chris Abrams' face staring directly at him. It hurt to hold his neck this way. He dropped his head for a moment before taking another look.

Abrams wasn't wearing a Ulysses uniform, but he was holding an M4. "Mister President?" Abrams said in perfect English.

The President relaxed and let his head hang. "Thank God," he said upon hearing Abrams' decidedly American accent. "What happened to the others?"

"You're the last of 'em," Abrams replied.

Always the politician, President Hatch thought carefully about his response. He imagined this moment would be re-enacted in a movie someday. "Well I hope you're a Democrat."

"No sir," Abrams replied, "I'm not."

He waited until the President strained his neck to look up again. Then he shot him twice in the face.

Chesapeake Bay
11:09 a.m.

The blue marlin leapt into the air, shaking its mighty head in hopes of freeing itself from the barbed hook in its mouth. It seemed to drift in mid-air for a moment before falling tail-first back into the Atlantic.

"You see that?" Dex Jackson said. A toothpick stuck out the corner of his mouth. "He's fading. Another half hour and he's dinner."

His son, LeBron, didn't seem so sure of that. The obese 12-year-old was strapped into a game fishing chair on the back of his father's Predator sports boat. LeBron was no outdoorsman, and the marlin was diving hard, taking up slack, whipping the rod tip around with supernatural force. The reel was actually smoking as the thick line spun out at more than ten feet per second. Dex trickled some bottled water over it to cool it off.

LeBron's palms were bleeding. "Dad," he said, "Can you take it? Please?"

"This ain't no video game," Dex said. "C'mon, boy. You can do this."

This summer, the 56-year-old Defense Secretary had vowed to get his youngest child off his soft video-gaming ass and into the great outdoors. LeBron was one hundred percent nerd. He was already on his fourth set of ever more powerful prescription glasses, a fact that Dex attributed to his all-nighters staring at game monitors. It was classic – LeBron had even gotten beaten up by jocks just before the summer break. When Dex asked the school's Vice Principal why it happened, he showed Dex his notes from the head bully: "We jumped LeBron cuz he's such a fat pussy."

Dex blamed himself. His own childhood had been 180-degrees from LeBron's, having racked up a 45-3 amateur boxing record prior to entering West Point, from which the structural integrity of his nose cartilage had never recovered. But since going into politics after a stellar military career, he'd let his work take over his life and left LeBron to a life of shopping with his mother and long nights of video gaming. But now he was going to change all that. The kid needed to build some muscle, see a few sunsets and breathe some air that hadn't been breathed before.

Angie Jackson was twenty years her husband's junior and many times more sympathetic. She stroked LeBron's forehead. "I'll get you some gloves, baby."

Something caught Dex's eye. A boat in the distance. He grabbed his binoculars.

It was a powerboat. He saw three men in black wetsuits, but they didn't look like recreational divers. They sure as hell didn't look like anglers.

Angie held the rod for LeBron as he quickly slipped the gloves over his lacerated hands.

Dex's phone rang. "ESC," the Executive Support Center within the Pentagon, came up on the ID. Shit. He'd been on vacation less than two hours, and his staff was already pinging him. He answered. It was General Wainewright's assistant, Corporal Hammond.

"We're evacuating to Site R," Corporal Hammond said without elaboration. "A Coast Guard vessel is en route to escort you back to shore."

"Are they in an unmarked boat?" Dex said, but Hammond had already hung up.

"Everything okay?" Angie said.

Dex picked up the binoculars again. The powerboat was coming straight for them. He looked at LeBron. The boy was finally getting into it, getting some leverage over the fish. Dex saw his boy changing before his eyes.

Then he looked out again at the boat and knew he had to stop thinking so much. That sure as hell didn't look like any Coast Guard patrol he'd ever seen.

"Let the fish go," he said.

LeBron was incredulous. As much pain as he was in, he wanted the fish. He wanted to prove something.

"Let it go, boy," Dex said. "I'm not asking you."

Martha's Vineyard
11:10 a.m.

Eva Hudson's plastic oversized sunglasses covered nearly half her face. She peered into the window of an upscale boutique in Edgartown, a quintessential Martha's Vineyard village – complete with an old red brick lighthouse – that had remained largely unchanged for more than a century. She walked past the famous Whaling Church, with its white Greek columns and fortress-solid structure that had been crafted by shipbuilders one hundred and fifty some-odd years earlier. After a bit of shopping, she planned to take in the 11:30 a.m. church service. Nothing in the world left her feeling more centered than an hour with a hundred strangers praying in unison.

She loved Edgartown's white picket fence sensibility. It was a bit more upscale than Oak Bluff, the island village that former Presidents and several notable rap stars liked to frequent. Last year, she and the President had stolen away from the watchful eyes of his security detail and squeezed into a local tour of the historic homes of long-dead whaling captains. After a couple years of sneaking around the White House, the unsupervised three-hour tour had felt as good as a prison break.

She lifted her sunglasses and leaned into the storefront glass, getting a good look at her face. Damn. That tanning salon had gotten her *way* too orange. And the crow's feet were back. She'd have to make another appointment with the dermatologist. It was well known that Presidents aged visibly – and quickly – during their time in office, but she swore this term had been harder on her than on Hatch.

As her eye traveled downward, she found that she was much happier about the rest of her. The Treasury Secretary had been running seven miles a day for the past month in hopes of having a bikini-ready bod for her planned weekend sneak-away with the President. Now that the President was going to Camp David instead, Eva was more determined than ever. Her fantasy for this morning was to buy a skimpy swimsuit, have someone take a photo of her in it, and make the President insanely jealous.

It would never happen. The paparazzi would prevent her from actually wearing it on the beach. Upon her arrival at her private rental two hours earlier, the maid had spotted the tabloid press boats already gathering about one hundred yards off the shoreline.

All the fuss was a bit stunning. Without advance reservations, Martha's Vineyard was relatively hard to get to in the summertime. The island's airport was tiny. Flights were expensive and booked solid from June through September. The ferries were fully booked months in advance. Eva figured the photo bug vermin must have boated in from New York's Fire Island or maybe Providence. She tried to convince herself that it was just as well the President hadn't come.

This was daily life since *Vanity Fair* had dubbed her the World's Sexiest Fed. Suddenly, her professional image had seemed to melt away, and she appeared in the same gossip rags as Hollywood actresses. It got worse when one of the President's nannies had come forward, selling a story to the *New York Post* that she and the President had a romantic relationship when serving together in the Virginia Governor's mansion.

Eva heard a car slow behind her. Fearing paparazzi, she looked up, using the boutique's storefront glass as a rearview mirror.

Then she saw him – Special Agent Hector Rios, the President's personal security chief. He was impossible to miss among the throngs of summery tourists – six-foot-ten and 260 pounds, down from his NFL playing weight of over three hundred, in a regulation black suit, earpiece and sunglasses.

Eva spun on her Sunday heels and tramped across the street. "Agent Rios!" she fumed as she bored in on him. "What do you think you're doing here?"

"Morning, Madam Secretary," Rios said as politely as he could. "The POTUS asked me to come."

"To keep tabs on me?"

"No ma'am," Rios said. He wondered where the hostility was coming from. He had never had anything but sunshine from Eva. "For your personal security, of course."

"Tell the President that number one, I don't like to be watched, and number two, his personal security detail is funded by the taxpayers to provide protection for him and his family."

"Yes ma'am, but…"

"I don't qualify as family, Agent Rios. Period. If Isaac wants to send his personal security detail to Martha's Vineyard, then he needs to get his presidential ass here. Got it?"

Agent Rios remained calm behind his sunglasses. "Yes ma'am. I'll be sure to let him know."

Eva stormed down the street. Rios waited until she was nearly out of sight. Then he pursued her, keeping his distance.

Chesapeake Bay

The powerboat was closing the distance on Dex Jackson's marlin boat.

"Cut the line," Dex growled at LeBron in the same low, insisting tone Dex used on their Rottweiler at home when it misbehaved. LeBron let the Marlin reel line away from the pole's spindle, undid his seat belts and pried himself from the sweat-soaked chair. The line on the reel soon reached its end. LeBron reached for the wire cutters to snip the line, but it was too late. The pole yanked out of its holder and flew into the boat's wake.

"Dex?" Angie said, looking out at the powerboat. Her voice welled up with fear. "What is it?"

"The anchor!" she cried up to the cockpit, where her husband had already fired up the engines, and was trying to put distance between them and the other boat.

Dex put the boat in neutral and climbed back down. He shoved LeBron and Angie aside and began craning up the anchor. He had it into the boat in under a minute.

Angie picked up the binoculars and looked out at the oncoming powerboat, which was now barely two hundred yards out. She spotted two men in black wetsuits with M4s. "Dex," she said, her voice shaky. "They have guns! Oh my God!"

He climbed back up to the cockpit and put the engines on full ahead. The boat suddenly jerked forward. Angie wasn't braced for it. She plunged over the back of the boat and into the drink.

LeBron called to his father, who had his full attention on maneuvering the new boat that he was only now becoming familiar with. But over the roar of the surging engines, and the distraction of the fast-approaching vessel full of apparent assassins, he didn't hear.

LeBron climbed up to the cockpit and threw the boat in neutral. "Mom's overboard," he said hysterically. "We have to go back." By then she had drifted half a football field away.

Dex shifted the boat down to one-quarter ahead and made a U-Turn with his left hand. With his right, he trained his binoculars on the assassins. He saw a man with a Stinger missile and two others brandishing assault rifles.

They were so close now. Angie was halfway between the two vessels. Dex looked at the gunmen, and at his wife, and his son. Back and forth.

LeBron saw his father contemplating the unthinkable.

"Dad?" he said. "Dad!"

*

From the deck of the little power boat, and through the scope of his Stinger Missile launcher, Elvir Divac spotted the woman flailing in the cold Atlantic. She was halfway between them and Defense Secretary Jackson's weekender. Elvir wiped the stinging salt from his cheeks. The pale Bosnian's complexion was already sunburned.

"Hey," he called up to Ali, his partner, in stilted Muskogee. "Slow down."

Ali cut engines altogether. The boat steadied and Elvir took another look in the scope. Who was she? Secretary Jackson's wife, maybe? Was she hurt? Could she swim?

He felt Ali's narrow brown eyes glaring at him. "What are you waiting for?" he demanded. Ali had been increasingly nervous about getting caught for the past two weeks. "Fire the missile!"

Elvir found the boat in the viewfinder. He wished he had another weapon for this mission. The heat-seeking Stingers were best suited to shooting down aircraft, not watercraft. He switched the launcher to manual and disabled the infrared targeting system. He aimed, took a deep breath, and released the rocket.

The weapon took flight, zipping about thirty meters behind the vessel's aft. He took another missile and reloaded the launcher. When he looked up again, an orange buoy shot from the Secretary's boat, well short of the woman's position in the water.

"Hurry!" Ali said.

He raised the second Stinger to his shoulder and steadied it. The waves were getting bigger now. It took him a few moments to find the horizon, and then the weekender, in the scope. When he did, he was astonished to see Secretary Jackson powering away at full speed away while his wife treaded water. She didn't appear to be wearing a life vest, and the current was carrying her away from the float tube.

Ali saw her now too. "Forget her," he said.

Elvir again fixed on the target. The message in the scope this time: **WARNING** TARGET OUT OF RANGE**

He fired anyway, raising the launcher's nose. The projectile made a gentle arc over the water, falling well short and exploding at the water's surface. He looked back at the woman. The current carried her toward them. She tried to swim against it, but it was no use.

Ali raised his rifle and advanced a round into the chamber.

"No," Elvir said, putting his hand over the muzzle. "This was not the plan."

Martha's Vineyard
11:11 a.m.

Eva stepped into Mocha Mott's and went to the counter. "Double espresso, dash of maple syrup, no foam." She swiped her debit card and was quickly distracted – along with the wait staff – by the CNN broadcast on the wall-mounted television. The sound was muted, but a red ticker appeared at the bottom of the screen that read: JUST IN - REPORTS OF A CAR BOMB IN MONROE. HUNDREDS FEARED DEAD."

The footage onscreen was an aerial shot, presumably from a helicopter, of what looked like an entire city block in ruins.

Eva felt someone watching her. She looked outside. Agent Rios stood across the street. Before she could get angry, her phone buzzed. She took it out of her purse. The display read "THREAT LEVEL RED. SECRET SERVICE EN ROUTE."

What do you mean en route? Eva thought. I'm looking at him.

Outside Mocha Mott's, Agent Rios read the emergency directives sent from the Homeland Security Acting Director Davis on his mobile phone. Rios' orders were to leave the Vineyard immediately and rejoin the POTUS' security detail, which was regrouping in Washington D.C.

This struck Rios as odd. For starters, he'd been told that morning that the POTUS was en route to Camp David, and in the event of an imminent threat, the POTUS was to enter the tunnels there and be transported via underground shuttle to Site R. He would absolutely not return to govern from Washington D.C. at a time like this. That would be contrary to the administration's emergency plan.

Secondly, he was standing across the street from Eva Hudson, a sitting cabinet secretary and member of the National Security Council. She was fifth in line to the POTUS, just behind the Veep, Speaker of the House, President pro tempore and Secretary of State. Securing the top five in the line of succession was a well-understood priority during red status.

Just then, a convertible jeep pulled up to the curb. Two men got out quickly. Among the flocks of well-heeled tourists, they were as out of place as he was – dark suits, buzz cuts, sunglasses. As they neared the entrance of Mocha Mott's, they reached into their jackets. It looked an awful lot like a weapons draw.

Rios instinctively reached for his Glock 9mm and shouted across the street. "Freeze! Hands up!"

Both men spun around firing. Shots ricocheted against the brick wall behind Rios. But the Secret Service agent's marksmanship was dead accurate. Four shots. Both men took two rounds square in the chest and collapsed on the sidewalk. The entire firefight was over less than two seconds after it started.

Birds flew. Traffic froze. Pedestrians froze in fear. Then the first rivulet of blood trickled from the bodies on the sidewalk. Now the screaming started, and within seconds the mobs ducked into stores and behind telephone poles.

Rios dashed across the street to check on Eva. He went inside Mocha Motts with his gun drawn. He found her hiding behind the counter, trying to raise the President on her cell phone.

Over North Carolina 11:12 a.m.

The U.S. Army C-130 cargo plane flew like a winged whale over the verdant North Carolina countryside. Agent Carver, Agent O'Keefe and the esteemed convict Nico Gold sat on a bench that ran along one side of the plane. The federal agents were still in their suits from the night before. Nico had been allowed to change into the civilian clothes that he had been arrested in – a pair of jeans and a vintage Atari t-shirt that both still fit, although he had not worn them since his first day of incarceration 39 months earlier. A dozen paratroopers sat on the row opposite, talking only amongst themselves.

Carver hated hitching rides on military transports. The conditions were rarely comfortable, but he could hardly afford to use his scant budget to buy airline tickets when perfectly good military planes were crisscrossing the country 24/7.

Nico did not wait well. He fidgeted and sighed, wishing for something – anything – to read or do. He had been allowed to take just one personal effect from the Federal Pen– a photo of moon-faced Madge Howland.

"Pen pal?" O'Keefe asked after seeing him obsess over Madge's photo.

"Fiancé," Nico corrected, shoving the photo back into his jeans pocket.

O'Keefe eyed Nico's tattoos – the block letters E-V-A, on each forearm. "Eva," she read aloud. "That's her name?"

Carver, who had fully researched Nico Gold's past before recruiting him, answered for him: "Eva was his mother's name."

Nico shook his head. "You're half-right, snoop. Eva's the name of the woman who put me into the world. It's also the name of the woman who took me out of it. "

O'Keefe squinted in puzzlement. "What? Now I'm confused."

"He means Eva Hudson," Carver explained.

"As in the Secretary of the Treasury?"

"Bingo. She was Assistant Director at the IMF when Nico went on his little Robin Hood kick."

"I can speak for myself," Nico said. "The IMF and the World Bank are nothing more than self-serving bureaucracies. I was simply taking what belonged to the world and redistributing it to people that really needed it. There's a full explanation in my autobiography."

"Which is lousy, by the way," Carver said.

Nico grinned for the first time all day. "You actually bought my book!"

"Don't flatter yourself. I borrowed it from the library."

O'Keefe checked her watch. It was coming up on a quarter past eleven. "We might as well tell you where we're headed now. We're going to Fort Campbell, Kentucky. There's a joint op effort between the feds and Army Intelligence."

"Army Intelligence? That's an oxymoron."

Agent Carver picked up his attaché and pulled out a folder full of coded transcriptions stamped CLASSIFIED. He handed them to Nico. "You might as well get started."

Nico pushed his eyeglasses up the bridge of his nose, looked over the transcriptions for all of two seconds before pushing them back at Agent Carver. "These are beyond comprehension. I need to hear the original audio files."

"Our people put a lot of time into those."

"If your people were all that great, you wouldn't have hauled my ass out of jail."

He had a point. Carver had been utterly confounded with the G-linguists who were supposed to be such effective code breakers. The NSA was the nation's single largest employer of mathematicians and had some of the world's most powerful supercomputers. Twelve cryptologists had already failed to produce any results. Carver subsequently had them all replaced with contractors. Three weeks later he regarded them as a bunch of overpaid, greedy academics with no real world experience.

Agent Carver's and O'Keefe's cell phones buzzed at the same time.

A paratrooper sitting across from them growled as the two startled federal agents whipped out their phones. "Hey! Cell phones off during flight!"

Carver ignored him. He had been told by his Air Force buddies that the concept of cell phones interfering with flight navigation was a myth that had been perpetuated by commercial airline pilots. Quiet passengers made for more enjoyable travel, and considerably happier flight attendants.

His face darkened as he read the first text message: ATTEMPT ON CAMEO INCONCLUSIVE. Carver had, unfortunately, seen this type of message many times before. "Attempt" was fed-speak for an assassination attempt. "Cameo" was the codename for the Vice President. "Inconclusive" meant that there were casualties, but there was a chance of survival. Had the Vice President been dead, the message would have read "Conclusive."

The other messages followed in rapid succession: ATTEMPT ON H MAJ LEADER CONCLUSIVE; ATTEMPT ON SENATE MAJ LEADER CONCLUSIVE; ATTEMPT ON SECDEF INCONCLUSIVE; ATTEMPT ON SECTREAS NONSTARTER.

O'Keefe's eyes welled up. She turned to Carver. "We're too late."

He smiled. "I love your optimism."

"Optimism?" O'Keefe said in an angry whisper. "How can you joke?"

"I wasn't joking," Carver said. "Only an optimist would assume the worst is already over. But that would be the best-case scenario."

"What are you saying?"

"This might be just the beginning."

The Pentagon
11:14 a.m.

Marines deployed retractable SAM batteries along the five edges of the Pentagon's massive 28.7 acre rooftop. Within the five floors and six million square feet of office space below them, some 23,000 military and civilian employees were ordered to stay clear of all window-facing offices. The building had been hastily constructed in the 1940s as a temporary military headquarters, and as 9/11 had proved, it was hardly impenetrable. The Pentagon had been built on the cheap during one of the most trying economic times in American history, right down to the several thousand pounds of horsehair used as insulation. In recent years its windows had been upgraded with Kevlar overlays to provide some measure of protection against a sniper or exterior blast. The SAM batteries had been added to defend against suicide pilots.

Deep beneath the Pentagon's ground floor, General Wainewright's staff gathered in the National Military Command Center, or NMCC. This was the subterranean vault from which the Joint Chiefs directed military operations during DEFCON 3 situations. Should the crisis go to DEFCON 2, plans called for strategic command to be evacuated to Raven Rock.

The officers gawked at several gigantic monitors, where the drama unfolded on live television. FOX was running a montage of the late Congressman Bailey. CNN depicted a 2008 still image of Holy Grace

Baptist Church, then cut to live aerial footage showing the smoldering city block where the church and two adjacent buildings had stood only an hour earlier. General Farrell, the Vice-Chairmen of the Joint Chiefs of Staff, turned up the volume. *"You're looking at what once was Speaker of the House Bill Bailey's home church,"* the news anchor said, *"where it is reported that the congressman was killed while attending services today."*

"They don't know the half of it yet," General Farrell snorted.

General Wainewright hurried into the NMCC with his waifish assistant, Corporal Hammond, trailing behind him. The blast doors closed behind them and the officers sprang out of their chairs. Wainewright peered over his reading glasses at the group. "The TV goes off," he said. "Status!"

Farrell began a sober tally of the morning's events. His voice was permanently hoarse from four decades of chain smoking and barking out orders. "We have several concurrent, seemingly coordinated assassination attempts," he began. "The Vice President is in critical condition: Unverified rocket attack on his car in Wyoming. Speaker of the House Bailey is believed dead: Car bombing in Monroe. Senator Thomas is believed dead: Blast at his vacation residence in Kennebunkport."

The brass volleyed a dozen questions all at once. "When did the attacks begin?" someone shouted.

"This morning," Farrell responded. "Between ten and eleven, and the situation is ongoing."

"What do you mean coordinated?" came General Shufford's voice over the speaker phone. Shufford was one of four Joint Chiefs, representing the Air Force, and had called in from a base in Europe.

Before Farrell could respond, the blast doors swooshed opened. The meeting's latest arrival wore running shoes, black spandex leggings and a snug gray athletic shirt with GWU emblazoned across the chest. Her long raven hair was pulled back into a pony tail. She carried only a Blackberry.

Haley Ellis had been in downward dog position at her Sunday morning yoga class in Rock Creek Park when she received an NIC alert on her phone. It had taken her just seventeen minutes to make it to the Metro Center subway station and out to the Pentagon. Despite a rock star security clearance that provided access to nearly any government facility, the Pentagon MPs had – as they always did – hassled her at the security checkpoint, delaying her arrival by several more minutes as they pretended to confirm her identity.

Ellis was used to the outsider treatment. She was the Senior Liaison for Pentagon-White House Affairs at the National Intelligence Center (NIC), a position created by President Hatch to foster greater oversight of Pentagon operations. But while the White House referred to her as a liaison, the Pentagon brass regarded her as little more than a civilian snitch. This came despite the fact that Ellis was herself an Iraq War veteran who had led a platoon during some of the most dangerous fighting in Ramadi. A war wound had earned her a purple heart and successive desk jobs at the DIA, CIA and now the NIC.

General Farrell watched disdainfully as Ellis walked to the back of the room and began typing notes into her Blackberry. General Shufford's voice resumed over the room speaker. "I asked what you meant by coordinated," he repeated.

"All the victims," Farrell replied, "were attacked shortly after returning to vacation homes or in transit. And far as we can tell, all the attacks occurred between eleven-hundred hours and eleven-hundred fifteen hours."

The room erupted in side conversations. Farrell spoke over it, adding another to the tally: "A chopper has picked up Defense Secretary Jackson. He and his son are on their way to Bethesda Naval Hospital for evaluation. His wife's status is unclear."

"Has the POTUS been evacuated?"

"Waiting on status," Farrell replied. "We have not heard from the President's security detail." The Vice-Chairman decided it was time to put Ellis on the spot. "Any news on your end, Miss Ellis?"

She looked up as the brass' eyes fixed upon her. Ellis felt self-conscious of the perspiration marks on her yoga shirt, but she had already made several calls on the way over. "I talked to the First Team chief," she said, referring to Special Agent Rios. "He wasn't with the President and hadn't heard from today's detail."

Wainewright's lower left eyelid twitched. "Has Admiral Bennington been notified?" Admiral

Bennington was the fourth Joint Chief, representing the Navy.

"Affirmative," Bennington's dour voice called out over the speakerphone.

A private entered behind Wainewright with a sealed envelope. His hands shook as he handed the message to Wainwright. The General opened and read the one-line message: MARINE ONE SHOT DOWN: POTUS BELIEVED KILLED.

There were no details. Wainewright calmly passed it to Farrell, who read it briefly, without showing any emotion, and turned to the private. "Who's seen this?" he demanded.

"Myself and the duty officer in the ESC."

"The media doesn't have it?"

"No sir."

Ellis beckoned to the messenger. "Bring the note here," she said. "I need to see it."

Wainewright gripped the messenger's right arm, holding him in place. "Negative," he told Ellis. "This one's beyond even your security clearance." He turned back to the messenger. "You'll stay in my presence until MPs can escort you safely off-site." Then he turned to Farrell. "Find that duty officer. Isolate him and anyone he's had contact with. Shut down the whole ESC if you have to."

"General," Ellis said, "Are we suppressing casualty information?"

"Fact: the less our enemies know, the safer we are." Wainewright turned to the group. "Confiscate all personal mobile devices in your units. The National Command Authority has been disrupted. The Joint

Chiefs will assume temporary command of the Armed Forces."

"You'll need to explain that," Ellis said. "Is there something I should know?"

"You said yourself that nobody's heard from First Team. The Vice President is at best incapacitated. The House Speaker is deceased and the line of succession beyond him is not clear. Therefore the chain of command is not intact. We are running the show, Miss Ellis."

General Farrell looked up at the Chairman, allowing himself a moment to admire his longtime friend's resolve. Then he stood up, sticking to the well-rehearsed script. They had drilled this situation at least a hundred times. "Protocol requires moving to a secure location. Transport NCA communications staff to Rapture Run. Let's execute."

Ellis watched the brass rush toward the exits. "Excuse me, General," she said, running after Wainewright. "I'm not familiar with the codename Rapture Run."

Wainewright paused and glanced over his left shoulder. "Just go home, Miss Ellis. There will be no further need for your services."

Corporal Hammond followed the General upstairs to his office. Like the rest of the staff, Hammond had never heard of Rapture Run. He had always assumed that they would be safe from attack in the NMCC, which had recently been reinforced to withstand the latest in bunker-busting missile technology.

Wainewright looked around the room and began rattling off a list of items to pack. "Laptop. Data cards. Three utility uniforms and five dress uniforms. Every item in my desk drawers. And those," he said, pointing to two framed photos on his desk. The first was of the General himself standing atop a burned-out Iraqi tank during the first Iraq war. The other photo depicted a young man in his West Point graduation photo. Although the General had never talked about it, Hammond knew from the other staffers that the young man was Wainewright's late son, who had been killed in action during a covert op somewhere in the Middle East. Hammond lingered on the photo for a moment. Packing family photos had an air of finality that made him uncomfortable. He wondered if the General knew something that he did not.

He wrapped the photo frames in soft cloth and packed them carefully but quickly between the General's uniforms. Then he moved on to the other items. He was finished in less than a minute. He stood at the doorway with the General's luggage, watching as Wainewright opened a transparent airtight display case on his desk that held a pair of antique optics.

"Sir, I've been meaning to ask you about those binoculars," Hammond said.

"Not binoculars," Wainewright corrected, "Opera glasses. They belonged to Abraham Lincoln."

"Seriously?"

"He was holding them at Ford's Theatre when he was assassinated."

The General unlocked the cable securing the display case to the desk, opened it, and delicately picked up the opera glasses. He pointed to a small brown splotch on the left rim.

"Is that Lincoln's blood?"

"So I'm told."

"My God. Why aren't they in the Smithsonian, sir?"

"They have great sentimental value to my family. My great-grandfather was loyal to the Confederacy. This is all that's left of his connection to the cause." Wainewright slipped them into a tattered leather carrying case and put them into his lower jacket pocket. They proceeded out the office door and down the hallway.

Hammond surged ahead to swipe his security pass on the next set of doors. "Besides," Wainewright explained, "They are a constant reminder of how we must be vigilant in the destruction of our enemies, even in the face of apparent victory."

"Lincoln's opera glasses remind you of that, sir?"

"Fact: Lincoln had received death threats even before taking the Presidency, going so far as to travel and lodge in secret prior to his inauguration. He continued to receive threats all throughout the Civil War due to his abolitionist tendencies. Again, he was sufficiently cautious. With me?"

"I think so, sir," Hammond said as they walked.

"But when the South finally conceded the War, Lincoln let his enemies go home. He could have crushed them, rooting out all militant elements while he had the upper hand. And so, while Lincoln was planning on enjoying his first evening at the theatre in years, John

Wilkes Booth was plotting to throw the country into upheaval. When your enemies are down, it's not enough just to shame them. You have to exterminate them."

"Yes, sir. I understand."

Wainewright was still thinking about the opera glasses as they entered the elevator. "Fact," he said. "John Wilkes Booth had the presence of mind to shoot Lincoln after the play's funniest line, when the entire house was laughing. If he hadn't jumped onstage like a fool, he would've gotten away with it."

"What was the line, sir?" Hammond asked.

"You sockdologizing old man trap."

Hammond laughed, but it sounded forced. Wainewright suddenly turned and grabbed him by the necktie. He lifted the tie up, as if to lynch him there in the elevator. Hammond gasped for breath, let go of the luggage and groped at the General's massive hands.

"You don't even know what sockdologizing means!" Wainewright roared. "Why did you laugh? Why?"

Hammond sputtered. "I-I don't know, sir."

Wainewright released the necktie and watched the red-faced Corporal cough until he got his legs under him. "Don't ever be insincere with me again."

Hammond straightened. He tucked his shirt in, picked up the General's luggage and followed Wainewright toward the rooftop helipad.

Camp David
4:45 p.m.

Speers drove slowly toward the Camp David checkpoint. The rental car's hood and rooftop were pockmarked with blackened softball-size dents from the exploded church's debris. Through the cracked windshield, Speers saw a razor wire barrier and a pair of Bradley armored vehicles parked in a defensive posture. It was hardly the cozy Camp David greeting he had grown accustomed to. Then again, he hadn't been to the executive retreat since last year, when the elite Marines had been replaced by Ulysses MPs.

A voice came over a loudspeaker: "The facility is closed to visitors. Turn back."

Speers did not heed the warning. He parked the car and got out slowly, holding his White House ID Badge above his head. There was no wind, and there was no birdsong. As he stepped toward the Ulysses MPs, he became suddenly and inexplicably conscious of his own appearance. His pants, shirt and tie were sullied by black ash. The grime was even under his nails. He could only imagine what his face and hair looked like.

The Bradley machine gunner released the safety on his weapon. The sound of provocation was unmistakable on such a still, noiseless day.

"Wait!" Speers yelled. "I'm Julian Speers! White House Chief of Staff!"

A helmeted Ulysses soldier rose up from the Bradley's gun turret.

"Get in your car and turn back," came the directive over the loudspeaker.

"The President asked me to come," Speers insisted. "Come look at my credentials. Please."

Another Ulysses soldier bobbed up from the Bradley. With his weapon at the ready, he came to Speers to inspect his identification, which he read in full before handing it back to Speers.

"What happened to you?" the soldier said as he regarded Speers' grubby appearance.

"I was in Monroe."

The soldier scrunched up his nose. "Don't you know to never walk up to a checkpoint? You got lucky. We shoot first and ask questions later."

Speers didn't like the soldier's attitude. "Well, the President is waiting for me. You're wasting his time as well as mine."

"The POTUS isn't here."

"What? Well what about the Iranian delegation?"

"There ain't no delegation," the soldier said. He spat yellow phlegm dangerously close to Speers' feet.

This made zero sense. Speers whipped out his cell phone and said "CIC" into the receiver. The phone's voice recognition software dialed the President's mobile, but the call went straight to voicemail. He dialed the Vice President. It also went straight to voicemail. Next, he tried Dex Jackson and got the same result. He was about to try Eva when the Ulysses soldier snatched the cell phone from his hand, removed the battery, and returned the now-useless handset to Speers.

Following his long-held practice not to piss off anyone with a gun, Speers didn't dare protest further.

"Wait here," the soldier said. He went back to the Bradley. Speers saw him pull up the vehicle's black jumbo-size phone receiver and talk into it. Several minutes went by. Speers leaned against the hood of his rental car. He longed for a shower and change of clothes.

One of the soldiers lit a cigarette. Speers' lips actually puckered. It had been the President himself who had given him the discipline and motivation to quit during the first term. The President had given him six cases of lollipops for Christmas that year to keep his mouth occupied. "Suck on these," the President had said, playing into Speers' weakness for sweets.

"I'll have to marry a dentist," Speers told him.

"Better her than the undertaker."

Finally, the soldier called to him and waved him toward the gates. "That was DOD," the soldier said, moving aside a row of razor wire so that Speers could pass. "We're relocating you to Site R."

Knowing nothing of the other attacks, Speers wondered what had prompted the President to take to the bunker, and weirder still, why he was finding out about it from a lowly Ulysses MP. He was on the first-team evac list. "Okay then," he said, "Let's go. Where's my chariot?"

"You're lookin' at it," the soldier said, pointing at the Bradley.

The other soldier popped his head up. "He ain't riding in here," he told his colleague, eyeing Speers' clothes. "Check out those blast clothes. Guarantee if you take that tie to the lab you'll find fifty people's DNA on it."

Speers hadn't thought of this. He had conveniently assumed the ash covering his clothes, body and car was nothing more than tiny bits of exploded masonry, insulation, wood and the like. But the soldier was right. Much as it horrified him to think of it, the ash was undoubtedly composed not only of building materials, but also tiny bits of human skin, bone and blood.

"Here ya go," the other soldier said as he mercifully tossed a gym bag at Speers. "There's a pair of sweats and a t-shirt in there. Go on. It's okay. Those clothes ain't been worked out in yet."

Baltimore
Hamilton Arms Apartment 309
5:35 p.m.

They were going to kill her. Of that, Angie Jackson was certain. She sat tied up with her back against the wall. Mrs. Defense Secretary Dexter P. Jackson wasn't scared. She was far too angry to feel any fear. Dear God, she thought. Do what you want with me. Make sure LeBron is safe. Do what you want with my husband. He's yours to judge.

Apartment 309's windows were covered in tin foil. There was no furniture in the living room except for a couch that had been found in a dumpster outside, and the little TV, which sat on top of a rusted milk crate. CNN played endless live coverage of the crisis, which the network had already branded: *A Day of Terror,* complete with an animated red, white and blue logo that played the opening notes of "Battle Hymn of the Republic" each time it swooshed onscreen. The tag line: *America Mourns.*

Elvir sat next to her eating from a can of sardines while Ali slept in the next room with the rest of the crew. Angie sized up Elvir's lean frame, which was wrapped in a too-tight wife beater t-shirt, and guessed his weight at about a buck sixty. Her eyes searched his arms and shoulders for some recognizable tattoo or mole, but all she saw was black hair. Elvir had to be the hairiest man she had ever seen. She took in all these details and committed them to memory. In the event that God spared her life, Angie vowed do her best to identify her captors and bring them to justice.

The assassin felt her staring. His eyes broke from the TV.

"Hungry?" he said in Bosnian-accented English. Angie nodded. He scooted closer and pulled back the tape covering her mouth. He spooned a sardine into her in a dispassionate, measured rhythm.

They had not planned on taking a prisoner. In fact, the client had said nothing about the Secretary of Defense's family being aboard the little sport fishing boat. Dex Jackson was supposed to be alone. In the heat of the moment, Elvir had decided to save Angie's life for fear that he would not collect his money otherwise. In Bosnia, where he had been a teenager during the civil war, there were sometimes financial penalties for inflicting collateral damage.

Besides, his employer had proved to be extremely particular. Given the very unusual nature of the assignment, he felt sure that they would not want Mrs. Jackson to die. He had vague hopes of earning some type of bonus for his heroism.

Suddenly, his prisoner's face was on live television. The anchor on TV put on a sympathetic face: *"Though our focus has been on the drama of the multiple attacks today, our thoughts at this hour, by the way, are of course with all the victim's families. In a new development, we have word that Secretary of Defense Dexter Jackson and his son LeBron Thomas Jackson are at Bethesda Naval Hospital being treated for a routine medical evaluation after gunmen attacked their boat in Chesapeake Bay. The White House has confirmed that his wife was killed in the attack."*

Angie recognized the photo of herself. It had been taken at the Foreign Correspondents' Press Dinner a year earlier.

Elvir turned up the volume. "You see?" he said. "Everyone thinks you are dead." They continued watching as the anchor eulogized her, detailing her years working as a policy analyst in the Pentagon before meeting and ultimately marrying Dex Jackson. "You should be happy," Elvir said. "He's saying such nice things. How does it feel?"

Angie didn't have to think about her answer. "Like being buried alive."

Over West Virginia
8:45 p.m.

The Ulysses helicopter approached slowly, uncertainly. The pilot was under strict orders – no running lights, no searchlights and no radio. The sliver of waxing moon illuminated nothing but a vast sea of cornstalks. Dex and LeBron were still in their boating clothes. "I thought you said we were close," Dex croaked.

"Sorry, Mister Secretary," the pilot said. "We're hovering over the coordinates CENTAF sent us, but I can't see anything."

Nearly as soon as he spoke a helipad lit up directly beneath them. Thousands of cornstalks fanned as they descended. By the helipad's dim glow, Dex could make out the outline of a tiny building surrounded by farmland. There didn't seem to be any roads.

The helipad dimmed as soon as the chopper landed. Two Ulysses soldiers wearing night vision goggles appeared and opened the doors. "Welcome Mister Secretary," they said as Dex and LeBron exited. In near darkness, the soldiers led them down a short, narrow path lined on both sides by cornstalks. There they entered the concrete structure and stood in front of two chrome elevator doors. There were no exterior buttons. Dex put his hand on his son's shoulder as they waited. The boy shrugged him off.

The doors opened. General Wainewright stood before them, wearing the same elegantly decorated military dress uniform that he had worn to the White House earlier that day. "Welcome to Rapture Run," he said.

Dex and LeBron stepped inside the elevator. The soldiers held the pilot back, although there would have been plenty of room for everyone. The doors closed and the elevator began to descend.

Dex braced himself as the elevator vibrated and groaned ever lower. "Where the hell are we?"

"This is Site R."

"Site R? What happened to Raven Rock?"

"You'll find that this facility is a major upgrade."

Dex grunted disapprovingly. "How is it that the Secretary of Defense doesn't know about the construction of a new emergency bunker?"

"Don't take it personally. Google Maps doesn't even know about it yet."

The elevator doors opened to reveal a cavernous underground defense operations center. The room was easily the length of a basketball court and three stories tall. Touch-screen monitors built into the walls tracked troop and weapons movements around the world. Dozens of uniformed Ulysses communications personnel sat at workstations around the room.

"Sweet Jesus," Jackson said. "It's as big as NORAD."

"You have no idea. We carved the command room out of an old Cold War missile silo that the Soviets never got wind of. The facility joins up with a natural cave to the north and a retired coal mine 'bout half a mile south. We could keep an entire brigade down here for years if we needed to."

Dex took note of all the Ulysses uniforms in the room. "General," he said, "I don't see many regular military personnel."

Wainewright smiled. "Dex, you're a Republican. You of all people should appreciate that the private sector will outperform the public sector every single time."

The General motioned for Corporal Hammond, one of the few regular military personnel in the bunker, to come to Dex's assistance. Hammond carried a titanium briefcase with one hand and saluted with the other. "Secretary Jackson," he beamed, knowing nothing of Angie Jackson's disappearance into Chesapeake Bay. "Happy to see you safe and sound, sir."

Hammond. The imbecile that was responsible for all this. Dex clinched his fists and took a swing.

Dex's right hook connected with the Corporal's left eyebrow, sending him to the deck with a rivulet of blood trickling into his eye.

Wainewright shoved Dex backwards. "What's gotten into you?"

"This is the little prick that called me on the boat. He told me to stay put. That hesitation killed my wife."

"The Corporal here was just the messenger, Dex. He had no way of knowing."

Hammond got to his feet, wiped the blood out of his eye and swallowed hard. "I'm sorry about your loss," he said. "I really had no idea." The Corporal plopped the briefcase atop a workstation and opened it, revealing several dozen phones with the names of their owners written on sticky notes. "I'm afraid I need your phone, Mister Secretary."

"You don't know when to quit, Corporal."

"He's not trying to antagonize you," the General explained. "There are no personal phones allowed down here. Not that you could get reception anyhow."

Jackson reached into his pocket, produced his phone, and grudgingly handed it over. LeBron's phone – outfitted with little grips for playing video games, tucked into the carrying strap on his backpack – didn't escape the Corporal's prying eyes.

"Sorry, kid," Hammond told LeBron. "Rules are rules."

Dex's jaw tightened. "He's just a kid."

"Let him be," Wainewright cut in. "He lost his mother today."

The Coal Mine
8:47 p.m.

After spending six gut-busting hours in a Ulysses Bradley armored vehicle that chugged along at sub-highway speeds, Julian Speers was led into an abandoned coal mine that had been fitted with blast-proof shielding. There the Ulysses soldier that had donated his gym clothes bid him good riddance and passed him off to a pair of MPs that led him down a long, gradually sloping tunnel. They passed through two additional sets of shielded doors and took an elevator and a rail car through what the MP described as the "ass end of the bunker."

They finally came to the Rapture Run command room. The cavernous operations center had the same awe-inspiring effect on him as it had on the other two hundred personnel that had first passed through its doors that day.

Speers recognized Corporal Hammond, the little terrier of a man who often waited outside the White House cabinet room for General Wainewright during Security Council meetings. "Welcome to Rapture Run," Hammond said with a smile. "I'll need to check your phone."

The Corporal obviously didn't recognize him. "I'm Julian –"

"Speers. I know. You're cleared to enter, Chief, but I'm afraid there are no exceptions to the policy on mobile devices." The Corporal held out his hand for the phone.

The Chief shook his head. "I've got data on this phone that is way above your security clearance."

Hammond leaned close and whispered into Speers' ear. "Compliance with the rules is *very* important here. There is a zero tolerance policy." Speers looked over his shoulder. He was surrounded by four armed Ulysses soldiers that were carefully observing his every move.

Don't piss off the guys with the guns, he reminded himself. Especially these guys. They don't just have guns. They've also got stock options.

As he surrendered his phone, he realized he had forgotten to call his neighbor, Ms. Tenningclaus. By now she was way out in Arizona, and the way this was going, those cats were going to have to catch their own dinner.

The Corporal put Speers' phone into the titanium briefcase that held several dozen others. He then led Speers through the command room toward the emergency NMCC. There, Speers recognized Major James Dobbs from CENTAF. Dobbs was supervising a small group of air traffic controllers. Speers left his chaperone and went to the mustachioed air traffic control czar.

"Major Dobbs?" he said. "Julian Speers. We met last fall. You were testifying before the Armed Services Committee."

"I think everyone here knows who you are, Chief." Dobbs looked Speers up and down, frowning at his track suit.

"The President told me to meet him at Camp David," Speers said. "When I got there they told me he'd never arrived. Nobody will give me a straight answer."

Dobbs turned to a junior officer. "Take the con. I'll be back in five."

Dobbs took Speers by the arm and led him to an empty conference room adjacent to the command center. He shut the door. "What I'm about to tell you isn't public knowledge. I haven't even been debriefed yet."

The Chief of Staff sat down. He could tell by the look on Dobbs' face that whatever story he was about to hear wouldn't end well. His mouth seemed to fill up with cotton as he listened to the Major's story. Dobbs described how he had generated a flight plan for Marine One that morning, and then tracked Marine One and its three identical decoys into the Maryland hills until they suddenly disappeared from radar. "I scrambled a pair of F-35s," he said. "I notified General Wainewright."

"You said three choppers went down," Speers interrupted. "That means one survived."

Dobbs shook his head. "You want to know if the President is alive. The answer is that I honestly don't know. The NMCC took over communications with the surviving chopper on a secure channel. We weren't even allowed to eavesdrop. Next thing we know, our entire squad of controllers was relocated here. We were told not to ask any questions."

"Was it the Iranians? " Speers said.

Dobbs was puzzled. "What Iranians?"

"That's the reason the President was going to Camp David. To meet the Iranian Ambassador. You see where I'm going with this. They request the meeting, then the Speaker of the House gets vaporized, then someone takes a shot at Marine One..." Speers tolerated Dobbs' blank look for less than a second. "Don't tell me nobody's put that together yet."

"Chief, you're mistaken. If there was an Iranian delegation en route to Camp David, I would've been told. Anytime foreign heads of state visit Camp David, we tighten up our air patrols. It's protocol."

Speers held his weary face in his hands. "Okay. Besides you, who could've known the flight plan?"

"Nobody. The flight plan isn't decided until Marine One takes off. I request a plan, one is randomized from the Pentagon database, and then I communicate that orally to Marine One."

The Chief had been on Marine One dozens of times, but he had never given much thought to the security procedures regarding flight plans. "What about the decoy pilots?"

"The formation adapts to the flight plan mid-air. That way, even if an enemy catches onto a codename, there's no time for them to get in place. We take no chances."

"It had to be rigged somehow. Was there anything unusual about today?"

"I don't think so, Chief. It worked just like always. I pushed a button and received the plan. But like I said, you didn't hear the story from me. I've gotta get back to work."

Dobbs opened the door and headed back to the command room. Speers remained seated. His mind filled with more questions. The only thing he knew for sure was that it had only been twelve hours since he'd left the White House Security Council meeting. And in those twelve hours, the nation had come apart.

Fort Campbell, Kentucky

Standing outside the base's screening room, Agent Carver could hear the voices of twenty-six unhappy contract linguists. On Carver's orders, the linguists had been rounded up and flown into Fort Campbell under a clause that allowed the Feds to retain any former military employee contractor during a national emergency. Most of them had families that were upset about being uprooted during the crisis.

Carver wasn't exactly psyched to see them either. They were the same virtual team that had tried and failed to crack the coded transmissions Carver had given them during the investigation. Still, except for Nico, they were all he had.

It had been more than twelve hours since Carver had heard from Speers. Without the benefit of the Chief's input, Carver had decided to continue pursuing the original investigation. If nothing else, he wanted to explore the possibility that Lieutenant Flynn might have had ties to the assassins.

"Hello Word Nerds," Carver said as he entered the room. He held a tiny video projector. "I realize that this isn't exactly convenient, but frankly, we blew it, folks, and a lot of good people are dead." The room fell silent as O'Keefe and Nico entered. The skin of Nico's wrists was red and irritated from wearing handcuffs during transit. "That's my colleague Agent Meagan O'Keefe. With her is Nico Gold. Yes, the *infamous* Nico

Gold. He'll be working with you on this case. If that isn't incentive to try harder, I dunno what is."

O'Keefe dimmed the lights. "This aired on Al Jazeera thirty minutes ago."

Faruq Ahmed's brown, clean-shaven face came onscreen. He wore a headscarf and began speaking in Arabic. As he talked, clips of desert training camps played behind him, showing teenage recruits destroying mock U.S. and Israeli targets. In less than three minutes, it was over.

Carver stopped the DVD. "Translation?"

"It's a suicide tape," one of the linguists said. "His name is Faruq Ahmed. He says he represents Allied Jihad. He is from Yemen, has been living in West Virginia for six months, and takes responsibility for masterminding the assassinations of several top leaders, although he gives no specifics. Plus the usual garbage about Muslim youth rising up against the evil empire."

"That's it?"

"The usual promises of seventy virgins in the afterlife to any martyrs that rise up within the U.S."

Carver turned his gaze to Nico. "Your thoughts?"

"The Koran cites seventy-two virgins for holy martyrs, not seventy."

"Okay. Is that significant?"

"I'd say. It means Islam is running low on virgins."

The linguists laughed. Carver waved his hand dismissively. "Get your Ivy League asses back on those intercepted transmissions. Agent O'Keefe will hand out the assignments."

The agitated linguists filed out into the next room. Nico remained in his seat. A sly grin spread across his face.

"What're you waiting for?" Carver asked him.

"My Presidential pardon."

Carver's expression went blank. He folded his hands on top of his head. "What…You mean you cracked the code already?"

"About that," Nico said. "It's not a code."

Rapture Run

The elevator wobbled as it descended deeper within the vast subterranean complex. It stopped abruptly between two floors, doors opening to reveal a cold, black nothingness that frightened young LeBron Jackson. The Ulysses MP pressed the D button repeatedly until the door shut and the elevator began moving again.

"What grade you in?" the MP said. He towered over LeBron's short, chubby frame.

"Eighth," LeBron said.

"Jesus. World's going to hell sure as I'm standing here."

The elevator came to a rest and opened. "Welcome to the dungeon," the MP said without any hint of humor in his voice. LeBron saw a long row of blue LED lamps that seemed to stretch forever. He felt the cavern's cool, moist air and heard someone's cries echoing off the wet rock ceiling.

An MP got up from a chair and came to greet them. The metal of his rifle glowed blue in the lamp light. "What's this?" he said, looking at LeBron.

"This is SECDEF Jackson's kid," the other MP said. "General Farrell wanted him brought down here."

"What'd you do?" the MP said, still looking at LeBron. "Stay out past curfew?"

"He ain't done nothing," the other MP said. "General said it's for his own safety."

The MP grunted. "Okay. Number nine then."

As they walked past several occupied isolation cells, LeBron heard someone crying softly. The MP kicked the door and the noise stopped. They came to the ninth cell. There was no light in the cell – only the dim blue glow from the lamp in the corridor. LeBron could make out four walls, an exposed toilet, a floor mattress and nothing else.

"This is home, kid," the MP said.

"Does my Dad know about this?"

The MP gently pushed him in and closed the cell door behind him.

*

Speers stood next to Major Dobbs and gazed up at the tremendous, awe-inspiring monitors in the operations room. Touch-screen maps tracked real-time enemy troop movements worldwide. One showed an aerial view of a truck convoy tracked by satellite. A descriptive overlay read: YEMEN. SUSPECTED ALLIED JIHAD CONVOY. TARGET SPEED 46 MPH. CONFIDENCE 70%.

Speers looked around in wonder. This place was a veritable Death Star. And it had been built right under their noses.

Suddenly, General Wainewright's talking head appeared on every monitor in the command room and every screen in the Rapture Run complex. "This is General Wainewright. We are now moving to DEFCON Two," he said. "Fact: the last time we saw DEFCON Two? Cuban Missile Crisis, 1962. The Soviets opened up torpedo tubes on us."

All work stopped. All eyes went to the General's image onscreen. "Momentarily," he continued over the internal broadcast system, "Martial law will be declared across the U.S. The last time that happened? 1865. The Civil War."

Wainewright signed off without further elaboration. Monitors cut back to normal. The Ulysses command personnel went back to their work without a word.

Corporal Hammond came to fetch Speers and Dobbs. "You're needed in the NCA meeting," he said, referring to the National Command Authority. Dobbs again handed temporary CENTAF command to his junior officer and followed Corporal Hammond to a large conference room. Speers recognized many of those seated at the table. The Secretary of the Interior. The head of the House Foreign Intelligence Committee. Several high-ranking generals. The junior senators from Texas, Florida and Utah.

Hammond pointed Speers and Major Dobbs to chairs at the back of the room.

As Dex Jackson walked in, the brass stood and applauded. "Mister Secretary," they said in near unison. Speers, who hadn't yet heard of Dex's surviving an assassination attempt, and who had only that morning advised the President of his possible role in weapons disappearances, wondered what the Defense Secretary had done to become so popular.

The room got quiet as Dex sat in the lone remaining chair at the big boy's table. Hammond closed the door behind him and, with a touch of a button, frosted the glass separating the conference room from the command center.

Wainewright broke the ice: "Our condolences regarding your wife, Mister Secretary."

"Noted and appreciated," Dex replied. "Is the POTUS en route?"

Everyone looked to Wainewright, who broke the news: "It's my solemn duty to inform you – and anyone else who hasn't yet heard – that the POTUS has been killed."

The news hit Speers square in his chest. His stomach was empty, but he nevertheless felt the urge to vomit.

"But the radio…" Dex said. "There was nothing about it on the radio."

"We're delaying the news cycle," Wainewright said. "The public only knows the half of it and people are already losing their shit."

Dex looked around the table. "Where's Number Two?" he said, meaning the Vice President.

Again, the room turned to Wainewright, who said, "He was attacked in Wyoming."

Dex jerked upright, his chair clapping to the floor behind him. "Christ almighty! Will someone just tell me who's in charge?"

"We're calling the shots," Wainewright said coolly.

Dex paced alongside the table. Speers wiped the perspiration from his brow in the suddenly close room. General Farrell lit a cigarette and offered the rest of his pack, but there were no takers amongst the obsessively fit, gum-chewing leadership. Speers took a lollipop from his pocket, unwrapped it and popped it into his mouth.

"Get the Secretary of State on the phone," Dex growled at Corporal Hammond. No sooner had the corporal picked up the wall-mounted phone than Speers took it from him and placed it back on the receiver.

"The Secretary of State was born in Australia," Speers said from the back of the room. "She's not eligible to assume the Presidency."

Jackson stopped pacing and cast his full eyes onto Speers. "With all due respect, Chief, I'm of the opinion that your job died with the POTUS. You shouldn't even be here."

Speers wasn't having it. "Not so fast," he said. "In the event of Presidential assassination, the President's personal staff, including the Chief of Staff, remains intact until the succeeding Commander-in-Chief relieves them of duty."

"Well I don't mean to be presumptuous, Chief. But if the Secretary of State is ineligible, I'd say you're looking at the new President."

"I'd like to challenge that," Speers said. He stood and went to the whiteboard on the far side of the room. He grabbed a blue marker and wrote POTUS, with a flow chart arrow to the word VEEP. "The line of Presidential Succession is as follows..." he began as he illustrated an org chart several layers deep. "If the President is deceased, the Vice President ascends. If the

Vice President is deceased, power falls to the House Speaker. Next in line, the President pro tempore – the late Senator Thomas."

Dex had no patience for this. "As we've heard, those four leaders are deceased. That means leadership falls to the Cabinet Secretaries."

"Right. But the order of ascension for Cabinet posts is State first, then Treasury...and *then* Defense."

General Wainwright looked like he had just taken a gut punch. Dex's eyes turned a deeper shade of red. "Eva Hudson outranks me?"

Speers drew a red circle around Eva's place on the flow chart. "Yes sir," he replied. "Looking at this in a historical context, you can see why. Until 2003, the Treasury Department was a fixture of National Security, directing both the Secret Service and NSA."

General Wainewright cleared his throat. "But that was before Homeland Security was created. The old line of succession doesn't make a lick of sense now."

Dex wanted back into the debate. "Show me where in the constitution it says that Treasury trumps Defense," he demanded.

"It's not in the constitution," Speers replied. "The line of succession comes from an act of Congress, specifically President Truman's Succession Act of 1947."

The room phone rang. Corporal Hammond put the receiver to his ear and answered in a low murmur. "Put me through to the President," the shrill voice demanded. Hammond turned to the room. "Excuse me, gentlemen. As luck would have it, Treasury Secretary Hudson is on the line. Shall I put her on speaker?"

"Negative," General Wainewright said.

Circling overhead, Eva Hudson was a passenger in a small Air National Guard helicopter whose pilot was searching desperately for the landing pad. "I'm tired, I've been shot at, I'm starving and generally annoyed that nobody bothered to tell the Security Council about the new Site R," she complained to Corporal Hammond. "Transmit landing coordinates right now, Corporal!"

Hammond turned again to the room and said, "Secretary Hudson is requesting permission to land, sirs."

"Tell her to hold," Jackson said, feeling the dark joy that came with keeping the late POTUS' girlfriend at bay.

"Are you there?" Eva demanded.

"Yes ma'am, I'm here," Hammond replied into the phone.

"Someone tried to kill me today, Corporal. I'm not in a patient mood."

"I'm doing everything I can," Hammond said as the Joint Chiefs' conversation swirled behind him.

"Corporal," Eva said, "I am a sitting member of the National Security Council! My secret service escort was recalled to Washington, and I practically had to hijack this aircraft to get here! I demand to know why I wasn't informed of the new bunker location!"

Hammond put the phone on mute and watched the debate around the eight-sided table. "With all due respect," General Farrell said to the group, "during a time of war, I'm not inclined to take orders from a glorified banker."

"If it's not in the constitution," Dex interrupted, "then there's wiggle room."

Speers wasn't about to give in. "That would be for the Supreme Court to decide," he argued.

"We don't have that kind of time," Wainewright said.

Hammond pointed at the ceiling. "Sirs," he cut in. "Permission to light up the landing pad so that Secretary Hudson can land?"

"Negative." Wainewright snapped. "Divert her to Fort Campbell. We'll be in touch."

FORT CAMPBELL
10:25 p.m.

Eva's chopper landed amongst an expanse of identical battleship grey buildings. Like all U.S. military bases tonight, Fort Campbell was on alert. Even at this hour, armed troops walked the fenced perimeter in the distance.

There was no welcome party. A lone officer wearing a short sleeve khaki utility uniform stood in the wet-hot Kentucky night. His hair was gray and his lips were pursed, and he was surprisingly pear-shaped for a former Green Berets. Had it not been for the brass birds on his lapels, Eva would have taken him for a career enlisted man.

He held his hand out to shake hers. "Colonel William Madsen," he said. "Garrison Commander. That means I run this place."

"Eva Hudson," she said. "Treasury Secretary."

"You need no introductions," Colonel Madsen drawled as he led her across the heliport to a modest single-story command post. "I've never met a celebrity," he added, eyeing her in wonder. Eva had heard that one before, but she still hadn't devised a polite reply. She just held her tongue.

As they walked, Eva tried all the speed dials on her phone. The President wasn't answering. Speers wasn't answering. The Vice President wasn't answering. Even her little sister wasn't answering. She had only been able to raise her rather useless deputy secretary, who along with every other federal agency employee, had been told to stay away from the federal offices until the threat level slid back down to orange.

They entered the command post and began down a hallway lined with framed photographs of past Garrison Commanders. "First time on a military base, Miss Hudson?" Colonel Madsen said.

"Hardly." As a child, Eva's Air Force father had dragged her all over the world, but it wasn't worth getting into with the Colonel. "And please address me as Madam Secretary."

"Fine, Madam Secretary," he said. "Will you be needing an office?"

"I'll be needing much more than you have."

"I know you think you've been exiled to the boonies, but we think we've got some of the finest Intel resources in the armed forces."

Eva stopped. "Intel? I thought this was a combat training base."

"That's what we're known for. But last year we inherited some Army Intel brain trust from Fort Huachuca and now we've got the Feds working a joint op too."

"No offense, but why here?"

"This is a bureaucrat-free zone. We focus one hundred percent on disrupting the enemy. Our people go out and execute. We're players, not planners."

"Can I have a look?"

Madsen pointed down the hall to the briefing room, where Agent Carver's linguists were filing out into the hallway. "Couple feds are working on that Allied Jihad suicide tape." Eva looked through the glass and recognized Agent Carver. Though she didn't know him by name, she had seen him leaving the Oval Office with Julian Speers on at least two occasions.

She stopped in her tracks at the sight of the tall, lanky man with dark hair and wire-rim glasses. Her arms were instantly covered in goose bumps that prickled to the point of being painful. She turned to Madsen. "Nico Gold."

"You oughtta be on a quiz show," Madsen said. "World's most notorious hacker, right here on the base. Not many people remember his case."

She cocked her head to read the twin tattoos on Nico's forearms that read EVA. "I'd say he remembers me too."

*

In the briefing room, the incredulous Agent Carver asked Nico to repeat himself for the third time.

"This code you've been trying to crack," Nico repeated as patiently as he could, "it's not a code. It's a language, y'see?"

"No. I don't see."

"Muskogee. A Native American language. An *oral* language. The thing is, nobody speaks it anymore. The actual tribe died out decades ago."

Carver's face was suddenly full of malice. He stepped into Nico with both hands and lifted him by his shirt collar, throwing him back against a table. "You knew what it was right off, didn't you? Back in Virginia. You knew!"

"How could I?" Nico said as he tried to fight Carver off. "You gave me those crappy transcripts, remember?"

O'Keefe pushed her index and middle finger into a pressure point just below Carver's right shoulder blade. His left arm suddenly dropped to its side. O'Keefe easily pulled him off, smiling at the perfect execution of a move she'd learned in her weekly jujitsu class.

Carver smiled too, despite the lingering pain. O'Keefe had only been taking those classes for a few weeks.

"You," she chastised Carver, "behave!"

She turned to Nico. "Now explain. Slowly. You said it's an oral language?"

"*Was.*The last survivor was coaxed into transcribing a phonetic version for archival purposes. No small feat. Muskogee is full of smacking sounds and tongue clicks and guttural sounds."

"Yet you claim that you can read it. Explain."

"Back then I was looking to develop a new programming language. Something spybots couldn't recognize. I saw a writeup about Muskogee in a linguist's community site. I ended up bribing a professor just to get a photocopy of it. Guess I wasn't the only one in the world with that idea."

Carver's left arm was still tingling from O'Keefe's pressure point move. He rubbed his forearm back and forth, coaxing the feeling back into it. "Just tell us how this relates to the codes."

"Look, it's an old trick. Some coder adopts an obscure tribal language with a completely alien syntax. Like when the Americans used Navajo against the Japanese in World War Two. The Japanese went the rest of the war trying to figure out this impossible code, which was really a Native American language with a sentence structure unlike anything they'd ever seen. Same idea here. You were busy cracking a code, when all you had to do was learn Muskogee."

*

Colonel Madsen took Eva to an office with wallpaper depicting bald eagles flying around snowcapped mountains. It contained a government-issue mahogany desk, a file cabinet and a computer docking station. Madsen nodded to a full-length couch against the wall with a set of blankets carefully folded at one end. "These are my old digs," he said. "That couch will do for tonight, and we can get you a hotel off-base in the morning. "All I need tonight is an outside line," she said.

Madsen nodded toward the desk phone. "There 'tis. You need anything else, I'm down the hall. I'll be bunking in my office tonight in case more hell breaks loose."

Eva lifted the desk phone receiver and waited for the Colonel to exit. She dialed the Iranian Embassy in

Washington. To her surprise, the Ambassador took her call despite the late hour.

"Madam Secretary," the Ambassador said, his British-accent indicative of his Cambridge University education. "I'm happy to hear you are alive and well. I was expressing my concern about your health to my colleagues."

How touching. Eva didn't buy it for a minute. "Mister Ambassador, I was calling to get your perspective on your meeting this morning with the President."

The Ambassador was quiet for several moments. "Pardon?" he said. "Perhaps something is lost in translation…"

"Camp David. This morning. You and the President were scheduled to meet."

"Madam Secretary, you have been misinformed. We have not yet had the honor of a Camp David invitation. To say such a thing is to rub salt in the wound."

"I meant no disrespect. I was just told that…"

"You are incorrect. And if you will excuse me, we are following the developing military situation quite closely, and if I can say, with much approval."

The Ambassador hung up. Eva's head mushroomed with questions.

She closed her eyes and tried to quiet her mind. She imagined that her anxieties and unanswered queries were white noise, like static on an old terrestrial radio station. It was usually a matter of concentrating, very hard, and imagining herself turning off that radio. In these meditations, she sometimes had to turn the radio off a few times. Eventually she would think about nothing. After some time, she would cease thinking altogether.

Tonight was different. The white noise was unbearable. It had only been this loud once before, after leaving the governor's mansion to take the IMF job a few years back. That time she was unable to quiet her mind for days at a time. She ended up needing medication to take the edge off.

She picked up the phone again and dialed her sister. The phone rang seven times. Finally her brother-in-law answered. He didn't even ask if she was okay. He just started in with the questions.

"Eva, what's going on out there? Are there going to be more attacks? The news is saying maybe we should wrap the house in plastic in case of chemical attacks. Is there any truth to that at all?"

Eva should have known. Nobody wanted to hear about her fears. Not even family. They had their own bitter little world to worry about.

Rapture Run
11:19 p.m.

Chief Justice Stanford P. Dillinger entered Rapture Run in the same bewildering way that Speers had before him – driven blindfolded through West Virginia hill country, and then escorted into the retrofitted former coal mine on an underground subway. Unlike Speers, he had been permitted to bring a duffel bag with two changes of clothes, which he carried on a strap around his shoulder. Two Ulysses soldiers brought him past the enormous CENTCOM command room and to an isolated chamber. It was uncomfortably chilly. Nevertheless he sat alone at a plain folding table, soothing himself by stroking the enormous beard that hung like a gray fox's tail from his chin.

General Wainewright entered the room twenty minutes later. He sat opposite the Chief Justice and folded his hands before him as if to pray.

"Your Honor," Wainewright said. He regarded Dillinger's jeans, wing tips and button down shirt. The country's leading constitutional authority looked incredibly small without his black robes. "Can we get you some tea or coffee? Maybe something to eat?"

"Don't gimmie this gimcrackery," the 85-year-old Dillinger said. He looked like a doddering old man, but his mind was sharp. "The President should have made a statement by now, and the networks are spewing disinformation. Cut the crap and tell me how bad it is."

Wainewright nodded. "All right then. A series of coordinated terrorist strikes have effectively beheaded our country's senior leadership and disrupted the continuity of government."

The Chief Justice absorbed this for less than two seconds, the scowl on his face unchanging. "That's the most deliberately obtuse bullshit I've ever heard. Just tell me who's dead and who's alive."

"Suffice to say, we'll need you to swear in the next President of the United States within the next twenty-four to forty-eight hours."

Dillinger pounded a scrawny white fist on the table. "Are you dense? I'm asking you for names, General."

Wainewright bristled, but managed to stay professional. "We've managed to maintain the National Command Authority, but due to the security situation, the planned model of Presidential succession just won't meet the country's needs."

The Chief Justice shook his head. "I'm getting the impression that you brought me here to bless military control of the country."

"Rest assured, the next POTUS will be a *civilian,*" Wainewright assured him. "A sitting cabinet member. You have my word."

"More bullshit. The fact that you won't name this mythical future leader is most disconcerting. Yes, most disconcerting indeed. Sounds like a black market auction, with the job going to the highest bidder."

"Presidential succession isn't a constitutional matter," Wainewright said, aping what he'd heard Speers say earlier.

"If you're going to flagrantly disrespect the laws this country has created, why are you wasting my time?"

Wainewright grinned. He thrived on this type of banter. Especially when he held all the cards. "You're the high priest, sitting in your temple of truth and justice with your fellow disciples. People respect you. If we've got any hopes of keeping the country together, I need you to swear in the new President."

Dillinger considered his options. The General was technically right. The Presidential Succession Act had come out of Congress, not the Constitution, and as of now, the Legislative Branch had no say over who took the throne. And if the situation was as bad as the General suggested, there could be riots, economic failure, anarchy. He had no intention of taking orders from the military, but on the other hand, if the High Court refused to participate in the process, they'd be permanently weakened. If anything, withdrawing the Court from the process might further fuel the country's burgeoning police state.

"A sitting cabinet member," Dillinger repeated.

"Yes your Honor."

Dillinger knew that this was the very kind of back room deal that changed civilizations. He only hoped that this was the lesser of two evils. "I'd make you swear on a stack of Bibles, but everyone in Washington knows you're an atheist."

Wainewright laughed, took Dillinger's hand and shook it. He had just cut the second most important deal of his career; The first had been persuading President Hatch to give him authority over Ulysses contracts.

*

Corporal Hammond led Dex Jackson down a low, dark corridor, lit with blue LED lamps, that reminded him of the nuclear submarine that he had served on after his graduation from Annapolis.

Hammond stopped and opened a small door to his right, which was much better lit.

"I'm afraid these are your quarters, sir. It's not much, but I'll get you some clean clothes."

Dex went inside, regarded the four walls, bunk, the small desk with a chair on either side, the video screen and the airplane-sized bathroom. He sat down on the bed and put his head in his hands. He was exhausted, but for the first time in his life, he feared sleep. Dex knew that when he closed his eyes, he would see his wife Angie flailing in the Atlantic.

"Dex," someone said. It was General Wainewright, standing in the doorway. "Got a sec?"

The room seemed much smaller as the General shut the door behind him and sat in the plastic desk chair. Dex had never been alone with the General, and he was awed by how much oxygen his presence seemed to require. The four stars on each shoulder of Wainewright's uniform did not seem nearly enough.

"I'm concerned about LeBron," Wainewright said without preamble. "He's blaming you for Angie's death."

Dex thought on this. "Well of course he is."

"That's between you and your conscience. Bottom line, we can't let him go on record saying you left Angie for dead."

We can't let him go on record. Dex thought about that statement for a few seconds. He didn't understand who the General meant by "We" – the Joint Chiefs? The Pentagon? And Dex took offense at anyone but him trying to parent his child. Still, this was the Chairman of the Joint Chiefs he was talking to. And for now, Wainewright seemed positively Czar-like. America didn't know it, but Wainewright was running the country from a secret bunker that he didn't even know the coordinates of, and he could do anything he wanted. This was no time to pick a battle.

"Don't worry," Dex said. "I'll talk to LeBron."

"Do yourself a favor," Wainewright said. "Let him sleep it off. Then let the chaplain or the staff psychologist have a crack at him. You'll have your hands full here with us."

Wainewright slapped Dex on the back and stepped into the corridor, where he spotted the glowing cherry of General Farrell's cigarette. He grabbed the smoke from Farrell's mouth and stomped it into the floor. "Don't be such a dinosaur," he chastised him.

They walked down the four-foot wide corridor single file. As always, Wainewright walked in front. He had been one year Farrell's senior at West Point, and had remained one step ahead of him his entire career. The nation's second-most powerful military man was happy in his friend's shadow. Farrell regarded himself as merely a great military mind, but thought Wainewright to be a true visionary, as evidenced in the way he had deftly outmaneuvered the President and DOD to feed Ulysses USA, his very own private army. Over the next week, they would have their chance to return America to its former greatness.

"The Allies are demanding communication with the POTUS," Farrell said. His voice was raspier than usual from shouting orders in the command room.

"Soon," Wainewright said confidently. He had planned out every eventuality of the operation months earlier, storing them in a virtual decision tree that he updated on his mobile device every hour. So far, they were doing remarkably well. The fact that Eva Hudson was alive was the only significant glitch. But even that was something that could be remedied in short order.

His counterpart wasn't satisfied with Wainewright's pat answer. "The general public is starting to panic," he said. "They're already stockpiling food and gas in Los Angeles and there are reports of militias on alert in Michigan and Texas. Some people on the East Coast are already lining up outside banks."

Wainewright took Lincoln's opera glasses from his pocket and clutched them as he walked.

"These remind me of what not to do," Wainewright said.

"What's that?"

"Deviate from the plan. Fact: after Booth shot Lincoln, he jumped from the Presidential box onto the stage. He was shouting 'death to all tyrants.'"

"He was showboating."

"That too. But at the core he was deviating from the plan." Wainewright stopped as he imagined the scene at Ford's Theatre a hundred and fifty some-odd years earlier, closing his eyes as he spoke. "Booth broke his leg with that stunt. He should have escaped out the back. It was dark and there was a horse waiting for him. Nobody would've seen his face. He could've led the resistance, just as he'd envisioned, and taken over Washington while the Union was reeling from the loss. All the pieces were in place. Security in the Capitol was light. Secretary Seward was incapacitated from his own stab wounds. Johnson was a closeted Confederate and was ready to take power. The timing was right. If only..." The General opened his eyes and stared at his shoes as he thought about his own plan. He looked up at Farrell, who had turned to listen to his ramblings. "You see where I'm going with this?"

Farrell was operating on too little sleep to indulge the civil war allegory. "No."

They resumed walking. "My point is that we need to stick to the plan," Wainewright said. "Dex Jackson is the next POTUS, just as we discussed. But we have to swear him in before the politicos can get organized."

"Speers made quite the case for Eva Hudson today. That bitch will be warming the President's desk before the devil knows he's dead."

"Relax. I've come to an understanding with Justice Dillinger. If we say Dex Jackson is our guy, the Court will bless it."

"Dex is a wreck. We need at least a day to get him straightened out. Then there's the matter of security."

"So we buy a day. "

Farrell stopped. "You mean the video?"

"Damn right the video. Call the networks."

PART II

"The next war in the Middle East will be fought over water, not politics."

Former United Nations Secretary General Boutros Boutros-Ghali

Fort Campbell
Monday, 3:03 a.m.

Seventeen hours after the car bombing in Charleston, Eva Hudson's cell phone echoed in the command post ladies' room. She crouched low to look under the toilet stalls. She was alone. "Hudson," she answered in an unintentionally husky voice. It was her Under-Secretary calling from her house in suburban Maryland. The President was going to be on NBC in five minutes.

Worries lifted. Her heart soared. If the President was going to be on TV, that meant he was alive.

But as Eva washed her hands in the sink, her mood quickly swung back to outrage. Seventeen hours since the Monroe bombing. He hadn't even bothered to call. Forget the fact that they were in a serious relationship. She was a cabinet-level secretary who, incidentally, had nearly been assassinated yesterday. He was punishing her for not going to Camp David, she decided. Letting his personal feelings get in the way of national security. There was no other explanation.

She wiped down her phone's keypad and used a paper towel to open the restroom door. As she walked toward Colonel Madsen's office – he had a TV – she speed dialed the President's personal cell phone. It went immediately to voicemail.

She remembered the rules she and the President had set for themselves: Don't put anything to the President in writing, because even if the tabloids didn't get hold of it right away, it would eventually be public –

framed in the Isaac Hatch Presidential Library ten or twenty years from now. More importantly, don't leave the President personal voicemails. Considering the circumstances, this was a rule she was ready to break.

And after the beep, she tore into him: "It's me. I can appreciate that we are in crisis mode, but denying me entry to the executive bunker is a violation of Security Council protocol and regardless of your personal feelings, I will not stand for it. I expect to hear from you."

Hanging up didn't make her feel any better. She took a breath and went down the hall to Colonel Madsen's office. Eva knocked but got no response. Madsen had said he planned on sleeping on the couch in his office until the crisis hit some breaking point.

Eva opened the door and flipped on the overhead lights. Sure enough, he was out cold on his couch. She went straight for Madsen's TV, powered it up, and switched to ABC.

"And now," the network anchor said, *"a special message from the President of the United States."*

The screen cut to a tight shot of the Presidential Seal, then cut to the President himself, where he was shown seated at a desk with only a gray wall and an American flag behind him. *"Good evening,"* he said. *"It's with a heavy heart, but with faith in the freedom that we cherish and our democratic republic, that I address you tonight. The Federal Government is operating smoothly and efficiently from a secure, undisclosed location."*

Madsen sat up on the couch, rubbing his eyes. He took note of Eva's body language – arms folded tight across her chest, leaning forward, pupils way too close to the screen.

"It's only natural," the President continued, *"that your hearts are filled with fear, thoughts of vengeance, and concern for our military men and women."*

"We ask that you do not panic," the President said. *"Any type of disorder, including looting, hoarding supplies or other criminal activity only diverts attention from our common enemy and makes it harder for us to respond. Please know that our emergency systems are working as planned and our government is taking all necessary measures to ensure your safety. More developments will be revealed as soon as possible. Good night and God speed."*

The screen abruptly cut to black and then to the Presidential Seal.

Eva flipped the TV off.

"He didn't get my vote," Madsen piped up, "but I gotta admit it's a relief seeing him in charge." Eva sat hugging herself. Her mind raced. "Penny for your thoughts."

She reached for words. She didn't want to cause more alarm. But she needed to talk it through. "The President hasn't looked like that since his first few months in office."

"What're you saying? The tape's not authentic?"

"I'm saying it wasn't recorded lately."

"Well, you would know."

Eva glared at him. "And that means what?"

"I don't buy the tabloids, but my wife does."

Eva imagined a scorpion's tail rising up behind her. "As the highest ranking officer on base," she said, "that's the last time you'll speak to me with disrespect."

"No offense, but you're —"

"Not military? Please. We know the Senator Pro Tem and Speaker of the House are dead. The Vice President is rumored to be crippled, and the Secretary of State is foreign born. That makes me, at the very least, the likely acting Vice President of the United States."

The Colonel broke off eye contact. "Hadn't thought of that, Secretary...I mean Madam Vice President."

"Madam Secretary will do until we know more. Not a word of this leaks out."

"Yes ma'am."

"Get your senior officers together at oh-six-hundred."

Fort Campbell Stadium Track
4:05 a.m.

Agent Carver woke in an empty office where he and Agent O' Keefe had slept for three hours on matching cots. His mind quickly went into gear, flooding with leads that had to be investigated, politicos that wanted updates and bits of Muskogee that Nico had taught him the night before. It was all coming back too fast and too early. He needed to break a sweat. Get his thoughts in order. Organize.

He opened his eyes and touched the outline of O'Keefe's undershirt, then tapped her gently. "Hey," he whispered. "Hey. You wanna go run some laps?"

She rose up on her elbows and checked her watch. "Bastard." She punched Carver in the arm and went back to sleep.

Since converting O'Keefe from an NSA desk jockey to a field agent, he'd managed to talk her into weapons training, jujitsu classes and brisk walks. But he still couldn't convince her to do any serious cardio.

He put on his shoes and slipped out of the building, making his way across the dark commissary parking lot toward a stadium he had spotted from the transport plane window. The sliver of moon provided his only illumination. Carver arrived at the football field less than ten minutes later, and having no access to gym clothes, he stripped down to his boxers and folded his suit, tie, shoes and socks neatly on a bleacher.

The feel of his feet against the track triggered a memory of the dirt road he had grown up on. A visceral memory of childhood was all it took to wrack Carver with guilt. It had been several weeks since he had called his parents. He was a bad son. Both were still living in Joseph City, a rancher's town off I-40 in Arizona, where his father had operated a feed store for three decades. The relationship had never been the same since Carver had decided to leave the Mormon Church, ruining his parents' vision of an afterlife where they were sealed for eternity as a family and would one day rule, like gods themselves, over their own private celestial kingdom. It wasn't that he didn't believe in God, as Carver had tried to explain over breakfast at the Joseph City diner one morning. He just wasn't sure that the LDS Church had gotten all the details right.

His career in the CIA had not helped family relations. There had been long stretches of service overseas where he had been prevented from contacting any family members for fear of compromising his identity or whereabouts. Not that he was resentful. It came with the job.

He picked up the phone and dialed the area code. He stopped himself. It was only 1:05 a.m. in Arizona. It was typical. He always seemed to be in an inconvenient time zone, calling at the worst possible time, or dropping home unannounced when his parents themselves were headed out of town.

Shut off the mind chatter, Carver told himself. Just run. He began a fast clip around the quarter-mile track. A military transport plane flew low overhead as it came in for a landing on the airstrip a half-mile to the east. Its thunderous screech passed slowly, but completely, until the only noise was the sound of Carver's bare feet against the track.

As he ran, he replayed a single conversation with Julian Speers in his head. Several weeks ago, Speers had just drafted Carver and O'Keefe into the covert investigation of the apparent DOD arms smuggling. They were at the Chief's house, where he had cooked some garlic-heavy spaghetti and meatballs. Speers and O'Keefe had downed three bottles of wine between them, leaving the very sober Carver to listen to their drunken ramblings.

"Thailand has had seventeen military coups since World War Two," Speers ranted. "Seventeen!" Thailand's Prime Minister had been out of the country on vacation as tanks rolled through the streets of Bangkok. Those loyal to the PM had been quietly notified of the impending changes in their offices. Meanwhile the King, who had apparently given tacit approval for the takeover in advance, made no public statements. As Speers described it, the public had grown quite used to occasional military takeovers. "Why not here?" Speers raved.

"Americans transfer power peacefully," Carver had told him. "That's what sets us apart from the developing world."

"Oh, grow up," Speers slurred. "Twenty-five flag-draped coffins come home every week. President's never fired a gun in his life. Military types didn't vote for him in the first place, now they blame him for the quicksand. The SECDEF's berating him publicly. He's got a twenty-two percent approval rating. The market's in the toilet. Dollar's at half the Euro. Thirty-eight percent of the population thinks he should be impeached. Nine percent will actually admit to hoping he gets assassinated. Need I say more?"

Insight into the extent of Speers' political awareness wasn't the only interesting thing that happened that night. He recalled walking O'Keefe back to the subway stop that night. He commented that the Chief of Staff had a dangerously free-ranging, undisciplined mind for someone in such a powerful position. O'Keefe, herself quite drunk, came to Speers' defense, saying that he was only stating what everyone already knew – that the President was losing his grip on power, and if he didn't step gracefully aside, Congress was going to do something about it. They began to argue. O'Keefe called him a narrow-minded puritan. He called her unpatriotic. She shouted something back. But by now he wasn't listening. He was too consumed with how beautiful she was. He couldn't stop watching her mouth.

He kissed her. She kissed him back. Regret instantly washed over him. He broke their embrace as O'Keefe gazed up at him with a mischievous spunk that only her ex-boyfriends had known.

"Look, Meagan…" It was the first and only time he had ever used her first name.

"No," she scolded him. "No first names. That's rule number one."

"Rules?" he said, laughing. "You're making up rules now?"

"We have to maintain professional distance," she teased. Then she kissed him again.

"Last subway's coming. You should get home."

"You should come with me."

He grinned. "We should be good."

"I'll be good. I swear."

"That's not what I mean. If we're going to slip, let it be when you're sober. And trapped in a government car on a stakeout somewhere."

"Surveillance sex?" she said, bursting into hysterics. "You want surveillance sex?"

"No. I've just got a thing for cars. Government cars. That's how patriotic I am."

She kissed him and backed away, slowly, giving him one last wave before heading down the escalator at Foggy Bottom Station. Carver's soul felt a little lighter that night. He actually felt giddy.

But by morning the feeling had given way to regret. He had cheated himself out of a rare chance to feel intimate with someone. Something he had needed for far too long.

Now he finished his run, slowing to a walk for the last lap around the track. He didn't bother to stretch. He put his suit back on and walked across the grass to the makeshift barracks to see if O'Keefe was awake yet.

The memory of the night at the subway station filled him with a kind of music. All these weeks later, he could still taste her mouth on his. I could slip, he told himself. I could slip right now. The sky is falling, the world is coming undone, and I could slip.

But back at the barracks, he found her sitting upright on her cot, holding her phone to her ear.

O'Keefe's mind was on business. She signed off brusquely and hung up.

"That was the Bureau," she said gruffly. "They found evidence in Faruq Ahmed's home linking him to six other Allied Jihad cells in four cities. They're making arrests right now."

Carver's pulse quickened. This was unexpected. Nico's assertion about the tape rang true with him. He didn't believe Ahmed was who he said he was. And all those assassinations weren't just the work of some crafty terrorist cells. There had to be an insider. "I need to see the evidence."

"That's what I said. They're saying our security clearance isn't high enough."

"What? The wolf is at the door, and they're going to quibble about security clearances?"

She nodded. "They found another body. Some cop at a drag strip outside Monroe. They're saying Ahmed was practicing there. They figure the cop was in the wrong place at the wrong time."

He sat down on his cot and thought for a moment. "They want us to back off, don't they?"

"Those weren't his exact words."

"We're resuming our end of this investigation. Screw the Bureau. We only answer to Julian now."

Rooftop, Baltimore, Maryland 5:45 A.M.

Elvir sat atop a five-story brownstone office building, watching McAlister Park through the scope of a sniper rifle. There were thunderheads on the horizon. He was sweating. It was too damn early to be this damn hot.

He spotted Ali. His partner wore a white cap and came across the street to enter the park's green space. Elvir switched his phone on and talked into the receiver fixed in Ali's ear. "Twenty meters at two o'clock. See the van?"

"Got it," Ali replied.

"Just get the money. If they invite you to go with them, walk away. Don't say anything. I've got you covered."

Ali went to the van and knocked on the door. It opened. A man in a black jump suit and sunglasses sat inside. Elvir could hear the man's voice through Ali's Bluetooth. He sounded white.

"This won't do," he said. "We hand the money off to Elvir directly. Take us to him."

"No," Ali said. "I get the money here and now. That is the deal."

Elvir found the man's face in the scope of his rifle. He wasn't in uniform, but he had a jarhead haircut. He had big horse's teeth. "Why don't we go get some breakfast?" the man asked Ali. "Somewhere we can negotiate."

Just as Elvir has instructed, Ali turned to walk away, but the man grabbed him around the neck from behind and shoved a gun into his face. The click of the gun's safety switch releasing was audible over the radio.

"Tell me where Elvir is. I'll make you rich. Or you can die. Your choice."

Elvir put pressure on the trigger of his sniper rifle, but he hesitated. Killing the man meant they might never see the last payment. Then, out of the corner of his eye, he spotted two more men get up from park benches and walk towards the van. Why hadn't he spotted them before?

Ali saw them too. "Okay, okay," he said. He was cracking. And they hadn't even hurt him yet.

No, Elvir thought. No, Ali. Don't make me do this. Just stay still long enough for me to pick these guys off.

Elvir found the man's face again in the rifle scope. His finger found the rifle's trigger. "It's an apartment," he heard Ali say. "Third floor."

There was no alternative now. He moved the scope one-eighth inch to the left. That was all it took to put Ali's chest in the scope's crosshairs. "I forgive you." He took the shot, blowing a hole through Ali's right lung. The armor-piercing bullet went straight through Ali's slight 130-pound frame and into his attacker and through the van, lodging into one of the park's mighty oak trees.

Elvir's second shot missed. He repositioned for a third, trying to target one of the other goons, but the familiar flash of an enemy muzzle stopped him. He ducked just as returning fire blew brick fragments into his eyes. The former Army sniper scrambled away from the roof's edge, temporarily blinded, retracing his steps to the fire escape on the other side of the brownstone.

Fort Campbell

Carver hated meetings. Or at least the kind that he and O'Keefe had just been summoned to. It was always the same. A bunch of Washington bureaucrats wanted thousands of case hours boiled down into a 60-second oral report and a 200-page written report that would never be read. On the basis of that, the bureaucrats would make a decision that would affect the fate of the operation. Nine times out of ten, they ended up killing it.

Eva Hudson was the new sheriff in town, and it seemed that she wanted to get her mitts on Carver's investigation. There was no way that was going to happen. Julian Speers and the President had requested that the operation stay off-the-grid, and it was going to stay there until they said otherwise.

He and O'Keefe made their way down the hallway toward Colonel Madsen's conference room. They had spent all morning going over Nico's assessment of the Muskogee translations. The news wasn't good. They were dealing with a bunch of nameless suspects that had been careful not to give up their locations or contacts in any of their transmissions. Carver felt strongly that the key was finding the language geek who had taught them Muskogee in the first place. It wasn't like Muskogee experts were a dime a dozen.

His phone buzzed. It was Madison, the receptionist at the K Street office. "Madison," he said. "How are you today?"

"Terrible," she said. "I'm all worried about what's been going on. Couldn't sleep. How are you, Mister Danforth?"

Madison was still under the impression that Carver and O'Keefe were consultants. She had never asked what kind. She was young, unambitious, preoccupied with her social life, and completely uninterested in the services that the company performed for its clients. She was one of those people who just wanted to punch in and collect a paycheck and get health care. A perfect fit for a front company.

"We're on our way to a client meeting," Carver told her as he winked to O'Keefe. "What's up?"

"I heard on the news that lots of companies are closed today because of the attacks. And I was wondering…"

"Stay home," Carver said. He was trying to be practical. And since the Georgetown field house had been compromised, he knew that they could expect a break-in on K Street as well. They wouldn't find anything, but there was no reason to put Madison in harm's way. "And don't worry about coming in the rest of the week. We're on the road anyhow."

"Uh, okay, but I don't want to use up all my vacation time. I'll still get paid, right?"

For God's sake. Carver was trying to save the country from further attacks and he had to worry about some receptionist's paid time off. He had told Speers from the start that these elaborate dummy aliases were more trouble than they were worth.

*

The markets were due to open shortly. The Treasury Secretary walked with an attaché in one hand and her phone in the other. On the receiving end of Eva's call was the Federal Reserve Chairman, who sat in an office high above the New York Stock Exchange trading floor, where nervous stock runners talked incessantly into cell phones to anxious brokers who feared the worst.

This wasn't the 72-year-old Fed Chair's first rodeo, and he was predicting a massive sell-off that might send the already troubled economy into a tailspin.

"Mister Chairman," Eva said, "I think that if we can manage the message before the opening bell, the markets should open as usual."

"Eva," the Fed chair countered, "in my neighborhood there was a line a hundred deep outside Bank of America. And that was at five a.m."

"And you think closing the markets will make them any more confident?"

Eva knew that the President had fantasies about forcing the old man's resignation, but the Chairman was an institution, having survived twenty-two years and four different administrations. Eva liked the old codger. He was a little conservative for her taste, but there was something to be said for someone who worshipped fundamentals. His favorite book remained Graham's *The Intelligent Investor*, and to Eva's mind, everyone needed a cynical old coot like that in their camp. If the Vice President was truly dead, God rest his hateful soul, Eva wished the President would call her and make her the Veep already. As the mere Treasury Secretary, her relationship with the Fed Chair was little more than one friend talking another down from a suicide jump.

"If you close the markets," she explained patiently, "and you cut people off from their investments, it's only going to make it worse."

"How about early closure?"

"No. Just listen to me. Call the major analysts. Get them to go on the networks advising a strong buy on any defense contractor and aerospace. You also pitch high-tech, natural resources, and precious metals."

"Those sound like protracted war investments. Are you trying to tell me something? Should I be thinking about war bonds?"

"You must've seen the Allied Jihad tape by now," Eva said. "If I know the President, he'll open up another front on those barbarians before the week's out. Point is, if we can get the talking heads invested in the idea that more fighting is good for the economy, we might avoid a crash today."

She hung up just as she entered Colonel Madsen's conference room and sat at the head of a cheap fiber-board table. Colonel Madsen and his senior staff sat at her flank. The American flag, the Kentucky State flag and the Army flag hung in a row behind her.

Agents Carver and O'Keefe came in just as Colonel Madsen began addressing his staff. "I'd like to inform everyone that Treasury Secretary Hudson is using this base as a temporary command post for a joint investigation into yesterday's events." He waited a moment for the officers to absorb the idea that the Secretary of the United States Treasury had effectively taken over command of the base. "And as Garrison Commander, I'm prepared to do anything in my power to see that she has our full cooperation."

"Thank you, Colonel," Eva said as Madsen sat down. "Everyone, I'd like to introduce NSA case officers Carver and O'Keefe. Carver is formerly of CIA counter-terrorism and will be leading the investigation."

"With all due respect," Carver said, "This is news to me, Madam Secretary. Agent O'Keefe and I are engaged in a classified operation that reports directly to the White House."

Eva folded her arms across her chest. "The White House?" she said. "To whom specifically?"

Carver was afraid to name the President, and not just because Eva was the President's not-so-secret girlfriend. The investigation was strictly off-the-grid.

"Well?" Eva said.

"We report to Chief of Staff Julian Speers," Carver replied.

"Have you had direct contact with Julian in the past twelve hours?"

"No ma'am."

"I'll be honest," Eva said. "We don't know where the Chief of Staff is now. He hasn't responded to calls. Considering the state of emergency we're in, I'll take full responsibility for the disclosure of your classified mission. Now I'll give you a chance to transfer operational details to me in private."

She excused Colonel Madsen and his staff. They rose uncertainly and began filing out. O'Keefe leaned close to Carver, whispering in his ear. "Are you sure we can trust her?"

"No," Carver said, "but the fact that she dismissed the brass is probably a pretty good sign that we should throw her a bone or two."

Eva tapped the table with her pen. "Before we get off on the wrong foot, I need you to explain why Nico Gold is on my base."

Carver was caught off guard. He was used to getting his way, and it was clear that Eva was significantly more hands-on than Julian. "Nico is a specialist in rare languages as well as computer…"

"I'm painfully aware of Nico's qualifications. I'm asking how a notorious international criminal found his way onto this base."

Carver didn't care how hot Eva was. He didn't like anyone baiting him. "Again, his skill set…"

"Let's get some history out of the way," Eva said. "When I was Executive Director of the IMF, Nico Gold hacked into our systems and drained our coffers of billions. I wasted two years of my life chasing him in some of the world's most unpleasant countries. We finally caught him in Syria, where he was living with a group of Iranian dissidents and learning Farsi. I pushed to prosecute him in Saudi Arabia, where he would've gotten the death penalty. I was overruled."

Carver's neck grew hot. He had done his homework. He was quite familiar with Eva and Nico's tangled past, but never thought this operation would by on anyone's radar. "Nico Gold isn't politically convenient," Carver said, "but he solved in one day what our agents couldn't crack in a year."

Eva considered this for a moment. "Fine. I'll allow you to use him while we're in crisis mode. But whatever deal you made, know I'll break it when this is over."

Rapture Run

Julian Speers walked through the cavernous command room and lingered between two rows of workstations occupied by eight soldiers on each side. He pretended to look for a network printer – General Wainewright had given him some bullshit assignment to draft legal documents regarding military power during martial law – but he was really just snooping. He looked over the shoulder of a Ulysses communications specialist and saw satellite imagery of several Iranian armor brigades. A massive formation trucking across Syrian territory toward Israel.

Speers leaned so close to the specialist that he could smell the man's cucumber-scented shaving cream. "Is that for real?" he said. "I mean, that's not some war game, right?"

"Oh it's real," the specialist confirmed a little too eagerly.

Syria didn't even border Iran. Had Iran sent armor through Turkey or Iraq to get to Syria, it would've been an international incident. The fact that nobody knew about it had to mean that Iran had been airlifting its tank battalions into Syria quietly for months, and with Syria's full cooperation.

And there was only one reason Syria would allow Iran to build up such a massive force in its territory – to eliminate a common enemy.

Then the Specialist turned and gave Speers the once-over, and seeing his civilian clothes, said, "Interrogative: should you be here, sir?"

Speers straightened up. "I sent a document to a printer called V11XT. Any ideas?"

The specialist pointed to a large multi-function machine near the Con, where General Wainewright sat on an elevated throne of steel.

Speers found his print job incomplete due to a paper jam. As he cracked open the machine, General Farrell and Dex Jackson converged on Wainewright's perch at the same time. Speers decided to linger at the machine and see if he could pick up anything juicy.

"Get any shuteye?" he heard Wainewright ask Dex.

"Nah. I heard Fort Campbell debunked the Allied Jihad tape. That set my mind off on all sorts of tangents."

"Nonsense!" Wainewright shouted. "Fact: Faruq Ahmed was Yemeni, for chrissake, and we have evidence that he personally carried out the suicide attempt on Speaker Bailey."

"That's bunk," Dex shot back. "Our embeds within the Allied Jihad say they never heard of the guy."

Speers loitered a little too long at the printer. Wainewright made him, shooting a glare so cold that the Chief of Staff's chin quivered. He tapped Farrell and Dex and pulled them into an adjoining room. Wainewright frowned at Speers through the Plexiglas before frosting the glass.

He turned his attention back to Dex. "We have proof," Wainewright said now that they were alone. "The suicide tape."

"How's that?" The corners of Dex's mouth and the corners of his eyelids succumbed to gravity's pull. He wore every bit of his trauma on his face.

"Fact: we have a tape made by the Monroe suicide bomber, Faruq Ahmed. He says he speaks for the Allied Jihad. We handed it over to CNN, and they're running it every fifteen minutes."

Farrell lit up another cigarette and held it between his thumb and middle finger. "And we've located some targets," he said. "In Yemen. Suspected Allied Jihad cell. The public wants this."

"Meaning?"

"Meaning we're going to take out the target. The American people need this."

Dex's face tightened. "Since when do we kill to make the public feel good?"

Wainewright sat at the table and folded his hands before him.

"Dex, the country is in an unprecedented crisis. We need leadership, and there's no clear line of succession. We're prepared to make you the next President of the United States."

Dex leaned back in his chair and took in the proposition. His heart was flapping within his chest at breakaway speed, but he managed to mask his exuberance as he spoke. "What makes you so sure I'd want the job?"

Farrell laughed with abandon. "What do you take us for? We all heard that audio file going around congress during the last election."

Dex looked up. "What audio file?"

Farrell was enjoying this. "The recording of a certain telephone conversation..." He paused, enjoying seeing Dex squirm. "...featuring a certain Defense Secretary calling the GOP Committee Chair, probing about support for a Presidential run."

Dex's face turned red. "So I'm ambitious," he admitted. "I was critical of the President's policies. That's no secret."

"This would be a chance to be your own man for a change. Do things your own way."

Dex didn't trust Farrell, and that went double for Wainewright. But he had always wanted the Presidency, and this administration's incompetence in foreign policy had made him want it more than ever. Dex hesitated for a moment longer, if only to think about the most graceful way to say I do. "If called," he uttered lamely, "I will serve."

Wainewright grinned. "Then demonstrate that you'll take our advice seriously."

"If you mean Yemen..." Dex said in a near whisper.

"Dex," Wainewright said firmly, "understand that we don't need your permission to do this. We're calling the shots right now, and nobody on God's green earth could stop us."

"But we'd rather work as a team," Farrell told Dex. "We'd be the brains, you'd be the face. Offer's on the table."

Dex shook Wainewright's hand, then Farrell's. "I'll support the strike," he said. "But we'd better have something credible to take to the press."

Farrell smiled and dragged on his cigarette.

Yemen

Five men sat around a campfire, telling jokes. The camp smelled like goat dung and saffron-spiced stew. There was absolutely no wind.

At night they cordoned the camp off with temporary fencing that they transported on a sled pulled by a pair of horses. The fencing allowed the children to play at night without their mothers chasing after them. It also allowed the herders to sleep without worrying about predators getting to the flock.

Suddenly three of the horses trotted out from behind a canvas tent. They were spooked. One of the men stood up, clutching a Kalashnikov rifle and gently shooed them away with one hand. Then more horses came through camp, picking up speed as they approached the perimeter. They were out of control. The man with the Kalashnikov aimed at the first horse as it leaped over the fence. Not because he wanted to shoot it. But because he hoped to prevent the others from following it into the black yonder.

The other men shined their lights in the opposite direction, looking for the predator that had made the animals restless. There was no sign of anything.

They heard the high-pitched screech an instant before everything vanished in a flash of white light.

Fort Campbell
10:15 a.m.

The base's Joint Ops media center was a cramped trailer with a low ceiling and the décor of a charter school library. Eva found Carver there at his laptop. He was hooked into the CIA Ethernet, which, for security reasons, still required a regular Ethernet cable. Eva glimpsed an Oklahoma State University faculty dossier on his monitor before Carver sensed her presence and clicked to a safety screen.

Eva stood behind him with her hips cocked to the side. "Anything I should know about?"

Carver tried to hide his annoyance. "No, Madam Secretary."

"You do realize who you're talking to."

Carver figured that given the high level assassinations, Eva was now the second or third most powerful person in the United States, depending on whether the Vice President survived his wounds. But he had sworn his silence and loyalty not only to Speers, but to the President himself. "With all due respect," he told her, "you're a paper billionaire."

"You'll have to spell that out for me."

"Regardless of what glorious title you might inherit, you're not at Site R with the President right now. That really limits your influence."

Eva pulled up a plastic chair and sat across from him. "I'm going to tell you something that I haven't told anyone. The President's broadcast last night was shot at least two years ago."

Carver revealed nothing in his expression. "Go on."

She switched on her phone and showed Carver a satellite image of a farming area on West Virginia's eastern border with Maryland. "See that mountain?" she said, pointing to a digital GPS marker she'd placed there. "Last night my helicopter was hovering right over this area, where Rapture Run is supposedly located."

"I'm still listening" Carver said as he memorized the longitude and latitude.

"Two years ago, Congressman Bailey presented a bill that would protect this area as a wildlife preserve."

"That must happen all the time," Carver said, although his mind was racing with possibilities. He already knew that Congressman Bailey was connected to both Lieutenant Flynn and SECDEF Jackson.

"Not like this," Eva said. "I just pulled up Congressman Bailey's bill. It had a rider that contracted Ulysses to completely seal off the wildlife preserve with a massive fence. We're talking a border fence. Like the one we're building between us and Mexico."

"Typical pork barrel spending," Carver said dismissively, although he knew better.

"This is different. Rapture Run was built without the knowledge of the Security Council. I can't even say for sure if the President knew. Yet Congressman Bailey and obviously someone high up in Ulysses knew that a military installation was going to be built there."

"And then Bailey turns up dead," Carver said, deciding to give Eva some validation. He wasn't about to tell Eva about Lieutenant Flynn and the missing Stingers. Not yet, anyhow. Until he could speak to Speers, or the President, it was way too early to trust anyone.

Rapture Run Cafeteria

Deep beneath the cornfield that masked the bunker's very existence, the Rapture Run cafeteria operated as if it had always been there, with eight cooks standing behind a counter and a lunchroom that could seat a hundred at a time. Speers grabbed a tray, but he wasn't here to eat. He was here for information. He inserted himself into line next to Corporal Hammond, who was managing two trays of food. "So," Speers said. "How long you think we can stay down here before Wainewright starts eating the enlisted men?"

Corporal Hammond eyed the gut that hung over Speers' belt. "I'd say we've got more to fear from you than him."

A dozen servicemen stood in the chow line on either side of them, each shuffling along with assembly-line precision. Speers and Hammond first came to a pile of egg salad that looked positively regurgitated. Speers covered his mouth to avoid taking in the odor.

"Guess you never had to eat in a mess hall," Corporal Hammond said.

"Once. I went with the President to Camp Pendleton on a campaign stop. We ate with the Marines."

Hammond smirked. "Didn't I see that on TV?"

"Oh I'm sure every conservative in America saw the President puke on the base commander. In slow-motion, no less."

Hammond put a double helping of the egg salad on one of the trays. "The General loves this stuff," he said.

"So," Speers said, feeling a bit of camaraderie build between him and the Corporal, "Is the Joint Chief's office a good career stop?"

"Big time," Hammond said. "Plus, it beats combat. I like my arms, fingers, legs. I like to keep 'em attached to my body."

The first cook looked at Hammond and said, *"Tofurkey or Soy burger?"* Hammond took both and advanced in line. Speers rapped his fist on the aluminum surface and said, "Hit me."

He caught up with Hammond, who was waiting for sweet potatoes. He edged close to him. "Y'know, I've been with the President since he was Governor."

"It's gotta hurt," Hammond said.

"General Wainewright seems to be taking it well, don't you think?"

Hammond kept his gaze on the food in front of him as he neared the salad. "The General can't afford to get emotional. He's just doing his job."

"We both know he's doing a little more than just his job."

"Make time, Corporal!" the cook scolded. Hammond took two of the little Caesar salads and bolted for the dessert area. Speers kept on his heels, his tie brushing the pair of chevrons on the Corporal's sleeve.

"I like you," Speers lied, "so I'm going to give you a chance to save your ass."

Hammond turned around and peered up at the Chief. "Look around. I'd say you're the one in hostile territory."

The cafeteria was full of armed Ulysses soldiers and yes, they all seemed to be watching. But Speers was undeterred. He leaned in close and whispered into Hammond's ear. "You all can't stay down here forever. And when you come up for air, Wainewright won't be able to save you from the CIA. Fact is, he'll probably sell you out just to save himself."

"They wouldn't be interested in me."

"They'll be interested in everyone involved in the conspiracy to assassinate the President and commit treason. Both offenses are punishable by death." Speers grabbed Hammond's right arm and squeezed it hard. "I don't think they'll have trouble finding a vein."

The Corporal broke free from the Chief's grip. His hands shook as he lifted the two trays and looked for the exit.

Fort Campbell Intel Lab
1:40 p.m.

Agent Carver stormed into the lab cubicles where Nico sat at a computer wearing headphones as he sifted through mountains of intercepted Muskogee audio files. He was going to shoot the person who had given Nico unsupervised access to a computer. Nico saw him coming. He took his headphones off. "What's up, Spook?"

"Hacked into my pension yet?"

"I'll make a nice deposit if you can get me a Presidential pardon."

"If you've gotta use a restroom, do it now," Carver said. "I've requisitioned a plane." The truth was that he had forged a travel authorization in Eva Hudson's name. The Treasury Secretary had turned Fort Campbell upside down so quickly that people were willing to believe anything you told them. "We're going to Norman, Oklahoma."

"What for?"

"Professor Emeritus Hitchiti. The last living Muskogee speaker."

"He's still alive?"

Carver smiled. "Still kicking at ninety-six. He doesn't teach regular classes anymore, but he had nine private students last semester. All from out of state."

Baltimore
2:15 p.m.

Angie Jackson sat slumped against the living room wall. Her hands were still duck-taped behind her. One of Elvir's associates – a thick-bellied goon with low-rise jeans that left half of his rear end showing – sat on the carpet beside her, cradling a 9mm while watching the never-ending crisis coverage on TV. Between commercials, Angie could hear the residents of the apartment next door screaming at each other in Spanish.

The Market Report was on TV. The anchor rested her chin on her thumb and forefinger, gazing into the market analyst's eyes. *"What advice do you have for people who are afraid? We're hearing from a lot of people who are of the mind that they should cash out while they still can."*

The analyst: *"It's never smart to panic. If you think you're in for a fall, it's much better to simply move your money into new opportunities in the market. Historically, you look at World War Two, even 9/11, the people who put their money into high tech, aircraft manufacturers, defense contractors, by and large, they did very well."*

The anchor was momentarily distracted. Someone was obviously speaking into her earpiece. Her face turned serious as she turned to face the cameras. The animated red/white/blue logo for A Day of Terror: America Mourns swept onscreen. The anchor seemed genuinely stunned as she announced to the country, for the first time, *"Government officials have just confirmed rumors that the Vice President has succumbed to his wounds."*

A patriotic video montage of the late Vice President began, accompanied by a narration track that had clearly been prepared well in advance. The dead bolt on the living room door began to turn. The goon leaped up and positioned himself behind the door as it opened.

He put the gun down. It was only his boss, Elvir.

Elvir shut the door quickly behind him, opening it one last time to peek down the hallway and make sure he hadn't been followed.

"Where's Ali?" the goon demanded in Muskogee.

"It was a setup," Elvir replied in his native Bosnian. He tossed his backpack onto the floor, unholstered a pistol from within his jacket and slumped into the lone armchair in the room.

"Where's Ali?" the goon repeated.

Elvir shook his head. "He gave me no choice."

"Shit! Shit! Shit!" The goon smacked his forehead repeatedly. He sat, enveloping his little head in his huge hands for a moment. "Listen to me Elvir. I have a friend with a small plane. He can get us to Mexico, and from there, we can get back to Bosnia."

Elvir shook his head. He switched back to Muskogee. "If we run, we'll never get our money."

"But how can we ever get the money now?"

Elvir looked at Angie and saw dollar signs. "They'll be very interested in our guest here," he explained.

Norman, Oklahoma
4:30 p.m. Central

They flew into the University of Oklahoma's Westheimer Airport under dark, threatening skies. All commercial traffic had been suspended since the attacks, rendering the tiny airport deserted. There were no aircraft controllers in the tower to guide them in, nor were there landing strip personnel to meet the Cessna U-27A as it taxied off the runway.

A hard summer rain fell as Agents Carver and O'Keefe exited the little military turboprop. O'Keefe turned to help Nico out of the aircraft. He was cuffed at the wrists and dressed in street clothes that were a little baggy on his slight frame. They sprinted to the main building where, as expected, the lone rental car counter was unmanned.

Carver jumped the counter and searched behind it until he found a locked cabinet. One hard tug busted the flimsy lock, revealing the keys to twenty Ford economy cars attached to numbered key rings. "Lucky number?" he said to O'Keefe.

"Eleven."

He chose the #11 key.

Fifteen minutes later they pulled up Cavalry Street in the blue rental car. "That's it," O'Keefe said, pointing to a modest two-bedroom Craftsman with faded blue shingles.

Carver parked the rental car a short distance down the street. He adjusted his rear view mirror and glanced at Nico, who sat in the back seat. He figured they had no reason to fear their white collar prisoner. But Nico was still a flight risk, and if this operation turned into a door-buster, or a shootout, they wouldn't be able to keep their eyes on him.

Carver climbed into the back seat, flipped out a small blade from his pocketknife and cut into the fabric rooftop until he hit a piece of metal framing. He then cinched Nico's right cuff around it, effectively locking him in the car. "Where's the love?" Nico protested. "You can't do this. It's against the law to leave me in a car by myself."

"Who's going to stop me? Child Protective Services?"

The two agents cut diagonally across the front yard's Kentucky Bluegrass lawn. "Door's ajar," O'Keefe said.

Carver put his hand on O'Keefe's shoulder. His touch sent butterflies swarming in her belly. "Let me take point," he told her.

"You don't have to do that. I'm wearing Kevlar."

Carver thunked his knuckles against something hard under his shirt. "I'm wearing armor. Besides, you have to let me be chivalrous once in a while."

They drew their pistols and approached the front entry. Carver went in first and regarded the ancient-looking man with long gray hair and eyeglasses in the overstuffed armchair. "Professor Hitchiti?"

The old man didn't answer. As O'Keefe cleared the other rooms, Carver drew closer and switched on a lamp.

A single bullet hole gaped on the Professor's forehead. Flies buzzed in and out of the wound.

Fort Campbell

Eva sat in her office studying bond market reports that the Under-Secretary had faxed in from her home in rural Virginia. She had been able to establish contact with a half dozen members of her staff, most of whom were now working from home or coffee shops. The Joint Chiefs had ordered all Federal Agency Internet and VOIP networks shut down, citing security threats. The fact that military bases were conveniently unaffected wasn't lost on her.

In the desk drawer sat a prescription for Ativan, an anti-depression and anti-anxiety drug that she had taken with some success after her husband's death. The base pharmacy had graciously sent it over without a prescription. The fact that it was there was comforting. But she tried to think of it as a fire extinguisher, glass only to be broken in the event of an extreme emergency. Important decisions had to be made. Her judgment had to be sound. The question was whether her critical thinking skills were more effective with or without the pills.

Madsen appeared in the doorway. He was red-faced and slightly out of breath. "We just hit targets in Yemen," he said without preamble.

Eva sat upright and ran both hands through her brunette hair. "We?" she said. "According to whom?"

"Rapture Run." He tossed a memo onto the pine desktop. "The U.S.S. John McCain launched cruise missiles against Allied Jihad training camps. There's an announcement going to the press as well."

"Didn't they get our intel report? We advised them last night that the tape couldn't be authenticated as Allied Jihad!"

"They got the report. They just didn't like what it said."

Eva stood, paced once around the perimeter of her desk, then leaned over it and rested on her elbows. Despite her official role as Treasury Secretary, she was accustomed to having the President's ear in every foreign policy situation. The fact that she was so far removed now, when the world was coming unglued, was unbearable. "Let's get Rapture Run on the line," she said.

Madsen shook his head. "They're still not taking our calls. General Wainewright's little assistant – what's his name, Hammond? – he said 'Don't call us, we'll call you.'"

Rapture Run

General Wainewright sat behind a collapsible desk in Rapture Run's Executive Quarters. It wasn't exactly the Oval Office, but it was roughly three times as large as Dex Jackson's quarters, complete with a full-size bed and private shower and satellite television feeding into three monitors.

Wainewright sat working on the Presidential Inauguration Speech. Lincoln's opera glasses sat on the desk beside his computer. He heard footsteps in the corridor and reached instinctively for his sidearm. He never sat with his back to the door, nor did he stray more than an arm's length from a loaded weapon. During the first Iraq war, after his tank battalion had crushed the Iraqis under the leadership of General Schwarzkopf, he had been celebrating with the officers one night when a psychotic tank commander – who had come unhinged at the sight of several charred Iraqi bodies – tossed a grenade into the tent, killing two of his colleagues. Wainewright had escaped with metal fragments in his thigh.

The lesson wasn't lost on him. He knew that there might be some among his staff who were plotting to kill him even now. He carried his sidearm at all times. And Lincoln's opera glasses. Always the glasses.

Corporal Hammond entered. He was ashen-faced and his waistline looked tinier than usual. "General," he said, "I have something."

"Shut the door."

Hammond entered and closed the door behind him. The General pressed a button on his desk that frosted the glass.

"It's Angie Jackson, sir. She's alive."

He handed Wainewright a message he had received from Elvir Divac, along with a full-color photograph showing Dex Jackson's wife on a carpeted floor against a bare wall. Looking glumly into the camera, she held a copy of that day's Baltimore Sun with the headline PRESIDENT URGES CALM IN TV ADDRESS. A man in a mask stood behind her holding a machine gun.

"They're asking for a great deal of money," Hammond said. The Corporal took comfort in the General's unflinching expression as he absorbed the message. There was no fear in him.

"We could both use a drink," Wainewright said finally. "At ease."

Hammond sat in a plastic folding chair on the other side of the General's desk. Wainewright pulled a mostly empty bottle of Irish whiskey from his desk drawer and poured the remainder into two glasses. He picked up one of the glasses and raised a toast at the photograph of his dead son in uniform.

"Did I ever tell you how he died?" the General said.

"No sir."

"Hezbollah was firing rockets into Israel," Wainewright said. His voice was softer than Hammond had ever heard it. "We had a few clandestine units in Lebanon, though we had plausible deniability in case they were captured. My son was a Second Lieutenant.

He located the rocket launchers, called in the air strikes that saved Haifa. He was a hero."

The General paused to finish the rest of his whiskey, then resumed in the same melancholy tone. "A few hours into it, an Israeli pilot comes in, drops his bombs fifty yards out of the target zone. Takes out my kid's entire unit. And for what? Hezbollah was back within days. Hamas was back in months. Syria still wants revenge. And what do we get for our blood?" He looked at Hammond earnestly, still speaking from somewhere dark and deep within himself. "I'm asking you as a man, Corporal. What do we get for my son's death?"

Wainwright stared at him for a moment, awaiting a response. Hammond was too timid to provide one. The General sighed and picked up the photo of Angie Jackson that Elvir Divac had sent.

"Anyone else seen this?" he said in a much louder voice.

"By your directive, I share sensitive information with you and you alone, sir."

Wainwright detected a lie. "I'm glad I can trust you," he told Hammond. "There's another bottle of whiskey in that footlocker. Fetch it for us."

Obedient as ever, the Corporal scurried alongside the General's desk and bent down to open the footlocker. Wainewright kept a 14-inch long, heavy black flashlight, the type that the Military Police had used long ago, in his desk. As Hammond bent fully over, Wainewright grabbed the flashlight, turned and cracked the unsuspecting Corporal on the back of his skull as hard as he could. Hammond fell unconscious.

The General turned Hammond over with his foot, then took the pillow off his bunk and smothered him with it until he stopped breathing.

The General calmly went to the door and locked it. He returned to his desk, picked up the phone and the ransom note, and dialed Farrell.

He hung up before Farrell could answer. The news about Angie Jackson was far too sensitive, he decided. It would be better if Farrell stayed focused on his own tasks.

Instead, he dialed Chris Abrams directly. Abrams answered on the first ring. "Baltimore has turned out to be more enterprising than we imagined," the General said into the receiver. He looked down at the Corporal's body, which lay slumped on the floor. "Don't delegate this, Mister Abrams. I want you to take care of the problem personally."

Professor Hitchiti's Home
5:30 p.m. Central

Professor Hitchiti's stiff corpse sat upright in the armchair in the living room, awaiting an agency forensics team. Carver and O'Keefe wore latex gloves as they sifted through the murdered professor's files and mail. From the scant knowledge of forensics Carver had picked up over the years with CIA, he figured that the professor had been dead more than one day but no more than three. The lack of stink and the presence of maggots told him that much.

Nico sat at the kitchen table hunched over the murdered professor's computer. He quickly located, on a Ukrainian hacker's site, an old spyware program called Thor that he had once used for desktop intrusion. Thor was hardly the latest or greatest, but Nico knew it well and figured it would be adequate for resurrecting any files that the 93-year-old professor had deleted.

The screen went blank for a moment, then came back with an image of a hammer squashing a hapless rodent. "Oh the power!" Nico said, shooting his hands up into the air. "You don't even know!"

Seven seconds later, he spotted something in the professor's deleted instant message files. "The Professor sent a study pack to someone named Elvir Divac. The address is in Baltimore."

Carver went to his side. "How recent?"

"Five months ago. It's the same address used by another one of the professor's students. The Hamilton Arms in Baltimore. Apartment 309."

"Who's the other guy?"

"Ali Lahari."

Carver sat down to think, angling his chair so that it faced the door. They would need to go to Baltimore, and they would need plenty of backup. He didn't dare go to DOD, and Speers was completely AWOL. He would need Eva's help, but he still couldn't divulge details of the investigation. Not without Speers' consent.

"Nico," Carver said, "Eva just got a brand new dot mil email account for use on base. She's been using it to boss Madsen's staff around. How hard would it be to spoof it?"

"So…You're asking me to forge a military email message in Eva's name?"

Agent O'Keefe shook her head. "I don't think that's what Agent Carver meant."

"It's exactly what I meant," Carver said. "And Eva doesn't know it yet, but she's going to thank me later. So can you do it or not?"

Nico smiled. "The Chinese have a saying: If you're born with fangs, don't pretend to be a panda."

Washington D.C.
7:42 p.m. Eastern

Apartment 3C was answered by a woman with a pierced lip and a neck tattoo. Special Agent Rios figured her for a student. Even in this day and age, Washington was too conservative for someone like that to get any sort of real job. Even the President made waves when he dared to work without a suit jacket in the Oval Office.

"You must be Hector," the woman said. "Come in. I'm Jenna. Haley's sister."

Rios stooped his six-foot-ten frame low enough to squeeze under the doorway. The apartment was fully furnished, but only half as nice as he had expected for a woman of Ellis' position. He had no idea what she made over at NIC. Low six figures at least.

"I'll tell Haley you're here," the sister said. "You want something to drink?"

"No thanks."

The sister disappeared into the rear of the house. Rios stood in the living room and looked over a collection of books on a shelf. They were mostly political biographies, but there were a few mainstream romances thrown in too. And some sailing books. He and Ellis had lunched together at least fifty times over the past two years. Rios had never heard anything about sailing.

Moments later, Haley Ellis appeared in the kitchen. It was the first time Rios had seen her long raven hair out of a pony tail. He liked the way the wispy ends flared around her shoulders, framing her angular face.

She hugged him like she meant it. Why was it, Rios wondered, that athletic women with curves gave warm, lasting hugs, while skinny women acted as if they were afraid of touching anyone?

"You look awful," she told him.

"You don't," he said.

"Stop!" she said. "Thanks for coming. You want some tea?"

"I'd love some," he said, "but curfew's at eight." He tapped his watch. "Don't have much time."

"Curfew?" she said. "Don't tell me curfew applies to the Secret Service."

"Those Ulysses guys, they shoot first and run credentials later. Know what I mean? Better to play it safe."

"Hector, the reason I called…I had a disturbing incident in the NMCC. Just after the attacks. After that we were evacuated from our offices and I'm unable to get onto the network. My entire address book is on that network. I haven't been able to get hold of anyone. The Director's still not taking my calls."

"Join the club," Rios said. "It's chaos right now. Agencies are pretty much not doing anything, and that's across the board. So much for disaster preparedness."

"So, about the NMCC…The Joint Chiefs were talking about commanding from someplace called Rapture Run."

Rios looked over Ellis' shoulder. "Uh, your sister…"

"I rent the back bedroom out to her. She's back there now. I made her promise to wear her noise-cancelling headphones until after you left."

Rios smiled. "Never heard of Rapture Run. Probably just a new codename for Site R."

"That wasn't all. General Wainewright said -- I'm trying to remember the exact words – something like the 'chain of command is not intact.'"

Rios' expression did not change, but his voice shifted lower. "What else did the General say?"

"They were suppressing casualty information."

Rios considered this for a moment. "Back to the chain of command. It might not mean what you think it means. A chain of command can be considered less than intact just because communications have broken down."

She smiled at him. "You lead the President's personal detail. Don't tell me you don't know what's going on."

"Look," he said, "Truth is I didn't get back to Washington until a few hours ago. The President put me on special assignment. I'm out of the loop."

"What was the assignment?"

Rios smiled. He liked Haley. He had always liked her. He wanted to tell her – to tell someone, anyone – that he had gunned down two would-be assassins and saved Eva Hudson's life. And he wanted to tell her that he had not heard from First Team since Sunday morning, and that he had no idea what was going on, and that the President might be dead, and that it scared the hell out of him.

Instead, he would have to make small talk. "Your furniture," he said as his eyes turned to the living room. "It's…well…"

"Beneath me," Ellis said. "I know. I'm saving my money. That's why I live with my sister, in case you were wondering."

"What are you saving for?"

"Don't laugh."

"I'm going to go now."

"A boat," she said. She waited for a reaction, but Rios only listened. "I'd like to quit my job and sail around the world."

"I saw the books."

"I'm taking lessons every Saturday."

"So come with me tonight," Rios said, an invitation that surprised even him. "I live down at the marina."

"What?"

"Serious. I live on a boat. A sailboat."

"Shut up."

"A thirty-two footer. Are you in?"

"What?"

"You should come with me. What are you gonna do here? You're locked out of your office. Locked out of the network. It's not like you're going to get anything done." He checked his watch. "Those Ulysses patrols are starting in just a few minutes. So what's it gonna be? Another night at home with the sister, or a night with ex-Jacksonville Jaguar first round draft pick Hector Rios?"

He blushed, embarrassed by the fact that he had just used his status as an ex-NFL player to seduce Ellis.

It wasn't his style. But maybe it was a sign of how badly he wanted her.

She stared at him for a moment. Sizing him up. The former football player. She had never been with anyone like him. And there had never been a week like this. It was like the world was coming to an end. Or at least her world. She couldn't remember the last time she had done something just because. Just for her.

She got up from the table. She took a bottle of Sauvignon Blanc from the rack. She grabbed her keys, already imagining the rhythm of the gentle marina waves lapping up against the hull.

Baltimore

The apartment had taken on the permanent odor of mushroom soup and baked beans. They had eaten the combo for every meal, and Angie had come to dread the sound of pots and pans in the kitchen. But maybe the fact that they were feeding her meant they weren't going to kill her after all.

Elvir came to her with yet another helping. "Hungry?" he asked her.

She nodded wearily. Then she smiled – not because she liked him, but because she thought that he might be less willing to kill her if she was nice. To her surprise, he held a container of honey vanilla yogurt. "This is the good kind," he said as he opened it. "No corn syrup."

He spooned some into her mouth. She swallowed. He pushed another bite toward her, but she moved her head aside and spoke. "Just tell me one thing," she said. "You were trying to kill us. So why didn't you let me drown?"

He contemplated his words carefully before speaking. He spooned more of the yogurt into her mouth and said, "I am fully trained on the Stinger missile. Trust me, Misses Jackson. Had I wanted to kill you and your family, my aim would have been true."

PART III

"The only matter that could take Egypt to war again is water."

Assassinated Egyptian President Anwar Sadat

Baltimore Outskirts
Tuesday 4:45 a.m. Eastern

Two Maryland National Guardsmen stood next to an eight-wheeled Stryker fighting vehicle. Three hundred feet of razor wire and a few construction barricades stretched across the six-lane interstate leading into Baltimore. Less than 60 feet away, the remains of a Chevy pickup truck burned. They had blown it up an hour earlier.

Two stray dogs chewed a foot that had been blown off the driver near the debris. One of the construction signs flashed TURN BACK - CURFEW STRICTLY ENFORCED.

A set of headlights appeared in the distance. The sight of the burning truck had warded off every single approaching vehicle since they had attacked it around midnight. But this one – a black Humvee – came within fifty yards before it eventually stopped.

The two guardsmen squinted as Chris Abrams stepped out of the Hummer. His arms were raised above his head. The sun was rising in the east, but the half-light made it twice as hard to see. One of the guardsmen switched on the spotlight, and they saw Abrams' closely cropped head and his Ulysses uniform. He was clutching an ID card.

They kept their guns on Abrams even as he drew close and they could see his battle fatigues.

"La Familia?" one of the guardsmen said, meaning Ulysses.

"Yep," Abrams said. "Joint Ops called us into Baltimore. You wanna see the orders?"

He handed over his ID and manufactured travel authorization. The guardsmen passed it between them although they scarcely examined it. "Look how ripped he is," one of the guardsmen said in astonished Spanish. "Even his head is ripped!"

Unfortunately for the guardsmen, Abrams understood Spanish perfectly. His head was not in fact "ripped," at least not in the traditional sense. Facial wasting, a side effect of his particular strain of HIV, caused his body fat to be improperly distributed. Abrams was incredibly self-conscious about it, as he was often falsely accused of being on steroids. Some years ago, he'd even undergone painful collagen injections to beef up his facial features, but the improvements were only fleeting.

Abrams was not the name he had been born with, but it was the name his employer had given him. For the past few years he had inhabited Christian Merrill Abrams so completely that, for the most part, he had forgotten that he had once been known as Henry and had been a prison guard in a small Wyoming town. After racking up too much debt, he had left his family for a year to make a hundred thousand dollars working for Blackwater, the American contract militia that had become so notorious on the streets of Baghdad.

The first thing that surprised him about Iraq was the heat. Abrams had trained in Yuma, Arizona, during the month of May, which was positively hellish for a man who had been brought up in Wyoming. But the training did little to prepare him for the 130-degree heat that hit him like a hydrogen blast upon arriving in Baghdad.

More surprising was that his crew was under fire nearly every day. It didn't help that they were assigned to protect an Iraqi interpreter who had been discovered cooperating with the Americans. The interpreter lasted about three weeks. He was killed by an RPG when Abrams was off duty. Abrams was called to an unrefrigerated morgue to identify the man's face and one of his colleagues. After that, he volunteered for units that took "proactive" assignments to ensure a target's safety.

Sixteen kills and twelve months later, Abrams returned to find that his wife and young son had suddenly relocated and did not want to be found. Abrams' wife had left a terse note explaining that she had transferred everything he had earned from the joint bank account, but that she had carefully signed over the house and both cars to him and left the papers in a folder on top of the refrigerator. Abrams searched for his family for three weeks, interrogating friends and relatives, sometimes at gunpoint. During one such episode, in which he tied up one of his wife's cousins in her mobile home, he had actually shot a Golden Retriever.

He served a four-month prison sentence for gross animal cruelty in Wyoming. It was there in the state pen that Abrams reckoned that he contracted HIV from another inmate, although he did not show symptoms for at least another year.

During his incarceration, government contracts were there for the taking and need for experienced soldiers was dire. Some of the major American security firms had taken to trolling the prison system for able-bodied former military with combat training and imminent release dates. A rap sheet with murder, grand larceny and anything sexually related automatically disqualified a candidate. But fortunately for Chris Abrams, Ulysses was able to look past animal cruelty. His prior combat experience and lack of family ties made him an ideal candidate.

He was offered jobs of varying levels by three firms in the weeks before his release. Having read about Ulysses' rapid rise in a Web news article, Abrams held out for a hefty salary and a big signing bonus. Not because he would have refused a lower offer, but because he enjoyed the negotiation. The truth was that he wanted nothing more than to get back into the action. He would have done it for free.

By the time that his HIV was discovered by the Ulysses medical staff, his reputation as a strategist who could also personally execute complex assassinations was considered essential. He was guaranteed the best possible medical care and a promise not to share his secret with anyone.

Now Abrams eyed the charred truck. "What happened to those guys?" he asked the guardsmen. "They get a little too close for comfort?"

The taller of the two handed Abrams his Ulysses ID. "No habla ingles."

Abrams laughed, stunned at the idea that the National Guard was employing active duty soldiers that didn't speak any English at all. He switched to Spanish. "You've gotta be shitting me," he said in a Juarez, Mexico dialect. "I knew recruiting was down, but this..." He felt the men tense up. "I mean, holy shit, right?"

The guardsmen didn't find this funny. They had been picked up by the border patrol in June and given a choice between being deported to Mexico or cutting an amnesty deal that would include six years of National Guard service. At the end of their service, they were to receive green cards. Neither men had thought twice about the decision, even though they realized they could be deployed to a combat zone.

Yesterday they had been quickly – and quite prematurely – declared fit for duty after only four weeks of basic training. Last night they had received a crash course in checkpoint security procedures by two retired Iraqi War vets. With no relief scheduled, the soldiers took turns sleeping in the Stryker. For food, they had raided the walnut grove on the other side of the interstate. Around midnight, a pickup truck had approached with no sign of slowing down. On the vets' advice, they had fired on it. The truck's driver and three passengers were killed instantly.

"Okay then," Abrams told them, "I'll just wave my guys through, then we'll be on our way. Okay?"

The guardsmen nodded and lowered their weapons. Abrams waved the Hummer through and put some distance between himself and the guardsmen. The Hummer rolled forward, its windows tinted as dark as a limousine's. As they drew close, the Hummer's passenger-side windows rolled down, revealing the barrels of M4 carbines that opened up with deafening thunder and twittering flashes of light.

The guardsmen were cut down before they could even get a shot off. Abrams opened the rear driver's side door and high-fived his USOC crew. "Freaking National Guard doesn't even speak English," Abrams said to his colleagues in the SUV. "You believe that?"

Abrams heard a ruckus coming from the Stryker, which was parked some 20 feet away. The Stryker's engine groaned to life and someone inside threw it hastily into gear. Abrams braced himself for the wrath of its 105mm machine gun, but the vehicle did not fire. It merely began moving away.

Abrams pulled a Javelin anti-tank weapon from the Humvee and knelt down on the asphalt. It took him less than two seconds to take aim and launch the missile. A millisecond later the Javelin slammed into the Stryker, transforming it into a hunk of flaming scrap metal.

The third Guardsman scrambled from the burning mess, his uniform aflame. He ran at full speed toward the walnut grove. Abrams marveled for a moment at the sight of the Guardsman, who looked like a streaking two-legged asteroid. He watched for a moment longer before pulling his sidearm and placing a single shot through the man's spine. "Damn!" somebody shouted. Indeed. At more than fifty yards, with a pistol, it was a hell of a shot.

Abrams spat, clicked his weapon on safety, piled back into the Humvee and raided the cooler for something to eat. He needed to pack in a couple thousand calories between now and their arrival in the city. He chugged the first of several protein shakes as they rolled past the lit sign that read WELCOME TO BALTIMORE.

Fort Campbell
5:05 a.m.

Eva's Under-Secretary was in hysterics. "Are you seeing this?" the squeaky voice on the phone said. "Greenbacks are down by double digits against the Euro, the Yen, the Yuan, the Pound, even the Canadian dollar. We're down a full ten percent against the Canadians."

"Finally," Eva said as she walked toward Colonel Madsen's office. "At long last, America's seniors can stop crossing the border to buy cheap prescriptions."

The Under-Secretary didn't appreciate Eva's gallows humor. "With all due respect Madam Secretary, we've can't absorb further currency erosion. This is a major emergency."

Eva stopped just outside Madsen's office. She was on her last nerve, but she had to remind herself that the situation looked far different here at Fort Campbell than it did in a living room in Northern Virginia. It was time to delegate some busy work. "Great idea," Eva said. "You've got my support to get the team together. I expect a full proposal by this time tomorrow."

"Really?" the Under-Secretary chirped. "I'm on it! Thank you so much!"

With her staff temporarily appeased, Eva hung up, peered into the Garrison Commander's office and found Madsen just getting off the phone himself. He looked up at Eva with bloodshot eyes. "The two Special

Ops units you authorized are with Carver and O'Keefe in Baltimore," he said.

Eva looked like she'd been broadsided. And she had been.

"Special Ops," Madsen iterated. "I said those units you authorized are with Carver and O'Keefe now. In Baltimore."

Eva realized she was living on a couple of power naps and a dozen energy drinks, but she was quite sure she hadn't ordered any supporting units to Baltimore.

"Something wrong?" Madsen said. He handed her a printout of the email from EHudson@fortcampbell.mil ordering two units of Green Berets to Baltimore. "You wrote this, right?"

But of course she had not. Still, she considered her options. Admitting that Agent Carver had pulled an end run would undermine the Colonel's confidence in her authority. She decided to avoid the question and take the matter up with Carver upon his return. "Is there anything else, Colonel?"

"Uh, yeah. Are you ready for this one? Intel ID'd the guys that went after you up in Martha's Vineyard. Their names showed up in the database."

"Which database?"

"DOD's. Both were retired Marines."

She remembered seeing the men's bodies on the Edgartown Street moments after Agent Rios had gunned them down. She envisioned the tide of fluids running down the sidewalk and the thickets of brown hair atop their heads. But she had not looked at their faces. Despite Carver's assertions that this was not the work of Allied Jihad, she had subconsciously assumed the assassins were foreign. Russians, maybe, or North Africans or extremist Saudis. Those nationalities fit the stereotypes. Those ideas were somehow palatable. Now she was faced with the possibility that her own countrymen – soldiers, no less – wanted her dead.

"Not active duty?" Eva said.

"No."

"I need to see their files for myself."

"For some reason, the files are sealed. The Joint Chiefs could authorize a look. Barring that, you'd have to call the President and get an executive order."

An executive order. That would be nice. That would be everything.

Eva thanked the Colonel, walked back to her office and dialed Agent Carver. As the phone rang, she opened the drawer and took out the bottle of Ativan. She removed one pill and broke it in half. Just to take the edge off.

Baltimore
5:15 a.m.

Carver, O'Keefe and the twelve Special Ops soldiers of Viper Squad gathered next to a pair of grey Humvees on the city's western edge. In what was easily the most dilapidated slum Carver had ever seen, it was still dark enough that the strike force blended into the shadows. Except for a few lunatics jawing on the other side of the street, the streets had been emptied by Ulysses patrols sent in to enforce martial law.

Master Sergeant Hundley, a square-jawed soldier who resembled a walking side of beef, handed out battle gear. Green Berets had the best of the best – state-of-the-art body armor, night-vision goggles, hands-free radios and a new prototype assault rifle that carried forty-round clips and weighed less than five pounds.

This wasn't Carver's first mission with Hundley. While in CIA counter-terrorism, Carver had led a joint op with Hundley's recon unit in the mountainous border between Pakistan and Afghanistan. Hundley had seemed far too fearless for his own good, and Carver was somewhat surprised to find that the Sergeant was not only still alive, but also that he still had the arms and legs he had been born with. All but one of the Green Berets in Hundley's unit were combat veterans; three had prosthetics, including a Staff Sergeant with artificial legs that were every bit as nimble as the real thing.

"Saddle up," Carver called out. The men and women of Viper Squad slid into either side of the unit's Humvees. Nico was cuffed into the second vehicle – not because they needed him for this leg of the operation, but because there was nobody else to babysit him.

Carver's phone buzzed. He answered without thinking and found himself on the line with Eva Hudson. She sounded pissed.

"I give you credit for ingenuity," Eva started, "but unless you clue me into what's going on right now, I'll have Colonel Madsen order the Green Berets to take you and O'Keefe into custody."

He considered faking a bad connection. He couldn't risk having her stop the operation now. They were too close.

"If you hang up, the next person I dial is Sergeant Hundley."

Carver was cornered. He checked his watch. It had now been nearly forty-four hours since he'd heard from Speers. That was far too long. He was likely dead. It was either clue Eva in and accept her authority, or risk the operation.

Carver spotted a pay telephone across the street. "I'm calling you on a land line," he announced. The public phone wasn't exactly secure, but it was probably safer than his lightly encrypted cell phone. He went to it and called Eva. He gave her the sixty-second version of how the President himself – through Speers – had ordered him to investigate Ulysses.

"And there's something else," Carver added. "Someone from the Bureau called O'Keefe and asked us to back off of the investigation of the Monroe bomber, Faruq Ahmed."

"That shouldn't surprise you. Typical FBI territorialism."

"But it wasn't. I made a few calls. Right after the attacks, Ulysses evacuated the West Virginia field office. The person who supposedly called me hasn't had basic phone service since the attacks. He hasn't even been able to log into the network since yesterday morning."

"You're swimming in deep waters," Eva said.

"All I know is that I need to get to Elvir Divac before they do."

"I'll give your operation my blessing, but I've got a mission of my own. I'm prepared to offer Nico Gold a pardon when this is all over if he solves one riddle."

"But we're about to mobilize," Carver protested.

"Then mobilize. Have someone get him in front of a computer. Then have him call me. The future depends on it."

Carver hung up, checked his watch, and turned to O'Keefe. "Eva wants to use boy wonder to check something out. It can't wait."

"Guess I'm with baby," O'Keefe said cheerfully.

"Don't sound so disappointed."

"I'm a thinker," O'Keefe said, "Not a fighter."

Rapture Run

The enlisted barracks was a cool, wet limestone cavern some 200 feet below ground and 50 yards southwest of the bunker's subterranean command center. It was linked to the main complex by a stone floor hallway with real stalactites hanging from the ceiling. The Army Corp of Engineers had not yet wired the barracks for electricity, so battery-operated LED lanterns were spaced every twenty yards along the treacherous walkway. In the barracks themselves, two hundred bunk beds were arranged in clusters of eight. Buckets collecting dripping groundwater sat everywhere.

Julian Speers slept on a bottom bunk in the middle of the cavern. Something woke him and he shot up, smashing his head against the metal bed frame. A large hand covered his mouth as he cried out. "Shhh," a Ulysses soldier whispered. "My turn to sleep." Speers focused, recognizing the soldier as his designated bunk buddy. Rapture Run was overcapacity, and the White House Chief of Staff had been asked to share a bunk with the rank and file.

Speers slowly pulled himself upright. The exhausted soldier wasted no time in sliding under the still-warm wool blankets. Speers rubbed the growing knot on his head and stood in the middle of the barracks, getting his bearings.

He had been dreaming about Eva Hudson. She was the rightful next in line, and the way the Joint Chiefs were operating, she'd never find out. He had to contact her. How he would do this was another matter. Not only had Corporal Hammond confiscated his work phone, but he had also been denied use of the facility phones.

After a few minutes of searching, he eventually found Hammond's empty bunk. With bed space at such a premium, Speers found it odd that Hammond wouldn't have given someone else a chance at his shift. Speers ambled down the slippery lamp-lit limestone corridor until he came to the Command Room. It was still fully-staffed, even at this early hour. The officer on watch was the junior officer, a Second Lieutenant, in Major Dobb's CENTAF unit. He busied himself by reviewing a list of DEFCON 2 communication protocols.

"Excuse me," Speers said. "I'm looking for Corporal Hammond."

"Check his bunk," the Lieutenant said.

"Hasn't been slept in. Last time I saw him, he was on his way to see General Wainewright. But that was hours ago."

The officer didn't look up.

"Mind if I check the exit logs?" Speers pressed.

"Don't bother. Nobody's left the facility."

"Sure about that?"

"Nobody gets out without a signed authorization from General Wainewright. And nobody's presented one on my watch."

Speers grabbed the file folder and flipped through them. Among the pile, he found a series of blank authorization forms signed by the General himself. Speers waited until the duty officer was distracted. As he turned to answer a question from a fellow officer, Speers slipped one of the pre-signed forms into his jacket pocket in case he needed it later. Even if he could locate his phone, he'd need to get out of the bunker somehow to get a signal.

Somewhere across the command room, two men were arguing. Speers couldn't see them, but it sounded intense. "Gotta call my family," someone was shouting. "Gotta call my family. Gotta call my goddamn family."

As if tossed by a giant, a metal file cabinet came crashing across the command room. Then an officer in a short-sleeve khaki uniform flew into the air. Speers saw him smash spine-first into a large monitor. He collapsed to the ground like a sack of oranges. Blood pooled around his head.

Speers ran to an aisle and, looking down the row of workstations, saw an enraged, acne-scarred Ulysses soldier whose biceps were so massive that Speers wondered how the man could wipe his own ass. "I got a family, man! Gotta call 'em! Gotta call 'em!"

It had been only a matter of time before someone snapped. The crew at Rapture Run was hundreds of feet beneath ground level, in a facility that only a small handful of outsiders knew about. They bore the burden of being the only people on the planet that knew that the POTUS was dead. They alone watched Iranian tanks as they moved unchecked toward Israel.

An MP appeared in the doorway behind the crazed soldier. He leveled his rifle and filled the soldier's chest with a quick burst of lead. The shots echoed throughout the cavernous former nuclear missile silo, bringing all activity to a stop.

General Farrell burst into the room and walked toward the scene. All eyes were on him. There was absolutely no sound, and when the General stepped in a puddle of urine – it was pooling from the pant leg of a communications officer – everyone stopped breathing. Farrell looked at his shoes once, but did not single out the offender. He calmly proceeded toward the gory scene and said, in a measured voice, "Good enforcement, soldier. Now let's clean it up."

Everyone returned to their stations. A sense of normalcy – or at least Rapture Run's extreme version of it – slowly resumed.

Speers wasn't cut out for the kinds of things he'd seen in the past forty-eight hours, starting with Lieutenant Flynn's interrogation in Georgetown, the car bomb in Monroe, and now this. He stumbled back down the long corridor to the enlisted barracks cavern. His senses felt muted. A growing numbness came over him. He wondered if this was what post-traumatic stress disorder felt like.

Secluded as the barracks were, Speers was astounded that neither the shots nor the shouting had awakened anyone there. Even so, he walked among the soldiers as if they were a den of sleeping rattlesnakes. He returned to Corporal Hammond's bunk, knelt before it and slid his hands beneath the bed frame. There he found the briefcase full of confiscated cell phones. Speers opened it and located his phone among all the others. He realized he had no charger with him, so he quickly found two other phones of the same model and pulled the batteries from each.

As Speers closed the case, he heard footsteps behind him. He closed his eyes. He remained on his knees. His time was up.

"Won't get a signal," a whispered voice said. "Not down here."

He turned and saw Major Dobbs, the CENTAF air traffic czar who had tipped him off about the President's demise. But Dobbs didn't look so friendly now. Although Speers had never been in a fight in his life, he often sized up other men by asking himself if he could take them down. Dobbs was a burly man who looked like he could manhandle just about anyone.

"Please, Major," Speers whined softly. "This is more than just a phone. I have classified documents in here. For God's sake, I work for the President."

Dobbs leaned closer. "*Worked,*" he said. "You *worked* for the POTUS. He's gone. He can't help you now." Dobbs exhaled a stinky breeze into Speers' face. Speers tried not to throw up. "I'm the next officer on watch," Dobbs said before turning away. "Come see me at oh-five-thirty."

General Farrell stood watching as the MP pulled the slain family man's body into a black body bag. Wainewright came up behind him, whistling so as not to spook either. He had seen the entire incident via camera from his quarters. He wasn't concerned. It was to be expected.

"Report." Wainewright's request didn't have anything to do with the dead man. He didn't give a shit about the dead man. Wainewright was good about keeping his mind on his priorities. Farrell understood this.

"Abrams' crew is rolling into Baltimore now," Farrell replied as they walked through the command room. "They should have it pretty much done within an hour."

"Good. And the withdrawals?"

They went into the adjoining conference room and shut the door behind them.

"Thirty C-130 transports landed in Kuwait City this morning," Farrell said. "Ten more have already left Baghdad. Two strike units left Lebanon this morning. The secret bases in Israel bugged out this morning. The heavy armor—"

"There's no time to pull out the armor. Destroy it and leave it in the sand. Syria opened up the border to Iranian armor divisions. There's no turning back."

Farrell lit a cigarette. "I'd feel better if we had some progress on the Allied Jihad situation."

Wainewright pulled the cigarette from Farrell's mouth and stamped it out. "Fact: elite Revolutionary Guard units are moving into Afpak right now. The Iranian Ambassador knows that if they don't produce results within a week, the deal is off. We'll have no choice but to send the Carrier Strike Group in to cut off the campaign in Israel."

"How do we know the Iranians won't seize the opportunity to invade Pakistan altogether?"

"We should be so lucky. Their economy can't handle fighting a two-front war. As long as they keep the Allied Jihad busy for awhile, and give us the desalination technology, I'll keep our end of the bargain."

"You sure about that?"

"Trust me. We're going to need the water."

*

Speers' stomach was a queasy ball of nerves as he entered the command room at oh-five-thirty on the dot, just as Major Dobbs had suggested. He clinched his last lollipop between his teeth. He had been rationing them.

Dobbs sat on the throne-like chair in the command room. Beside him, his deputy – a young Lieutenant who looked like he had been shaving for a year at most – talked through a list of bunker procedures. When Speers came into view, Dobbs turned to the Lieutenant and interrupted his monologue: "Take my shift, Lieutenant. Wainewright's sending us offsite."

The young Lieutenant looked puzzled. "Right now, sir? I wasn't aware of a change in schedule."

"We're at DEFCON two," Dobbs reminded him. "Information's on a need-to-know basis. Get used to it."

Dobbs led Speers toward the entrance. "Just go along with whatever I say," Dobbs whispered. "You'll live longer."

They came to the cornfield entrance elevators. Two MPs stood before them with rifles held diagonally across their chests. Speers immediately recognized one as the MP who had gunned down the family man. "Authorization?" the MP asked, without even the pretense of respect.

"See these?" Dobbs said, pointing to the brass clusters on his lapels indicating his rank. "And these?" He pointed to a brass globe on his shirt pocket, adorned with an early model jet aircraft and Olympic-style laurels, signifying him as the CENTAF commander. "These are all the authorization I need."

The MP smirked with an arrogance that surprised even Speers. "There are at least fifty officers down here with higher rank. And all of you still need a little yellow piece of paper with General Wainewright's signature on it."

Dobbs stepped into the MPs face, spitting as he spoke. "Choose your words carefully, Corporal, or I'll have you court-martialed for insubordination to an officer."

"Ulysses has deemed this a combat situation," the other MP said as he launched into a well-rehearsed response: "During combat situations Ulysses troops are not subject to U.S. military law except those laws that are specifically expressed by the Joint Chiefs or the President. By order of General Wainewright, we are also authorized to enforce martial law upon pain of death, regardless of U.S. military rank."

Dobbs stayed in the MP's face, muttering obscenities in a low growl that struck Speers as particularly vile and abusive, even for the military. As Dobbs distracted the MP with his verbal assault, he slowly reached for his sidearm.

Speers cut in before it could devolve into more senseless violence: "I think I have what you need." He produced the yellow signed authorization he had lifted from the officer on watch's folder hours earlier. He had simply time-stamped it and filled in CLASSIFIED as the reason. Dobbs' eyes were big, and his fingers still fondled the pistol-grip of his still-holstered .45. Speers sucked hard on his lollipop as the MP scrutinized the form.

"Have you arranged transport?" the MP said.

"It's already on the pad," Dobbs snapped.

At that, the MP switched on his radio and spoke into it: "This is two sixty. Can you confirm transport on the cornfield helipad?"

"Affirmative," the radio voice chirped back. "The helipad is occupied."

The MPs grudgingly moved aside so that Dobbs and Speers could enter the elevator. They did not look back as the doors closed behind them. Speers spotted the elevator's surveillance camera and was careful not to smile or speak. He felt his ears pop as the elevator muscled its way up several hundred feet to the surface. When the doors finally swooshed open, Speers took in the smell of cornfields and felt dizzy with the rush of fresh air. Dobbs grabbed him by the arm and led him toward the clearing, where there was indeed already a helicopter on the pad, its rotors spinning against the yellowing eastern sky.

The pilot wore a bandana around his neck and, although it was only sunrise, sunglasses as well. He grinned and stretched out his hand. "Morning Major," he said. "General coming with?"

"Negative," Dobbs replied, "and you'll be less familiar with me from now on."

"Sir, yes sir."

He shoved Speers into the passenger seat while he sat behind directly behind the pilot. "Take us due east at eighty miles per hour," Dobbs said.

"Sir yes sir. Destination?"

"More as you need it, Lieutenant."

"Sir yes sir."

The chopper pulled up and away from Rapture Run. Speers kept his eyes on the golden cornstalks and the tiny bunker entrance until they were high enough that he could no longer see it. Convinced that they had completed their escape, he breathed a little easier.

Dobbs apparently did not share his relief. "Get to four thousand feet," he told the pilot. "And quickly."

"Sir yes sir."

Baltimore
5:39 a.m.

Dawn broke over the city's buildings, flickering out street lamps. Faces peered out from tenement windows as the two battleship grey U.S. Army Humvees rolled through the desolate city streets. Martial law, which imposed a curfew until six a.m., had, if nothing else, eliminated traffic. Four Ulysses units patrolling in Bradley Fighting Vehicles had made sure of that.

Viper Squad was split into two six-man units. Carver rode in the lead vehicle, his typically smooth face darkened by more than two days without shaving. "We'll stage two blocks east of the target," he said into the radio. "Copy that," Sergeant Hundley reported from the second Humvee.

They passed a young Asian couple that had been shot dead on the sidewalk. They had no doubt been caught out after curfew. "Ulysses got some last night," Private Scott, Carver's driver, said. He slowed the vehicle down and gawked at Ulysses' bloody handiwork. "Heartless, man. Just heartless."

"Maintain speed," Carver told him. "Focus on the mission."

They rounded a corner and came upon a mob scene. Looters were carrying TVs out of the shattered front window of a large electronics store. Carver counted at least twenty men and women helping themselves to the latest in home theater equipment.

"Keep driving," Carver insisted.

But Private Scott braked. "All due respect," he said, "We're under martial law. We should get busy on these assholes."

"Nobody shoots," Carver said into his radio. He turned to the private. "Now get this convoy moving before somebody does something dumb."

Two shots rang out from the second Hummer. Carver flinched and crouched out of instinct. Then he recognized the sound of the M4. Damn. It was one of theirs.

He unfurled and peered out the window. One of the looters was down on the pavement, clutching his leg. Blood pooled all around him.

The other looters dropped their wares and fled on foot up the street. Carver reached into his holster and took out his SIG. He levered a round into the chamber and got out and walked to the second Hummer. Twenty yards behind him, the wounded man screamed in agony. Blood streaked the sidewalk as he pulled himself with his hands up the fractured concrete sidewalk.

Carver kept his attention on the Green Berets inside the vehicle. Viper Squad was a frightfully unified fighting machine. Each assumed an identical posture – assault rifles across their laps at matching angles, eyes locked on Carver, mouths stretched tight and expressionless. Only the plume of bluish rifle smoke lingering alongside the rear driver's side of the vehicle gave the shooter away.

Sergeant Hundley sat at the rear driver's side window. Carver leveled his gaze at him. "Sergeant Hundley?" he said. Hundley did not respond. For

Carver, that was as good as a confession. "Step out," Carver said as the wounded man's screaming echoed throughout the near desolate street. Hundley unfolded himself from the cramped Hummer. Carver snatched the soldier's M4 and slung it over his shoulder. He pushed his SIG underneath the Sergeant's chin, stripped his grenade belt away with a quick jerk, and then stepped back to a safe distance. "Empty your clip," he said. He pointed to the sidearm that Hundley kept in the pocket of his cargo pants.

Hundley obeyed without question. He had seen Agent Carver at work with enemy prisoners in Afghanistan. He had learned then that the ex-CIA agent had a highly quantitative mind that, in fractions of a second, weighed the eventualities of any action and followed the path with the most upside. He would not hesitate to kill one person if he could save two.

"You gonna shoot me?" Hundley asked.

The looters had gathered about a hundred yards up the street, and the size of the mob had grown. The early morning shadows were still dark enough for Carver's eyes to play tricks on him, but he thought he saw weapons in their hands – guns, bats, tire irons, bottles.

"You disobeyed a direct order," Carver said.

"Yessir," Hundley replied. "I don't like thieves."

"I like riots even less. The way I figure this, I can either demonstrate that your actions are not condoned by the United States government, or a lot more people end up dead."

The mob kept their distance, but they began screaming out for vengeance. It was the first time Carver had ever seen the Sergeant scared. "Sir? What are you going to do?"

"You once told me you ran a 4.4 fifty yard dash," Carver said. "For your sake, I hope you were telling the truth."

He left the Sergeant unarmed on the sidewalk and climbed back into the lead Hummer. Private Scott reluctantly stepped on the gas.

Over West Virginia
5:55 a.m.

The Blackhawk chopper Major Dobbs had appropriated at Rapture Run enjoyed clear morning skies as it clipped along at 2200 feet. With all commercial air travel grounded, they had the skies to themselves. But Dobbs wasn't aboard to enjoy the view. From his seat behind the pilot, Dobbs eyed the instrument panel and saw that the directional was pointing northeast.

Speers' knuckles were bone white as he gripped an exposed piece of the chopper's frame. The Chief of Staff's only other helicopter flights had been with President Hatch aboard Marine One. It was like going from a luxury cruise ship to a jet ski.

"Mister Speers," Major Dobbs said suddenly, "I'm about to give the pilot the details of our itinerary. Please pay close attention."

Speers looked to Dobbs just in time to see him leveling his .45 automatic at the base of the pilot's neck.

Speers shouted "No!" at the exact instant that Dobbs pulled the trigger. The bullet entered the pilot's cerebellum and exited his left eye socket and ricocheted off the chopper's steel framing. Multi-colored giblets of brain, bone and blood splattered across the front glass.

The old Julian Speers would have hyperventilated or thrown up. Now, after all he had seen in the past two days, his primary instinct was merely to stay alive. He immediately overcame the shock of the Lieutenant's sudden execution as the pilotless chopper began to pitch slightly. He looked around the cabin in hopes of spotting a parachute.

Dobbs, however, had no plans to bail out. He had started his career thirty years earlier as a helicopter pilot, had flown combat missions in a Huey attack chopper during the invasion of Grenada, and despite moving into an administrative role in CENTAF's air traffic command, he had still managed to log a few dozen flying hours each year. Now he learned forward from the back seat and took the chopper's control stick in one hand. Then he half-climbed onto the dead pilot's lap, unfastened the corpse's safety harness and pushed the body against the door. The pilot's dead weight carried itself out. Dobbs resisted the urge to watch the body fall to earth.

He could hardly see out the windscreen. "Gimmie your tie," Dobbs said. Speers untied his half-Windsor and handed it to the Major, who used it to wipe the pilot's spatter from the glass.

"Okay there, Chief?" Dobbs said.

Speers found his voice. "I'd like to know why you're helping me."

"Rapture Run was starting to feel a lot like Jonestown," Dobbs replied. "And if there's two things I can't stomach, it's murdered congressmen and poisoned Kool-Aid." Speers couldn't argue with that. "Our pilot was circling back to Rapture Run," Dobbs went on. "We're officially AWOL during martial law, and that makes us targets, Chief. I am prepared to kill any treasonous, Ulysses-loving SOBs that get in our way."

The Major pushed the stick forward. The chopper descended toward the tree line. Speers drummed his fingers nervously on his legs.

"Now then," Dobbs said. "We've gone to a lot of trouble so that you could make a phone call. I think it's time you make it."

Speers pulled the phone out of his pocket, powered it up and found Eva Hudson's mobile number in his contact list.

Fort Campbell

The Federal Reserve Chairman's head looked enormous on Eva's monitor. His 72-year-old chrome dome twittered ever so slightly as he jawed at length about the financial implications of the crisis. "I hope you can convince the President to act on this pronto," the Chairman yelped over video chat. "His predecessor was granted certain emergency powers that he shouldn't be shy about using."

She didn't have the stomach to tell the Chairman that she hadn't spoken to the President since the church bombing in Monroe, and that she didn't know a soul who had. "I'll do my best, Mister Chairman."

Colonel Madsen abruptly opened Eva's office door. "Chief of Staff Julian Speers is on line one."

Eva didn't have to be told twice. "Mister Chairman, I apologize. Call you back." She cut the video feed and picked up the phone. "Julian?"

"Eva, it's good to hear your voice."

It was good to hear Julian's voice too. But there was only one thing on Eva's mind. "Is the President with you?" she said. "He hasn't returned my calls." Eva heard a familiar whirring in the background. "Chief? I hear rotors. Are you on Marine One?"

"Eva," Speers began with a foreboding tone. "This isn't easy for me to say…" Speers choked up, unable to speak.

So it was true. Eva had suspected as much from the moment she saw the emergency tape. She felt the tears coming, but she couldn't let herself go there. She resolved to hold herself together. There was no time for grieving. Not now. There was a leadership vacuum. She had to find out the details and act on them. "How did it happen?" Eva said.

Speers relayed the story that Major Dobbs had told him, and then offered his speculation that Marine One's flight plan randomizer had been rigged ahead of time. It was the only theory that made sense. The signal dropped before Eva could respond.

She took out the bottle of Ativan. She took the other half of the pill she had ingested earlier and calmly swallowed it.

Eva sat for a moment, absorbing what she had heard. Not a surprise. But a blow nevertheless. The biggest blow.

She looked at the Ativan bottle. Taking it had been a mistake, she decided. She needed a clear head. The fog might numb the pain a little, but it wouldn't fix anything.

Eva pulled the wastebasket close to her, leaned over it, and stuck her right index finger down her throat. Her gag reflex kicked in immediately. The anti-anxiety pill and what remained of last night's dinner came out with force, filling the bottom two inches of the trash can.

She sat up, reached calmly for a Kleenex and wiped the corners of her mouth. Then she dropped the rest of the pills in the garbage. There would be no more crutches today.

Baltimore

Four short minutes after Carver had left the unarmed Sergeant Hundley as a sacrifice to the city's vengeful looters, the Viper Squad convoy pulled within two blocks of the Hamilton Arms. A figure in jogging shorts and a blue hoodie emerged from a parked car and approached the lead Humvee. Carver rolled down his window.

"Nobody's been in or out since three a.m.," the man said. He was CIA case officer Celon Wise. Carver had only last night picked Wise out of a CIA directory in hopes of finding someone local to stake out the Hamilton Arms. To Carver's surprise, Wise was better than just local. He had a high school acquaintance that was a super in the building next door, so he had been able to set up an observation post without any problems.

Wise pulled the hood back, revealing the speckled charcoal complexion and left-veering nose that Carver recognized from his agency profile photo. "Tin foil's on the back windows," he went on. "I counted four people in the thermal goggles."

"Any weapons?"

"The three men have assault rifles. But they've got a lady in there with 'em. Pretty sure she's not there by choice."

Carver switched on his radio. "All units, we have a possible hostage situation. Use discretion."

Sergeant Hundley's second-in-command responded from the second Hummer. "Interrogative, Agent Carver: what is the definition of discretion?"

"It means don't shoot an unarmed woman," Carver said. "And be careful with other residents that might be coming out of the building. Thanks to Sergeant Hundley, we missed our strike window. Curfew just ended."

Celon Wise donned his hood and got back into his car. Viper Squad scrambled from the Humvees and proceeded toward the building. "Unit one, cover the building's rear entrance. Unit two secures the lobby. Nobody gets in or out. Unit three's with me."

Carver led his troops into a lobby that had last been redecorated in the 1980s. A few elderly residents sat reading in pleather chairs. Others were playing poker around a glass coffee table. Their eyes got big when Carver entered with his armed-to-the-teeth Special Forces unit. Two Green Berets split off immediately, securing the lobby at both ends.

"Hey fella," an old man said. His dyed black hair was swept back tightly against his head. Carver could smell the shoe polish from several feet away. "You're here for those jerks in 309, yeah? I called the cops days ago."

Carver went to the table. "What's going on in 309?"

"Rough lookin' C-U-Next-Tuesdays. Last week they were carrying these long gym bags, like they was going to play lacrosse or something. But I saw the outline of a gun stock pressed up against the fabric of the bag. They was carrying rifles, all right. And I know there ain't no hunting season in August."

"We'll check it out." Carver addressed all the residents. "Ladies and gentlemen, I'm sorry about this, but you need to get some fresh air right now."

"Like hell," the old man said. "Ulysses shot up a handful last night. Saw it on the Internet."

"Curfew's over," Carver said. "And trust me on this – you'll be much safer outside than in here."

The residents got up – some of them with great difficulty – and made their way to the front doors. Carver took two Green Berets with him up the stairwell and left four to cover the lobby.

*

Chris Abrams pulled his unmarked Humvee alongside the other two sitting down the street from the Hamilton Arms. The four men in Abrams' crew were eager to get out. Two stood on lookout as the others began inspecting the other vehicles. "They're from Fort Campbell," one of them said. "You figure they're here on patrol?"

"Not a chance," Abrams said. "These things didn't drive themselves all the way from Kentucky. And the Army wouldn't just airdrop any unit's vehicles into Baltimore."

The four men in Abrams' crew had already added it up in their heads. "Twelve Green Berets," one of them calculated, "versus five of us."

"Like those odds," Abrams said as he opened a protein drink. After shooting down Marine One and personally assassinating the leader of the free world, Abrams equated himself with Iron Man and the rest of his crew as slightly lesser, but still lethal, superheroes. So far, their engagements on U.S. soil had been vastly easier than anything they had been asked to do in North Africa or Iraq. They were careful to always maintain the element of surprise. The constant intermingling of corporate defense contractors such as Ulysses and the traditional armed forces had nearly wiped out any suspicions that might have existed previously.

He parked the Hummer right behind the others, so that the vehicles looked to be part of the same convoy. The crew readied their weapons and approached the building on foot. Now it was time to divulge the details of the mission to his crew.

Abrams pulled three photographs of Angie Jackson from his pocket and handed them to the men.

"She goes by Angie," Abrams explained. "Make sure she's dead. We'll take the body with us."

"What if she's in pieces?"

"We'll vacuum her up if we have to. Don't leave a single scrap of DNA."

*

In Apartment 309, Angie Jackson sat in the living room propped up against two floor pillows. Her ankles and wrists were duct-taped together and the television had been her only companion for hours. The pundits on TV, a pair of retired Generals who had once served under General Wainewright, paraded on-and off-screen like a couple of buffoons trained to recite from the same script. *"The foreign press wants you to believe these strikes in Yemen are somehow reckless or without justification. But let's recap what we know about Yemen. First off, it's long been a harbor for terrorists. Second, the government has been openly sympathetic to extremism."*

Elvir entered the room looking like he had just woken from a too-short nap. He had large puffy circles under his eyes. An M4 was strapped around his shoulder.

"I gotta pee," Angie told him.

"When don't you have to pee?"

He sighed and helped her to her feet.

"I can't feel my fingers and toes," she complained.

He used a kitchen knife to cut the duct tape around her wrists and ankles and walked behind her to the bathroom. They passed the apartment's lone bedroom, where two men slept on a floor mattress snuggling machine guns like teddy bears.

Angie went into the sparse, windowless bathroom and shut the door behind her. She stooped to look under the door to see if Elvir was waiting outside. As evidenced by his boots, he was. She turned the sink faucet on full and opened the medicine cabinet as quietly as she could. She wasn't sure what she hoped to find – something sharp, maybe– but the cabinet was empty. Deflated, she sat on the commode and peed and, when she realized that she had to do much more than just urinate, noticed that the toilet paper roll was gone. In its place, a magazine with several pages ripped out rested sadly on the vanity. She dreaded the feel of the glossy pages against her bottom.

She mindlessly tapped her feet, a habit she had picked up as a child when her mother taught her how to make sure her feet didn't fall asleep on the toilet. Then she felt it – something cool and round grazing the ball of her foot.

*

In apartment 209, the unit directly below 309 where Elvir Divac held Angie Jackson, Agent Carver stood on a living room table. He used a whisper-quiet drill with a two-foot masonry bit to bore a quarter-inch hole in the ceiling between the two apartments. He had not needed the masonry bit after all. The ceiling was impossibly thin and the insulation was non-existent.

209's residents sat on a loveseat in the corner watching him work. Like many other elderly couples, they were too broke to move out of the crime-infested building. Carver had urged them to go downstairs, where they would presumably be out of the line of fire, but they had insisted on keeping an eye on their possessions.

Carver inserted a 20-inch fiber optic probe into the hole. Then he attached a small viewfinder to the end. By twisting the probe in a circular motion, he saw the entirety of 309's living room. The apartments' floor plans were identical. Carver saw the newscast on the TV in the living room and circled the probe around slowly. The room looked empty.

One of his men whistled twice from the bedroom. Carver dismounted the table, made his way down the hallway and regarded the Green Beret standing atop the old couple's bed. He was looking into an identical viewfinder. "Two men," the soldier whispered while keeping his eyes on the prize. "Both asleep. Both armed." He twisted the optic another two inches. "Another in the hallway. Just outside the bathroom. Also armed."

Carver went into the bathroom, where another solider stood on a crate. The soldier put his fingers to his lips. "Female in the bathroom," the soldier twanged in a hushed Louisiana accent.

"Is she armed?"

"No sir. I'd say civilian."

"Hostage?"

"Sir, I'd..." the soldier stopped. His face turned red. He turned away from the viewfinder.

"What's the problem?"

"She's on the crapper, sir."

Carver frowned. There was no time for chivalry, privacy concerns or squeamishness. He pushed the soldier aside, stood on the milk crate and peered into the fiber optic probe for a moment. Then he stepped down, astonished.

"That woman," he said, "is Angie Jackson."

"Who?"

"Angie Jackson. As in Mrs. Dexter Jackson."

"The SECDEF's wife? No sir. She's dead. Saw it on the news."

"Believe nothing." Carver twisted the optic and took another look. This time he found himself looking directly into Angie Jackson's brown eyes. "Uh-oh. She's onto us."

*

Angie grabbed the optic probe and tugged on it. She managed to get about ten inches of it above the carpeted bathroom floor – just enough to realize that she was holding a tiny camera. She was being watched. Or videotaped. In the bathroom. She dropped the fiber optic and pulled up her pants.

Elvir knocked at the door. "What are you doing in there?"

"My stomach's upset," she called through the door. Were her captors actually videotaping her bathroom visits?

She tried to push the probe back down into the carpet. No dice.

"No more time," Elvir said. "I'm coming in."

Angie took the magazine from the counter and tossed it onto the floor just as the door handle began to turn.

*

Chris Abrams forced a grin as he slowly opened the Hamilton Arms lobby door. He and his men walked upright, at ease. Although their rifles were live, with rounds in the chamber, they did not assume an attack posture. Looking like friendlies was key to their success.

There were four Green Berets in the lobby, kneeling behind a barricade of stacked furniture. Their backs were to the main lobby door, rifles trained on the building's primary escape routes – elevator and stairwell. When Abrams' men came into view, sporting U.S.-issue weaponry, Ulysses uniforms and shaved heads, the Green Berets stood and dropped their weapons to their sides.

"Who called in Ulysses?" one of them cracked.

Abrams' reply was a burst of M4 fire that cut two Green Berets across their waists and sent the other two diving over a couch. Both were quick to respond with grenades, which was a risky move at such close proximity. Abrams' crew dropped and rolled to either side, seeking cover.

Both grenades went off simultaneously. Abrams felt a stinging jab to his left side that stunned him. He opened his eyes in time to see a long, square segment of metal ventilation shaft falling from the ceiling. He rolled behind it as the surviving Green Berets sprayed the cloud of smoke, dust and bodies with gunfire. He pressed his hand to his aching side. Though his uniform on that side was frayed, and his fingers pressed through the riddled body armor to his tenderized flesh, there was no blood.

Just three feet from him, a dismembered, claw-like hand twitched. Abrams considered playing dead and then surprising his attackers as they rose to count their kills. But these were Green Berets he was up against. They were too smart for that. Unless Abrams' crew started firing back, and with a vengeance, the Green Berets would only keep lobbing grenades into the debris until there was nothing left of it.

Abrams removed the pin from one of his own grenades and flung it in a high arc to the other side of the room. It never made it that far. Abrams heard the sound of metal-on-metal as his grenade lodged into a piece of fallen ceiling. It hung there for three seconds until it exploded, bringing more chunks of the second floor raining down on them.

*

Elvir was baffled by the echo of explosions and gunfire downstairs. He had half-expected the government to come looking for Angie Jackson, but she was here before him. The two remaining members of his crew woke not ten feet from him. So who was fighting whom?

He flung open the bathroom door to check on Angie. He found her in the bathtub, wielding the shower curtain rod like some medieval jousting lance. "Easy, woman," he yelled. "Remember for a second who saved you!"

His eyes searched the room and eventually came to rest on the magazine on the floor. He kicked it aside. He recognized the optic probe immediately.

He put his foot over the probe's lens and looked at Angie. "Who's watching us?" he demanded. Angie did not know the answer. She had thought the camera was Elvir's.

An M4 salvo ripped through the floorboards. A round passed straight through the sole of Elvir's boot and came to rest within the ball of his foot. Angie released the shower curtain rod and cowered in the tub just as another burst of automatic gunfire came from the apartment below. Elvir collapsed to his knees, bleeding from his groin.

Through the open bathroom door, Angie watched as Elvir's cohorts rose from bed and got to their feet. But gunfire sliced through the carpet and cut them down before they could escape.

*

Carver stood looking through a series of holes in the ceiling that he had made with his own gunfire. A familiar face from Apartment 309 stared back at him.

And he knew without a doubt she was the SECDEF's wife.

"We're pinned down," came the frantic voice over his radio. "Two down in the lobby."

Carver turned and barked at the two Green Berets. "Go up to 309 and get that hostage safe. Use the fire escape. I'm headed to the lobby."

He was down the stairwell in thirty seconds. The door separating the stairwell from the lobby was blown clear off, and Carver was stunned to see that some of the second floor had caved in. The room was a haze of dust and smoke, but he spotted two surviving Green Berets, both half-buried in collapsed drywall. At the opposite end of the lobby, three guns returned fire near the main entrance. Carver shot from the third stair step and was sure he saw a spray of blood as the muzzle flash went dark.

Through the murkiness, Carver saw a uniformed figure sidewinding across the entrance. He readied his rifle to fire on the rushing attacker, and then saw a flash of an Army airborne uniform. It occurred to Carver that this could be some horrible friendly fire catastrophe – two units sent after the same target, cutting each other to bits because there was no central command authority. Carver realized he would only have himself to blame. This was the very definition of a skunk works operation.

He lost the figure in the smoky air for a moment. Then Carver saw a knife blade, its shank glimmering in the reflection of a half-destroyed chandelier that sagged low to the ground. The enemy gun went silent.

The other gun went silent around the same time, but it was difficult to see what was happening from Carver's vantage point. Finally someone called out. "Cease fire! Cease fire!"

The voice was one he hadn't expected to hear again. It was Sergeant Hundley.

Viper Squad's returning fire slowly petered out. "Sarge?" someone said.

Hundley stood up straight. "Damn straight."

Carver came down the stairs. He and the Sergeant locked gazes.

Hundley held a bloody 10-inch buck knife. The Sergeant stooped down and picked a rifle from one of the dead Ulysses soldiers. He held it in the ready position, with his finger on the trigger. The Sergeant's huge deltoids twitched underneath his shirt. It occurred to Carver that Hundley could take his revenge now if he wanted to, and he was in no position to stop him.

"So you made it," Carver said.

"I still run a four-four," Sergeant Hundley replied.

"Lucky for us."

"Agent Carver, tell you what. I'm prepared to forget about that incident on the street if you are."

The idea of making a deal with a loose cannon like Hundley didn't sit well. On the other hand, if Carver were to refuse, Hundley would shoot him on the spot, and the other Green Berets would undoubtedly cover for him. And there was the little matter of the national emergency to tend to.

"I don't say this to be vain," Carver said, "but you're looking at the only person in America who can catch the assassins."

Hundley grinned. "You're an even bigger egomaniac than I am. So are we good?"

"No," Carver said. "Seriously, Sergeant, I can't pretend you didn't shoot that looter. Twenty other people saw you gun that guy down. But I can tell the Army about the other things you did here today. Maybe they'll go easy on you."

Hundley lowered the rifle. "I can deal with that."

Carver climbed over the debris. "So who were we fighting?"

"Ulysses," Hundley said. He kicked one of the dead Ulysses soldiers in the ribs. Carver looked over the bodies. He picked up a Ulysses ID on the floor and regarded the photo of Chris Abrams' chiseled head. He turned over the four bodies one by one.

Their faces were intact, but none matched the man on the ID.

8th Precinct, Baltimore

The police station was oddly quiet as O'Keefe ushered Nico to reception. The Desk Sergeant, a rail of a man with bushy, graying eyebrows, was the only person in sight. "Morning," he said. "What's a nice couple like you doing in a dive like this?"

O'Keefe's left wrist was cuffed to Nico's right. She jerked them to eye-level for the Desk Sergeant's benefit.

"My mistake," the Desk Sergeant said. "You looked like a couple lovebirds holding hands."

O'Keefe flashed her old NSA badge, having learned the hard way over the past several weeks that it carried far more weight than the generic-looking credentials issued from Speers' office. "Where is everybody?" she said as she peered around the near-empty station.

"Sleepin' it off," the Sergeant said. "We're not staffed to enforce martial law, but we were doin' just that until the Ulysses boys showed up a few hours ago."

"Everyone okay?"

"One of our guys fell asleep behind the wheel, smashed into a daycare. Thank God no kids were there at the time. Chief had seventy cots set up downstairs an' they're all full up. But now we got scattered reports of looting coming in, and I'm thinkin' naptime's over. Know what I mean?"

"Sorry to trouble you," O'Keefe said, "but I need a secure Internet connection."

"What, NSA don't have wireless?"

"She said secure, genius," Nico quipped. "That means a land line."

"Pardon my colleague," O'Keefe said. "Now can you help us?"

"Third office down the hall, right side. Knock yourself out."

Just as the Sergeant said, they found a small meeting room with an outdated public-use computer. Nico stood before the ancient machine, nervously chewing the nails on his free hand as he gazed at his EVA tattoos.

O'Keefe picked up the telephone and called Eva's extension at Fort Campbell. Eva picked up on the first ring. "Put me on speaker," she instructed before launching into an explanation of Speers' theory that someone inside the military had pre-selected Marine One's flight path on the President's fatal flight. "If we can find out who did this, we can follow the trail all the way up the command chain. Can you do it?"

Nico began chewing on his nails again. "So let me get this straight," he said. "You're asking me to do the very thing that you put me in prison for in the first place?'

"I'm asking you to help solve a murder. If you can pull this off, then you'll get your pardon. Can it be done?"

"I can do anything given enough time."

Eva let out a short, sharp laugh. "You don't have any. We needed this yesterday."

He sighed. "At least give me a contact at CENTAF. Then it's at least like looking for a needle in a haystack."

"As opposed to what?"

"A needle in a stack of needles."

Over West Virginia
6:45 a.m.

Major Dobbs piloted the Blackhawk chopper at treetop level over the rolling West Virginia countryside. Speers held a handkerchief over his mouth as the rollercoaster-like trajectory played havoc with his stomach. Looking out the window, he spotted a herd of deer scattering across a rocky ridge beneath them. The ridge soon gave way to a valley of green farmland and, below that, a pig farm and a river of winding brown sludge.

A small town was nested at the far end of the valley. "Where are we?" Speers said over the grinding hum of the rotors.

"That's Martinsburg."

"Does the MARC run out here?" Speers said, referring to the commuter train that ran from West Virginia and through Maryland to D.C. "I gotta get back to the District."

"Risky," Dobbs said. "If they haven't done it already, the Joint Chiefs are going to break out the bloodhounds. Count on it."

"But they've severed my VPN connection," Speers explained. "I've gotta get on the network. The only way is to go to the office."

Dobbs eased off the throttle and set the chopper down in a cattle pasture. Three dozen bewildered cattle ran for the hills.

"There's a MARC station on the other side of that river," Dobbs said. "Watch out for water moccasins when you cross it."

"Wait - you're not coming?"

"Negative on that, Chief. I wanna live."

"What's your plan?"

"I'll set this baby down on the other side of the Canadian border and wait for the Mounties to come."

"Political asylum isn't all it's cracked up to be these days. As an attorney, I'd have to advise…"

"Save it, Chief. And for God's sake, find some deodorant. You stink."

Speers reluctantly shook the Major's hand and wished him good luck. He ran, crouching, as he exited the chopper until he had cleared the expanse of the rotor blades. He stood watching as Dobbs took off again and flew due north. He put his nose to his underarm and flinched. Dobbs was right. He smelled absolutely putrid.

He walked past awestruck cattle toward the river. His patent leather shoes squished deeply and loudly into the mud.

Aside from a city park, Speers had never actually been in a forest. The closest that the 42-year-old had been to experiencing the great outdoors was with a car window rolled down while antiquing in rural Maryland. Raised as an only child by his late mother in D.C., the sum of his boyhood adventures had taken place in museums and theatre houses and video games. He had never been camping, nor had he, like most of his colleagues, taken up running or hiking or kayaking.

He gazed at the river in the distance, which looked at least 20 feet wide. "How in Hades am I going to get across that?" he said aloud. Even at this distance, he could hear the roar of the water. It was like the audio file of nature sounds that helped him sleep at night.

The unmistakable whirr of helicopter blades roared overhead. Speers looked up smiling, expecting to find that Major Dobbs had decided to join him after all. He was mistaken.

Two Apache AH-64 attack helicopters flew so low that Speers could have hit them with a rock. Speers ran backwards toward the tree line, unable to take his eyes off the twin airships. The Apache on the left wing suddenly released two white sparrow missiles. They dropped perhaps six feet before emitting a shower of white flame and hurling northward at breathtaking speed.

It was then that Speers spotted Dobbs' chopper, still barely visible on the horizon as the missiles rushed toward him. Speers stood at the edge of the field. Even to his non-military eye, it was clear that Dobbs was flying far too low for effective evasive action. He banked the Blackhawk as hard as he could and released a torrent of flares.

The flares did nothing to deter the laser-guided sparrows. They locked onto the Blackhawk anyhow, striking its underbelly like flying snakes. Dobbs' chopper was transformed into a comet that plummeted into a barn on the hillside.

Speers didn't have time to grieve Major Dobbs' violent death. He sprinted for the tree line as the Apaches rose and turned in sync eastward. The real forest was nothing like Speers had imagined from the comfort of his TV screen. The trees were thin-trunked and far too dense with underbrush for any serious running. Poison ivy was everywhere. The best he could do was squirm several feet into the thick foliage and lay down to hide. The Apaches circled overhead twice, in large circles, so low that the trees swayed in the breeze from their rotors. Speers felt something – chiggers, probably – biting his ankles, but he did not dare move.

His phone buzzed in his pocket. His heart soared as he realized he had regained signal. He longed to answer. He wanted to tell someone that he was being hunted like an animal. But even if he did, what good would it do? There was no defense against the Apaches except to hide. And it occurred to Speers that the phone was perhaps a liability. What if Wainewright's goons had used it to track his location? What if they had listened in to his brief conversation with Eva? He reached into his pocket and held his thumb over the power button.

8th Precinct, Baltimore
6:52 a.m.

The air was close and hot in the little room. Nico sat with his orange jumpsuit unzipped to the waist as he pounded multi-colored code onto a black computer screen. O'Keefe watched over his shoulder and pulled at the ends of her long strawberry-blonde hair to stay awake.

"This is spooky ironic," Nico said. The speed of his rapid-fire typing didn't suffer as he spoke.

"You mean hacking into government records for the very same person who put you in the slammer for hacking into government records?"

"Not only that," Nico said. "I'm hacking into government records in a police station. The cops are actually helping me commit a crime. Twisted, right?"

O'Keefe took off her Kevlar-lined jacket for the first time today, revealing a gray t-shirt with the NSA emblem across the chest. "Too bad you'll never be allowed to put this in your memoirs."

The computer emitted a shrill buzz. Nico stood and kicked a trash can across the floor. "What?"

"CENTAF cyber sheriff booted me out. This is too much pressure. I can't believe Eva's doing this to me. Double-crossing beotch."

"Watch it," O'Keefe warned. "That's the future Veep you're talking about. Be nice to her. She's got half a mind to hand you over to the Saudis."

Nico went pale. "She really said that?"

"You know what the Saudis do to hackers, right?" She held up her arm and made a slicing motion across her wrist.

He returned to the machine and began again. His heart wasn't in it. It was a futile exercise. Neither O'Keefe nor Eva understood that anyone with clearance to work on CENTAF's systems could have rigged Marine One's flight plan without leaving obvious digital fingerprints. Forensic IT work was difficult and labor intensive. It would take days or weeks to find anything conclusive.

O'Keefe walked to the other side of the table and stretched her arms high above her head and yawned. She yawned again. And a terrible idea popped into Nico's head.

"At least switch off the lights," he told her. "Screen glare's killing my eyes."

She did. Nico typed with a bit more force now. His cuffs knocked loudly against the keyboard. He kept this up for several minutes. Then, exasperated, he turned and held his wrists toward her. He rattled his cuffs for good measure. "I can't work in these."

"C'mon. Don't put me in that kind of position."

"You're torturing me."

"Melodramatic."

"I'm in serious pain. Have a look if you don't believe me."

She took a peek at the skin of his wrists. It was indeed red from the cuff's constant chafing.

O'Keefe pulled the key from her belt and freed Nico's wrists. "Just get back to work."

Nico turned back around and began pounding the keyboard again. Shortly, a site with Cyrillic alphabet displayed on the screen.

O'Keefe sat up. "That's not one of our sites. What're you doing?"

"Easy, spook. This is just a Hungarian site for coding geeks. I gotta download some spyware. And stop looking over my shoulder. It's makin' me all edgy."

"How much longer?"

"Couple hours at least. Might as well get comfortable."

O'Keefe sat in a wooden chair against the wall. She put her loafers up on the desk, looking sleepy. Nico began working again. He typed in a deliberate, rhythmic canter. Slow. But steady. Like a resting heartbeat.

Gangplank Marina, Washington D.C. 8:11 a.m.

Rios was still asleep when his phone jarred him from a dream. A good dream. He was sailing down in the Florida Keys with nothing but blue ocean and sunshine ahead of him. Plenty of beer in the ice chest and nothing but chips, guacamole, homemade salsa and fried shrimp to eat. Samba played loud – too loud – over the stereo. His knees didn't even hurt.

His Blackberry rang. The reality of a city under martial law came flooding back to him. He opened his eyes on the second ring and gazed at his right hand, remembering that he had used it to kill two men the day before. He sat up and saw the row of boats out the porthole, realizing that he was safe aboard the Little Santa Maria, at slip #74, just like always.

Except when he was traveling with the President. The President. He had not heard from First Team since Sunday. He grabbed the phone and answered as fast as he could.

"It's Rios," he said.

The man on the other end identified himself as the CSO from Homeland Security. Rios had met him once, maybe twice. While he technically reported to HS, they didn't bother him too much. The President had always insisted that Rios run the show.

"You're needed at the Willard," the CSO said.

The Willard was one of the oldest and most prestigious hotels in Washington. It was near the White House. "Okay. What's up?"

"VIPs will be taking occupancy tonight. Your team has already been notified and will meet you at the hotel. Instructions will be disseminated at that time."

"Wait. You mean First Team?" Rios said. "First Team will meet me there?"

"Just show up," the CSO said. The line went dead.

Rios was left looking at the receiver as the sailboat gently rocked beneath him.

"Who was that?" said the voice behind him.

Rios shot out of bed and spun around, fully naked, his heart sputtering. He found himself looking at Haley Ellis, naked under the sheets of his queen-size bed.

She looked hurt. "You actually forgot I was here, didn't you? Last night was that memorable?"

Rios shook his head and looked for his pants. "It's just…I'm not used to having company. It's been a long time."

"You usually kick them out before dawn?"

"It's not like that."

She groped the floor for her clothes. "This isn't exactly business as usual for me. I was brought up a good girl and I am a good girl. Iraq didn't even ruin me. I just want you to know that."

"Don't worry about it. I guess martial law makes you do crazy things." Rios got his pants on and watched as she did the same. "Call it what you want," he added, "but I had a good time last night."

She turned and made eye contact. Goosebumps went up her arms. "Me too."

He sat back down on the bed. They shared a slow kiss. He had to force himself to break away. His head hurt. They had drunk a lot of wine last night. And he was late. And a little scared.

8th Precinct, Baltimore
10:21 a.m.

O'Keefe awakened from deep REM sleep and tried to focus. A man looked down on her. He was shaking her shoulder gently. "Oh jeeze," she said as her vision slowly came into view. It was Nico. He was standing over her, breathing through his mouth. His breath was heinous.

"How long have I —"

"Two hours."

"Oh God." She groaned as she righted herself in the chair. Holy Mary Mother of God. She had fallen asleep while supervising a federal prisoner. She could lose her job for this. "I'm impressed you didn't try to escape."

He blushed, looking somehow guilty. "Actually, I didn't want to leave without saying goodbye."

She instinctively reached for her weapon. It wasn't there. She looked down and saw her agency-issued cuffs looped around her right ankle. The other cuff was tightened around a support beam underneath the table. Nico held the key in his hand.

O'Keefe let out a long, sustained scream at the top of her lungs. Nico put his fingers in his ears, sat back and waited patiently for her to stop. Half a minute later, O'Keefe stopped the noise long enough to catch her breath. "I don't get it," she huffed. "How come nobody's coming to help me?"

"They used this room to question suspects. It's completely soundproof."

"How'd you know that?"

"They've got old floor plans and office assignments on the precinct wiki. There used to be an observation window on that wall, but they bricked it up."

Fear welled up in her. She hadn't had a chance to look at Nico's intel file. She hoped he didn't have any latent mental health issues.

He saw it. "Hey now, don't be scared. I'm a pacifist. Robin Hood criminal."

"So why are you still here?"

"I just had to tell you how sorry I am. I couldn't do it."

"Couldn't do what? Bring yourself to help Eva?"

"No, no, no. I mean I literally couldn't do it. I'm not a forensic IT expert. It's a completely different specialty."

"Maybe if you explained it in those words. I could talk to Eva for you."

He shook his head. "We both know that if she actually gets to go back to the White House, she'll hand me over to the Saudis the first chance she gets."

O'Keefe folded her arms across her chest. "You think you're in trouble. Just wait until the agency finds out that I lost an international cyber criminal. My career's ruined."

Nico nodded sympathetically. "I thought of that. Which is why I'm giving you a consolation prize."

Nico handed O'Keefe a freshly printed stack of records. "Hector Joaquin Sanchez and Damien Griffith LaSalle."

"Who?"

"The guys that tried to kill Eva up in Martha's Vineyard. I decided to hack into Veteran's Affairs and see if I could find something from there. They've got these ancient legacy systems that are virtually held together with paper clips, so it was pretty easy."

"Are they extremists?"

"As far as I can tell, they're just mercenaries. They began their career as part of an elite Army sniper unit called the 1-501. After a tour of duty in Iraq, they both left to join the USOC unit. Pay was way better, I can tell you that. They were put under the command of a man named Chris Abrams, who was an unspecified consultant."

"Never heard of him."

"Back to Abrams in a moment, but moving on, please turn to page twelve of your handout." O'Keefe flipped to page twelve as Nico resumed his story. "For kicks, I looked up our favorite Baltimore resident, Elvir Divac. Lo and behold, the name Chris Abrams pops up again. I looked up his partner in crime, Ali Lahari. Also listed as assigned to—"

"Chris Abrams?"

"Cha-ching. But strangely, there is no VA file for Chris Abrams, which I thought was odd for a Ulysses consultant, since they tend to hire veterans as a rule. So I looked him up on the Social Security database, and there was no man by that name within his age group."

O'Keefe wriggled in her seat. "I know I'm a captive audience, but you're boring me. Cut to the chase."

"On page eighteen of your program, you'll find what I discovered in the log files of a site called *PrivateMilitaryNews.com*."

O'Keefe turned to the printout. It was a photo of General Wainewright with Chris Abrams. The article caption: *General Wainewright with Chris Abrams, one of Ulysses' top guns in Indonesia*.

"This is the guy?"

"It is. But what's interesting is that nobody knows this page still exists. It never made it to the live site. It was held in an editor's queue in the Web site's content management system, but it still lives on through the wonders of Web dev versioning software."

"Just tell me what it means!"

"The article's a smear piece, showing that Wainewright owned millions in Ulysses stock options and was thus violating anti-trust laws by pitching them DOD-financed contracts. Abrams' inclusion as a Ulysses employee in the pic was just a happy accident."

"Proves nothing," O'Keefe said. "General Wainewright is very open about how pleased he is with Ulysses' performance."

"With one crucial exception. The General's photo with Chris Abrams. I found myself wondering why someone went to such lengths to make sure it didn't get published."

"What lengths?"

"Double homicide."

"You lost me."

"Turn to page twenty-six." O'Keefe did. "I looked up the name of the journalist to see if there were any follow-up pieces that saw the light of day. Instead, I found what you're holding on page thirty-two."

O'Keefe flipped to the page. It was an obituary. "Go on."

"The writer was stabbed in a supermarket parking lot the day before the article was due to be published. That night, his editor was killed by a hit and run driver."

Had she not been cuffed to the table, O'Keefe could have kissed him. Nico had found a direct link between Eva's would-be assassins and Ulysses, and it even had a name – Chris Abrams. Even if Abrams was just a blunt instrument, O'Keefe figured if they dug deeper, there would be a connection to their own investigation of Ulysses as well. She shuffled anxiously through the rest of the files Nico had printed up.

Static hum erupted over the room speaker. Then the Desk Sergeant's voice cut in: "Riots in 8th Precinct. All hands reports."

Right on time. Nico himself had hacked into the precinct messaging account moments before waking O'Keefe and issued the emergency broadcast.

He stood. "So I guess this is goodbye."

O'Keefe nodded. "Thanks, Nico. This was nice of you. All things considered, I mean."

He slipped out of the soundproof room and switched off the light on his way out. Around the corner, he found the open cabinet with a half dozen riot helmets, Kevlar vests, and shields. He put a helmet on first. Then, as police ran past him, he calmly dressed in full riot gear and made his way toward the building's entrance, where similarly costumed police officers were making their way to the street. Walk with purpose, he told himself. Stay with the pack. You are a cop in riot gear. Be the riot gear.

He continued following the other officers until he saw a public phone in front of a library. He went to it and lifted the shield on his riot helmet and picked up the receiver. When the operator came on, Nico said "Collect call to Burlington, North Carolina, please. Margaret Howland. H-O-W-L-A-N-D. You'll have to look up the number.

Rapture Run
10:49 a.m.

General Farrell felt his intestines tighten as he entered Wainewright's quarters. He was accustomed to being the calming influence in Wainewright's life. But he didn't feel calm now. Wainewright looked up and saw the rage in Farrell's face. "Shut the door," he said as he pressed a button on his desk to frost the door glass.

"Why wasn't I told about Angie Jackson?" Farrell demanded.

Wainewright leaned back in his chair. "Your plate's full. You didn't need any more distractions."

"Abrams' crew failed, and now Eva Hudson's people have Angie. I think we can count on Eva going public with this."

"We can't let that happen."

Farrell's voice turned wobbly. "We've already played our hand. We've got to tell Dex his wife is alive. What choice do we have? Better that he hears it from us first."

"Calm down."

"Don't tell me to calm down. Eva's alive, and that means she's next in line. Maybe before we could've forced Dex into office, but not now. We're going to have to make some kind of deal with Eva. Maybe tell her we'll support her presidency in exchange for immunity. We could maybe give her Jeff Taylor. Or Abrams."

Wainwright peered up at Farrell with red eyes. "You've completely lost it."

"Don't you see how this is going to look? The plan was to blame this on the Allied Jihad. That's falling apart now. It looks bad. We look bad."

The Chairman remained calm. "Get a grip. We look golden. Besides, if we give up now, the country would be right back where we started. Bogged down in the Middle East for a generation. Vilified by the world. Buying our water from Canada or going to war with Mexico to get it." He stood, walked around the circumference of his desk and spoke mere inches from Farrell's face. "The most patriotic men in America are standing right in this room. I really believe that. And I'm not afraid to put my reputation, and my very life, on the line for the good of our country. Are you?" He poked his index finger into the middle of Farrell's chest. "Are you? Because it sounds to me like you're only concerned about saving your ass."

Farrell stepped back. He took an unfiltered cigarette out of his pocket and lit up. Thick ropes of smoke roiled throughout his esophagus and lungs.

TEN MONTHS EARLIER
Northern Colorado

The Chairman's private hunting cabin was nestled within sixty private acres of golden windswept plains and dense aspen forests. It was not accessible by road. Being an avid hunter, General Farrell had been angling for an invitation for more than a year. With armies in three war zones, a single weekend off for any of the Pentagon brass was a rarity.

Wainewright finally relented in early October, just in time for deer season. They had come in on a Wednesday morning by private helicopter. The 110-year-old outpost had been a remote ranger station until the late 2000s when the State of Colorado, its tax revenue crippled by the housing bubble collapse, had been forced to sell off chunks of prime public land. Wainewright snapped the place up for just over a million in cash.

The Pentagon's most powerful duo spent the afternoon in an aspen grove overlooking a busy game trail. They saw deer by the dozen and elk by the truckload. By dusk they had both bagged big bucks. They butchered the animals themselves, hauling the prime cuts out on their backs and leaving the rest for the coyotes.

They spent the evening eating venison, drinking 12-year-old cognac and smoking Dominican cigars by firelight. As always, the conversation eventually turned to politics. Wainewright was candid about his feelings about the President's policies. That was no surprise. He waited until Farrell's third glass of cognac to veer into the unexpected.

"Ed," he said, using Farrell's first name for the first time in ages, "There's a movement among certain members of congress to remove the President."

Farrell shook his head. "There's not enough votes for impeachment. Trust me, I'm following it too."

"I'm not talking impeachment," Wainewright said.

The Vice-Chairman sipped his liquor. "Then what are you talking about?"

"Removal."

Farrell laughed. "Careful," he said. "If I didn't know better, it sounds like you're talking—"

"Removal," Wainewright confirmed.

Farrell was quiet for a moment as the implications of the conversation dawned on him. He set his drink on the table, extinguished the cigar in an ash tray and replaced it with an unfiltered cigarette. "I take it you didn't bring me out here just to hunt."

The Chairman puffed his cigar and looked up at a bison head that his great-grandfather had killed. "If it makes you uncomfortable, we don't have to discuss it. No pressure at all."

Farrell knew better. Wainewright had no patience for anyone that wasn't rowing in the same direction that he was. This conversation was a test. If he didn't seem amenable, he'd find himself out of the Joint Chiefs – or worse – by the end of the year.

"General," Farrell said, "you're a registered Republican, right?"

"I'm beyond the party system, Ed."

Farrell took that to mean that Wainewright now considered himself a revolutionary. "So these members of Congress..." Farrell said, treading as lightly as he could. "They theoretically advocate drastic measures."

"Not theoretically. It's real, Ed. It's obvious to everyone that the executive branch has accumulated too much power. Fact: we're on track to suffer twelve thousand combat casualties this year, and we'll have nothing to show for it but more enemies. Fact: our annual foreign aid to Israel and its neighbors alone costs us more in one year than it would cost to fix social security for the next ten years."

"I'm sure that's true. But still—"

"Fact: twelve states are running out of clean drinking water, and the President is doing nothing to stop it."

The Vice-Chairman tried to make sense of what he was hearing. Was this the cognac talking, or was Wainewright for real?

"General," he began, not quite comfortable with calling Wainewright by his first name, "these member of Congress you mentioned. Maybe we could help them get the votes they need."

"Impeachment?" Wainewright laughed. "The Vice-President would just continue the same policies."

"Point taken. But the line of succession would be the same regardless of how the President left office."

Wainewright smiled. "We think alike, my friend. Which is why I told them that their plans were far too conservative. Removal by assassination is too short-sighted. They're not thinking big."

Farrell felt dizzy. "Big?'

"We've known each other for thirty-five years You know I'm no secessionist, and I'm sure as hell not a socialist. You know I love this country. But you have to admit that we're being outmaneuvered by emerging governments that combine free markets, a strong military and strong central government."

"You mean China."

Wainewright nodded. "Not just China. Fact: Russia is buying our debt and selling it back to us at prices we can't even afford." He pounded his fist on the table. "Russia, Ed!"

Farrell lit another cigarette. "I think it's important to remember that we still live in the greatest country in the world."

"Not even close. We're at best the nineteenth or twentieth greatest country in the world. But there's a powerful movement afoot, Ed. The fog is lifting."

That night, Farrell went to bed so shaken that he could not sleep. By morning he had developed several stress boils on his neck, shoulders and back.

The cabin phone rang at 10:36 a.m. with the news that a car bomb in Santa Monica had killed 170 people. The Joint Chiefs were summoned to the White House for an emergency Security Council meeting. A helicopter took them to Fort Collins, where they boarded a private jet bound for Washington.

The NSC convened five hours later at the White House, where President Hatch informed them that, in response to Indonesian radicals claiming responsibility for the bombing, they would open up a new military front in Indonesia. The decision came despite the fact that the U.S. military was already stretched beyond capacity. It came without any proof whatsoever that Allied Jihad forces battling the government in Indonesia were behind the bombing. It came without any room in the country's three-trillion-dollar deficit. But the public wanted revenge and the President had decided to take the fight to the terrorists. He wasn't interested in the Joint Chiefs' arguments to the contrary.

After the meeting, the two Generals shared a car back to the Pentagon. They were quiet until they entered the Pentagon parking garage. "About what you said last night," Farrell said. "I'd like to discuss that more."

Eleven days later General Farrell received an invitation to attend a private dinner at General Wainewright's home near Alexandria. He was specifically instructed not to bring his wife or any other date. Upon pulling up to Wainewright's home – a six-bedroom estate with Greek columns in front – a parking attendant led him inside, where Wainewright's assistant, Corporal Hammond, swept his clothes with a metal detector and placed his phone in a safe near the front door.

He was led to a dining room where the other two Joint Chiefs – General Shufford of the Air Force and Admiral Bennington of the Navy – were already seated, along with the head of the House Foreign Intelligence Committee, the Secretary of the Interior, and junior senators from Texas, Georgia and Utah. The room was lit with ancient chandeliers and the walls were paneled with red and black leather.

"Welcome," Wainewright said, gesturing for Farrell to sit next to him at the head of the table. He closed the door and locked it, leaving Corporal Hammond outside. "FYI, the walls and ceiling are soundproofed and the room was swept for bugs less than an hour ago. We are quite free to say what we must."

General Wainewright spent the next 45 minutes explaining in detail how he had already arranged for the construction of a secret command facility in West Virginia from which to operate during the early stages of the operation. Then he outlined how he planned to utilize Ulysses and, indirectly, the Iranians to help achieve their goals. "This is nothing less than a second American Revolution," he said.

Admiral Bennington was the first to raise his hand. His jowls framed his 62-year-old pale face into a nearly perfect rectangle. "I agree that our relationship with Israel is hurting us," he said. "The drain on our economy is undeniable. But I'm not too keen on the Iranians."

"I should remind everyone that during the first American Revolution, nobody wanted help from the French either."

"I still don't."

The Chairman laughed. "Admiral, in your opinion, why will most of the wars be fought in the next hundred years?"

"That's an easy one," Admiral Bennington said. "Water."

Every head at the table nodded.

"Water," Wainewright repeated. "H2O. Fact: at our current consumption rate, factoring in steady population growth, the United States won't have enough clean drinking water for the western United States within twelve years. Think about it. We already import everything from labor to matchsticks. Do we really want to import water too?"

The Secretary of the Interior, a small, wiry man who had once been an executive at Exxon, agreed. "The Canadians are already ratcheting up their prices," he said. "They're sitting on enough water to supply the U.S. for the next hundred years, but it's going to bankrupt us."

The head of the House Foreign Intelligence Committee checked her watch. "General, I have to leave in ten minutes. You were asked about Iran, and I'd like to hear the answer."

"Everyone assumes that Iran has had its best scientists working on building nukes for the past decade," Wainewright said. "That's just a sideline. They have in fact been focusing on a breakthrough in desalination. I visited the plant near the Caspian Sea personally last month."

Farrell gasped. He, and everyone in the Federal Government, had been told that Wainewright had been in Afghanistan, not Iran.

"The Iranians are building massive underground reservoirs," Wainewright went on. "Trust me. I drank water that had been in the Caspian Sea just one day earlier. This innovation is as seminal as when we split the atom. But the Iranians aren't dumb. They realize this is more valuable than oil."

"They're going to export it?" Farrell asked.

"Sure as I'm standing here," Wainewright said. "Now you understand Iran's true motives. They don't just want to destroy Israel. They want to occupy it for their new business."

"From Israel they could build a pipeline to Saudi Arabia, Egypt, Jordan, Lebanon, Turkey," said Admiral Bennington. "And they'd have a port right on the Mediterranean. They could ship water anywhere in Europe."

A congressman with a bad combover cleared his throat and leaned his elbows on the table. "Does President Hatch know about the desalination technology?"

"Of course," Wainewright said. "But he'd rather bankrupt the country by buying water from the Canadians instead of dealing with Iran."

Bennington was getting impatient. "You've made it plenty clear why the Iranians need us," he said, "but you still haven't answered my question: What do we get out of this?"

"The technology," Wainewright said. General Shufford guffawed, but the Chairman stayed on message. "I know it's difficult to accept that we might actually need technology from a country like Iran. That isn't supposed to be the way the world works. But none of the desalination techniques we've been working on come close. What the Iranians have done will solve all our needs. And they're going to give it to us. We don't even have to help them fight Israel. We just have to stand aside while they do."

The congresswoman from South Dakota raised her hand. "General, from the time we get the technology, how long will it take to build the desalination plants?"

"Took the Iranians fifteen years once they figured it out," Wainewright said. "They think we can get it done in two."

Union Station, Washington D.C.
7:15 p.m.

The commuter train slowed as it entered the D.C. suburbs. Julian Speers sprawled in a business class booth. The conductor's voice crackled over the speakers: "This is Union Station. Union Station." He woke from a snatch of dreamless sleep and shook his numb left arm awake. With his right, he scratched the chigger bites on his neck.

He saw the Capitol Rotunda out the window and forced himself alert. Soon Union Station, the most celebrated Beaux-Arts structure in the country, came into view.

"Attention," the conductor's voice broke through again. "Attention please. The District of Columbia and its outlying areas are under martial law. All private citizens are required to remain indoors after eight o'clock p.m."

As they pulled into the station, the Ulysses MPs and their German Shepherds soon came into view. Speers got up and went directly to the restroom, where he locked the door and sat on the toilet. He didn't have to go. He hadn't had anything to eat or drink all day. He only needed to stay hidden until the MPs completed their sweep.

Speers listened to the passengers disembarking. Someone tugged on the door – it sounded like an old woman – pounded on it briefly and pleaded for him to hurry. Speers did not reply. He did not move.

Eventually he heard the woman move on, complaining to anyone who would listen.

Moments later, Speers heard heavy boots on the linoleum floor and the click-clack of canine claws. Again Speers waited as silently as he could. He sat so still that his legs went to sleep, and he had to flex his calves to keep the flow of blood rushing through them. Chunks of dirt fell off his mud-caked shoes.

Sixteen minutes later he heard the whirring of an industrial-strength vacuum and opened the door a crack to peer down the aisle. A cleaning lady was cleaning up a spilled beverage. He opened the door further and, through the window, saw the MPs and their dogs congregated at the far end of the platform.

The cleaner, a rotund brown woman in a tent-like blue smock, spotted Speers as he returned from the toilet. "'Bout time," she shouted as she grabbed a bottle of anti-bacterial spray and some paper towels and slid past. Speers waited for her to shut the tiny bathroom door. Then he snagged her cleaning cart – full of mops and brooms and cleaning supplies – and pushed it out of the train ahead of him, using it as a shield as he headed for the station entrance.

He had been on hundreds of local trains through Union Station in the past three years, and he had twice been led on evacuation drills by the President's secret service through the station's underground tunnels. But only now, entering from the commuter train platform, did he understand the extent to which the station had been converted into a huge indoor shopping mall. Dozens of chain stores and eateries stretched out before him.

Union Station was a massive temple of marble, gold leaf and virgin white granite. He had seen figures stating that four million passengers passed through each year, and it seemed to Speers that all four million of them were now scrambling to get home before the rapidly approaching curfew.

It had been two years since the last evacuation training. Speers looked for the bookstore where the portal into the tunnels had been built. He stopped at a station kiosk and saw no less than four bookstores on the directory. None of the names rang a bell.

Nothing on this level looked familiar. He pushed through the throngs of black-and-grey-clad government workers, lobbyists and Hill aides. Two Ulysses MPs chatted not 30 feet from him. One of them followed Speers with his eyes as the other kept yakking.

Finally, nestled between the Jamba Juice and Agent Provocateur, Speers found Capitol Books. The tunnel entrance.

During President Hatch's first term, Speers had learned the real reason behind the station's $70 million dollar restoration effort completed during the Reagan administration. It had been true that the station's once-magnificent stone inscriptions had gathered mold, and the homeless had colonized like so many rats under the decaying platforms. But beneath all that, the administration had orchestrated an extension of the Capitol's evacuation tunnels. The enhanced labyrinth of escape routes linked Congress to Union Station, the Eisenhower Building, the White House, the Pentagon, Mount Weather, and Arlington Hills.

The tunnels had been upgraded in each succeeding administration. Now the Union Station tunnel entrance required both a code and a retina scan, and there were but five retinas in the Hatch administration that could gain access: President Hatch, the Vice President, Speers, Agent Rios, and General Wainewright. Speers felt both honored and grateful to be in possession of one of those precious eyeballs.

Three customers perused Capitol Book's magazine rack. Speers pushed past them, stepping on toes, past the checkout counter and into the back of the store, where a single employee on break watched a TV show on his cell phone. The employee leaned against an unassuming white door with a digital keypad.

"Excuse me," Speers said, and when the employee didn't move, he used his forearm to clear the employee out of the way. The startled clerk pulled the headphones out of his ears and watched Speers punch a string of numbers into the keypad. On the advice of the previous administration's Chief of Staff, Speers had kept the code extremely simple – it was his late mother's birthday, the same code he used at ATM machines. The logic behind the easy-to-guess code was that it was likely to be used just once – and that was only if things got really bad. Under conditions like these, five-digit codes were way too easy to forget. Besides, the real security was in the retina scan behind the first door. And the fact that only a handful of people in the world knew of the tunnels' existence.

"You management, huh?" the employee said. "Ya'll got an executive toilet back there or somethin'?"

The door opened. Speers wasted no time. As he turned to close the first door behind him, he spotted a tall jarhead in plainclothes talking into his radio. The guy was clearly reporting Speers' position. He fumbled with the knob and pushed the door shut.

Speers came to a set of stainless steel blast doors. He bent his frame slightly to put his eye to the retina scanner. The scanner had been specific to one eye. But which eye?

Behind him, the doorknob to the store entrance jiggled, causing Speers to blink. The scanner buzzed and displayed an error message: COULD NOT READ. Behind him, the door shook with a series of heavy blows. It sounded like someone was pounding the lock with an anvil. Speers steadied his nerves and waited for the scanner to reset. Then he bent again and held his eye open with his thumb and index finger. The door displayed another error message: FALSE MATCH. Ugh. Wrong eye.

The door was throbbing now. It sounded as if someone on the other side was throwing dozens of kitchen sinks at it. Speers' hands shook as he waited for the scanner to reset. As the error message once again transformed to read READY, he tried his right eye, again holding the lid open so as to avoid blinking.

That did it. The scanner lit green. The door locks whirred and the entrance to the tunnels beneath Union Station swooshed open just long enough for him to get through. The five-foot thick portal closed behind him. It was built to withstand a nuke. He was safe. At least for now.

The station tunnel was eerily spotless, perfectly silent and lit with amber LED lamps that branched off in four directions. And narrow. Four feet wide and eight feet tall.

On each tunnel branch were cryptic signs in painted white lettering. The first read "Pickup Silver," code name for a baseball field in Silver Springs, Maryland. The second tunnel read "Salon," which led to a secret entrance beneath the Capitol Building. This portal was intended to evacuate members of Congress in the event of a direct biological or terrorist attack. The third tunnel was labeled "Camelot," which led to the President's personal fallout shelter beneath the White House itself. Speers' main office was right next to the President's private study in the West Wing, but he was betting that Ulysses agents were already waiting for him there. The fourth tunnel was marked "Papa," codename for the Eisenhower Building, where Speers maintained a second office for days when he needed a quiet place to work. In order to prevent pop-in traffic, he had purposely kept its exact location a secret from all staffers except Mary Chung and the President. He was hoping it would keep Ulysses guessing for a few more hours.

Fort Campbell Infirmary
7:20 p.m.

Elvir Divac was far paler and smaller than Eva had envisioned. His nostrils were filled with clear oxygen tubing. An IV was spiked into his arm and his ankles were shackled to the bed frame. A lone physician checked his vitals. His disheveled white lab coat and stained t-shirt rankled Eva. One of the few things she appreciated about the military was the ability to know someone's status by the stripes on their sleeves or the brass on their lapels.

"Where's your uniform?" she asked the doctor.

"This is it. I'm a civilian. My company's on contract with the base." He fished a business card out of his white coat and offered it to Eva.

She turned her gaze back to the prisoner. "Wake him up."

The doc shook his head. "He's under general anesthesia. We just dug a bullet out of his groin."

He motioned Eva behind a tall white divider, where Angie Jackson also lay unconscious. So it was true. Eva didn't know Angie well, but they had exchanged pleasantries at a few State dinners. Eva examined the yellow plastic ID bracelet around Angie's wrist. It read *Jane Doe*.

"We just sent some hair to the lab as a DNA sample," the doc said. "The poor thing was in shock. She thinks she's the Defense Secretary's wife."

Eva heard the thumping cadence of Agent Carver's voice in the background. He was arguing with the MP at the door.

"Let the Feds in," Eva told the doc. "Then clear the infirmary."

There was a slight hunch in O'Keefe's posture as she followed Carver around the white divider. She barely made eye contact as she looked across Elvir's bedside. Eva's arms were folded across her chest and she wore her judgment like armor.

"Madam Secretary," O'Keefe said, "Nico's escape was entirely my fault."

"No," Carver said. "I take full responsibility. I'll find him personally."

After all the gut-busting globetrotting, food poisoning, vaccinations, time and resources she had spent tracking down Nico Gold and putting him on trial, Eva wasn't about to relieve the federal agents of their shame. "The world's most dangerous cyber criminal is on the loose, and you think you're just going to turn over some rock and find him? You really have no idea who you're dealing with, do you?"

It wasn't a question. She was just rubbing their noses in it. Rather than endure Eva's wrath, Carver decided to change the conversation. He pulled Chris Abrams' Ulysses ID out of his shirt pocket and handed it to Eva.

"He was in Baltimore today," Carver added. "We're working under the assumption that he was there to kill Angie Jackson."

Eva held the ID, but she couldn't focus on it. Nico Gold was on the lam. Years of effort down the tubes. Once the crisis was over, she would need an army of programmers to safeguard the nation's security grid.

Colonel Madsen entered the room with a sealed envelope. He was out of breath. "General Farrell sent this by personal messenger from Rapture Run. He asked me to run this across base personally. You're supposed to open it right away."

Eva did. There was a sheet of paper inside on which Farrell had handwritten a ten character alphanumeric pass code and a domain name. Eva recognized it from a National Security Council meeting. It was a private video chat site to be used in case of national emergency.

Fort Campbell Gym

The old gym was located behind the stadium track in a red brick building that had not been entered for six years. Carver picked the front door deadbolt and flipped the switch. Three dusty fluorescent tubes flickered to life and twittered like strobe lights on a dance floor.

Carver lifted the dust cover off an ancient incline weight bench. Like all the equipment in the once-flooded gym, its legs were badly rusted. Carver figured it would still support a lightweight like Elvir Divac.

He placed the still-comatose prisoner on the incline weight bench. His hospital gown hung open, revealing post-surgery bandages around his thigh and groin. He cuffed the prisoner's wrists to a barbell mounted on the rack above his head. Two hundred pounds in free weights were mounted on either side.

He poured ice water on Elvir's face. The native Bosnian, who was still under general anesthesia, coughed in his sleep but didn't wake. Carver had anticipated this. He pulled a syringe from his pocket, raised the hem of Elvir's gown and injected his prisoner in the thigh. The serum was a favorite among CIA interrogators.

Elvir came suddenly awake, screaming at operatic volume, his eyes dilated like big black saucers. He struggled mightily against his handcuffs, nearly dislodging the barbell from the rack over his chest.

Carver leaned over the barbell and looked down at him. "What do you think of our wake-up serum? I've heard the sensation is like falling from a skyscraper."

Elvir tried to spit. His mouth was too dry.

"Tell me who sold you the Stingers," Carver said. "Then you can sleep. Promise. I've got a drug for that too."

Elvir muttered something in Bosnian.

"Drop the act," Carver said. "I know you understand English. We have your file. You were born in Bosnia. Crossed enemy lines and joined the U.N. Forces during the war in Croatia. Applied for amnesty in the U.S. First you were denied, then they made you a deal – citizenship in exchange for five years in the Army. After 9/11, the Army was looking for anyone who spoke Arabic. They put you in Special Forces in Afghanistan. Then six months in Iraq. You were discharged for battle fatigue syndrome. Benefits paid crap."

"You like the sound of your own voice," Elvir said in English.

"Chime in at any time."

"My attorney's name is Thomas Myers. He lives in Fairfax."

Carver pulled a pair of dental pliers from his pocket. He had bought the pliers, along with some other medical supplies, from a subway station sale in Tokyo, where a vendor sold enamel scrapers right alongside kitchen knives. At-home dentistry struck Carver as somewhat bizarre in a westernized country. Carver had always assumed fear of the dentist was a worldwide phenomenon. The thought of an untrained family member doing it was even scarier.

"I'm going to ask you again," Carver told Elvir. "Lies cost one molar each. Ask for an attorney again, and it'll cost you one of those beautiful front incisors."

*

Eva entered the 10-digit login Colonel Madsen had given her into the computer. She was immediately launched into a video conference session. General Farrell appeared onscreen. Although they had been to dozens of Security Council meetings together, this was the first time Eva had looked him square in the face. His teeth were yellower than she remembered. The President had once said that Farrell was a hero during the 1980s invasion of Panama, but he said very little at the Security Council meetings. Mostly he seemed to be Wainewright's yes man.

"Eva!" Farrell exclaimed as if he were happy to see her.

"General."

"You look a little worse for wear."

"You really know how to charm the ladies."

"Word is you've got the brass at Fort Campbell on bended knee," he said. "They're calling you Queen Eva."

"I'd say what they call you, but the FCC might revoke my video conference privileges."

Farrell's face fell. "Madam Secretary, we're reconvening the Security Council in a few hours. We need you at Rapture Run."

Eva had reason to be suspicious. Angie Jackson was in the infirmary and she didn't know who to trust. "I'm afraid my hands are full here, General."

The General didn't hide his exasperation. "Eva, don't make me spell this out on video conference." Eva put on her best poker face. She stared straight ahead, saying nothing. "Fine," Farrell finally snapped. "You must have heard about the POTUS by now. You're next in line. We need you here with your team ASAP so we can begin the transition."

There, he had said it. They wanted to swear her in. She was going to be the next President of the United States. "General, you can imagine how that sounds. I've been completely stonewalled for two days. You can imagine how it looks from here."

"Paranoia is understandable. The truth is, we don't know who to trust. It took some time for us to clear you."

"Clear me?"

"Everyone has been re-screened. We think there's someone high up within the Pentagon working against U.S. interests. We feel you'll be safest here. My personal plane is landing at Fort Campbell as we speak to bring you to Rapture Run."

"I'm not entirely comfortable with the idea of going to a bunker that was built without Security Council authorization. I suggest we meet at the White House instead."

Farrell shook his head. "Out of the question. It's a security risk. Until we find the conspirators, the government will operate from Rapture Run."

Eva shook her head. "I've assembled a very effective Joint Operations task force right here."

"You really have no choice. Are you really going to make me send the Secret Service to extract you?"

"I haven't accepted the job."

The General didn't hesitate. "If you're not up to the job, Madam Secretary, Dex Jackson is."

She sighed. She wasn't about to concede the country to the likes of Jackson. "Very well. I'll be bringing my team."

"And another thing…We'd like you to bring Angie Jackson." Eva's poker face betrayed her. How could they know about that? "I'm sure she'd like to see her son. He's here with Dex."

The video screen cut to black. Eva ran her fingers through her hair. She picked up her desk phone and dialed the infirmary. The Doc answered. "Get the prisoner ready to travel," she said.

The Doc was silent for a moment. "Madam Secretary, I was told he was with you."

Hagerstown, Maryland
7:32 p.m.

The Greyhound Bus Station had been a hub for Hagarstown's homeless population ever since the local government started issuing free "Go West" vouchers. The vouchers, which provided free one-way bus tickets to Los Angeles, San Francisco and Phoenix, were the principal means by which Maryland sought to solve its homeless problem. The program was a miserable failure. As word of the vouchers spread, Hagarstown quickly became the hottest homeless destination on the East Coast.

Margaret Howland drove her truck into the Greyhound lot. Her headlights panned slowly across the dozens of hungry, unshaven faces. She rolled her window down. "Anybody seen a guy named Nico?"

"Hey lady," a veteran in a fungus-tainted Army uniform yelled. "I've got a bus ticket with your name on it. L.A.'s beautiful this time of year."

"God bless you," Madge called back diplomatically. The truck's headlights finally found Nico's clear-framed eyeglasses and thin lips and slight chin. He stepped out from the curb wearing ill-fitting khakis, a gray t-shirt and blue sneakers that he had found at Goodwill that afternoon. He opened the truck's passenger door and took in the sight of her. She wore the same size-fourteen floral print blouse she had worn during her last visit to the prison. Her hair was up in a bun. And as usual, she had not tweezed her eyebrows and her nails were unpainted. She was just the way Nico liked them – plain, round and unpretentious.

"I can't believe you came."

"It'll cost ya," Madge said with a wink. "Get in here."

Nico climbed into the truck. He kissed her tentatively at first. Then again, and with more confidence. She smelled like tea tree oil shampoo.

They drove wordlessly through town toward the I-81 South. Madge did not ask Nico how he happened to be out of prison some fifteen years ahead of schedule. The Lord worked in mysterious ways.

Madge was a mid-level programmer for a local Methodist Children's Hospital. Two years earlier, she had been moved by a story written in *Technology Weekly* about Nico's exploits called "Rise and Fall of an Activist Hacker." The next week, she had written him a letter that began, "Dear Mister Gold, I read about the unfortunate turn of events in your life, and would like you to know that I for one am praying for your eternal soul."

Although Nico was an atheist, he did not mind Madge's attempts to convert him to Christianity, which had never waned in the sixty-one letters and fourteen visits to the Federal Penitentiary that followed their first contact. He found her relentless devotion to faith fascinating, even comforting. He was attracted to her earnestness. And while he knew that Madge was far from the coding genius that he was, the common language of programming gave them something to talk about.

They entered the I-81 South toward Burlington. "Are you hungry?" Madge said.

"No," Nico replied, although in truth he was famished. The last thing he needed was to get recognized in some roadside diner.

Twenty miles down the road, they pulled into a truck stop. Nico waited in the pickup while Madge went inside, purchased four microwavable burritos, nuked them, and brought them out to the truck with a pair of cokes. They sat eating them in the parking lot until, having forgotten to grab napkins, Madge licked one of her chubby fingers. Nico grabbed her hand and licked her other fingers for her. One thing led to another in the expanse of the king cab's spacious back seat.

"I didn't plan that," Madge said as she buttoned up her shirt, "and I'll have to pray on it. But Jesus my savior knows that my heart's been with you for a long time. It's only the liberal justice system that's kept us apart."

A few more miles down I-81, they passed a Ulysses convoy. "Isn't it terrible what's been going on?" she said.

"Awful," Nico said. He did not elaborate. He knew that if he told Madge what had really happened – that the President was dead, and that there was no such terrorist cell in Yemen responsible for all the carnage – that she would not believe him. That's tomorrow's conversation, he thought. Enjoy tonight.

Eisenhower Building
7:35 p.m.

Speers emerged from the tunnels through the narrow portal in the Eisenhower Building's basement stairwell. The massive blast-proof door slammed behind him, and he froze. He held his breath and listened for boots, voices or gunfire. The Old Executive Building was an extension of the White House itself. It flanked the West Wing and had been renamed the Eisenhower Building decades ago, although most people still used the old name. The building had been completed in 1888 and was originally the State, War and Navy Building. Speers kept a cubicle in the West Wing for times when it was strategically important to be near the President. But on most days, he preferred to work here, where there were fewer interruptions.

Having heard nothing but the frantic booming of his own heart, Speers decided it was safe to proceed. He pulled his security badge from his pocket and swiped it on the elevator panel. The doors swung open. The elevator arrived at the third floor. Speers held the doors open. He craned his neck into the corridor to see if anyone was there.

By the look of the office, it was clear that the staff had been evacuated in a hurry. Doors were flung open. Lights were left on. Personal items – gym clothes, unused movie tickets, grocery lists – were out in plain sight. Piles of shredded paper and partially eaten breakfasts were everywhere.

Speers was famished. He could not resist a half-eaten Danish sitting on a colleague's desk. He shoved the rubbery pastry into his mouth as he made his way toward his own office.

It was a relief to see that the office had not been ransacked. He booted up his computer and unlocked his lower desk drawer, which was full of grape lollipops. He unwrapped one and popped it into his mouth. His eyes rolled back into his head as the sugar began flowing through his body.

"Curfew in twenty minutes," a voice boomed. "You have twenty minutes to get indoors. This is a zero tolerance curfew." Speers peered out the blinds and looked down on 17th Street. The voice was coming from a speaker mounted atop a Ulysses patrol vehicle.

Speers turned his attention back to his computer as his mail came online. He spotted the message he had been looking for:

> FROM: Corporal Hammond, Office of the Chairman of the Joint Chiefs of Staff
> TO: Julian Speers
> FW: RE: CONFIDENTIAL

There were two attachments. Speers clicked on the first, a document containing a series of mechanical diagrams that were annotated in Farsi. The engineering schematics were beyond him, but he switched on a Farsi-to-English translator in his browser and soon realized that he was looking at a proposal for a state-of-the-art, Iranian-built desalination plant that had been prepared for General Wainewright. Further into the document, he came upon a map of the California coast. Xs near Mendocino, Eureka and Cambria seemed to mark future desalination plant locations.

The second attachment triggered a video on a private Web server. It took Speers several seconds to recognize Angie Jackson holding a copy of yesterday's newspaper. She had the vacant look in her eyes of someone who had resigned herself to certain death. The video's sound was scratchy as she put the newspaper down and began reading from a prepared script. Speers boosted the volume on his desktop speakers.

"Yesterday," she began, "I was rescued from Chesapeake Bay. It was clear that these men had no reason to harm me."

Suddenly, the overhead lights flickered out, followed by the computer and printer. Speers went to the window, hoping it was some type of blackout. It wasn't. The streetlights in the surrounding buildings were all on.

A banging noise sounded from one of the lower floors. Speers grabbed the few pages that had come out of the printer, crammed them into a folder and escaped down the hallway just as red laser targeting beams cut through the darkness.

Escape routes were few and far between. Getting downstairs to the tunnels would be tricky. The building had several staircases, but they were probably crawling with Ulysses. Elevators were also out of the question.

His thoughts turned to the late Vice President's office in the large corner suite facing the White House's West Wing. The office featured a hand-operated dumb waiter from a bygone era that was large enough to hold an entire Thanksgiving meal. The kitchen staff used it to send a regular stream of coffee and snacks up to the office whenever the Veep was in residence.

Speers made it to the corner office and found that the dumb waiter was deployed. Good. But as the building's emergency lighting finally kicked in, he found that the contraption looked smaller than he remembered. Speers climbed in head-first and crammed his legs into the rickety platform, cursing himself for not losing the 30 pounds his doctor had prescribed last winter. Once his limbs were safely tucked in, he gripped the steel cable and began cranking himself slowly down.

His forearms were cramping by the time he arrived in the basement kitchen. He unfolded himself, wrung his hands and went once again to the tunnel entrance. He stooped and held his eye open for the retina scanner. "Access Granted," the scanner said pleasantly as the portal opened.

Once back in the tunnels, Speers allowed himself a moment to rest. It was then that he realized how much pain he was really in. His body wasn't cut out for this. His arms ached. His sinuses felt ready to burst. The balls of his feet were swollen and his socks were wet with the pus from the broken blisters on his toes and heels.

He eventually made his way through the tunnels until he came upon the portal to the Metro Center subway station. There he slipped seamlessly into the stream of passengers rushing to get home before the 8 p.m. curfew. The Blue Line to Franconia swooshed into the station.

Ulysses could not be far behind. Speers cut to the head of the line. Despite a palpable agitation among the passengers enduring a third night of martial law, nobody challenged him. In fact, his fellow commuters gave him wide berth. What was this, some show of respect? He wasn't used to being recognized on the street. Outside the Federal Buildings, he was a nobody.

When the subway pulled in and Speers glimpsed himself in the car's metallic reflection, he understood. He saw the chigger bites on his neck and head. The grass-stained shirt. The mud-caked shoes. The Albert Einstein hairdo. He smelled the mildew on his shirt. Nobody got out of his way out of respect. No. Quite the opposite.

Fort Campbell Gym

Elvir Divac writhed on the tattered brown incline weight bench. Agent Carver stood over him and clamped his dental pliers around one of Divac's rear molars. The Bosnian was close to cracking.

Torture was far from Carver's standard operating procedure. During his career with CIA, he had gladly employed psychological conditioning tactics to weaken prisoners' resolve. He had never resorted to physical torture, however, and although the Supreme Court had decided that pulling a prisoner's perfectly healthy teeth was simply called dentistry, Carver had no such illusions. What he was doing was not just morally repugnant; it was evil.

But the country was not merely suffering terrorist attacks from some foreign coalition or a few madmen. This was far more serious. Carver didn't have the luxury of time, and he was willing to do anything he had to – including hurting Elvir Divac for a while – to get to the bottom of it.

Carver gave the molar a final yank and stood with the bloody prize between the tool's pincers. Divac screamed so loud that Carver could hardly hear himself speak. "That's two," Carver said as he dropped the molar to the floor, where it bounced like a wet marble. "Just twenty-six more to go."

Divac pursed his lips, determined not to let Carver's pliers back into his mouth. Carver took hold of Divac's right nipple, squeezed and turned it to the left. He waited until Divac screamed, then jammed the pliers in and gripped a third molar. He put his knee on the prisoner's chest for leverage, and then began to tug on the tooth in earnest.

Divac muttered something that sounded like surrender. Carver pulled the pliers out and wiped the sweat from his forehead. The prisoner spit a mouthful of blood and saliva out onto his hospital gown.

Carver let him catch his breath, then asked for the third time, "Who gave you the Stingers?"

"They're going to kill me for this."

"I'll kill you too, but much, much slower."

The Bosnian spit more blood. His left cheek was puffy, pushed out by the swelling of his gums. "I was back from my third tour," he started. "They had me in Walter Reed Hospital. I applied for a visa back to Bosnia. I just wanted to go home. One day a man came. I swear I don't know his name."

"What did he look like?"

"His head was smooth…shaved. He looked like he worked out a lot. I could see his muscles even in his neck, his face. Like one of those muscle men, sort of. But he also looked a little thin. And a little sick. I don't know how to explain."

Chris Abrams, Carver thought. He seemed to be everywhere. "Why did he come see you?"

"I thought it was for the visa, but no. Instead he offered seven hundred and fifty thousand dollars."

"For what?"

"To learn a dead language. And stage a mock attack on the Secretary of Defense."

"*Mock* attack?"

"In Chesapeake Bay, yes. Secretary Jackson was to believe his life was threatened. But no one was to get hurt."

"You're lying."

Divac was insulted. "I have fifty-six kills between Bosnia, Afghanistan and Iraq. I shot down four helicopters. All my kills were by sniper rifle or Stinger Missile. Sometimes in winter weather. I ask you, how could I miss a white fishing boat on such a clear day?"

Carver heard the door. He looked up and saw Colonel Madsen. Eva was close behind him. She surveyed the bloody scene with an expression that was somewhat cold and practical.

The doctor was not so forgiving. He ran in behind her, spotted the bleeding prisoner, and pushed Carver away. "This is a war crime!" he said as he searched his medical kit for a piece of gauze. "I'll be reporting this."

But Eva had no time for it: "Doctor, get Mister Divac ready to travel. And you'll be coming too."

"Travel?" the Doc shot back. "This man has been tortured!"

"He's living, breathing proof of a conspiracy to overthrow the government," Eva said. "I'm not about to go into Rapture Run empty handed."

Washington D.C.
11:10 p.m.

Just a block away from the typically hopping Adam's Morgan nightlife, Speers crawled from a storm drain, scurried to the dark side of the street and stretched his back. The sidewalks were empty. Somewhere in the distance, machine gun fire crackled for an instant and then went silent. He eventually straightened himself and began walking cautiously toward home.

It was another hot and humid evening in the swampy Capitol city. The Chief got to his feet and made his way to the sidewalk. For the first time in years, Speers' pants were actually a little loose around his waist. He stopped to tighten his belt a notch and fell off-balance, realizing his own exhaustion. Apart from the lollipop that he salvaged from his Eisenhower Building office, he had not eaten a meal in nearly twenty-four hours, and he had eaten only sparingly in the day and evening before that.

He spotted a water fountain. It had been at least eight hours since he had taken a drink of anything. He bent over the fountain's cool stream of city-treated water and stood there a good long while to quench his thirst until his belly was so full that he felt the water sloshing inside as he began walking again.

Someone whistled. Speers looked left and saw a man with a dirty face peering out from a cardboard box. The man motioned him closer, but Speers kept his distance. "Stay out of the light," the man called out.

"They're patrolling this street every couple minutes They tried to knife me, but I got away from the bastards."

"Who?"

"Ulysses!" the man cried. "It's martial law, loser! Where've you been?"

Speers crossed to the other side of the street, where there were fewer lights. He stank of perspiration. He had been absentmindedly scratching the chigger bites on his neck, arms, legs and thighs for hours. He needed a shower and fresh clothes, and more than anything else, shoes. But the stores had long closed, and Speers reckoned it was perhaps fifteen minutes walking to his Georgetown brownstone. Problem was, his home wouldn't be any safer than his Eisenhower Building office had been.

He considered DC310, the field house where there was an entire closet full of new shoes. But any government location was fraught with its own set of risks. Besides, Ulysses' people had already been there to kill Lieutenant Flynn.

Then he thought of his neighbor, Mrs. Tenningclaus. The morning of the attacks, he had promised he'd look in on her cats. That had been Sunday. Three days ago. He hoped they hadn't clawed each other's eyes out from hunger.

He kept to the shadows until he reached his own neighborhood. He cut through a neighbor's driveway and jumped a fence into Ms. Tenningclaus' back yard. Hers was a three-story brownstone directly across from Speers' condo. He went to her back door, finding the hidden key under the rock where Ms. Tenningclaus had left it for him.

The odor of soiled kitty litter hit him instantly. The cats wailed and emerged from the shadows to rub with feverish intensity against his pant legs. They soon turned, hissing savagely when Speers tried to pet them. By the amber glow of the nightlight in the kitchen, the Chief saw that their bowls were empty. He fed them and poured some fresh milk before seeking anything for himself.

Mrs. Tenningclaus' fridge was empty except for a granola bar and a Mountain Dew. Speers took them and went upstairs and – careful not to turn on any lights – perched himself by the attic window. His own condo was directly across the street, and he watched his kitchen window closely as he ate. His windows were dark except for the faint amber hue of the stove light in his kitchen. Initially, he saw no cause for alarm. He began to yearn for his own bed, his own clothes, his own shower.

But he was patient. He chewed slowly. He drank slowly. Some three minutes later, the light in his window changed ever so slightly. To Speers' astonishment, he watched as his fridge opened. He could make out the silhouette of a man. That man is waiting to kill me, Speers thought. The Grim Reaper. And he's raiding my fridge.

Speers retreated to the safety of Ms. Tenningclaus' guest bathroom and took a long shower by candlelight. He was tired of running. But he had no choice. He couldn't stay here. He noticed a used razor sitting in an empty soap dish.

It took him fifteen minutes to erase the Van Dyke goatee he had worn since college. He then found some scissors and went to work on his hair, cutting it into short, choppy locks. He slid the shower curtain open and gazed at himself in the mirror. He didn't recognize himself.

When he was finished, he used baby powder talc from head to toe and tended to his abused feet with Aloe Vera gel and bandages. For the red welts from his chigger bites, he found calamine lotion in the medicine cabinet.

Ms. Tenningclaus' husband had died less than two years earlier, at the age of sixty-three. When Speers went to the master bedroom, he was relieved to find Mr. Tenningclaus' wardrobe still completely intact. Speers pulled on a pair of too-large Khaki chinos and cinched them tightly at the waist with a leather belt. He went commando, for he could not stand the thought of wearing a dead man's underwear. Then he donned one of Mr. Tenningclaus' classic navy polo shirts, which fit perfectly. Shoes were not an option – Mr. Tenningclaus was a size 12, two full sizes larger than his own. Stuck with the footwear he had come in with, he wrapped the beaten soles with duct tape from Mrs. Tenningclaus' hall closet.

He sat briefly on the edge of the mattress to plot his next move. His eyes burned. He closed them for a moment. That was all it took for exhaustion to overcome him. He slipped quickly into REM sleep, falling into the recurring nightmare that had haunted him for two years – a military coup in the United States that cost the President his life.

Speers' eyelids snapped open twelve minutes later. One of the cats was curled up on his chest. He petted it to confirm it was real. Then he touched his face and felt the clean shaven skin. He got up and went to the window to look across the street at his condo. The assassin had turned on the stove light and sat at the kitchen table, wearing green latex gloves, flipping through the August issue of *National Journal*.

PART IV

Over Kentucky
Wednesday 12:09 a.m.

Agent Carver felt the Gulfstream G650 bank hard to the south. They had been in the air just a few minutes. He rose from his seat and went to the cockpit entrance, where two Air Force pilots were snuggled into black leather seats, surrounded by an instrument panel and console that wrapped around them on both sides like a tightly tailored jacket. It was an impressive but cramped, womb-like enclosure that was a far cry from the roomy luxury in the main cabin. Unlike the civilian Gulfstream jets, the military version had been retrofitted with seating for two additional crew members directly behind the pilots. Carver sat and stared out the two-piece curved cockpit window at a layer of wispy clouds gleaming in the moonlight.

"Evening, gentlemen," he said. "What's our ETA?"

The co-pilot, who looked nearly as weary as Carver, turned and shook his head. "We don't even know our destination. CENTCOM is drip-feeding us new coordinates every fifteen minutes."

A hand on Carver's shoulder broke his irritation. It was O'Keefe. He could smell the sharp bite of caffeine emanating from her pores. "Eva would like to see us."

Carver turned and followed O'Keefe back through the cabin, where Elvir and Angie Jackson were both asleep in their seats. In the back of the plane, Eva and Colonel Madsen were gathered in an airborne office with an actual desk and computer.

"Sit down," Eva told them. "This is going to be a difficult conversation. I know we've all had our suspicions, but I can tell you now that they were correct. The President is dead."

The news wasn't a surprise, but Eva's composure was. "And you've been sitting on this for how long?" Carver said.

"The Chief told me this morning. But frankly, I was reluctant to believe him. He said he had only heard it secondhand. General Farrell confirmed the news about an hour ago."

O'Keefe spoke up. "So what happens now?"

"I'm next in line," Eva said with no trace of pleasure in her voice. "The Joint Chiefs have established a secure operations base at Rapture Run. They're going to swear me in."

Carver's eyes got wide. "Or at least that's what they told you."

Rapture Run

Air Force fighter pilot Alexandro Chuy Rodriquez, whose call sign was Bearcat, was led down the blue-lit corridor leading to the senior officers' quarters. He had not seen the light of day in the four weeks since he had unwittingly killed eight Ulysses soldiers in a friendly fire incident in Indonesia. Friendly fire incidents were an unfortunate reality of war, but Captain Rodriquez had hardly been without fault: he had been flying while under the influence of locally grown opium. In the weeks since the incident he had been made to describe the events over and over again, beginning with his shooting the drug into his buttocks before takeoff and ending with his air-to-ground missile slamming into an American transport.

The Ulysses MPs escorted him into Wainewright's quarters, where the General's eyes seared through him from behind the bunker's largest desk. By now Rodriquez had grown quite used to constant hostility from his fellow soldiers. He braced himself for more of the same.

General Farrell sat in a corner of the room, holding a very small computer. Rodriquez saluted out of protocol, but he did not really know who Wainewright or Farrell were. The Joint Chiefs operated from such lofty heights that they were only recognizable to soldiers that closely followed Washington politics. And after all, Rodriquez had been in the presence of Four-Star Generals before – the military seemed to have hundreds of them. He had to admit, however, that he had never seen so many decorations on anyone's uniform.

"Been a rough month for you," Wainewright began in a voice that was almost sympathetic. Rodriquez showed no emotion and, as his attorney had advised him, spoke humbly and robotically in hopes of receiving a light sentence. "I have no excuses, sir. I am ready to be held accountable for my actions."

"You know," Wainewright said softly, "my own son died in a friendly fire incident."

"I'm sorry to hear that, sir." Rodriquez waited a few seconds, but there was nothing further from Wainewright. "Interrogative, sir: Am I here to begin my court martial, sir?"

Wainewright smacked his lips. "You're here to redeem yourself." He paused to see if the Captain would bite, but there was no response except for a slight quiver of the Captain's lip. "If you do one job for me, I'll personally make sure that you never stand trial. Sound good?"

"Sir, yes sir."

"Your assignment is to shoot down a government jet."

"Interrogative, sir: a jet from which government, sir?"

"Ours."

Rodriquez paused. "May I ask why?"

"The passengers are traitors that threaten our national security."

Rodriquez' resolve wavered momentarily. He would rather have done anything than kill more friendlies. But the chance for redemption was too great. "Sir, yes sir. I'll do anything to protect my country, sir."

"Good." Wainewright looked to Farrell. "General Farrell here is now responsible for the success of this mission. You will report directly to him."

*

Deep in the bowels of the Rapture Run complex, the elevator descended to the isolation wing. Dex Jackson stepped off the elevator. Twenty cells sat along a corridor lit with blue LED lamps. A lone MP straightened himself. He recognized the Secretary of Defense and snapped to attention.

"Where's my son?" Dex snarled.

The MP took him to LeBron's cell, where the kid was curled up in fetal position on a mattress, wearing a regulation white t-shirt and underwear. He was shivering. "We acted on Corporal Hammond's orders," the MP explained. "He said the boy couldn't sleep with the soldiers. He said it was for the boy's own safety, sir."

Dex delivered a chopping blow to the MP's Adam's apple. The soldier fell to the floor, gripping his neck, struggling to get air back into his crushed windpipe. Dex opened the cell door. LeBron sat up on his elbows. For once, he was happy to see his father.

Burlington, North Carolina
12:20 a.m.

Nico was asleep by the time Madge pulled the truck into the driveway of her three-bedroom home. "Nico," she called gently. He opened his eyes, taking in the beauty of the moonlit v-neck of her plus-size floral blouse. Madge blushed, and then said, "You flatter me. Now let's hit the hay for real. It's way past my bedtime."

The living room was adorned with school photos of her nieces and nephews, as well as a life-size print of the Shroud of Turin. "You'll have to pardon the house," she said, although the house was very tidy. "I wasn't exactly expecting guests."

"I'm beat," Nico said.

"You'll be in there." She pointed to the guest bedroom, where a day bed was covered with a homemade comforter with a cowboy theme. "I know it doesn't make much sense given what happened and all, but I don't feel right about sleeping in the same bed."

"No worries," Nico said. "I get it." He actually didn't get it at all. But he had bigger things to worry about right now. His eyes were already fixed on the computer and tiny desk in the living room corner. "Uh, do you have an Internet connection?"

Madge's eyes were serious for the first time tonight. She looked at the computer, then back at Nico. "I was wondering how long you were going to be able to stay away from it."

"I don't want to make trouble," Nico said.

She kissed him on the forehead. "Go on. Use it. But if you find yourself tempted to fall back into old patterns, wake me up. I'll get up and pray with you."

Washington D.C.
1:17 a.m.

Speers crept along dark Georgetown side streets in hopes of avoiding the Ulysses patrols. He had kept his phone off for the past several hours in fear that Wainewright's people might use it to track him. But as he came within sight of the George Washington University campus, he spotted one of the last remaining public phones in the city. He went to it. He called Eva.

Eva answered right away, although the connection was shaky. "Where are you?" he said.

"At about thirty-five-thousand feet," she said. "We're on our way to Rapture Run."

"Eva, listen to me. You've got to get off that plane."

"The Joint Chiefs reached out," Eva said over the scratchy connection. "And I have a prisoner here who claims that the attack on Dex was —"

"Faked," Speers said. "I know. Corporal Hammond sent me some very illuminating items."

"I'll need the Joint Chief's assistance to get resources on this. I need to convince them in person."

"Eva, you've got it wrong. The Joint Chiefs are keeping Dex in the dark. Even now, he probably thinks his wife is dead."

Speers' words didn't compute. "Chief, I can't comment on Dex's situation, but General Farrell acknowledged that I'm next in line."

"Next in line for the cemetery, maybe." Speers looked over his shoulder as a Ulysses patrol rambled down the far end of the street. It was time to end the conversation before it got ended for him. "Eva, trust me. Just get off that plane."

Rapture Run
1:21 a.m.

The lone surviving Marine One helicopter was docked in a subterranean hangar that was concealed fifty yards below ground and built to withstand a direct hit by a ten megaton nuke. Wainewright and Farrell sat inside as a crew readied the deluxe chopper for the flight to Washington. Despite the late hour, the Generals wore full dress uniforms. In just a few hours, they would be orchestrating the most dramatic political event ever to appear on live television.

Dex Jackson and his son came to the door and peered inside the spacious cabin. "My son will be joining us," Dex said in a tone that reeked of resentment.

Wainewright looked at the boy. "Very well. Sit up front with the pilot."

The pilot started the chopper's engines. The massive hangar roof parted overhead. Cornstalks fell over the side into the hangar and were shredded into confetti as they passed through Marine One's churning rotors.

Dex took a seat in the booth opposite the Joint Chiefs and buckled himself in as the chopper rose steadily.

"Whose idea was it to put LeBron in the isolation ward?" Dex said. "At least you'd give a bum a blanket and a hot meal."

"I asked that he sleep separately for his own safety," General Farrell said.

"Well I expect the MP on duty to be court martialed."

"Consider it done," Wainewright said. He pushed a document across the table. "Your inauguration speech."

Dex flipped through the speech's first pages and pushed it back to Wainewright. "When JFK was assassinated, Johnson had the decency not to turn the passing of the torch into a spectacle." Wainewright nudged the speech back across the table. "And he spent the rest of his term running JFK's playbook."

Dex scanned the speech's first page more closely: *We gather here at the Lincoln Memorial to usher in a new era.* The idea of such a public gala still did not sit right with him. He looked up. "What about security?" he said. "The people that tried to kill me are still out there."

"Trust me," Wainewright said. "So long as you stick to the script, your life is not in danger."

Over West Virginia
1:22 a.m.

Captain Rodriquez, aka Bearcat, flew his F-35 Lightning at 35,000 feet near the Kentucky/Virginia border. He had been given the expected trajectory and altitude of the Gulfstream G650 jet, as well as the ideal intercept location. Rodriquez wondered how so much could be anticipated about the flight plan of a government jet that was supposedly full of mutinous traitors.

Bearcat was forbidden from making radio contact with any entity – airborne or terrestrial – except CENTAF, which was operating from Rapture Run. He was only to intercept the target, take it down, and return to the unnamed private airfield in rural West Virginia where he had taken off.

"Bearcat this is Escort Six," the CENTAF controller said to him over the radio. "You should register the target on your screen in four…three…two…"

Right on cue, a blip appeared on Rodriquez' radar some 20-odd miles in the distance. It was flying at 12,000 feet.

"Please confirm that the target is in range," CENTAF said. "Bearcat, do you copy?"

"Copy that, Escort Six," Rodriquez said. "Closing in for visual confirmation."

"Negative, Bearcat. The FAA has grounded all commercial aircraft. This is a CENTAF-authorized target."

Rodriquez' voice grew edgy. "Protocol for a hijacked friendly requires a visual."

"Negative, Bearcat. General Wainewright has authorized a long-range kill...Do you copy?"

*

The Gulfstream co-pilot looked nervous. He was on the radio trying to hail CENTAF. They had not received the scheduled coordinates update. It had been more than twenty minutes since their last communication. Something was wrong.

Eva and Agent Carver approached the Gulfstream's cockpit and sat in the two crew seats behind the pilots. "Where are we?" Eva demanded.

The co-pilot turned. "We just crossed into West Virginia."

The radar bleeped to announce an approaching aircraft. "Single F-35," the pilot called out. "Twenty miles out and closing fast."

Relief shot across the co-pilot's face. "Must be an escort."

"Why would they send just one?"

"That's no escort," Carver broke in as he buckled himself into the crew seat. "Does this thing have any anti-radar or anti-missile capability?"

"Sure. All the new DOD-owned Gulfstreams do."

"Crank 'em up. And take us down to a thousand feet."

The co-pilot reached for the radio. "Let me check with CENTAF once more."

There was no time to convince the pilots that their own government was trying to kill them. That would have to come later. Carver unfastened his holster, pulled out his SIG and pressed the gun metal against the back of the co-pilot's head. "Don't touch that radio."

Nothing commanded obedience quite like a drawn weapon. The co-pilot crossed his heart as the plane began a rapid descent. "Kill the running lights," Carver said. While Carver had never taken flying lessons, he had sat through enough closed security briefings to know what happened in battle once a pilot's radar failed him. He would try to establish a visual. "Kill the running lights," he demanded.

An eerie howl arose from the fuselage as the plane began its plunge and disappeared into the night sky.

Marine One
2:08 a.m.

They were less than fifteen minutes from Washington, where they planned to survey inauguration preparations on the National Mall. General Wainewright sat quietly annotating a touch-screen map of the D.C. area. Several major security enhancements would be needed after the inauguration. In particular, he was worried about the growing number of privately-owned submarines on the market. It would be so easy for the Allied Jihad to park one 50 miles offshore and launch a dirty bomb into the Capitol. He planned to grant Ulysses a massive contract to install a state-of-the-art undersea detection network around New York and Washington. It was just one of many similar projects. There was so much that had been neglected during the last administration. It might take a decade or more of military control to truly make the country safe again.

He sensed he was being watched. He turned and saw General Farrell's eyes on him. Farrell was holding a small computer, and his eyes looked suddenly hollow. Something was wrong. "What is it?" Wainewright snapped.

"Eva's plane," Farrell began. His droopy eyes drifted downward as he completed his thought: "They disappeared from radar. We don't have a visual confirmation, but we expect to find wreckage."

Wainewright knew he had just been lied to. Or at least there was more to the story than Farrell was letting on. Wainewright had realized from the start that his Number Two was far from the most courageous man in the military, but he could not tolerate lies. He resolved to contact Rapture Run to get more details. As for Farrell, he would deal with him later. Today was not a time to make rash decisions about senior personnel.

Marine One's videoconference system hummed. The words CAPTAIN JAMES WHITE: DO YOU ACCEPT? appeared on the wall-mounted monitor. Wainewright sighed and accepted the session. Captain White's tan face appeared onscreen. White was Captain of the Carrier Strike Group U.S.S. Ronald Reagan, the youngest CSG Captain in recent history.

"Captain White," the Chairman growled, "this is highly irregular. You report directly to Admiral Bennington. You've got no business hailing this aircraft. I'd like to know who at the Pentagon put you through."

White proceeded reluctantly. "Sir, I apologize. No disrespect to the Admiral is meant. But I have an emergency situation and I have been unable to reach him."

"Go on."

"We're tracking five divisions of Iranian armor on the Israeli-Syrian border. All hell's raining down from Southern Lebanon. The U.S.S. Reagan is standing by to begin Operation Wailing Wall, and –"

"Operation Wailing Wall is cancelled," Wainewright said. "Direct the entire strike group to move out to international waters."

White couldn't believe what he was hearing. "General, as the POTUS must be fully aware, our NATO pact dictates that an attack on one member is an attack on all."

"Move away from the war zone, Captain."

"With all due respect," White said, "If we're defying NATO, shouldn't the POTUS announce it publicly?"

Wainewright's face flushed red. Had the Captain not been two oceans and thousands of miles away, he might have used his fists to get his point across. "Fact: I am the Chairman of the Joint Chiefs of Staff. Fact: I am temporary Commander-in-Chief of the Armed Forces during this crisis. Fact: We are at war, and as such, I am ordering you to take orders as directed, upon penalty of death."

Captain White's disconcerted stare froze onscreen for a full second before the monitor cut to black.

The Mediterranean

The U.S.S. Ronald Reagan floated in the middle of a vast Carrier Strike Group 14 miles off the coast of Israel. The stench of burning oil mingled with the salty Mediterranean air, and the seamen of the U.S.S. Ronald Reagan had been suited up and waiting for the order to engage since last night. At 0900 hours local time, two fighter pilots had gone to the bridge demanding to know why Captain White would not give the order to attack. The Captain refused to see them.

Three dozen carrier pilots sat on the flight deck, most squatting on their helmets, watching the pyrotechnics display along the Israeli coast as Syrian and Iranian jets dropped ordnance directly into civilian areas. Rows of F-18 Hornets queued for takeoff, each fitted with AGM-84 Harpoon air-to-surface missiles for enemy tanks, as well as AIM-120s for air-to-air combat.

It was the ease with which the enemy planes hit Israeli targets that surprised and disturbed the sidelined American pilots. While the Israeli Air Force was equipped with aging F-16 Fighting Falcons, the Iranians were thought to have only a handful of Russian-made MIGs scattered amongst the hundreds of ancient American-made F-5s and F-14 Tomcats given to them in the 1970s when the U.S. armed them to fight Saddam Hussein's Iraq. The intelligence was dead wrong. The IAF had its hands full fending off the Iranian armored battalions pushing through the Holy Land to the east and recent acquisitions from China and Russia had brought Syria and Iran into the modern age. Of particular usefulness to the Iranians were dozens of new lightweight, radar-evading MIGs that were designed to emulate a crashed F-117 that the Russians had fished out of a Venezuelan jungle.

On the carrier's bridge, some 50 feet above the flight deck, Captain White raised his binoculars to take a last look at the Israeli coast's crumbling majesty. It wouldn't be long until black smoke rising up from the cities fully obscured his view. Nearby, a Hebrew translator sat with headphones on, listening to Israeli military air traffic controllers as they coordinated the counterattack.

The translator took off his headphones. "Sir," he said, scratching his neck, "the Israeli planes have been ordered to abandon ground targets. They're focusing on the enemy MIGs attacking Haifa."

The Captain heard the Ensign's boots come up behind him.

"Captain," he said, "The pilots asked me again –"

"No," the Captain said. "I already went over the Admiral's head. What part of *penalty of death* don't you understand?"

Just as soon as he said it, the phone chirped the pre-programmed ring tone – four bars of Wagner's Flying Dutchman concerto – of the Admiral of the Navy. Out of habit, the Captain's heels snapped together and his posture straightened as he answered.

"Yes Admiral," he said into the receiver. He listened for a moment as the Admiral chewed him out for going over his head and contacting the Chairman directly. Then he said again, "Yes Admiral," and hung up.

"Sir?" the Ensign said.

Captain White kept his gaze on the erupting coastline. "We're moving out to international waters. Tell the crew."

The Ensign was aghast. He flinched as a series of cluster bombs fell on a coastal village that, from this distance, sounded like a string of erupting firecrackers. "Sir," he said, "I got relatives over there. All my neighbors back in L.A. got people over there."

Being privy to far more intelligence than his men, the Captain knew the situation was far more dire than the Ensign even knew. Iranians and Syrians were attacking from the northeastern front. Palestinians were coming in from the east and south. Hezbollah agents were everywhere. Without U.S. support, he gave the nation of Israel three days max.

Washington D.C.
2:45 a.m.

Speers surfaced from the tunnels underneath Arlington Station like some artful rodent that kept cheating death. There was no activity in the station. The last trains had stopped running hours earlier under the disquieting spell of martial law. The Chief stole across the vacant platform, hopped the turnstile and made his way, slowly, silently, up the motionless escalator. As he crept out onto Memorial Drive, he found the humidity absolutely overpowering. The night air felt textured and heavy as it flowed into his body. But there were no Ulysses patrols in sight, and that was a relief. The streets were empty of pedestrians or cars, and there was virtually no noise except for the nagging buzz of mosquitoes flitting around his head.

Up Memorial Drive, he eyed the rolling green hills of the Arlington Cemetery. Unending rows of white tombstones glowed brilliantly under soft yellow lights. He looked over his shoulder as he walked up the gentle slope. The Arlington hillsides had a sweeping view of the Capitol. A mile across the Potomac River was the National Mall, a majestic two-mile stretch of green space that hosted the Lincoln Memorial, the Korean, Vietnam and World War II memorials, the Reflecting Pool, the Washington Monument, and at the far end, Congress itself. Across the Potomac and to the southeast was the massive Pentagon.

But he was not here to admire the view. He was here to hide. Out of respect for the nation's dead, Arlington Cemetery was one of the only places in the D.C. area without NSA-controlled surveillance cameras. And as Speers had expected, the guard booths at the cemetery gates were empty. The Army MPs who had once guarded Arlington had long ago been replaced by civilian security guards who were no doubt sequestered at home under martial law.

Speers scaled the eight-foot cemetery gates with some difficulty, huffing and puffing as he lifted himself high enough to drape his right leg over the top. The leg of his pants caught at the hemline, tearing as he pulled the rest of his body onto the other side. He crossed himself as he walked past the first rows of identical white tombstones in Section 26.

Over the past three years, Speers had taken it upon himself to know every nook and cranny of the cemetery. Not because he was morbid, but rather because he had, after the Santa Monica bombing, been tasked with overseeing the Administration's disaster evacuation planning.

He had first requested each previous administration's disaster preparedness plans from the National Archives. He'd expected five or ten records, beginning with the Cold War administrations. Instead he received thirty-seven such plans, dating back to 1811, when the primary national threats were considered to be British invasion, slave uprisings, plague and fire. Of those, only the British invasion had actually come to pass, during the War of 1812. As Speers learned, the hills where Arlington Cemetery now stood had often figured big in those plans.

Before Arlington had been formally turned into a National Cemetery, the hill had been the strategic highpoint of the Capitol and the Potomac region. It had been settled by a long line of military men descending directly from George Washington. Arlington House, the stately Greek-revival mansion on the cemetery's hilltop, had been built by President George Washington's grandson, George Washington Parke Custis. Custis had positioned himself as a pacifist, only to find himself firing cannons at the British before they eventually swarmed into the Capitol in 1814. Two decades later, in 1831, Custis' daughter married General Robert E. Lee, who lived in the home for thirty-years before the outbreak of the Civil War.

During his research, Speers had seen copies of letters from Union spies claiming that Lee had designs on defending Arlington House at the outset of the Civil War. Lee apparently envisioned a massive battle in northern Virginia, knowing the steep hill would have been an excellent firing position for his cannons upon the Union Army. Lee set his staff to building escape tunnels below the wine cellar in the event that they were overrun. It was soon evident that the Confederate Army would not be able to mount a defensive posture in time, and as Union forces began gathering in Washington, Lee resigned his post and set off for Richmond, where he assumed command of the Confederate Army. Upon Lee's departure, Lincoln directed General George McClellan to inhabit Arlington House with a Federal staff, setting up cannon positions on the hillsides overlooking Virginia. Three years later, in 1864, Union soldiers had been buried just outside Arlington House's front door. Speers tried to imagine Lee's anguish upon learning that enemy dead were buried in his own front yard.

In 1952, General Eisenhower's administration, fearing a Soviet attack, devised the elaborate labyrinth of subterranean tunnels beneath the Capitol, including one from beneath the West Wing to an underwater port in the Potomac, where a Polaris submarine manned by the Naval Administrative Unit would whisk Eisenhower out to the relative safety of the Atlantic and chart a course for London. In the event that the Potomac might be blockaded by Soviet warships, the CIA's Plan B involved burrowing a tunnel beneath the Lincoln Memorial, underneath the Potomac, and linking to one of General Lee's original tunnels underneath Arlington House, where Eisenhower could theoretically escape into the Virginian suburbs. Speers had himself written Lee's tunnel system into the current administration's evacuation plans, receiving in return a budget of two hundred thousand dollars to install the new retina scanners on each of the twenty-two tunnel entrances in D.C., Arlington and Silver Springs.

Now the drone of a low-flying helicopter cut through the otherwise silent evening. The memory of Dobb's final moments in West Virginia was all too recent. Speers crouched behind a hedgerow.

He could hardly believe his eyes when the ghost ship flew directly overhead. The VH-71 Kestrel skimmed the Arlington Hills at about 90 miles per hour, and Speers, who had often been a Marine One passenger, recognized the helicopter's unmistakable profile against the night sky.

His hands balled up into fists as he watched the Kestrel land between the Lincoln Memorial and the Reflecting Pool. The thought of someone other than the President requisitioning Marine One for personal use was maddening.

A fleet of vehicles pulled around the National Mall. They looked like Ulysses Bradleys, but it was hard to tell from this distance. Soldiers scrambled from the vehicles and began setting up a security perimeter.

Speers got to his feet again. His exhaustion was all-consuming, but so too was his curiosity. He would have to take a closer look.

*

A homeless couple munched potato chips and leaned against one of the Lincoln Memorial's 38 fluted columns. Behind them, the nineteen-foot, 175-ton white marble statue that deified Abraham Lincoln was surrounded by dozens of homeless families. The luckiest of them were in tents that had been supplied by the National Park Service. The less lucky squatted on blankets donated by a local shelter.

On the mall below, the convoy of Bradley personnel carriers four-wheeled across the grass. In the middle of the 2000-foot long Reflecting Pool, Ulysses contractors erected enormous scaffolding.

The VH-71 Kestrel came in low and loud over the Lincoln Memorial and touched down in the narrow strip between the steps and the Reflecting Pool, sending miniature tidal waves across the shallow water. Ulysses troops scrambled out of the Bradleys and formed two receiving lines. The soldiers saluted as General Wainewright, General Farrell, Dex Jackson and his son LeBron exited the chopper.

The entourage made its way to the base of the Memorial, where two Secret Service agents escorted Dex and LeBron into a waiting car. Wainewright and Farrell, with soldiers in tow, marched up the ninety-eight steps to the top. The cadence of stomping boots gradually woke the hordes sleeping near Lincoln's throne.

As he finally reached the top, Wainewright found himself winded and grumpier than usual. There he came face-to-face with a Forest Service employee who failed to salute. "What's all this?" Wainewright snarled.

"This is what martial law looks like," the Forest Service employee said as he gestured at the dozens of families behind him. "Last night your mercenaries shot a homeless family of four right over there on Pennsylvania Avenue. They're all dead. Even the two kids."

"The eight o' clock curfew is not complicated," Wainewright said. "We broadcast the rules in seven languages."

"The shelters were full," the Forest Service employee explained. He gestured toward the people gathered around Lincoln's statue. "We had to put these people somewhere."

"Cram 'em into Roosevelt's memorial," Wainewright said, nodding in the direction of the far humbler monument to President Franklin Delano Roosevelt in the distance. "This one is reserved."

*

A black armored SUV pulled up to 1401 Pennsylvania Avenue, where two Ulysses MPs stood with loaded M4s at the front entrance to the Willard Hotel. The taller of the two MPs stepped forward to open the rear door. Dex and LeBron Jackson exited the SUV as the soldiers all but shouted, "Good evening, Mister Secretary, sir!" Dex put his hand in the small of LeBron's back and ushered him past the MPs without so much as looking them in the face. They had no bags except for a single military issue duffel.

For the past 150 years, it had often been said that the Willard Hotel was the nation's actual seat of power. An easy walk to the White House, the hotel had long been the de facto lodging for visiting heads of state. Abraham Lincoln himself stayed there – under tight security – in the days before his inauguration, as death threats poured in from pro-slavery Southerners.

The Willard's lobby, with its high ceilings and gilded crown moldings, was one of Dex's regular haunts. He had taken to meeting foreign dignitaries in its lounge, where Ulysses Grant had enjoyed cigars and cognac.

But there was no time for leisurely pleasures tonight. The Secret Service agents hurried him and LeBron through the lounge and past the bar, where a large flat screen TV broadcasted CNN. Dex broke away and entered the lounge to see what was on television. It'd been three days since he'd seen any news that wasn't filtered by Wainewright's screeners.

A crowd of tense-looking hotel guests stood around with cocktails as the CNN anchor remarked, *"Next we'll show you how local volunteers are pitching in to save animals displaced by the Monroe bombing."*

"What is this Mickey Mouse feel good crap?" someone said. "Turn on the BBC."

The barman switched to the BBC, where the screen filled with images of the war zone developing in Eastern Galilee. The anchor read from a teleprompter *"Our correspondents in Jerusalem are seeing a heavy barrage of incoming Iranian artillery. The Israeli government is calling for the U.S. to honor the terms of its NATO alliance, but the American government has yet to respond."*

The Secret Service Agent tapped Dex on the shoulder. "Mister Secretary." Dex didn't budge. "Mister Secretary, we need to move."

The TV suddenly reverted to CNN's feel-good animal story. The crowd glared at the barman, who threw up his hands. "Don't look at me," he said. "I didn't even change the channel."

"Mister Secretary," the guard intoned. "For your sake, sir, let's go."

Dex and LeBron followed the security detail to the elevators. Inside, the senior agent pushed the fourth floor button.

"Top floor," Dex corrected him. "The Presidential Suite's on the top floor."

"You are correct, Mister Secretary, sir. But General Wainewright has reserved the Presidential Suite for himself, sir."

Dex swallowed his pride and adjourned to the fourth floor hallway, where another member of the detail held the room door open. It was a junior executive suite with a single bedroom and a small kitchenette. "You still have time to catch a few winks before the inauguration, sir. We'll be outside if you need anything."

The door closed. Dex and LeBron were alone together for the first time in months. Neither one looked at the other. LeBron went straight to the TV and flipped it on, searching for the BBC. It was nowhere to be found. The CNN broadcast was on every channel.

"What's going on?" LeBron asked his father.

"It's one of the little improvements General Wainewright has in mind for the country," Dex said. "It's called state-run TV."

*

All was clear at the Jefferson Memorial, where two National Guardsmen reclined near a Patriot missile battery, smoking unfiltered cigarettes and listening to club remixes of mariachi classics. Every fifteen minutes, their unit commander would check in over the radio –

speaking only in Spanish – to make sure they were still awake.

Speers crept up the back steps of the neo-classical monument toward a row of public telescopes with views overlooking the National Mall. He popped a quarter into one of the telescopes and focused in on several hundred people leaving the Lincoln Memorial. It would have been an odd sight on any night, but it was especially curious during martial law. The telescope's magnification told the story – Ulysses was marching a horde of homeless people toward the Roosevelt Memorial.

The Chief turned the scope back to the Mall, where two Ulysses units were unfurling massive rolls of temporary fencing. Behind them, more Ulysses soldiers propped up the eight-foot fencing and sledge-hammered posts into the ground. It looked as if they were attempting to seal off an area stretching from the Lincoln Memorial halfway to the Washington Monument and the World War II Memorial.

Further up the Mall, Speers made out four Ulysses soldiers carrying what looked like a hefty wooden box across the mall toward the Lincoln Memorial. It appeared to be made of dark wood and resembled a casket, only shorter. He watched patiently as the soldiers made their way along the footpath that skirted the Korean War monument, near the edge of the Reflecting Pool, and stood the wooden cabinet on its end at the foot of the Lincoln steps. He knew he'd seen it before, but couldn't place it. He wracked his exhausted brain for the memory.

He sat down and took several deep breaths. He rubbed the top of his ears between his fingertips, an exercise that his mother had taught him as a child to improve concentration. Three minutes later, he felt the memory returning like the distant smell of home cooking. He hopped back up to the telescope and watched as the soldiers struggled to get the cabinet up the memorial steps. Speers himself had stood not ten feet from the big hunk of wood. But that had been at congress, not at the Lincoln Memorial. Of course! It was the podium. The Inaugural Podium.

The Joint Chiefs were not only going to swear in their new puppet, they would wrap him in Lincoln's legacy and broadcast it on live TV.

He powered up his phone. He had to talk to Agent Carver. There had to be some way to stop this.

Over Rural Pennsylvania

The Gulfstream flew just above the treetops without running lights or radio. The plane let out a violent shudder. Eva grabbed Carver's forearm.

Agent Carver and Eva sat in the cabin behind the pilots as they headed due north. The others were in the main cabin. They had not decided where they were going, only that they needed to get as far from Rapture Run as possible and land in a safe location far from Wainewright's reach.

"Your nails," Carver said as Eva's grip on his arm began to hurt. She pulled away.

Carver imagined for a moment that it was O'Keefe sitting next to him. He would welcome her nails digging into his arms, he decided. To the point of bleeding. He wanted to feel her presence. Even if it hurt.

As for Eva, he did not even know how to address her. Madam Secretary no longer seemed to fit. Less than three days ago he had regarded her as a merely competent Treasury Secretary whose real power was in her private relationship with the President. He still found it hard to fathom that she, by all rights, should now be the Commander-in-Chief. But there was no doubt in Carver's mind that she was the right choice. Better an underprepared Treasury Secretary than some puppet appointed by the military.

Carver turned on his phone for exactly ten seconds, just long enough to download seventeen new messages. Sixteen were from former CIA colleagues, whom he automatically ignored –anyone at the agency could be compromised. But the last message was from Julian Speers. It read: IF YOU LOVE YOUR COUNTRY MEET ME IN SECTION 26 @ 0500.

Carver understood the second part of the thinly coded message perfectly – that Speers would be waiting for them in Section 26, the area of Arlington Cemetery where Union soldiers were buried near Arlington House, at 5 a.m. It was one of the few places in the Capitol that wasn't teeming with surveillance videos. As for the first part of the message, Carver could only guess that the window to save the country from military rule was closing fast.

He turned to Eva as the turbulence abated. "It's time to make a decision. Do we want to survive? Or do we want to retake control of the country?"

"I want both."

"Unlikely."

"I don't see it that way," Eva said. "We could get to Canada. Go to the media. Use international pressure to force the Joint Chiefs to relinquish power."

Carver smiled condescendingly. "The Joint Chiefs will never own up to it. They'll control Dex quietly. He'll be the face. They'll be the brains."

"I'll go to the media and tell my story."

"You won't live long enough to collect the advance on your autobiography. The Canadians will never be able to protect you from Ulysses."

"Your pessimism isn't helping."

"It's realism. Wake up. Even if they can't get to you physically, you've made it easy for them to completely discredit you."

"What are you suggesting?"

"Your inappropriate relationship with President Hatch makes you an easy target."

Eva turned red. Her voice quivered. "You're over the line, Agent Carver."

"They'll take every opportunity to depict you as the dead President's power-hungry mistress who would say anything to get back into the White House. They'll leak rumors that you ordered his assassination. They'll hire some hack to make a movie about it. And they'll stay on message until the entire world believes it."

Tears streamed down. "Okay, asshole. So we're doomed? Is that it?"

"No. We have one chance."

"And what would that be?"

"Join up with Dex Jackson."

Eva laughed darkly. "Dex and I hardly look at each other at NSA meetings. What makes you think he'd even take my call?"

"We have his wife."

Washington D.C.
4:10 a.m.

Speers arose from the tunnels beneath the Eisenhower Building, scurried across Pennsylvania Avenue and into the alley behind the Willard Hotel. He ducked behind a garbage dumpster that smelled like two-day-old shellfish. Soon a man in a cook's uniform popped out the service entrance. He was yammering on a cell phone. *"If Linda doesn't like the fact that we're seeing each other, then she can move out as far as I'm concerned."* He propped open the door with an empty wine bottle, then ambled down the alley as he talked.

Once the man was out of earshot, Speers slipped behind him and into the open Willard Hotel kitchen. A startled chef looked up and yelled "Security! Security!"

"Calm down!" Speers cried. "I'm with the Administration!" He flashed his White House credentials, but with his hair cut and beard shaved, and dressed in Mr. Tenningclaus' ill-fitting clothes, he looked nothing like the man in his Federal ID photo. The chef screamed again and banged a large pot with a soup ladle.

A Secret Service agent in a black suit entered with his weapon drawn. Speers closed his eyes and waited for the bullet to come.

"It's okay," Speers heard a familiar voice tell the cook. "Calm down. This guy is who he says he is. I got this handled."

The mountainous Special Agent Hector Rios took Speers by the arm and pulled him roughly into a walk-in freezer. As usual, Rios was immaculately put together. His uniform was tailored to a tee, he was freshly shaved and his hair was slicked back tight atop his scalp. The circles under his eyes told another story. That and his hands. They were trembling.

"Julian," he said, "I've got orders to use deadly force on your ass."

Speers broke away from Rios' grip and smoothed his shirt sleeve. "And you think that's reasonable?"

Rios shook his head. "I get orders, not explanations."

"You don't want to hear them."

"Don't feed me that line, Chief! I haven't heard from First Team in three days. Went up to Camp David myself but Ulysses won't let anyone near it. I'm taking orders from some assistant to the Joint Chiefs now. What the hell is going on?"

"The President is dead."

Rios spun around once on his heels and punched a side of frozen beef hanging from the ceiling. "I knew it! I *knew* it, man!"

"We don't have much time. Trust me when I say that more people will die unless you get me in to see Dex Jackson."

Rios, still reeling from the news, shook his massive head. "Doesn't make any sense." His thoughts turned to the men he gunned down on Martha's Vineyard. The smell of gunpowder was still fresh in his senses.

"Hector, did you hear me? I need to see Dex."

The frozen beef swung into the freezer sidewall as Rios pummeled it once more. "There's a half dozen agents between the kitchen and his room."

"Then you'll have to bring Dex to me."

*

Jack McClellan, the graying agent who stood on watch outside Dex's Willard Hotel suite, was less than a year from retirement. He had survived four administrations. He had also survived a gunshot from a would-be assailant during George W. Bush's presidency. The failed assassination attempt never made the press, thanks to media suppression from the CIA.

For a while after the incident, McClellan had been taken off security detail because there were questions about his ability to shake symptoms of post-traumatic stress disorder. He'd only made it back to the POTUS rotation this year. Even so, it was more of a retirement present. The other agents were careful never to leave him alone on duty.

Over the past three days, Agent McClellan's worst fears were all coming back to him. First, the high-level assassinations. Then that sketchy pre-recorded video of the President. Then the rumor that First Team hadn't reported in. A buddy guarding some high value targets at the Raven Rock bunker had told him off the record that POTUS had never showed there. Beyond spooky.

His earpiece crackled. "Agent Rios coming up."

The elevator tone sounded and the doors swooshed open. Agent Rios stepped out the floor pushing a room service cart full of covered trays.

"What," McClellan said, "Secret Service delivers food now? Where's the room service guy?"

"I was told no visitors." Although Rios was technically McClellan's boss, the elder agent didn't always treat him with appropriate respect. For the most part, Rios allowed McClellan his ego. He had earned it.

McClellan lifted one of the platters and regarded a plate of Maryland crab cakes. He locked back at Rios and shook his head in disbelief.

"I took a bullet for Bush Forty-Three," he said, "and now they expect me to be an errand boy? I refuse to take this crap."

"Take a break," Rios said. "I'll do it."

Agent Rios knocked on the suite door and stood directly in front of the peephole so that Secretary Jackson would recognize him. Rios pushed the cart past Agent McClellan, then past Dex, who was clad in a white bathrobe, and closed the door behind him.

"We didn't order room service," Dex said as he gazed up at the six-foot-ten secret service agent. LeBron slept behind him on the couch in front of the TV.

"If you'll please just sign this," Rios said. He took the black folder from the cart and presented the check. Dex pulled his reading glasses from his bathrobe pocket and saw the hand-scrawled note: "YOUR WIFE IS ALIVE." He looked at Rios over the eyeglass frames. His pupils darted from side to side like fidgety tadpoles. He re-read the note. YOUR WIFE IS ALIVE.

Dex went to the TV and turned it up loud. LeBron squirmed in his sleep, but did not wake.

"What's the meaning of this?" Dex whispered.

"Someone important knows where your wife is," Rios said. "I can take you to her."

Dex studied Rios' face before answering. "What would happen if I picked up the phone right now and asked General Wainewright about this?"

"You'd never know peace," Rios said. "You'd always wonder about Angie."

The would-be President couldn't hide his feelings. He was about to become the centerpiece of something that was far more sinister than he had even imagined. He was becoming acutely aware of the fact that he still didn't know the rules of the game or even who all the players were. He cast a worried glance at LeBron.

"Get your son dressed," Rios warned. "He's not safe here."

Over Northern Virginia
4:50 a.m.

The first hint of purple sunlight appeared through the Gulfstream's cockpit windows. The porch lights and streetlights of D.C.'s bedroom communities twinkled like constellations not 500 feet below the aircraft. It had taken some convincing, but the pilots had come to believe Carver's story that they had been targeted by CENTAF. Until now, they had stuck to Carver's orders to fly at treetop level, under radio silence and without running lights.

But radio silence also meant no contact with air traffic control. They weren't cleared to land at any airport – military, federal or civilian. The copilot turned in his seat to face Eva and Carver. "We're low on fuel," he said. "I've gotta radio in."

"No radio," Carver replied.

"You don't get it," the copilot said. "This is the Capitol we're talking about. The airports are surrounded by SAM installations. If we're not careful we'll get an ass full of Patriot missile."

Carver maintained his composure. "No. We need another option."

The copilot pulled at his hair and thought for a moment. "There's a small private airstrip near Valley Forge. My kid got his license there. With a little luck we could —"

"Too far," Carver said. "We need to get our team into the D.C. area immediately."

The pilot spoke up without taking his eyes or hands off the controls. "Not many cars on the beltway this time of morning."

The copilot shot him a dirty look. "Don't be ridiculous."

"I spent two years putting F-18s down on the U.S.S. Carl Vinson."

"Stop."

"That boat's just one hundred thirty-four feet wide. Runway couldn't have been wider than two freeway lanes. Floating, no less."

The pilot was for real. Carver looked to Eva. "What do you say?"

"I think we'll qualify as a carpool," she quipped.

The copilot began to recite Psalm 23 as the plane slowed and turned northeast. "Yea, though I walk through the valley of the shadow of death, I will fear no evil: for Thou art with me; Thy rod and Thy staff, they comfort me..."

They came in so low over Alexandria that Carver could see the face of a woman getting into her car for the morning commute. The Gulfstream jet skimmed the telephone poles as it came in over the I-495, the rumble of its engines triggering car alarms. It extended its landing gear as the first sight of light pre-dawn freeway traffic came into view.

Eva and Carver bent over in their seats with their heads between their knees, bracing for a hard landing. The co-pilot's recitations grew louder: "...Thou preparest a table before me in the presence of mine enemies; Thou annointest my head with oil; My cup runneth over." He stopped abruptly as he saw three economy-size sedans merge onto the otherwise wide-open freeway ahead of them. "Oh God!" he said. "Pull up and re-approach."

"Negative," the pilot answered. "We won't get a second chance."

The landing gear hit the asphalt hard. The sedans careened to either side of the freeway. The Gulfstream's wing flaps snapped to 90-degree angles as the aircraft braked, skidding across the median and into the path of two oncoming cars. The left wing dipped as they entered the wide, grassy median, clipping the windshield of an oncoming truck and slicing the cab clean off. The Gulfstream's left landing gear snapped on the uneven ground, sending the plane sliding in a shower of white sparks.

The grinding roar of metal on asphalt slowly petered out. The pungent odor of jet fuel filled the main cabin, snapping Agent O'Keefe alert. Pink hues of sunrise filtered into the cabin through smashed passenger windows.

Beside her, Angie's head was cocked back against her seat. Her eyes were shut and her hair was streaked with blood. O'Keefe slowly pushed the bangs back. There were no abrasions. Angie's eyes flapped open and locked with hers. She was alive. The blood belonged to someone else.

O'Keefe unbuckled her seatbelt and got shakily to her feet. Several chunks of scalp were blown across the seatbacks in the row in front of her. Crimson droplets were spattered on the cabin ceiling. She walked two rows forward and found herself gazing into the top of Elvir Divac's skull. A seatback tray had sheared it open like a watermelon.

In the window seat, the doctor's body slumped sideways. His lifeless eyes gazed skyward and the window was a smear of matted blood and hair. One row up, O'Keefe found Colonel Madsen. His eyes were closed. O'Keefe put her index and middle fingers on his neck, hoping for a pulse. His head tipped sideways, resting at an unnatural 90-degree angle atop his shoulders.

She feared more carnage as she wobbled on shaky knees toward the cockpit. Her fears were realized. From behind, she saw the pilots' arms hanging limply at his sides, elbow joints jutting out his blood-soaked shirt sleeves in a horrific compound fracture. Both pilots' faces were smashed grotesquely into the instrument panel.

An orange-tanned arm stretched out into view. O'Keefe recognized it as Eva's. She was alive.

There was one more passenger to account for. Agent Carver had been seated adjacent to Eva. O'Keefe entered the cockpit, afraid of what she might find next. As she rounded the corner, she found him standing in the corner of the cockpit, peering out a tiny clear prism of smashed window. A traffic chopper was hovering overhead.

"Smile," Carver said to his fellow survivors. "We're on TV."

The Willard Hotel

The Iranian Ambassador entered the Presidential Suite wearing a new black silk suit that would have been more appropriate in a European disco. He shook Wainewright's hand and wasted no time in getting to the point. "I could not risk telephone communications," he said with precise enunciation. "I received a call yesterday from your Treasury Secretary."

"Don't worry about her," Wainewright gruffed.

"But you leave me no choice. First, you assured me she would be dead by now. Second, the President obviously told her about the Camp David meeting despite my request for confidentiality. Now she is twice as dangerous."

Wainewright was distracted. The timing of so many things – including the inauguration and shifting of Ulysses forces to additional key posts – was dependent on the carefully timed release of influential information. He glanced at the muted TV, eager to see whether his personal press corp had managed to maintain control over the network news feed.

The Ambassador did not like to be ignored. "General, did you hear me?"

Wainewright's attention returned to the Ambassador. "You won't be hearing from Eva Hudson again."

"I'm delighted to hear that. As expected, NATO is calling on us to stop our invasion of Israel. We are prepared to justify ourselves in this cause, as always, but we cannot afford speculation that there is any connection with the American President's death."

"You hope for too much," Wainewright said. "Fact: Iran's an easy scapegoat for the world community. Fact: there will be rumors of your involvement no matter how good we are. We have to stick to our assertion that this was the work of the Allied Jihad."

The Ambassador's gaze fell upon the dresser, where Lincoln's opera glasses sat on a folded white handkerchief. "I have an eye for antiques," he said. "Mid-nineteenth century, yes?"

General Wainewright had never before passed up an opportunity to explain about his prized keepsake, but he had no time for it now. "What about the mountain campaign?" Wainewright said. In exchange for Wainewright's promise to abandon its pact to defend Israel, the Iranians had promised that elite Iranian troops would invade and destroy Allied Jihad bases in Afpack. Iran had been funding Allied Jihad operations for years, but their offspring had spiraled out of control. Nevertheless, the Allied Jihad were dependent on supplies from Iran, and the Iranians were in a unique position to squash their Afpak capabilities once and for all.

"We have already destroyed nine Allied Jihad camps," the Ambassador confirmed. "This is only the beginning. Within one week, Israel will be pushed into the sea. And by November, any Allied Jihad camps in the mountains will be exterminated and we will have accounted for ninety percent of its leadership."

Wainewright glanced at the TV and saw imagery from a live traffic cam aboard a network helicopter. The titles on the screen read LIVE FROM I-495. He grabbed the remote control and turned up the volume.

"Beltway commuters," the TV anchor said, *"you may want to think about telecommuting today. We are looking at live footage from our eye in the sky traffic cam. This apparently happened just moments ago. We have what appears to be a Gulfstream jet down on the Beltway. Yes, you heard me. A plane crash-landed on the 495 just minutes ago."*

Wainewright's phone rang. It was Farrell. "We have a situation," he said frantically.

"I'm watching it now."

Farrell hesitated. "That's only the half of it. Our people just went to wake up Dex. He's not in his room."

The Beltway

Carver stood in the middle of I-495 as a TV news traffic chopper hovered overhead. Adrenaline blocked the pain from the fractured collarbone he had suffered during the crash. Behind him, O'Keefe and Eva teamed up to pull Angie Jackson from the Gulfstream's fuselage. Her eyes were vacant and she hadn't uttered a word since the crash. She was ambulatory, but they were going to have to go at her pace.

They needed a car. It took Carver only a few seconds to spot a prospect: a middle-aged government worker in a navy blue Ford economy car that had slowed down to rubberneck. He was an IRS auditor, which was clear from the Internal Revenue Service badge around his neck. Carver raced across the median and pulled the driver's side door handle. The door was unlocked, and the auditor was so busy gawking at the plane wreckage that he did not see Carver in time to pull away.

Carver gripped the auditor by the collar of his blue oxford shirt and yanked him out of the vehicle as it continued to roll forward at idle speed. Carver slid into the warm driver's seat and braked so that O'Keefe could push Angie and Eva into the back seat.

The bewildered auditor regained his balance and began running alongside his car just as Carver began to accelerate. Carver pulled a business card from his jacket pocket and handed it to him through the window. "Call my office. We'll get you a new car."

The auditor stumbled and fell. He got up, brushed himself off, and held the card in both hands as he read the name aloud: "Ethan Danforth. FutureK Consulting." He looked up at his ride as it powered away.

Carver struggled to weave the American-made economy sedan through the light dawn traffic. The engine was sluggish and the handling was an abomination. "We should've waited for somebody in a BMW," he complained.

O'Keefe craned her neck out the rear passenger seat window. "Traffic 'copter's following us."

Carver was in no mood for a televised freeway chase. They careened onto the Georgetown Memorial Parkway off-ramp. The news chopper followed. Carver gunned it, racking his brain for some competitive advantage that a car might possibly have over a helicopter.

"Where are we headed?" Eva said.

"Arlington," Carver shouted back, knowing they wouldn't be able to drive there without leading the bad guys straight to Speers. He had to ditch the car.

A mile later he saw the exit for Turkey Run Park, where he often went running on weekends. He took the exit and wound the car under the first bridge, skidding to a stop under cover of the 200-foot long overpass.

O'Keefe and Eva jumped out. Carver helped Angie out of the car and pulled her by the hand toward a section of wooded green space.

They picked up a jogging trail that stretched under a thick canopy of poplar trees. Following Carver's lead, they went as fast as they could for the length of a football field before stopping. Angie was still foggy, but she moved well with O'Keefe's help. Carver crouched to peer between a pair of shrubs. The traffic helicopter was still hovering over the bridge where the car was parked. It had been joined by two Army Huey attack choppers.

"We don't have long," Carver said. "They'll have boots on the ground within ten minutes."

"It would suck if they released dogs," Eva said.

"We're one hill away from the Potomac Heritage trail. There's an oak and beech forest not far from there that runs all the way to Arlington. It's our only shot."

Washington D.C.
5:15 a.m.

Agent Rios led Dex and LeBron to the Metro Center station entrance as the day's first orange line train was about to arrive. The mid-career secret service agent's hands trembled. Sixty-six hours ago he had shot two assassins dead on Martha's Vineyard. For that, he had no regrets. It was the prospect of using his weapon again that bothered him.

They passed the turnstiles without incident and descended the steep escalator toward the platform. Rios' senses were highly attuned to the few souls scurrying about the station. He heard the conversations of strangers at impossibly long distances. He could smell the trash on the other side of the tracks. Everything seemed magnified.

His phone buzzed. The caller ID displayed a variation of a Pentagon telephone number. He answered.

"This is General Wainewright," the voice on the other end said.

It took all Rios' willpower to remain polite. The Secret Service did not answer to the Pentagon, but rather, to Homeland Security. Still, he realized all that could change depending on who occupied the White House by nightfall. It was best to be cautiously subservient. "Yes sir," he answered.

"Are you alone?"

"No sir." Rios did not elaborate further.

"I'm glad you didn't lie to me, Agent Rios. I hate liars."

Rios put his hands on Dex's and LeBron's shoulders and backed them up against a concrete column. He looked left and right, but did not see any cameras or enemy agents. He returned the phone to his ear as the train entered the station slowly and loudly.

"Is there something I can do for you, sir?" Rios told the General. "I'm about to get on the subway."

"Yes, Agent Rios. You and Secretary Jackson can report to me at the Pentagon and join my team."

"I work for the White House, sir. It's really not my choice."

"Don't play dumb," the General said calmly. "This is your last chance to play on the winning team."

The train doors swooshed open before them. Rios ushered Dex and LeBron inside with him. He motioned for them to stand near the doors, in case they had to jump off at the last moment. He took a moment to inspect the surrounding seats. Behind him, a masked Chris Abrams emerged from behind one of the wide concrete columns on the platform. He kicked Dex in the back and plucked LeBron from the train just as the doors began to close. Rios lunged for the exit. The doors clamped around his left wrist. His hand was saved only by a safety feature that caused the door to hiccup open for an instant before sealing again.

Dex managed to get to his feet to catch a last glimpse of LeBron struggling in Abrams' clutches as the train headed into the tunnel.

Agent Rios screamed into the phone. There was nobody there. Like LeBron, General Wainewright was long gone.

Burlington, North Carolina
5:20 a.m.

While Madge slept, Nico sat at her computer in the living room, navigating past a series of firewalls that would lead him to the Pentagon's virtual inner sanctum. As always, he did not attack his target head on. He had begun by finding the name of the IT firm that the Pentagon had hired to service their legacy network systems. He quickly found Novi Technical Group, a small company in nearby Fairfax. A look at the source code from their corporate site – a quick WC3 diagnostic racked up more than thirteen-hundred coding errors – told him that the company's employees had little time to spend on themselves. While the IT firm had undoubtedly been very meticulous in securing the DOD's formidable intranet, it was likely that the firm's employees were too overworked to spend any time on their own corporate security, where a copy of their work for DOD would certainly reside. It was a classic case of a hairdresser with bad hair.

By four a.m., Nico had hacked into the company's internal network and located an unencrypted Excel document containing one employee's login information for a variety of sensitive federal systems.

The old rush was returning. He felt invincible. Bulletproof. As fervent in his belief in what he was doing as ever. He hadn't felt this way in Oklahoma, where Agent Carver had asked him to break into the old professor's email. Nor had he felt it in Baltimore, when he had broken into the DOD's personnel files for Colonel Madsen.

This was personal. This was about ideology. Much as he hated the idea of anyone continuing President Hatch's foreign policy, the idea of military rule was far worse. But crippling the Pentagon's communications with a virus wasn't the answer. If only he could broadcast a simple message inside the Pentagon's network that would make the Pentagon sheep think twice about what they were doing.

The breaking news ticker flashed across the bottom of Madge's customized desktop: *Tragedy in Washington: President Hatch killed. Successor to be sworn in. Details forthcoming.*

So the Joint Chiefs were going public. The world was about to change. He had to hurry.

Washington D.C.
5:35 a.m.

Speers surfaced from the tunnels under Roslyn Station, where Agent Rios was due to deliver the Defense Secretary. He pulled the baseball hat low over his face as he stood in the shadows and watched the platform. A few early bird commuters – mostly men wearing gray suit jackets and ties despite the uncomfortably hot weather – stood staring into the screens of their mobile phones. The rumble of an approaching subway car shook the concrete. He spotted Agent Rios and Dex, both peering anxiously through the glass, as it rolled in. There was no sign of Dex's son.

Dex charged off the train and threw a looping right hook that cracked Speers on the cheekbone. Speers fell back and covered up, more stunned by the audacity of Dex's punch than hurt by it. Rios grabbed Dex from behind, easily subduing the much smaller man.

"They took LeBron," Rios explained as Dex retreated to a corner of the platform to compose himself.

Speers dusted himself off and touched his face, which was already beginning to bruise and swell.

"You said my wife was alive," Dex said. "You sure as hell better not be lying."

"She's with the two best federal agents in the entire country," Rios offered.

"I'd like to hear it from him," Dex said, pointing at Speers.

Speers wiggled his jaw from side to side. It seemed safe to talk. "Okay then. The so-called terrorists that attacked your boat were led by an ex-military man of Bosnian descent named Elvir Divac. They weren't supposed to hurt anybody. The Joint Chiefs hired them to make you a believer." Speers knew the story sounded crazy, but it was clear by the look of enlightenment on Dex's face that it rang true. "When Angie fell overboard, they didn't know what to do. They saved her because they were afraid they wouldn't get their money. But they were wrong. The Joint Chiefs were going to eliminate them either way."

Dex's eyes reddened. "Why did you bring me here?"

"I thought if you knew the truth, you might want to see her alive again. I thought you might help us."

"But they've got my son now." The next train pulled into the station. It was bound for the Pentagon. He headed toward it. "You're on your own."

The Pentagon
6:02 a.m.

General Wainewright's armored SUV entered the Pentagon's subterranean parking facility and stopped at the private entrance reserved for top brass. General Farrell stood in the concrete archway, smoking his fifth cigarette since the Willard Hotel's wake-up call had come at 4:45 a.m. He dropped the butt and stamped out the smoldering cherry just as the Chairman got out of the car. After losing Dex Jackson, it wasn't hard to imagine Wainewright blowing off his head for a simple infraction like smoking.

The two met each other with only a glance and walked at a quick clip. "Did you see the Ambassador?" Farrell said. He was anxious for any news on Iran's pledge to go after Allied Jihad camps in Pakistan. The two walked past a Lance Corporal distributing Kleenex to a trio of weeping civil servants. "What's their problem?" Wainewright said too loudly.

"They're grieving," Farrell replied as they rounded a corner toward the elevators.

"For who?"

"President Hatch," Farrell hissed. "It might be old news to you by now, but the rest of the world is just getting used to the idea."

The press release had come out of the Pentagon as scheduled at five a.m. sharp. It had been a deliberately terse and obtuse statement issued directly from the Pentagon:

> The President died at Camp David after a suicide pilot of Yemeni heritage crashed a plane loaded with explosives into the area. Also among the dead was Secretary of the Treasury Eva Hudson. The Pentagon is working with the other branches of government to maintain the continuity of our federal government. A pivotal ceremony at the Lincoln Memorial will take place before ten a.m. today. There are no further details available at this time.

"It never occurred to you to postpone the press release?" Wainewright said.

"We didn't notice Dex was missing until eight minutes after it went out."

The idea had been to give the public three hours or so to absorb the grim news – just long enough for the Pentagon to spin Dex's inauguration as a swift, necessary step to stabilizing the country. By the time opposing members of the Senate and the House figured out what had happened, they would realize that they were outnumbered, pitted against the Pentagon, the Judicial Branch, several members of Congress, and a reeling American public that would do anything for the sake of stability. If possession was nine-tenths of the law, then the White House would be theirs before anyone could contest it.

At least that had been the plan.

They stepped into a waiting elevator and descended four floors to the NMCC, where they would run the last stage of the operation.

"And if Dex doesn't show up?" Wainewright said.

"He'll show," Farrell said. "We have the boy."

The elevator doors opened at the entrance to the NMCC vault. Two Ulysses MPs saluted as the Generals entered. A crew of fresh communications specialists was on duty. All had been hand-picked by Chris Abrams. The previous crew was still sequestered at Rapture Run, and would be held there until Wainewright could ascertain whether they could ever again rejoin the general military population. In the event that the 279 Ulysses and Armed Forces personnel at Rapture Run were deemed a security risk, Wainewright was prepared to flood the bunker with nerve gas, then bury the entire facility under five-hundred tons of lime, concrete and dirt.

In the far corner of the cavernous command room, Abrams stood and saluted. He wore a black t-shirt and forest green cargo pants. On his right cheek was a four-inch square bandage that covered a grenade wound he had taken during the firefight in Baltimore. Wainewright and Farrell made eye contact with Abrams, but did not acknowledge him in front of the staff. Instead they went into a private conference room and waited for Abrams to follow.

As a rule, they treated Abrams like a walking weapon of mass destruction. His reputation in the mercenary trade was without equal, and he made as much money as the CEOs of many Fortune 500 companies. That made him far too dangerous to risk any public association. Until now, they had never met him in person. Instead they used pawns such as Corporal

Hammond to deliver messages back and forth and negotiate payments. With Hammond now dead and the other intermediaries confined to Rapture Run, Wainewright and Farrell had no choice but to communicate with him directly. These were desperate times, and Abrams was the only person in the world they could trust to take out the remaining targets.

As Abrams entered the room, the Generals watched him in the same way that a child might watch an exotic tiger in a zoo. He closed the door and sat at the far end of the conference table. Then he pulled a meal substitute bar from his pocket and began eating.

"You need to finish the job you were hired to do," General Wainewright told him.

The mercenary's mouth was full as he spoke. "If you had kept tighter reigns on your Treasury Secretary, General, Angie Jackson would be pushing up daisies."

Farrell, who prided himself on knowing when to play yin to Wainewright's yang, jumped in. "Let's just focus on next steps."

"We're tracking Blake Carver and his little entourage," Abrams said.

Wainewright was outraged. "Tracking them? I want Eva Hudson's head on my desk. Kill them now."

"Not yet, General. First, Agent Carver will lead us to Julian Speers."

"Exactly," Farrell chimed in. "Speers wasn't even on the original target list. But it's clear that he's going to be hugely disruptive."

"Unacceptable," Wainewright insisted. "I want immediate gratification."

Now finished with his meal, Abrams put a boot up on the table. His pant leg raised up just high enough for the Generals to glimpse his ankle holster. Farrell didn't have to look at Wainewright to sense his displeasure. He had already told the Chairman that terminating Abrams after the operation was not an option, since he claimed to have an elaborate scheme of retribution planned in the event that he was double-crossed.

Abrams remained calm. "It will happen like this. I will direct the operation from here. Our ground troops will corner them. Then we'll deploy the USOC team to take them out."

"You're scared. Otherwise you'd do this yourself."

The mercenary's face grew surly. It was true. Agent Carver had gotten the better of him in Baltimore. He had been lucky to escape with his life. Still, he didn't appreciate being called a pussy.

"Chris," Farrell chimed in, "I think what General Wainewright is trying to say is that he'd like you to handle this personally."

"Fine," Abrams said. "But it's going to cost you."

Haley Ellis watched as the tall, sinewy bald man with pockmarked skin sat at a laptop computer linked into the network. The monitors around the room lit up with headshots of Eva Hudson, Agent Carver, Agent O'Keefe and Julian Speers. Abrams addressed the room. "These are the people we're looking for," he announced. "You can begin sharing these profiles with our Ulysses field operatives."

Ellis watched helplessly as the message was dispatched to public and private units all over the city. The message below each read: WANTED FOR CONSPIRACY TO ASSASSINATE THE PRESIDENT OF THE UNITED STATES. LETHAL FORCE AUTHORIZED.

She jumped in her seat as a hand touched her shoulder. She looked up and locked eyes with General Farrell. "Miss Ellis," he said as he towered over her. His breath smelled like eggs Benedict and coffee. "I'm afraid there have been some changes in the command structure. Perhaps no one notified you. The NIC is no longer welcome here."

Force a smile, she told herself. "I'm aware of that, General. But I worked with Agent Carver at CIA, and I thought I could be of some help here today." It was the truth. Before accepting the post at NIC, Ellis had made a career stop at CIA, where she and Carver had worked two cases together. She watched as Wainewright chewed on the answer. She had no intentions of helping the investigation, but it was essential that she buy some time. She had to figure out what the Joint Chiefs were up to and get word to the Director.

"We already know a great deal about Agent Carver," Farrell said.

It was time to improvise. "We've implemented new facial recognition software onto the network over at

NIC," she said, referring to the network of surveillance cameras in the Capitol. "The system is barely out of beta mode, but it's already very effective. I think it could help us locate the targets."

Farrell nodded slowly. "Very well. You can stay."

U.S.S. Ronald Reagan
The Mediterranean

From his perch on the carrier's massive bridge, Captain White watched the Israeli coast burn as bright as an Arizona sunrise. His staff watched live footage of an Egyptian trawler firing rocket-propelled grenades at a Ferry full of Israeli citizens. Egypt had not officially joined Iran, Syria, Hezbollah or HAMAS in declaring war on Israel, but it had also done nothing to stop wave after wave of private Egyptian vessels with armed citizens taking potshots at the exodus of Israeli refugees.

The U.S. was still sitting on the sidelines. White couldn't believe it.

"We're tracking fifty-six boats leaving Tel Aviv," the Ensign reported. "All full of civilians. All packed to the gills."

"I see 'em," Captain White said as he followed the real-time satellite feed.

The carnage was happening well within striking distance of White's strike group, but he was powerless to do anything. All the treaties and alliances in the world seemed to have been tossed on the trash heap without explanation. If his orders stood, every one of those refugee boats would be sunk.

The U.S.S. Reagan's official motto was Peace Through Strength. Yet Admiral Bennington had ordered the carrier strike group to move out to international waters. The best White could do was cite engine problems with one of the CSG's destroyers, using this as an excuse to remain in the theatre. Bennington had not demanded a more detailed report, and Captain White took that to mean that his heart was not entirely into the order for defiance of the NATO pact either. White was going to maintain his position as long as he could and hope for a reversal.

Night had fallen, and Hezbollah had stepped up their rocket attacks to the north while the Syrian fighter-bombers continued their assault from the northeast. In Jerusalem, the Palestinians had met the Iranian armored divisions with open arms, and together they controlled both sides of the city, as upwards of twenty-thousand armed citizens and HAMAS soldiers alike walked behind six battalions of Iranian tanks.

The bridge phone rang. The Ensign picked up and passed the phone to Captain White. White listened wordlessly for less than two seconds. "I see," he said finally. "Thank you." He hung the phone back on its cradle and turned to the Ensign. His face was suddenly ashen.

"That was the Admiral," he said. "President Hatch has been killed."

"Killed? Killed how?"

He leaned against the bulkhead. The bad news out of the States never seemed to end. "I don't know. They're saying it was someone from Yemen."

White sat down. He did not feel grief, exactly, nor sadness. Like most everyone in the military, he hadn't voted for Hatch. But he felt shock.

"Yemen?" the Ensign said incredulously. "Why couldn't it be someone from Iran, or Palestine? At least then we could attack."

Arlington Cemetery
6:20 a.m.

Rays of orange sunlight broke through a layer of wispy clouds. Several ragged figures slouched up the hillside, threading themselves like needles through the endless rows of majestic, identical headstones. Without binoculars, Speers could not be sure that Agent Carver and Eva were among them. Don't move a muscle, he told himself. Not until you are sure.

He sat on the slope known as Section 26, just below Arlington House. It was here, in General Robert E. Lee's former front yard, that the cemetery's first Civil War veterans had been interred in the 1860s. Speers was careful not to sit directly on top of any of the graves. He positioned himself on the edge of one of the burial rows, behind a hedgerow that provided camouflage as well as a view of the city.

He counted nine helicopters combing the skies above the Capitol. They were concentrated in the airspace above the western district, Georgetown, Turkey Run Park and Rock Creek Park. Looking for Agent Carver, no doubt.

The Eternal Flame, where President Kennedy and his immediate family were buried, wasn't far down the hill. President Hatch would soon be getting a memorial here somewhere, Speers thought, albeit a much smaller one. He tried to remember the names of all the Presidents that had died in office. Kennedy, Lincoln, Harding, Franklin Roosevelt, Garfield, Harrison and McKinley. And now President Hatch. Speers did the math. That meant about 18% of all Presidents never left the job alive. Wow. Being President was the most dangerous job in America.

The fugitives grew closer. He distinctly recognized Eva's tall, composed gait, and Agent Carver's athletic strides. Behind them, O'Keefe pulled and prodded Angie Jackson up the hill. Angie's face was a frozen mask of pain and her eyes were half-shut and without focus, as if she was under hypnosis. But with O'Keefe's steady guidance, Angie's feet moved, albeit slowly. Speers' insides filled with dread as he wondered what to say when she asked him where her son was.

Speers whistled and waved from behind the hedgerow. When they reached Section 26, O'Keefe gave the Chief a hug. "I'm glad you're alive," she told him.

"It's nice to see some friendly faces," he admitted.

"You lost weight," Eva told him.

"It's the new three-day diet," Speers replied. "You can eat anything you want, but you spend the entire time running from bad guys."

The distant hum of helicopter rotors grew measurably louder. Speers hiked up the hill, leading them behind Arlington House and to what had once been General Robert E. Lee's back door. He let them into the Hunting Hall, a high-pitched, rustic room adorned with taxidermied deer.

"Is my son here?" Angie said.

Before Speers could respond, Carver glimpsed something terrifying from the south-facing window: Ulysses Bradleys pulling up Memorial Drive.

"It's a trap," Carver said. A pair of attack helicopters came in so low that he could see the faces of the pilots.

"Down here," Speers called out. He began down a rickety set of stairs to a 19th century wine cellar. Save for a few low-wattage light bulbs, the white-walled cellar had been restored to its former glory. Oak barrels stacked along the far wall, perfuming the room with their scent. Speers lifted one of the barrels, revealing an ancient wooden trap door over the stone floor. He opened it.

"What is this place?" Eva said.

"Trust me." Speers helped her down a wooden ladder that descended into a dark, cool dirt-floor chamber. She was followed by Carver and O'Keefe.

Angie trembled as Speers helped her descend the ladder. As he closed the trap door behind her, he heard broken glass and footsteps on the floorboards upstairs.

Carver whipped out his cell phone and used the screen's backlight to illuminate the otherwise pitch-black chamber. Nudging past Eva, Speers shined his phone on a large security portal that looked just like the one he had first entered yesterday underneath Union Station.

He punched his code into the door and it pushed open. At the second entry point, he held his right eye up to the retina scanner. He had performed the routine so many times in the past several hours that it was practically second nature.

Unlike the tunnels linking Union Station with the Eisenhower Building, there was no emergency lighting. "Light 'em up," Carver said as he waved his phone to reveal the claustrophobic passageway. "Don't worry – you can't make any calls down here, which means Ulysses can't track the signal." They all pulled out their phones except Angie, who had lost hers in Chesapeake Bay three days earlier.

This stretch of tunnel was six and a half feet high, providing barely enough headroom for Carver and Speers, and just four-feet wide. The floor was a mixture of hard-packed clay and mud, and the roof and sides were lined by oven-baked bricks and mortar. Many of the bricks had crumbled away from the walls during the past 150 years, forced out by tree roots that, at some places, had grown completely across the width of the tunnel.

Speers stumbled in the half-light, then recovered and set a pace that he hoped his sore feet could handle. He and Carver walked up front, with Eva in the middle and O'Keefe prodding Angie Jackson along in the rear.

"I've heard rumors about these tunnels," Eva said as they trudged along in the near-darkness. "I thought they were a myth."

"Nixon actually believed the Russians were going to park a sub in the Potomac," Speers explained. "He spent millions linking Lee's tunnels to the ones under the city."

"Who else has the code?" Carver asked.

"The question is, who that has the code is still alive?"

"Correct."

"Besides me? Hector Rios. And General Wainewright."

They heard the rats long before he spotted them Thousands of tiny clawed feet swarming the tunnel walls, squeezing in and out of the cracks and breaches that had been created by tree roots and seismic tremors. Carver shined his cell phone light ahead and waited for the wave of vermin to pass.

They moved on, the blue glow of their cell phones lighting only four or five feet in front of them at any time. The tunnel floor gradually became an ankle-deep sludge that grew several inches deeper with each passing minute. But it was much wider now. Up to 10 feet wide in some places. Carver welcomed the elbow room. But not the water.

"I don't like the looks of this."

"It goes under the Potomac," Speers explained.

"The Holland Tunnel goes under the Hudson. But it doesn't leak."

"You try getting budget to waterproof a tunnel that nobody ever uses."

"Get us out of here alive," Eva chimed in, "and I'll give you as much budget as you need."

They kept moving, slowly and without much speaking, as the water levels continued to rise. Something swam against Carver's leg. He decided not to say anything to the others.

He could not get his mind off the fact that General Wainewright had a code. If they were caught in a narrow section of the tunnels, they would be easily trapped, unable to flee or fight. Carver was not afraid of dying.

Carver believed in the afterlife. He was sure that his soul would be separated from his body and ascend to some blissful spirit world where Mormons and Athiests and Muslims and Jews would comingle with scant memory of what had divided them on Earth. But his greatest, most irrational fear lay in the mechanics of the soul's journey. When exactly did the soul separate from the body? Could it move through solid rock, or did it need a clear path to ascend to some unseen parallel universe? He did not want to die here, in a tiny tunnel far below ground. He did not like the idea of his soul roaming these dark tunnels for all eternity, endlessly looking for a way out.

"Where is my son?" Angie suddenly cried out. The voice loosened Carver from his own obsessions. He looked back. Angie was hyperventilating and her eyes darted around at frightening speed. This was someone who belonged under a psychologist's care. O'Keefe had been at her side since they left Fort Campbell, and the wear and tear was starting to show in her face.

"My turn," he said as he took Angie's arm. "We're getting closer with every step," he told her. His voice seemed to soothe her. "We need to keep going."

O'Keefe took the point. She drew her weapon. They kept moving.

The Pentagon
6:35 a.m.

From their private conference room adjacent to the NMCC, Wainewright and Farrell heard a wave of applause, followed by several ear-piercing whistles. The Generals burst into the room to see what good fortune had come their way. They found Dex Jackson standing in the middle of the NMCC, surrounded by Pentagon communications staffers who were lining up to shake his hand.

"Genius PR," Farrell whispered into Wainewright's ear. "Genius!"

During the past seventy-two hours, the Joint Chief's communications department – under the careful guidance of General Wainewright – had remade Dex from a bully Defense Secretary into a sympathetic hero who had lost his wife in the attacks but managed to save his son. Having been only drip-fed meaningful crisis information, and cut off from any other people-related stories that made for riveting television, the networks had lapped up every morsel of Dex's fabricated plight for survival in Chesapeake Bay. Dex Jackson was a household name. Wainewright would have what he wanted – a popular President that he could control.

"Back to your stations," Wainewright called to the staffers. As the applause petered out, Wainewright put on his best smile and crossed the room to shake Dex's hand. "You had us worried," he said.

"I need to see LeBron," Dex said. "*Now*."

Wainewright guided him into the conference room. General Farrell opened a silver titanium briefcase containing a tablet computer. Farrell switched it on. A time-stamped digital photo of LeBron appeared. It had been taken not thirty minutes earlier. The image had all the charm of a jailhouse mug shot, down to the dazed, depressed expression on the boy's face.

"He's waiting for you," Wainewright said. "Do what you promised, and you'll see him."

"And my wife?"

Wainewright shook his head. "In heaven, Dex. Where else?"

"I've heard different."

"You know, Dex, being a bachelor and the leader of the free world at the same time could have its upside. There's a lot of pretty White House interns who would give it up for a night in the Lincoln Bedroom."

Dex lunged at Wainewright's jugular with both hands. Farrell sprung into action, ramming his shoulder hard into Dex, managing to knock the much larger Defense Secretary off balance and into the door. A groundswell of boots pounded the floor outside.

"We're okay!" General Wainewright shouted through the door as he slicked his hair back with his hand. "Everyone back to their stations!"

Dex freed himself from Farrell's grip and retreated to his corner of the room. "All this will come to light," he said. "You'll be tried for treason."

Wainewright touched the photo screen and dragged his finger across it, grossly enlarging LeBron's face. "I don't think so. Your first act as Commander-in-

Chief will be to direct the National Archives to seal all documents and testimony pertaining to this crisis for fifty years."

Then General Farrell slid a yellow forty-six-page document in front of him. It was a supply order totaling $272 million in communications and security equipment for Ulysses to use in creating Rapture Run. It had Dex's signature on it, as well as that of Ulysses CEO Jeff Taylor. Dex remembered signing a document much like it more than a year earlier. He remembered Corporal Hammond bringing it to him personally, telling him that the order was for Raven Rock. He was accustomed to signing entire stacks of multi-million dollar contracts at a time, and he had undoubtedly signed this one after only a quick skim. It was all too easy for Dex to imagine how the Joint Chiefs would use it to prove that Dex had conspired with Ulysses to build the secret operations center without the National Security Council's permission. He figured it was just one of many smoking guns they would hold to his head if he chose not to cooperate.

Wainewright did not bother to explain what was already understood. "After the inauguration," he continued, "your security detail people will be staffed by personnel of our choosing. Just to make sure you don't get too big for your britches."

The fury in Dex's eyes turned to resignation. It was obvious that the Joint Chiefs held all the cards.

"Honestly, Dex," Farrell added, "once you accept this, you'll see we're giving you everything you wanted. We could have chosen anyone. The Number Two, Eva Hudson, even Congressman Bailey. But we chose you because we agreed with all your foreign policy arguments. You wanted a rebuilt military? You'll get it. You wanted out of Indonesia? Done. You wanted out of the Middle East? Except for the new base in Dubai, you're getting that too. All you have to do is be a good boy and do as you're told."

Abrams pushed the door open. He was scowling even more than usual. "We have a problem," he said. "My men had the targets cornered at Arlington House. Julian Speers was with them too. They all disappeared inside. Gone without a trace."

"Did you say Arlington House?"

"Yes."

Wainewright knew immediately where Speers had taken them. "Grab a wing man and some night vision gear," he told Abrams as he headed for the elevator. There was a tunnel entrance beneath the Pentagon. And he had a code.

Washington D.C.
7:02 a.m.

Agent Rios leaned against a tree near Lafayette Square, just blocks from the White House. He was exhausted. Up the street, a Ulysses patrol loudspeaker called for residents to avoid gathering in large groups. It was an absurd request on any day, much less this one. The city had woken up to the news that President Hatch had been assassinated.

Something cold and wet brushed Rios' hand. A Schnauzer muzzle. The dog was attached to a woman in her mid-40s with kind eyes and wide ankles. "Excuse me," she said. "Can I ask you a question?"

"Me?" Rios said.

"Well I see you work for the government." She gestured toward Rios' earpiece and black suit and tie. Rios pulled the transmitter out of his ear. "Can you tell me what's going on?"

"Sorry ma'am. I may know less than you do." It was the truth. He was completely out of the loop. There were a dozen messages on his phone demanding that he appear at Homeland Security headquarters to explain his actions. Suspension from the Secret Service was certain. Dismissal without pension was likely.

"My sister called from Peru," the woman added. "She said Israel is being invaded."

Rios shrugged. He hadn't seen or heard any international news. His phone buzzed and displayed a headshot of Mary Chung, President Hatch's longtime executive assistant.

"Thank God you're alive," she said, choking back tears. "Can you talk?"

"Depends," Rios said. "Did someone ask you to call me?"

"Heavens no," Mary said without hesitation. "I'm just trying to make sense of the Pentagon's press release."

"Haven't seen it."

"They say that Eva Hudson died at Camp David. But I knew that the President had asked you to shadow Eva on Martha's Vineyard."

"Eva wasn't at Camp David. The President never made it there either. I need you to tell me everything you know."

"I was just at the White House. The Uniforms are all gone," Mary said, using the shorthand for the Secret Service's Uniformed Division, otherwise known as the White House Police Force.

"Gone? You mean there's no security at all?"

"Oh there's security," Mary said. "Just not ours. The mansion is surrounded by Ulysses soldiers."

Rios wished he was surprised. "Go on."

"I went to the staff entrance," Mary said. "I was told my credentials were no longer valid." Rios waited as Mary choked up, then regained her composure. "But the strangest thing…"

"What?"

"Secretary Jackson's kid."

"LeBron Jackson? You saw him?"

"Saw him? Hector, they ushered LeBron right past me. He's in the White House right now."

The Tunnels
7:28 a.m.

Chris Abrams and Elijah Smith moved slowly and silently through the chest-level water. They had been in the tunnels for forty-five minutes, and all they had seen so far was a water moccasin as big around as a human thigh. They wore night vision goggles and held their M4s across the tops of their shoulders to keep them dry. The tunnel had widened to about twelve feet at its widest point, but seemed to be getting narrower again. The soles of Abrams' boots were slippery against the mossy tunnel floor. He longed for a pair of waders and the felt-bottomed boots that he wore on occasional river fly-fishing trips back to Idaho.

The two men did not know each other. With Abrams' crew having been killed in Baltimore, he had been forced to choose a wing man from the few available Ulysses MPs on duty at the Pentagon. None had any covert ops experience to speak of. Abrams knew only that Smith had done three years for Ulysses in Afpak after flunking out of ROTC. Not exactly the rock star he had hoped for, but at least he had actual combat experience, which was more than he could say for the others.

Abrams cursed under his breath as they came to a fork where the tunnels branched off into three directions. They were under instructions to follow the tunnels north until they found the HVTs, or High Value Targets. Wainewright had said nothing about a fork.

They didn't have a map, and they were too far underground for their GPS to work.

Then he heard it – a faint scream. A woman's scream. Then at least one deeper voice, maybe two. It was impossible to tell how far away. But it was coming from the left fork. Abrams looked at Smith and pointed toward the left tunnel and moved his rifle from the dry carrying position to a dry firing position, with the barrel pointed in the direction they were walking and the stock resting firmly against his shoulder.

Twenty yards further, the water receded to waist-level. Abrams stopped and motioned for Smith to do the same. The voices had stopped, but a faint blue glow appeared in the distance. He pointed Smith to the tunnel's far side, while he took up a firing position on the opposite wall. Abrams slipped once but managed to get his feet under him without splashing.

The distant light flared strangely through his goggles. He lifted them up to try with his naked eyes. Then the HVTs came into view – four cell phones and five humans, perhaps eighty yards ahead. Abrams licked his busted lower lip and stretched his neck from side to side. He felt a dull pain in his belly and realized it was hunger. It had been a little more than two hours since he had eaten.

"How much longer?" a woman's voice echoed. Abrams kept as still as death.

The tunnel curved in a serpentine path, and from Abrams' perspective the HVTs drifted in and out of view. It was unclear whether there were additional forks in the tunnel.

After the failure in Baltimore, Abrams had vowed never again to engage in a firefight with the esteemed Agent Blake Carver. They would wait until the HVTs were very close. Then they would slaughter them. All of them.

Abrams put his goggles back on and looked at Smith. He held his left hand in front of his face and balled it up into a fist – hold position. He then held his pinkie and thumb out and wobbled them from side to side to signal that they would ambush the targets. Then he flashed the numbers one and five, meaning they would wait until the targets were within fifteen yards to attack.

Abrams' right index finger danced around the M4s trigger as the HVTs slogged toward them. They were, for the most part, single file, and as they came closer, their cell phones created halos around their bodies. The target walking point was brandishing a handgun.

Abrams found her in his scope, placed gentle pressure on the trigger and tried to regulate his breathing as he waited for the targets to come within range. Ten more yards, and he'd put two rounds into the point target and reset his aim to one foot above the water. Combatants in water instinctively went neck deep when attacked. Rarely did they have the composure to hold their breath and swim underwater.

Then the unthinkable happened – Smith lost his footing and slipped below the surface. The sound of his splashes cut through the tunnel's silence like the ringing of church bells, spoiling the element of surprise.

"Lights out!" one of the HVTs shouted. The targets froze twenty five yards out and shut off the backlights of their cell phones. The glow lingered in Abrams' night vision goggles.

He pulled the trigger and placed two rounds squarely into one of the target's chest. Then he moved his barrel to the right and fired another burst, but the targets were not where they were supposed to be; they had dispersed to each side of the tunnel and vanished from view.

A lone body floated on the water's surface.

Smith got to his feet and, although his rifle was waterlogged, blasted half his magazine indiscriminately at the now-dark tunnel before him. Abrams braced for return fire, but none came. He was afraid that Carver & company would take advantage of the tunnel's winding path and slip away. He motioned to Smith to move quietly forward. Abrams hung back several feet, deciding to let Smith take the point.

The water broke just ten yards out. Ten more rounds flared out the end of Smith's rifle in less than two seconds. Both men retreated to the sides of the tunnel. Moments later, something floated to the top. The eviscerated remains of a massive carp. It twitched violently as some ancient-looking tunnel creature gnawed at it.

A figure rose up in Abrams' peripheral vision, impossibly close. The tunnel lit up once again with the flare of gunfire. Abrams recognized Carver's determined face only feet from his own.

Abrams' torso listed, throwing his return fire well off the mark. Hot blood pumped out his neck and chest. His legs split into a widened stance as he managed to stay upright long enough to watch Smith slip under water for the last time. Thousands of tiny tadpoles swam around him, eager to pick at his flesh.

*

Carver reached into the water and pulled the assailant's corpse to the surface. Abrams' face was ghoulish in the blue cell phone illumination and he wore a Pentagon security badge around his neck. Carver put the badge into his jacket pocket for safe keeping. If they made it out of here alive, he was going to link Abrams to every dirty Pentagon official he could find.

Something flipped on the surface. Carver felt a force pulling Abrams' body away from him. Carver fired into the tunnel water. Whatever it was let go and swam away.

Behind him, Speers cradled Agent O'Keefe's floating body. Her green eyes stared endlessly upwards. Strawberry-blonde hair bloomed around her like kelp.

Carver had lost plenty in his career. He had been at the scene of terror attacks, where civilian guts were splattered about like so much paint. He had even cut Lieutenant Flynn's corpse into luggage-size pieces for the sake of national security. But he could not look. This was O'Keefe. This one hurt. He should have never let her walk point. He should have never demanded that she take weapons training. He should have taken her home and made love to her that summer night at the train station. He should have said and done so many things.

"Blake," Speers said softly, "There could be more of them in the tunnel. We have to get going."

"Shut up," Carver snapped as he clung to Abrams' corpse. He had to think about next steps. That was how he was going to get through this. Next steps. Thought, action, result. Focus on what to do with the bodies. The Army always retrieved their dead, but it was different for intelligence agents working off-the-grid cases. Protocol was to strip the body of identification and destroy it. Like it never happened. Like the person had never lived at all.

But Carver could not bear the thought of surrendering O'Keefe to whatever tunnel creatures lived in this cesspool. He stowed his weapon in his shoulder holster and reached out to touch her hair. The skin of her scalp was still slightly warm.

"Blake," Speers tried again. "The inauguration…We have to move."

He looked past Speers' shoulder, where Angie stooped behind Eva like a frightened child. "We'll buddy up," Carver said at last. "Eva, you're with Angie."

Carver sized up Julian. The Chief wasn't strong enough to carry O'Keefe's body out. Carver took her in his arms and swung her over his right shoulder. With his free hand, he pulled Abrams' body toward Speers. "Julian, you'll take Abrams."

The Chief was mortified. "Why don't we leave this a-hole here? He's fish food."

"No. When this is over, the Pentagon is going to say Abrams never existed."

"So take a DNA sample."

"No. We need a full set of teeth, fingerprints, everything."

Speers gripped the dead man's collar and floated the body behind him. On the other side of the tunnel, something was boiling the water near where Mr. Smith had gone under. "Leave him," Carver said. "He's too small to keep."

Capitol Hill
8:40 a.m.

Special Agent Jack McClellan opened the door to the tiny backyard. His miniature Doberman Pinscher bounced past him and lifted his leg to pee on the wooden fence. The home was located just a few blocks south of the Library of Congress. Back in 1994, McClellan purchased the two-bedroom row house for $80,000 and became the first white homeowner on his block in twenty years. Now the house was worth more than ten times that. It was a good thing. Considering what happened at the Willard last night, he figured he could kiss his pension goodbye. He was going to have to sell the house just to make ends meet.

The Doberman's ears pricked up. Someone was at the door. The dog darted past McClellan and went to the front door. He didn't bark or growl. He wagged his tail. It was someone he knew.

McClellan peered through the peephole and saw Special Agent Rios staring at him. Of course it would be Rios. The last person he wanted to see.

He opened the door anyhow and looked up at his hulking colleague, who was still in his clothes from the night before.

"I'd like to explain about last night," Rios said. He looked past McClellan into the home, hoping the old veteran wouldn't make him beg for an invitation.

McClellan opened the door just wide enough so that Rios could turn sideways and squeeze in. Rios sat in the chair closest to the door. The Doberman came to him and laid at his feet, hoping for some attention.

"You know they suspended me for that bullcrap," McClellan said. He had whiskey on his breath.

"Not just you," Rios said. "They sent everybody home."

"What?"

"You heard me. There are no Secret Service agents in the White House. Uniformed Division, ERT, nothing. They've all been expelled. Right now, the White House is surrounded by about a hundred Ulysses MPs. Several hundred more are deployed on the National Mall."

McClellan sat back in his seat. "Well what the hell do you make of that?"

Rios told him all Speers had told him about Ulysses and the Joint Chiefs. When McClellan had absorbed that bit of news, Rios explained why he had snuck the DEFSEC out of the Willard.

"I don't know why I didn't see it before," McClellan said. "They planned this thing perfectly."

"What do you mean?"

"Summer recess," McClellan said, referring to the yearly ritual of Congress, the Executive branch and just about every other federal agency in Washington clearing out of the Capitol each August. "Homeland Security deployed six hundred agents to the President's ranch in advance of the recess. That's double the usual number. Another three hundred were sent out to Wyoming for Number Two. Made no sense. They only had a hundred acres to secure there. Another fifty were traveling with the Secretary of State in Hungary. Then you consider that half the Service takes their own vacations in August."

Rios shook his head in disbelief. "How many agents do you think we actually have in the Capitol right now?"

"Maybe a hundred White House Police and twenty Special Agents, but God knows what state they're in. Half of 'em are probably hung over."

"We'll need every single one," Rios said. "I'll get on the phone."

McClellan stood up. "No. let me do it. I know you were head of First Team and all, but when it comes to respect..."

Rios was more than happy to step aside for a moment and give Jack McClellan's ego its due.

"Fine, Jack. Go ahead. Round up a posse."

The Lincoln Memorial
9:15 a.m.

Chief Justice Stanford P. Dillinger stood behind a pane of bulletproof glass at the top of the Lincoln Memorial steps, where members of DOD, Congress and Ulysses executives milled about, gossiping in the already stifling morning air. Dillinger had trimmed his massive gray beard for the occasion. The Chief Justice was a reluctant one-man receiving line as the VIPs cleared security in pairs and came up the steps.

Jowly Ulysses CEO Jeff Taylor rolled toward him in a gold-plated wheelchair, the glint from his diamond cuff links momentarily blinding the Chief Justice. "So you're the voodoo priest that's gonna bless this shotgun wedding?" Taylor said as he shook Dillinger's hand. But Dillinger, all-too-conscious of the news network cameras and the power of long-range microphones, did not smile or comment. He concentrated instead on a two-star General coming up behind Taylor.

This wasn't Justice Dillinger's first inauguration. He had administered the oath of office to President Hatch some six years earlier, and again for the President's second term. He recalled the first inauguration as being filled with hobnobbing members of congress, celebrities, billionaires and religious leaders, all hoping to be part of Hatch's broadly themed Crusade for Change. Hatch's second presidency was made possible only because his opponent had been diagnosed with untreatable brain cancer just two months before the election. The irony – that the very disease that had taken his wife had made him a two-term President – was far from lost on him.

That inauguration had been considerably less jubilant. Gone were all the celebrities and religious leaders. But Washington's elite had returned, along with big business, if only to call in favors they felt the President owed them.

Congress had gone into recess a week earlier for vacation. It was now Wednesday and they still had not been recalled to Washington. Dillinger looked around and envisioned his future in the burgeoning police state.

He surveyed the mall, where a few dozen carefully vetted members of the media, and around five thousand invitees from various federal agencies, were solemnly gathering. Huge crowds were gathered along Constitution Avenue, kept at bay by Ulysses troops. Ulysses soldiers stood at the Memorial steps like bouncers at a concert trying to prevent fans from getting onstage. They also stood atop guard towers that had been hastily thrown up overnight using construction scaffolding. D.C. Metro Police helicopters hovered overhead. Dillinger found it curious that there were no Secret Service agents on hand.

"Harry," someone said, tapping Dillinger from behind. He turned and saw Justice Dominquez, President Hatch's most recent appointment to the bench. Dominquez had been closest to Hatch in terms of ideology, and he pulled no punches. "We've been talking," he said, meaning himself and the other Justices. "We think the terms of the inauguration are unacceptable. We think the Court should abstain from this ceremony."

"Oh?" Dillinger feigned surprise. He knew damn well that the terms were less than ideal. He was only doing this for fear that the country would otherwise descend into chaos. And only because Wainewright had promised to install a sitting cabinet member. The alternative was permanent military rule. "This isn't a constitutional matter," Dillinger correctly pointed out. "The Succession Act of 1947 is a congressional matter, and with congress in recess, I have a larger duty to the people of the United States to ensure that the country continues to operate with some sense of normalcy."

"You have a duty to make sure that the right person is sworn in."

"I have to go with my conscience," Dillinger argued. He had known General Wainewright for twenty years. Although he suspected that the Chairman had pulled off nothing less than a military coup, he knew going against him now would mean paying the ultimate price. He, for one, had no love for President Hatch, nor his Treasury Secretary-cum-girlfriend Eva Hudson, and he wasn't willing to succumb to Riacin poisoning – or sacrifice the Supreme Court – to preserve their legacy.

A groundswell of chatter rose up from the crowd. Justice Dillinger saw an armored stretch Humvee pulled up in the drive beside the Memorial. A company of armed Ulysses MPs sprinted toward it, assembling in two lines of security that stretched between the Humvee and the Memorial steps. General Farrell stepped out first, followed by Dex Jackson. They waved to the crowd, and then made their way up the steps.

Dillinger moved to the Inaugural Podium and readied the Presidential Bible.

Lincoln Memorial Archives
10:05 a.m.

Dust kicked up in a far corner of the six hundred-square foot archive room. Agent Carver ducked through a wooden door frame that would have been far too diminutive for Lincoln himself. His clothes were soaked to the chest with brackish tunnel water. He crouched there near the doorway with his weapon as his eyes adjusted to the room's harsh yellow lighting.

The room was a tall maze of wooden shelves packed with airtight containers. The unmistakably tinny sound of AM radio chatter came through an open doorway at the other end of the room. *"We are perhaps moments away from a landmark moment in history,"* a radio voice said. *"There really is no precedent for what the country is seeing right now. In a few moments the Secretary of Defense will ascend to the Presidency."*

The others were still waiting in the tunnel. Eva Hudson and Angie Jackson had both been reported as dead. So long as Carver could keep them alive, they alone were proof of a conspiracy to deceive the public and overthrow the government.

Carver waited until his eyes adjusted to the lighting and then proceeded to secure the room. He walked slowly to the end of the row, stopping every so often to peer through gaps in the containers. The sound of the radio grew louder as he approached the doorway. *"If memory serves, this moment has some indirect precedent. I'm referring to the time when President Ronald Reagan was shot in the 1980s and Defense Secretary Alexander Haig declared himself in charge."*

He stepped through the doorway and felt the cold metal of a Smith & Wesson .38 revolver press into his right cheek. "Drop to the ground," a voice said. "Don't do nothin' stupid."

If the timber of the old security guard's voice hadn't given away his age, then the choice of weapon would have. The .38 was an old-timer's weapon. A police sidearm in an era before steroids, genetically modified food and seven-foot-tall athletes made bigger criminals that required bigger weapons. Pawn shops across America were full of them.

"I'm a federal agent," Carver said. "ID's in my pocket. Go ahead. Take a look."

The rent-a-cop seemed even less comfortable with the situation than Carver was. "If you was a federal agent," he said nervously, "then you wouldn't need to be creepin' around my archive room, now wouldja?"

Carver didn't have time for this. He had tried it the easy way. "I surrender," Carver said. "Don't shoot. I'm going to put my wrists behind my back so you can cuff me."

As the old timer stepped back to give his subject some room, Carver used his superior hand speed to strike him on the forearm, knocking the revolver out of his grip and onto the floor. The old man came at him, swinging with a series of roundhouse punches. Carver kicked his overmatched opponent in the solar plexus – just hard enough to knock the wind out of him. He casually picked up the revolver, opened the magazine and emptied the shells into his pocket.

"I don't want to hurt you," Carver said. "I really am a federal agent. You all alone here?" The guard nodded. "Come on. I need some help."

Carver ushered the old-timer back through the archive room, where Speers, Eva and Angie Jackson were waiting at the tunnel entrance with the cold, stiff corpses of Meagan O'Keefe and Chris Abrams at their feet. To Carver's horror, O'Keefe's body was contorted with rigor mortis, bent at the elbows and the waist. Hardly the picture of eternal peace.

The old-timer went pale at the sight of the ladies. "You're supposed to be dead," he stammered as he pointed a bony finger at them.

The Pentagon
10:49 a.m.

On any other day, Haley Ellis would not have had to make excuses for leaving the NMCC. Her job allowed her to come and go freely from the most sensitive security areas in the federal government. But today was unlike any other day. If Wainewright had authorized deadly force on civilians violating curfew on the streets of Washington, he wouldn't hesitate to shoot dissenters within the Pentagon.

She grimaced and groaned, just loud enough to be noticed by the communications staffer at the next workstation. She held her stomach for several moments, resumed working briefly, then hunched over again. "Maybe something I ate," she explained as she rose from her workstation and headed for the exit en route to the ladies' room. She left her attaché as proof that she was coming back.

Ellis took the elevators to the DC Metro level and sprinted as fast as she could in designer flats. She arrived at the platform just as the Orange Line whisked into the station. She stepped on board, nearly out of breath, peering out the windows to make sure she wasn't followed. Ellis took a good look as the subway pulled away from the station, knowing it could be the last time.

She stood for the eight-and-a-half minutes until they reached Farragut West Station. The platform was nearly empty. A lone Ulysses MP with a German

Shepherd stood near the ticket booth. He seemed to be paying more attention to two young girls in hot pants than anything else. Ellis stepped on the escalator and dialed the NIC Director as she ascended toward the street. "Please answer," she said aloud. "Answer, answer, answer."

"It's Hummel," the Director said into the line. "Hold on."

"This can't wait," she blurted out.

It was a five-minute walk from Farragut West to the Eisenhower Building on 17th Street NW, where she had been assigned a small office for the past year. It was said that the building represented a symbolic – if not geographical – halfway point between the White House and the Pentagon. In truth, the location was a strategic move by the White House to keep NIC observers close and minimize the risk that they might be compromised or influenced by the Pentagon brass.

On a street that was crawling with Ulysses troops, two gum-chewing MPs were posted squarely in front of the building's front entrance. To Ellis' eye, they were in their late teens or early twenties. Something in their eyes – she had learned to recognize it, but had yet to name it – told her that they had never been in combat.

She held out her credentials. "Senior Pentagon Liaison. Third floor."

The MPs shook their heads. "Lady, nobody's been in this building since Sunday," the taller one said.

"You're wrong," Haley said. "There was a security breach last night at seven thirty-five p.m. Check the logs if you don't believe me." Ellis had already seen the incident log describing how a Ulysses unit had been sent into the building to pursue Julian Speers.

The shorter MP stopped chewing his gum. "How'd you know that?"

"It's my job. I need access to my office. It's a matter of national security."

The shorter MP turned his body sideways to let Ellis pass.

The building was completely empty, just as the MPs said it would be.

Ellis did not in fact go to her office. She instead pushed the second floor button, where the Secret Service had a small satellite presence, and swiped her badge to get onto the secured floor. In ten more paces, she came to another set of doors where she swiped her badge again.

Agent Rios' cramped, windowless office was sandwiched between two kitchens in a room that had once held the building's network servers. Ellis slipped her fingers under Rios' middle desk drawer, groping for the hidden key that Rios kept to the Secret Service weapons locker. The locker was located just outside Rios' office, and had been established some decades earlier to give the Secret Service an area to rearm in the unthinkable event that the White House was overrun by invaders.

The unthinkable was happening. Ellis opened the locker and took an M4 carbine and some ammunition from the rack. The last time she had held an M4, a car bomb exploded in a Ramadi market. It was 2006, her last day in Iraq. When the medics found her, a piece of the car's fractured radiator was lodged in her hip. Thanks to Director Hummel and a convincing doctor at Walter Reed, she never returned to combat duty.

Until today. She reached back into the weapons locker and took a rifle scope, a pair of binoculars and a satellite radio. She gathered them in her arms and headed for the roof. The high ground, she remembered. Always take the high ground.

The Lincoln Memorial
11:14 a.m.

A Methodist minister – a portly, pink-faced man with a Mississippi drawl – stepped up to the Inaugural Podium. Behind him, Chief Justice Dillinger stood alongside Dex Jackson, General Farrell and an entire row of Ulysses executives. Thousands of citizens huddled on the National Mall, peering into tiny phones carrying the broadcast. Thousands more stood along Constitution Avenue alongside legions of Ulysses soldiers.

"Let us pray," the Minister began in a loud, booming voice that echoed over the public address system as if he himself was a deity. His message was uncharacteristically succinct for an inaugural prayer. He asked the Almighty for guidance and wisdom. He asked that Dexter Adams Jackson be blessed in his endeavor to lead the country. And he asked that God begin an era of healing. *Amen.*

As tentative applause rose up the crowd, Chief Justice Dillinger took his place at the podium. It was time. General Farrell leaned into Dex's ear and spoke just low enough not to be heard by the VIPs around him. "Fifteen minutes from now you'll be with your son. Don't blow it."

"Secretary Jackson," Dillinger said into the microphone, "Come forth and place your hand upon the Bible."

Dex approached the podium as if it were a gallows. He lifted his right hand into the air, flattened it, and slowly, slowly, lowered it. The SECDEF found that difficult. He had been a member of the Church of God in Christ throughout his entire life. Until college, he had believed that the entire Bible was the literal word of God, and even now he believed that much of it had been channeled through Jesus. *Forgive me,* he thought as his hand slowly came into contact with the leather dust jacket.

The crowd let out a long gasp that slowly mushroomed into scattered applause. Justice Dillinger's white eyebrows arched into boomerang shapes. Dex turned to look behind him. He could not believe his eyes.

Eva Hudson – her clothes shockingly muddied and wet – walked barefoot in front of the DOD brass. As the cameras zoomed in on her, it was evident that the World's Sexiest Fed wore no makeup and her hair was pulled back into a ponytail. Agent Carver walked slightly in front of her, clearing a path.

Just behind them, Speers and the old timer accompanied Angie Jackson toward the front. Her eyes were fixed on some faraway point and she was mumbling.

They moved quickly by design. By the time General Farrell caught a glimpse of Eva through the crowd and moved to block their path, there were only 10 feet between Eva and the podium. Carver opened his jacket to reveal his SIG. Farrell backed off. The Ulysses MPs were both too far away and too confused to intervene. Dex stepped off the podium and gazed stupidly at his wife.

To Dillinger's horror, Eva leaned toward the microphone and began speaking into it for the thousands in attendance to hear.

"Your Honor," she started in a shaky voice that grew more confident, "CENTCOM has confirmed that the President, the Vice President, the Speaker of the House and the Senate President Pro Tem are all deceased, God rest their souls. The Secretary of State, who I presume to be still alive, is foreign-born and therefore ineligible for the office of Chief Executive. Therefore, under the terms of the Succession Act, I respectfully request that you swear me in as the next President of the United States."

PART V

The Pentagon
11:19 a.m.

General Wainewright had never given much thought to what it would be like to come down on the wrong side of history. But as he stood in the NMCC and watched his carefully laid plans unravel on live television, he realized that there was something even worse than tactical failure: letting the left-wing historians demonize him as an enemy of the state.

The room monitors displayed a life-size Eva Hudson standing in Dex's place at the inauguration. None of the Ulysses MPs lifted a finger to stop her. Wainewright's bloodshot eyes turned to the communications staff. "The HVTs are on camera! Take them out!" he shouted at nobody in particular All activity in the room stopped. Every head turned. "What part of conspiracy to assassinate the President don't you people understand?"

"Sir," one of the senior staffers said quietly. The man stood up. He had a face like a pancake and two protruding glossy orbs for eyes. "The Ulysses field commander has refused the order."

"Then tell him who's giving it."

"I've done that, sir. He has responded by saying, and I quote, he needs to hear it from the CEO." The staffer stepped back, as if fearing that Wainewright's reddening face might explode.

"Get me Jeff Taylor," he demanded. If the Ulysses troops wouldn't take a direct order, then he would get the company's CEO to intervene.

"I'm afraid I can't do that," the staffer stammered. "NIC Director Hummel and Deputy Homeland Security Director Davis are entering the Pentagon as we speak. They would like to assess the situation before any further orders are taken."

"Like hell they are! I'm in charge here! Somebody get Jeff Taylor on the phone!"

Nobody moved. Nobody breathed. Wainewright felt suddenly naked in front of the men. He wiped a layer of perspiration from his forehead, unfastened his holster, drew his .45 automatic and switched the weapon off safety.

"Hit the deck!" someone shouted. The staff dove under desks and workstations. Except for the senior staffer, who closed his eyes and awaited the inevitable. But Wainewright did not shoot him. With the gun in one hand and Lincoln's opera glasses in the other, the General opened the blast doors and exited to the waiting elevator.

He waited for the elevator doors to close, then swiped his security badge and pressed the elevator's HOLD button. Alone at last. He needed to catch his breath. He inhaled deeply and tried to clear his mind of clutter.

"I have options," he said aloud. "They think I don't, but I have *all* the options."

*

Jeff Taylor had seen enough. Aided by his designer cane and his wife, Taylor hobbled toward the Lincoln Memorial handicapped elevator. The botched spectacle of an inauguration wasn't over yet. But it was obvious that, with Eva Hudson in the White House, Taylor's career was.

The CEO's phone buzzed. General Wainewright's photo appeared on the display. Taylor's thumb flirted with the IGNORE button. Any correspondence with Wainewright or the other conspirators now was very risky. The coming witch hunt for the conspirators would be like none the world had ever seen. A hundred times bigger than the Kennedy conspiracy investigations. Still, he reasoned, Wainewright was dangerous. Better to keep him close, Taylor decided. He steadied himself on his wife's arm and answered.

Wainewright wasted no time in making his intentions clear. "Jeff," he said, "I don't have to tell you what an Eva Hudson Presidency means."

"They're fueling up my jet now," Taylor said quickly. "Meet me in Chantilly in twenty minutes."

"We will not cut and run," Wainewright said. "Your job isn't done yet."

As Taylor realized what Wainewright was suggesting, he began to lose his balance. His wife ground her heels into the concrete flooring and managed to steady him. "What is it that you want?" he said.

"Have your troops secure the White House perimeter and await my arrival," Wainewright pressed. "No one gets in or out without my approval."

Taylor had once considered Wainewright a strong ally and a personal friend, but he had never suspected that the General was such a radical. A back room conspiracy was one thing. But now Wainewright was staging a public coup. He was going to kill Eva Hudson in open view and take the White House by force.

The CEO figured he had nearly fifty million dollars divided among personal accounts in Europe and the Caymans. If his health held up, he might be able to buy his way out of trouble. "Ulysses is strong," Taylor said, "but it's nothing without the backing of the President."

"Wrong. The Pentagon will fall neatly into line behind me," Wainewright assured him, "And Ulysses will take its place at my side as my own private elite force." Taylor was quiet for a moment. Wainewright knew better than to give him time to process it. "Jeff," Wainewright added, "Don't think for a second that you can run from this. If Eva gets power, she will find you."

The General had a point. He recalled how Eva had proved her mettle as a global bounty hunter at the IMF. Taylor figured he might have to hide in a developing country – or at least one hostile to the U.S. government – that would sell him political asylum. He tried to imagine himself adjusting to life in a country like Syria. Or North Korea. He had been to both places on business. He hadn't seen a single handicapped ramp or parking space in either country, not to mention the state of the hospitals. Not ideal for someone with disabilities.

"Possession is nine-tenths of the law," Wainewright said. "Hold the White House for a single day, and the country is ours."

Taylor took the elevator down to his car. He dialed his local field commander, who had spent the past three days busting civilian heads in the Capitol. He explained that in light of what his men had already done to D.C.'s homeless population, and considering the Hatch administration's lack of popularity, the order to contain the White House perimeter came as a more or less natural extension of Ulysses' current role. Still, Taylor had to be realistic. It was possible that his employees would have to battle other Americans. That could have disastrous consequences on morale. Widespread desertion was a very real possibility. But every warrior had his price.

Taylor offered the field commander an eight-figure bonus – paid in cash – if he could hold the White House for forty-eight hours, or at least until reinforcements could be called in from Chantilly and elsewhere. He was to keep half the bonus for himself and distribute the rest among his squad leaders. They would be part of a new America, he explained. And they were going to profit from it.

The National Mall
11:24 a.m.

As the bewildered Pentagon brass made their way down the Lincoln Memorial steps, seventeen Secret Service agents formed a human perimeter around Eva and Speers. Seventeen was all Special Agent Jack McClellan could round up on short notice, not twelve hours since they had been dismissed by Wainewright's transition team.

McClellan met them in the middle of the circle of black suits and sunglasses. They knew each other well. McClellan had personally escorted Eva to three world economic summits, and it had been Speers himself who had persuaded Agent Rios to reinstate McClellan to First Team detail.

He was the first to address Eva by her new title. "Madam President," he said, his eyes scanning the Ulysses forces, "We have to move out."

They whisked her down to the Presidential car, nicknamed The Beast. The vehicle was straight out of Batman – five-inch thick armor, run-flat tires, blast-resistant undercarriage and an interior that auto-sealed during a chemical attack. McClellan hoped today wasn't the day that the Beast had to earn its name.

The security detail divided into groups and filed into six other cars. Typically, the Presidential motorcade would have been three times that number, including at least two decoy Presidential limos and four SUVs loaded with urban combat specialists.

"Eva!" a voice called out as she was about to enter the car. It was Dex Jackson. A Secret Service agent was holding him at the base of the Memorial steps.

"Let him through," Eva said.

Speers' hands balled up into fists as Dex cut through the semi-circle of Secret Service agents and came toward them. He was sporting a nasty bruise on his jaw from Dex's sucker punch earlier in the day. But as he got closer, Speers looked in the SECDEF's eyes. He was broken up inside.

"Where's Angie?" Dex said.

"On her way to Bethesda."

McClellan didn't like the looks of the Ulysses troops organizing just thirty or so yards away. "Madam President, we have to move now!"

The four of them – Eva, Dex, Speers and McCellan – piled into the back of the Beast. The motorcade proceeded down Constitution Avenue in the opposite direction of the White House. Without the usual legions of security, throngs of curiosity seekers were free to run alongside the limo and peer through the veil of deeply tinted glass.

"We're going the wrong way," Eva said.

"We're not going to the White House," Speers said.

"Someone care to tell me why?"

"Because they'll kill you," Dex cut in, talking over Speers. "Ulysses is shoring up positions around the Mansion."

The glow of accomplishment fell from Eva's face. "I'll have you hung for your part in this."

"No," Dex said. "You won't. You need me."

"Madam President," Speers interrupted, "I propose that we head to NBC studios. I think we need to go on camera and tell the country what's happening."

Again, Dex cut in. "We're way past the media war. This is a military coup. They only understand force. And without me, you've got none."

Eva frowned. "And I suppose I'm supposed to beg for your help?"

"Grant me full immunity and I'll start calling the Pentagon brass right now."

The Tunnels
11:27 a.m.

Agents Carver and Rios walked through the amber-lit subterranean corridor linking the Lincoln Memorial and the White House. They went single file, with Carver in front, as the tunnels were no wider than four feet in this stretch.

From the steps of the Lincoln Memorial, Carver had been among the first to notice the Ulysses troops melting away from the National Mall. Seconds later his phone buzzed in his hand – a text message from Haley Ellis telling him that Ulysses was marching up 17th Street NW toward the White House.

"A military dictatorship?" Rios said in disbelief. "The public wouldn't stand for it."

Carver knew the opposite to be true. "Everyone thinks that we've been brought to our knees by Islamic terrorists," he reminded Rios. "A lot of people will think a military man is just what the doctor ordered."

The tunnel portal opened to a private bunker some 100-feet below the West Wing. The main room featured an open floor plan and a dozen single beds separated by yellow shoji screens. Against the far wall, a private office was stocked with computers and communications equipment. The near wall was stacked to the ceiling with shelves full of MREs and emergency medical kits.

"The First Family's personal shelter," Rios explained. "They call it Camelot."

"They wouldn't head for Raven Rock?"

"Get real," Rios said. "If the Allied Jihad got themselves a couple of submarines and started launching nukes off the coast, there'd be no time to go anywhere but here."

Carver's mind was on the hundreds of Ulysses troops heading toward the White House Complex. "Any weapons?"

Rios led Carver to a weapons locker, revealing a half-dozen standard M4 carbines. Carver couldn't hide his disappointment at the slim pickings. He slung one of the carbines over his shoulder. "Anything high-impact? RPGs? C-4? Grenades?"

"Hardly."

"Then we'll have to get organic," Carver said.

Rios raised an eyebrow. "We're not here to fight, are we?"

Carver shook his head. "No, Hector. We are here to destroy."

The way Carver figured it, the White House – and specifically the Oval Office – was like the Sword in the Stone. Anyone that possessed it would suddenly inherit unimaginable powers that were only safe in the hands of a legitimately elected Chief Executive. Carver was still old enough to remember what came after the fall of the Soviet Empire. Mikhail Gorbachev had been a prince among world leaders. Idolized. Worshipped around the world. Then one day Boris Yeltsin stood on a tank in front of the Kremlin, and a couple hours later found himself in Gorby's old office getting drunk and fielding congratulatory calls from Gorbachev's old friends. It wasn't that anyone liked him all that much. They were just afraid of him.

17th Avenue
11:31 a.m.

Haley Ellis stood on the Eisenhower Building rooftop with a pair of binoculars. The midday sun beat down on Ulysses troops pouring in from every direction. They had effectively surrounded the Executive Mansion on Pennsylvania Avenue between 15th and 17th Streets, and had cut off the intersection of 17th and New York Avenue as well. Bradleys fortified their positions in the Ellipse, also known as the President's Park – fifty-two acres of public green space adjacent to the White House's South Lawn. Ellis counted at least four hundred armed soldiers and fifteen Bradleys so far.

Her headset buzzed. It was FBI Director Chad Fordham. "Just got off the phone with your boss," Fordham said, referring to the NIC Director. "You wouldn't believe the rumors flying around."

"All true," Ellis replied. "The question is what we're going to do about it."

"Do about what? I just received an explainer fax from the Pentagon. It says Ulysses has a contract to protect the Capitol during martial law."

Did she really have to spell it out? "They're not there to *protect* anyone," Ellis snapped. The FBI Director was silent on the line. Ellis took this as encouragement. "Mister Director, we have somebody inside the White House. You need to hear it from him."

*

The scent of spoiled meat permeated the West Wing kitchen. A row of salads had been left on the countertops in mid-preparation. Flies buzzed around a piece of cut blood sausage. Hundreds of tiny bugs swarmed over a vat of creamed corn that looked about as appetizing as a bucket of vomit.

"Looks like the staff was expelled in a hurry," Carver whispered.

Rios nodded. "Just like Mary said."

He opened the door to the Butler's Pantry. "Let's see if anyone's home." Once upon a time, the Butler's Pantry had been stocked with the President's favorite foods and wines. In the late 2000s, it had been transformed into a security monitoring room full of surveillance video cameras and corresponding remote controls for each. Except for bedrooms and the Oval Office itself, there was virtually no nook or cranny in the White House that couldn't be seen from the pantry.

Rios powered up the system and began scrolling through hundreds of camera views. Carver's phone buzzed. It was Ellis. "I'm conferencing you with FBI Director Fordham," she said.

Carver didn't have time to ask questions. He closed the pantry door and spoke in a quiet but stern voice, explaining that Ulysses had surrounded the White House in advance of a military takeover, and that within the hour, General Wainewright would be in the Oval Office. "The first thing we have to do," Carver explained, "is convince Ulysses that they're not going to get out of this without a fight."

"Let me get this straight," Fordham said. "You want me to commit FBI agents to fight our own people?"

"Not *people*," Carver asserted. "A rogue *corporation* that's acting against the interests of the United States."

Director Fordham was silent for a few seconds. "Call it what it is. You're talking about killing Ulysses employees," he said. "That means killing Americans."

Carver realized the magnitude of what he was asking. The FBI had managed to lose fewer than fifty agents in the line of duty during the Bureau's entire history. It had done that, in part, by sticking to its core mission, and that mission didn't typically involve urban combat. But the stakes were higher now than they had ever been. "Call it what you will," Carver said. "But if you don't help us, there won't be a White House to defend. And that's a promise."

"That sounds like a threat."

"It's a vow. If the rightful President can't occupy this house, then nobody will."

The Director sighed heavily. "Look, I'm not sure how many agents are even on the premises right now. Maybe a hundred."

"It's a start."

"Ulysses has heavy weapons. How are we supposed to deal with that?"

FBI Headquarters – otherwise known as the J. Edgar Hoover Building – was only a few blocks away. Carver had only been there once, in the mid-90s, to see a weapons demonstration the agency put on to attract recruits. The demonstrators had pulled guns from a large cache of confiscated criminal weaponry, including a large number of assault rifles that had been taken from gangs, terrorists, Mafia families and militias throughout the ages. He had even laid eyes on one of Al Capone's Tommy Guns.

"You still have that gonzo criminal weapons collection?" Carver asked.

"It's still there," Fordham confirmed.

"Open the entire collection up to any field agents that are willing to fight. Let them choose their weapon and all the ammo they can carry. Then get your people on the rooftops along 17th Avenue and start picking off these corporate knuckle-draggers."

Carver hung up. Behind him, Agent Rios toggled through screen after screen of surveillance cameras. "Cavalry coming?" Rios said hopefully.

"You're not off the hook yet. Let's move."

"Five minutes," Rios said. Mary had said that LeBron Jackson was being held in the White House. The kid's life was in jeopardy because of him. No way was he torching this place with an innocent inside. But he had nearly exhausted the six stories, 132 rooms, thirty-five bathrooms and eight staircases covered by surveillance.

Finally, Rios detected movement on the camera. "There," he whispered. "Second floor. The residences."

The camera zoomed in on two Ulysses soldiers sitting in chairs outside one of the bedrooms. They had pulled an antique side table between them and were playing a game of Hearts.

"Bored-silly babysitters," Carver quipped.

"The kid's gotta be in that room."

Rios stood. Carver pushed him back down. "I'll go," Carver said.

"There's two of them."

"Let me worry about them. You know this place better than anyone. Figure out how to blow it up."

Burlington, North Carolina
11:39 a.m.

As Madge snoozed in the bedroom, Nico watched MSNBC's coverage of the events in Washington turn ugly. A camera crew had been booted off the top of the Treasury Building by hostile Ulysses troops. A reporter had fallen to his death.

Nico was no fan of Eva Hudson, but the idea of enduring Ulysses' brand of military rule was unbearable.

He set to work on the Ulysses USA firewall.

Less than five minutes went by. Bingo. He received a pixel flare from a slave machine within Ulysses' headquarters confirming that the hack was successful.

So he was in. Now what? It wasn't like he had time to develop some killer malware that would wreak major havoc in their mobile combat systems. Nico knew nothing about the security giant's internal operations. He needed someone to tell him how to throw a wrench into the machine.

"Nico?" Madge's disappointed voice floated up behind him.

Nico spun around in his chair and absorbed the reality of Madge in the morning. Tracks of dried drool caked the corners of her mouth. Hair pulled back into an unflattering bun. She wore the bed comforter as a makeshift robe.

"How'd you sleep, sweetie?" Nico managed. He backed his chair up against the monitor in hopes of obscuring the screen. But Madge had already seen enough to know what he was up to. "Madge," he began backpedaling, "Babe, I can explain this."

Her disappointment morphed into palpable anger. "Nico, I told you to *wake* me if the old urges came back. This is *my* house! This is *God's* house! I can't *have* this in here!"

"God?" Nico said. "Madge, you're wrong. God would totally approve of what I'm doing. Can you please sit down? Please?"

She sat at the dining table. "I didn't listen to the radio in the car yesterday," she started. "I didn't want to know why you were out. I wanted to believe."

"I'm legitimately out of jail," Nico said, "and that's the truth. I'm just not legitimately out of *custody*." Madge sobbed. "Sweetie, just listen, please. I made a deal with two intelligence agents right after the bombing in Monroe."

"From what country?"

"What country? Ours! The National Security Agency. The N-S-A!"

An excited gleam twinkled in Madge's eyes. "Are you telling me you helped the government catch the terror cell in Yemen?"

It would have been easy to let Madge believe this. But, Nico decided, it was time for total honesty. "No, no, no. It's not like what you've seen on the news. There is no connection with Yemen. That's a big lie perpetrated by the Pentagon brass. I helped them find the terrorists, all right. Turns out, they're right in our own government." Nico stopped, waiting for Madge's response. She didn't blink. "I'm saying that Americans planned this. People in the Pentagon, Madge! After the President was assassinated…"

The rims of Madge's eyes grew red. "What?"

"Oh, right. Sorry. I forgot you didn't know. They announced it while you were sleeping. President Hatch is dead. They killed him."

Madge grabbed the remote control, pointed it at the little TV on the bookshelf and turned up the TV. A FOX News camera was trained on the Presidential motorcade, which was winding away from the White House. A ticker ran along the screen that said CHAOS IN WASHINGTON.

"Madge," Nico said, "Forget about the President for a sec. This isn't what I wanted to tell you."

"Forget about it? The President is dead!" Madge ran to the bathroom, slammed the door and locked it. Nico heard the sound of running water, then uncontrollable sobbing. As much as Nico wanted to comfort her, there was no time. Nico turned back to Madge's computer and resumed his exploration of the Ulysses network. There had to be something he could do, some wrench to throw in the machine.

The White House
11:43 a.m.

Agent Carver crept up the staircase to the Executive Residences. He slung the M4 Rios had taken from the weapons locker over his shoulder and held his SIG out in front of him. If given the chance, he would use his bare hands. He didn't want to draw attention to himself.

He stopped at the next corner and held his breath, listening. He heard the dry slap of cards against a wooden table. "Gin!" someone said. It was a man's voice, and he was just down the hall.

"Screw you, cheater," the other soldier said. "Shuffle 'em, will ya? I want revenge. Gotta take a piss."

Carver heard a chair slide backwards and footsteps on the floor runner. Carver backpedaled, ducking into a doorway that he soon realized was an open bathroom. He stepped behind the door just as the soldier entered. The soldier did not bother to shut the door behind him, nor did he bother to raise the toilet seat as he unzipped his cargo pants and sprayed his urine into the bowl, onto the seat and onto the floor.

A bronze bust of Jefferson Adams stood on a wooden nightstand beside him. It looked heavy, and the thought of using it to bash the kidnapping bastard's skull in brought a smile to Carver's face. But the soldier would inevitably clang head-first into the mirror or toilet bowl, which would alert his colleague. Carver was all alone. Stealth was key. Carver decided he would have to get his hands dirty. It was the only away.

Carver quietly holstered his pistol and took a towel from the hook behind the door. In one motion, he stepped out from behind the door and looped the towel tight around the soldier's neck, squeezing hard enough so that he could neither breathe nor scream. The only sound was the stream of urine splashing the vanity, wall and flooring. The urine flowed long after the point that the man's heart stopped. Bending to a near-squat, Carver settled the soldier's dead weight noiselessly down onto the bathroom floor.

He left the bathroom and crept back to the corner. He held his hand over his mouth and began coughing. "Mike?" the other soldier called. "You okay in there?" Carver coughed again, more violently. "Mike?" the soldier repeated. Carver launched into a series of choking sounds, the likes of which he had not tried since he was in seventh grade, when he and his friends would pretend to have asthma attacks to get out of algebra class.

He heard the other soldier's chair slide behind him, then footsteps. Carver kept up the charade until his target rounded the corner. Then he chopped him hard to the neck. Once he was on the ground, the soldier's face froze in shock as he grappled at his shattered windpipe. Carver put one hand over the man's mouth and used the fingers of his other hand to pinch off his nose, effectively shutting off his airways. The soldier blacked out thirty seconds later. In sixty seconds, he was dead.

Carver dragged the body into the bathroom, laid it next to the other Ulysses soldier, and shut the door. Then he proceeded down the hallway to the bedroom that the men were guarding. The door was slightly ajar. As Carver approached, he heard the bleeps and bloops of a video game. He nudged the door wider with his foot and saw LeBron Jackson in his native habitat – happily playing his first video game since his father had taken him and his mother on that fateful Chesapeake fishing trip.

Agent Rios knew very little about arson, and even less about making a bomb. But he knew that the White House had one of the most sophisticated smoke and chemical detection systems in the world. He wasn't going to be able to simply walk into one of the kitchens and turn the gas on, wait a few minutes, and light a match. The sprinkler system would have the fire out in no time. He would have to be more creative.

He took the elevator to the White House bowling alley and walked through the back, down the stairs, to the boiler room. Early in his career, he had occasionally accompanied city officials here to read the gas meter, and he remembered the pipes snaking overhead to every part of the White House complex.

The room was pretty much as he remembered it, except that the old steel gas pipes had all been replaced with new copper. He sat on the floor looking up at them, hoping for some type of eureka. It did not come. He opened up the janitor's closet and looked around. It was then that he spotted a can of WD-40. As a kid growing up in East L.A., one of his cousins had taken him out into the desert and showed him how to make a flamethrower using a lighter, some metal tubing and a can of WD-40, which was highly flammable. He remembered standing over a giant anthill, holding the flame in front of the aerosol can, and torching thousands of red ants. At the time, he had considered it the coolest thing he had ever seen.

He looked back up at the gas pipe.

The White House had twenty-nine fireplaces and three kitchens. It stood to reason that the gas pipe funneled natural gas to all those places, where it was bottled up and stored at one of many valve endpoints. If Rios could find a way to inject flame into the pipe from the boiler room, he saw no reason why the flame wouldn't be carried through the gas pipe to all the fireplaces and each of the stoves in the White House, causing fires in many or all of those places. He doubted even the White House's system had access to enough water pressure to put out 29 fires at once.

He went to work rummaging through the crates of tools for a drill, an ice pick, anything to inject fire into the pipe.

As he worked, thoughts of Haley Ellis drifted in and out of his mind. He realized how much he had looked forward to their lunches over the past year. The little things. Hoping she would show up with her hair down. Hoping she wouldn't bring up old boyfriends. Or new ones. But he never pushed anything.

He didn't want to die without spending another night with Haley. And he didn't want to be remembered as the man that had blown up the White House. But Rios understood duty. He would do what he had to.

Fort McNair, Washington D.C.
12:17 p.m.

The Presidential motorcade swung down Maine Avenue and took a right at P Street SW toward Fort McNair's gated entrance. Eva, Dex, Speers and McClellan shared the back of the Beast. Dex was on the phone with the commander of several Virginia National Guard units. "I am still the Defense Secretary of these United States!" he shouted. "I am relaying a Presidential Directive to deploy your troops to the White House immediately!"

The commander's response was evident in Dex's face. He had been unable to convince a single one to confront Wainewright's Ulysses forces in the streets around the White House. They were afraid of Wainewright's retaliation, and Dex didn't blame them. Unless they could somehow get Eva safely into the White House, and secure it, anyone who had ever opposed Wainewright was going to end up on the wrong end of a firing squad.

Dex hung up and turned his gaze to Eva. "He wants proof that you've got the support to take office."

"That's your job," Eva said. "If you can't deliver that, then you are useless to me."

Even if Dex had overestimated his sway with the military brass, Fort McNair held the keys to Dex's backup plan. The 200-year-old military outpost was neatly tucked into a Washington business district. Gone were the battlements that had once lined its walls. Gone was any trace of the gallows where the Lincoln conspirators were hanged in 1865, including Mary Surratt, the first American woman ever executed for treason.

These days the base was much more like a college campus, awash in military officers in casual dress going to and from classes at the National Defense University's War College. Other than a few armed MPs, there were no active combat units in residence. Which was why a pair of National Guard M1A1 tanks had caught Dex's eye when he had visited the previous week. The upgraded M1A1 was still arguably the most fire-resistant tank in the world, having a composite armor package that included depleted uranium. It was nearly impossible to take one out with a standard RPG. Most anti-tank missiles couldn't dent it either. Not in one hit, anyhow.

As the motorcade pulled up to the gates, two Army MPs hustled out from the patrol booth. Dex got out of the state car and gestured at the gates. "Open 'em up!"

Both saluted as they recognized the Defense Secretary. The gates opened. Speers ran after Dex, passing the patrol booth as the motorcade drove by. The pair of thirty-two-foot long, sixty-seven-ton tanks were still parked on the freshly cut grass.

"Who's authorized to drive those M1s?" Dex asked the taller MP.

"Two National Guard Tank Commanders are teaching a class in residence, sir. The tanks are for demo purposes only."

Dex wiped the sweat from his brow. "Like hell they are. Get those commanders out here on the double, and tell 'em to bring their gear."

Dex walked up to one of the tanks and touched his hand to the sun-heated armor. "These bad boys are going to get us into the Rose Garden."

"How's that?" Speers sputtered. "I see two measly tanks and two measly tank commanders. A battle-ready M1 has a crew of four."

The M1A1 had seen action in six war zones since 1990, and aside from roadside bomb attacks in Iraq and Afghanistan, there had been only two confirmed reports of M1A1 armor being compromised by enemy fire. In both cases, the tanks had been hit from behind, where the armor is thinner.

"Well?" Speers persisted. "How are these tanks going to do anything against twenty-some-odd Ulysses Bradleys without even a full crew?"

"We won't be slowing down long enough to fight."

Now Speers found himself in Dex's face, spitting as he spoke. "Eva's life has been in constant danger for four days. I'm not willing to go there again."

"Get out of my grill," Dex growled. He had already decked Speers once today, and the idea of tattooing the Chief's face with his fists again was tempting.

"Hey!" a voice shouted. Jack McClellan emerged from the Beast and jogged toward the tanks. "I just talked to the boys over at CS," he said, referring to the Secret Services' counter-sniper unit. "He's scrounged up about twenty snipers, maybe more. They're willing to fight."

Dex's eyebrows raised, but he stopped short of smiling. They were going to need a lot more help than that. "Coordinate with Haley Ellis."

"Who?"

"Haley Ellis. NIC snitch with some urban combat experience. She's taken up a position atop the Eisenhower Building. We might as well coronate her as the eyes and ears of this op."

17th Street SW
12:21 p.m.

It was ninety-six degrees along 17th Street with ninety-eight percent humidity. Heat flares rose up from the asphalt, mixing with exhaust fumes to create hundreds of tiny, fleeting rainbows that rose and evaporated like Technicolor ghosts. The civilian crowds melted away into the side streets as columns of Ulysses soldiers marched up 17th and 15th, which ran parallel on the other side of the White House Complex. A crew of five Bradleys sealed off southern access to the White House by setting up positions along the Ellipse. Haley Ellis thanked her lucky stars that Ulysses didn't have air power.

She watched through binoculars as FBI agents wearing bullet-resistant vests fanned out atop an office building at 17th and F Streets. Another group deployed further down 17th atop the old Red Cross mansion. FBI Director Fordham had managed to come up with just ninety agents – the best he could do on short notice. It was good that they were taking the high ground. Ellis had led urban patrols in Ramadi and been in exactly the position Ulysses was in now. Nothing had been more demoralizing than being pinned down from above.

Still, Ellis knew those numbers weren't going to be nearly enough should the crisis escalate into full-on combat. If nothing else, she hoped that the notion of fighting the FBI would be enough to make some of the greener Ulysses troops desert their posts.

In the past hour Ellis had also been on the phone with the D.C. Metro police. The local cops hadn't cared for the way Ulysses had taken over the city during martial law, and it wasn't hard to convince the DC Metro Police Chief to pitch in. SWAT teams were staging on the Blair House rooftop at the corner of 17th and Pennsylvania, and also at Lafayette Square. Riot police were assembling a few blocks away.

White smoke billowed along 17th from an FBI tear gas canister. Ellis trained her binoculars on the street, hoping to see the first signs of desertion among Ulysses' ranks.

A voice boomed over a mobile PA system that the FBI had been hastily mounted atop the Red Cross building further down 17th: "This is FBI Director Fordham. All Ulysses units are to disband immediately and leave the White House area. If you do not leave, you will be treated as hostile."

Having themselves been prepared to use tear gas during martial law, the Ulysses troops quickly donned gas masks. Ellis held out hope that they wouldn't have the gall to fire live rounds at Federal agents in broad daylight.

Two of the fifteen Ulysses Bradleys turned their 25mm guns toward the Blair House and unleashed a torrent of fire along the roof's edge. It's on, Ellis thought in wonder. This is really happening. Public versus private, brother against brother, God versus the Devil.

The FBI agents responded with a fierce salvo from the adjacent rooftops as the Ulysses troops were still struggling with their chemical masks. A handful went down in the first volley.

Her phone buzzed. She answered on Bluetooth, but it was impossible to hear the caller over the sound of the battle. She tore off the headset and pressed the phone close to her ear.

The caller was Special Agent Jack McClellan. "I'm here to help," the old man said. "I've got twenty counter-snipers and a hundred Emergency Response agents ready to rumble. Plus about fifty special agents, but they're pretty much only packing guts and handguns."

"Get your snipers on high ground near 15th and Pennsylvania. The D.C. police are already massing at the other end of the street."

"Got it," McClellan said.

"Also, Ulysses has managed to get on top of the Treasury Building. They need someone their own size to pick 'em off."

"Will do. I'll check in when we're in position."

Now that the game was on, Ellis wasn't about to be left out. She slid the M4 off her shoulder and steadied the barrel on the edge of the building overlooking 17th. She would have to limit her targets, as the M4's effective range was only about 160 yards.

On the street below, Ulysses troops were taking cover behind their Bradleys, having already figured out that the hostile fire was coming from the northwest and southwest corners of the street. Ellis decided to give them something to worry about from the east. She targeted a soldier reloading her weapon from behind one of those big Bradleys.

Despite firing her weapon dozens of times in Iraq, Ellis had, to the best off her knowledge, never killed anyone. This was to be the first. "God forgive me," she whispered. Then she exhaled and squeezed the trigger.

The White House
12:23 p.m.

The steady crackle of gunfire grew more audible as Carver opened the oak-and-walnut-framed door to the Oval Office. LeBron stayed close, his oversized hands trembling as he held fast to Carver's left arm. They stood before the couch where Carver and Speers had sat with the President on Sunday morning. Where so many pivotal meetings had taken place throughout history.

Carver realized that he had better put his reverence for the Oval Office behind him. Some things had to be destroyed in order to be saved.

He sized up the room from a defensive perspective. There were four entrance points – doors opened to the Rose Garden, the President's private study, Mary Chung's office and the West Wing corridor. None of the doors had locks, making it a less than ideal place to fend off an attack. The lone opportunity for cover was the Executive Desk, which looked to be made of heavy wood. From the room's south-facing windows he could glimpse Ulysses troops shoring up positions across the South Lawn and the Ellipse.

He laid his M4 across the Executive Desk and peered out the windows to the Rose Garden. The intensity of the firefight along 17th, 15th and Pennsylvania was encouraging, but it also came with risk. Unless Ulysses could somehow be cut off, they could decide to retreat into the White House itself. If that happened, Carver would have no way of holding them. Rios would have no choice but to blow the place.

He dialed Agent Rios to establish some ground rules. "Call me every five minutes," Carver said. "If I don't answer, or we get cut off abruptly, you know what to do."

"What if you lose signal?" Rios protested. "I can't torch the White House on a dropped call!"

"Then call the land line," Carver said. "I'm in the Oval Office."

"You're where?"

"You heard me. If I don't answer, it means Wainewright is already here."

He hung up. LeBron peered out the window like a nervous cat. Every pore in his adolescent body was crying out for survival. "Can I go?" he pleaded. He gazed up at Carver, who at thirty-eight was old enough to be the 12-year-old's father. "Please? I can run fast."

The kid didn't exactly look like a track star. He was all baby fat and dimples. "Get under the desk," Carver said. "It's the safest place. Unless they come in from the West Wing. If that happens, make a run for the Rose Garden," he said, pointing at the vast rows of flora planted along the West Wing perimeter. "Get behind a bush and stay there until the guns go quiet."

The boy nodded solemnly. "What if something happens to you?"

"Then make friends with whoever's still alive."

*

Down in the Executive Fallout Shelter, six Ulysses MPs stepped in from the tunnels and secured the room. Wainewright and Farrell followed, along with two journalists from *Stars and Stripes* – the military's "independent" news source. The journalists wore heavy packs containing cameras, computers and mobile broadcast equipment.

Wainewright instructed the Ulysses troops to guard the tunnel entrance. The two generals, along with the journalists, went up the staircase into the Executive Mansion. In less than five minutes they would enter the Oval Office, where Wainewright would address the world community as the leader of a new America.

Farrell regained phone reception and began downloading a series of reports. He sniffed the foul air. The ghastly odor of smoke, gunpowder, diesel fuel and tear gas – a byproduct of the street battle – wafted through the mansion's ventilation ducts.

"We are encountering some resistance," Farrell reported as he read a message from the Ulysses field commander. He yearned for a cigarette, then thought better of it. Wainewright was in a delicate mood. There was no sense in angering him.

"By who?"

"Certain elements of the FBI, sir." He found himself unable to provide the General with additional details, for fear that he would overreact.

"Authorize the use of indiscriminate force on all enemies of the state," Wainewright said. "Scramble a squadron of attack helicopters. I want the FBI headquarters reduced to rubble."

Farrell couldn't hide his shock. "There are civilians working in that building."

"Zero tolerance," Wainewright said. "It's the shortest path to stability."

Walking slowly behind his master, Farrell doubted the Air Force would obey the order. He also could not curb his cravings. He plucked a cigarette from his front pocket and reached into his front pants pocket for a lighter. He sparked the cigarette and inhaled, savoring the taste of the unfiltered tobacco. "Sir," Farrell said nervously, "I think this could be counterproductive."

The Chairman pulled the white antique Colt .45 revolver from his holster and shot Farrell through his smoking hand. The bullet passed through the back of Farrell's left hand, through his mouth and eventually lodged near his cerebellum. The Vice-Chairman of the Joint Chiefs of Staff crumpled at Wainewright's feet.

Wainewright lingered on the gory image for only a moment. He looked up at the horrified *Stars and Stripes* journalists. "Obviously we'll memorialize him as a hero," Wainewright said. "Start working on the story."

He began up the stairs. Wainewright's mind turned to the broadcast he would soon be making from the Oval Office. He would stick to the talking points they'd been feeding the networks since Sunday. He would reinforce what the public had already been told – that Allied Jihad cells from Yemen and other extremist countries had infiltrated the United States and struck a crippling blow to the country. He would say that the foreign perpetrators had been dealt with, and that additional names and details would be forthcoming.

Then he would tell the American public something new – that the terrorists had help from within the federal government, from right within President Hatch's own cabinet. Eva Hudson. Julian Speers. People the President trusted most had been unhappy with the direction the country was going and decided to overthrow the administration in a mad scramble for power. He would promise to prosecute these traitors and bring them to justice.

Burlington
12:26 p.m.

Nico watched the shaky, hand-held camera view of dark smoke rising from behind the Red Cross building along 17th, just a block from the White House. Since the FAA had grounded all news network helicopters this morning, news feeds amounted to a few frightened journalists delivering blow-by-blow reports from behind buildings and cars.

He refocused on the task at hand. It had taken longer than he would have liked, but he had been able to use the slave machine he had acquired in the Ulysses USA Chantilly headquarters to network into the company's combat operations center. From there, he would be able to send instant messages to ground troops that would appear to be from central command. Theoretically, he now had the power to manipulate the very forces that were blockading the White House.

Nico realized that there were two problems with this strategy. First, thanks to the spotty news coverage, he had no way of knowing what the battleground really looked like. Without the ability to see Ulysses troop positions, any bogus directives Nico might issue to Ulysses forces might inadvertently help them. The second problem was that his directives had to seem realistic. If he issued something that didn't smell right – like sudden withdrawal – it would only take seconds for a field commander to countermand the order. There had to be some slight but significant movement that would tip the scales against them.

He glanced up at the TV as a camera zoomed in on a lone figure atop the Eisenhower Building. She wore a t-shirt with the block letters NIC on the back.

Nico turned up the volume. A frantic, disembodied voice narrated the scene. *"We're looking across the street, although the smoke has made visibility quite poor. I'm told the woman you're seeing is NIC's Haley Ellis, whom C-SPAN watchers might remember from last year's intelligence congressional hearings."*

Nico drummed the desktop with his fingertips. He had just found his spotter.

17th Avenue
12:31 p.m.

A barrage of 25mm gunfire sliced off the southwestern corner of the Eisenhower Building rooftop. Ellis hit the deck as the tracer rounds edged closer, shearing tiny chunks off the historic building's ornate sixth-floor exterior. Scary as it was, Ellis took some satisfaction in being the target of this latest assault. It meant that her three kills had finally forced the Ulysses Bradleys along 17th to redirect some of their fire from the SWAT and FBI forces.

Now she felt the telltale vibration of her phone in her pocket. She pulled it out and read a text message from Agent McClellan: *base runner headed for home. south lawn. clear a path.*

Base Runner was the codename for a President in transit. Ellis hoped McClellan was mistaken. She had heard the President's limo, codenamed "The Beast," was heavily armored, but it wouldn't be any match for the Bradleys that were blocking access to the Ellipse and the South Lawn.

Ellis ran, hunched over, to the southeast side of the rooftop and looked over the side. From there she had a partial view of the West Wing and the Oval Office where Agent Carver waited with LeBron Jackson. She could also see the entire South Lawn, The Treasury Building some 300 yards to the east, and the Ellipse. The five Ulysses Bradleys were still there, parked end-to-end, gunners peeking out of their turrets like a row of armored gophers.

The phone rang in her hand. She checked the caller ID. It read CARVER. "Abort!" Ellis answered. "The path isn't clear!"

But the voice on the other end wasn't Carver's. "I can help you, Haley Ellis," the voice said."

"Identify yourself or get off the line. "

"I'm a friend of Agent Carver's," Nico Gold told her. He had managed to hack into the network to spoof Carver's mobile ID. It had been the only way to ensure that Ellis would take his call. "If you could wave a magic wand and make Ulysses do just one thing right now, what would it be?"

"Who is this?"

"Try me, Haley Ellis. There isn't much time."

Ellis ducked and spun on her heels, scanning for enemy spotters. The haze had grown too heavy on 17th. She could no longer see the opposing rooftops. She gazed across the South Lawn to the Treasury Building. Something was happening over there. She saw hunched over figures running back and forth. "I need to know who I'm talking to."

Nico's voice was steady and insistent. "Just try me, Haley."

The Presidential motorcade would be coming up the South Lawn any second now. To do that, they'd have to cross the Ellipse. "Okay," Ellis said. "Five Ulysses Bradleys are parked on the Ellipse. I need them gone."

"Gone where? Be specific."

Ellis didn't have to think too hard. "Tell 'em the HVT is at 15th and Pennsylvania. Tell 'em to stage there and await further orders."

"Stand by," Nico said. There was silence on the other end for a full ninety seconds as the firefight along the street intensified. Then the voice began in Ellis' ear again. "Done. Now take a look. Tell me what's happening."

Ellis crab-walked to the opposite side of the rooftop and peered over the park-facing side. Sure enough, the Bradleys were moving out, heading northwest across the Ellipse. "I'll be damned," Ellis said into the phone. "It's actually working. Who are you really?"

"A friend."

The Bradleys had just disappeared under a canopy of sugar maple trees when something new registered in Ellis' peripheral vision – two M1A1 tanks slicing across the National Mall toward Constitution Avenue.

Ellis took a gander through the binoculars to confirm that she wasn't delusional. Sure enough, the tanks bore National Guard insignia. But it didn't make any sense that the stretched-thin Guard would dare go against so many Ulysses units, nor did it compute that they would send only two tanks.

The M1A1s had just hit the Ellipse's green when Ellis saw the Presidential motorcade coming up behind them. Six cars, with the Beast smack in the middle of the formation.

Something moved atop the Treasury Building. Treasury flanked the White House's East Wing and was directly across the immense South Lawn from the Eisenhower Building. Whomever controlled Treasury could turn the South Lawn into a shooting gallery, and it looked like Ulysses units had somehow fought their way back to the top.

Looking through the binoculars, Ellis was pretty sure one of them was holding something long and lethal over his shoulder. The combatant dropped to a kneeling position with, sure enough, a Javelin anti-tank missile. The motorcade had been spotted. The bastard was just waiting for a clear shot.

"Hey," Ellis said into the phone. "You still there? I need another miracle."

"I'm here," Nico replied, "but the Ulysses net sheriff just booted me out of the network."

"Can you get back in?"

"It'll take time."

Time was one thing Ellis didn't have. She hung up and steadied the M4's muzzle on the roof's lip and found the soldier in her scope at 310 yards. It was twice the recommended distance for the M4, which was designed for close combat. But there were no other options. The SWAT snipers were too far away.

She lost the convoy behind a grove of southern magnolias for a moment. They soon broke into view as they sped across the park's zero-milestone.

Seconds later, a combined 120 tons of hulking steel ripped through the South Lawn fence at full speed. The iron barrier crumpled like blades of grass under the

M1's treads. The motorcade poured onto the South Lawn through the massive holes in the fence.

Haley understood now. Since she had been hanging with Agent Rios, she had been thinking in football analogies, and this was no different than a basic trap play. The M1s were like offensive lineman creating holes in the defense. The cars in the motorcade were blockers, the Beast was the running back, and the end zone was the Oval Office itself.

It was now or never. Ellis returned her gaze into the scope of the M4, found the Javelin operator atop the Treasury Building, and moved the scope up three inches above the soldier's chest, calculating a slight arc in the bullet's trajectory across the 310 yards.

She pulled the trigger. Dust flew from the rooftop over the target's left shoulder. Damn. Ellis readjusted her aim and squeezed the trigger again, but the rifle's recoil did not come. The M4 was jammed.

*

From the south-facing windows of the Oval Office, the very one where Presidents from bygone eras had watched as protesters massed outside the South Lawn gates, Agent Carver spotted the motorcade, complete with escort tanks, rolling up the green toward the West Wing. The Presidential limo – the Beast – was in the middle of the formation. Base Runner still had a lot of ground to cover before she would be safe.

White light flashed from atop the Treasury Building. An instant later, the Javelin anti-tank missile slammed into the Beast. A huge cloud of smoke engulfed the lawn, obscuring an entire acre. Carver pushed LeBron under the desk.

It was the end, Carver thought. He had been told that the Beast could withstand a full-scale attack by a couple of maniacs with machine guns and grenades. It could probably even survive a roadside bomb. But he was pretty sure the car couldn't hold up against an armor-piercing missile.

Moments later, he was amazed to see the Beast crawl, blistered and smoldering, from the haze. A chunk of its front-end was twisted and cockeyed, and the length of its chassis was crooked, but the long black behemoth was intact and still moving, albeit much slower.

What it couldn't take was another hit. So why weren't those tanks closing ranks to protect Eva's car?

The Javelin anti-tank missile operator held the launcher vertically and looked to be reloading. Odds were slim that Ellis was going to be able to pick him off from her perch on the Eisenhower rooftop.

"Stay under the desk," Carver told LeBron. "If I'm not back in five minutes, hide in the Rose Garden."

Clutching his M4, Carver exited the office's east door and sprinted into the Rose Garden in a low crouch. He scurried to the very edge of the foliage, closing within about 110 yards of the Treasury Building. Without a scope, this was going to be an awfully hard shot with the rifle he had. Getting closer would mean running in the open grass. It would be suicide.

A fusillade of small arms fire peppered the motorcade as five other shooters came to the roof's edge.

One of the black sedans burst into flames and veered off on a collision course with the Eisenhower Building. Two others closed in towards the middle, as if to shield the President's car from the shooters. One of the M1 tanks followed accordingly.

Raising to one knee, Carver took aim at the missile operator. The enemy had completed the reload and was already lining up the Beast in his viewfinder for a second shot.

Like Ellis, Carver aimed slightly above his target, correcting for distance, and switched his carbine from double-shot bursts to single-shot mode. He exhaled and pulled the trigger.

The soldier leaned sideways, drooping unnaturally as the 5.56mm round ricocheted off his clavicle and lodged within his left lung. The launcher fell from his hands and hung on the roof's edge. A nearby soldier lunged for it, getting a hand on the device as the others came to his aid.

The replacement soldier managed to launch the missile. It hit the Beast squarely, engulfing the lawn once again in a fiery explosion. Carver feared the worst. There was no way the car could have withstood a second hit.

Judging by the way the Ulysses soldiers were pumping their fists, he was right. Carver wasn't about to give these bastards a chance to enjoy their apparent victory. Having found his range, Carver now switched the carbine back to fully automatic and let loose with several bursts into the cluster of troops. Two Ulysses soldiers fell immediately and the others melted away from the building's edge.

Meanwhile, a cauterized M1 tank – it had been grazed in the second hit on the Beast – rolled ever closer, seeming to slouch across the final fifty yards of lawn toward the West Wing. Its unscathed counterpart slowed to its side, as if hoping to draw hostile fire.

Peering through a cloud of dissipating smoke, Carver finally saw a welcome sight – a half-dozen armored SUVs bursting over the South Lawn fencing that the M1 tanks had so effectively crushed. He recognized the plates as those of the uniformed Secret Service, heavily armed units of highly trained White House police officers. Considering that Wainewright had relieved them of duty just thirty-six-hours earlier, Carver was surprised that any of them were sober enough to drive, much less fight.

Even if they had managed to kill Eva, perhaps they had at least repelled a full-scale Ulysses occupation.

It was then that Carver remembered the phone in the Oval Office, and his proclamation that Agent Rios, who at this moment was ready to sabotage the gas piping in the boiler room, should destroy the mansion if he didn't answer the land line on the executive desk. Unfortunately, Carver knew Rios to be a man of his word.

Carver got to his feet and raced back through the Rose Garden. Even over the roar of persistent fighting on 17th, the phone's distinctive old-world ring could be heard from well outside the open French doors. Carver rounded the corner, sprinted inside and lunged for the phone. "Carver," he spat into the receiver as LeBron poked his head out from under the desk. The line was dead.

"Run!" he screamed at LeBron as he tried to raise Rios on his cell phone. The kid rose up but was paralyzed at the sight of the approaching tanks. "Now!"

LeBron sprinted out to the relative safety of the Rose Garden just as Carver heard the northwest Oval Office door open behind him.

He swiveled around to reach for his M4, which he had laid on top of the Executive Desk. He was too late. General Wainewright stood across the room with an antique Colt .45 pointed straight at him. The *Stars and Stripes* journalists stood wide-eyed behind him.

Wainewright flashed an irritated smile as he spoke. "Step away from the Resolute Desk."

Carver couldn't help but laugh. He was obviously about to be shot. God forbid he might bleed on the General's future desk. "Resolute?" Carver quipped. "You've given the desk a name?"

"Idiot," Wainewright snapped. "The desk was named in the nineteenth century. Fact: the desk was carved from the timbers of H.M.S. *Resolute,* an abandoned British ship discovered by Americans. Queen Victoria was so grateful for the find that she presented the desk as a gift to President Rutherford B. Hayes in 1880."

"Hayes, huh? I think your obsession with assassinated Presidents borders on unhealthy."

Wainewright took aim and pulled back the revolver's lever.

The floor trembled. The old mansion let out a moan. Carver smelled gas. Pipes rattled within the walls. Dust fell from the ceiling. Special Agent Rios had come through after all. Carver smiled, knowing that even if he died, he would take the General with him.

The floor bucked beneath the General. Losing his balance, he groped for the journalists. Both braced themselves against the room's north wall. The floor rippled again, sending a ten-foot stretch of copper pipe jutting up violently through the floorboards. An eruption of yellow and blue flame gasped from the fractured pipe, setting fire to a wall tapestry and both journalists' uniforms.

The sprinkler system instantly sprang to life, emitting bursts of water from the ceiling so powerful that they stung Carver's neck and face. Rios had grossly underestimated the mansion's ability to protect itself from sabotage. The fire was doused immediately, and everyone and everything in the Oval Office was drenched. The General held onto the chaise as the building shuddered once again and the room filled with smoke. Carver seized the opportunity, grabbing the M4 from the desktop. Holding the weapon at his hip, he fired as Wainewright lost his balance on the hardwood floor, felling both of the fire-bitten journalists standing behind him.

He turned the muzzle toward Wainewright, but the wet carbine jammed. Carver found himself looking down the barrel of Wainewright's Colt .45. The General squeezed off a round at close range that grazed Carver's neck, unleashing a geyser of blood. The wounded agent vaulted over the desk and tackled the General.

As tiny aftershocks rumbled throughout the mansion, and the sprinkler system streamed bruising ropes of water from above, Carver kneed the general in the solar plexus and immobilized his shooting hand by stepping on the soft underside of his right forearm. Wainewright rocked his legs up under him and sent the more agile but smaller Carver head-first into an exposed piece of pipe.

The mansion's sprinkler system finally let up. Carver dropped to the soggy carpet and swung his legs clockwise, sweeping the old warhorse off his feet. Lincoln's opera glasses slid from his pocket onto the glass coffee table as he fell. Carver followed up with a left-right combination to Wainewright's face. Crimson blood sprayed from the General's broken nose.

A hard heel to the chest knocked the General's wind from his body, and he remained on his back trying to get air into his lungs. Carver grabbed his right arm and pulled it straight back toward him, out of its socket. He stepped over Wainewright and did the same to his left arm. Wainewright's upper limbs fell to his sides like wet noodles.

The General had no more fight in him, but Carver wasn't content to let him live. A man like Wainewright was always dangerous. Even if the ragtag alliance of forces outside were able to defeat the Ulysses troops, and the military fell in line behind Eva's successor, Wainewright could still brew up a world of trouble from a prison cell. He would still have the sympathy of thousands of officers in key positions across the military.

Carver removed the damaged glass top from the coffee table and held the jagged end vertically over Wainewright's neck – an improvised guillotine. "Don't!" Wainewright rasped. Carver raised the sheet of heavy glass four feet into the air and let it fall. A wave of warm blood drenched Carver's pant leg as the General's severed head rolled to the side.

Intermittent explosions and gunfire on the surrounding streets and rooftops slowly crept back into Carver's consciousness. He heard boots on the paved walkway just outside the Oval Office and turned to see uniformed Secret Service units running past the south-facing windows.

He exited the east door and walked out into the Rose Garden. Smoke was gradually clearing on the South Lawn as SWAT units replaced Ulysses soldiers atop the Treasury Building. At the edge of the Rose Garden, uniformed Secret Service pulled the crew from the M1 tank's charred turret.

His heart jumped as he recognized the first figure to emerge from the tank. It was Julian Speers, followed by a very alive Eva Hudson. She never had been in the Beast. It had been the decoy all along.

Carver felt pain shoot up through his groin. He limped through it. His shoulders were full of knots and his neck was stiffening badly. He was bleeding, but he didn't know where the blood was coming from.

A team of ERTs met him at the lawn's edge. Carver told them that there was a gas leak in the mansion. He told them there were armed Ulysses soldiers on the lower levels. He said that Special Agent Rios was inside and was likely in need of a coroner.

He heard none of their questions. He felt none of their hands as they probed his injuries. He just kept lurching through the wisps of smoke that swept like dirty fog across the lawn. He glimpsed Dex Jackson, then lost him in the haze. His eyes roamed the grounds for a soft, shady place to lie down, vaguely aware that the sound of gunfire on the surrounding streets was growing more sporadic. A light breeze blew, sending a welcome chill through his blood-soaked clothing.

The U.S.S. Ronald Reagan
The Mediterranean

An explosion lit up the night sky just 100 yards from the U.S.S. John Kerry, one of four destroyers floating between the Ronald Reagan and the hundreds of Israeli vessels carrying refugees. Captain White saw the flash in the distance out the bridge observation windows. Only an hour earlier, White and his direct reports had been listening to the VOA news coverage from the Lincoln Memorial. But the broadcast had been suddenly interrupted with commercial-free classic rock.

Captain White turned the radio down as the Kerry's CO, Commander Deke Perkins, hailed the Rear Admiral on the radio: "Fishing boat just rammed the ferry closest to us. It's listing to stern. Tons of passengers are jumping overboard."

"Copy that, Kerry," came the Admiral's response. *"Monitor and keep your distance."*

"Negative," Perkins said. There was a small boat circling and shooting the survivors. "This is a rat kill."

"Repeat, monitor only."

"Negative," Perkins replied.

"You're disobeying a direct order?" came the Admiral's retort. *"You better get your dress whites out, Commander Perkins. I'm penciling in your court martial, son."* There was no response from Perkins, who turned the Kerry and began steaming toward the floating inferno.

Less than two minutes later, the ship's radio sounded again. White answered, expecting an earful from the Admiral. The voice on the other end was unfamiliar to him. "Captain White," the voice said, "this is President Eva Hudson. I'm with Defense Secretary Jackson."

"Captain, the Admiral has been relieved of duty," Dex said. "The President is directing our armed forces to provide immediate military assistance to Israel. You are to engage the Iranian air and ground units with indiscriminate force. Do you understand?"

When White issued the directive over the ship's PA, the crew's elation could be heard from every corner of the ship. Operation Wailing Wall was a go.

NINE MONTHS LATER

Eastern Cape, South Africa
6:45 p.m. local time

Carver drove through scattered rain over twisting one-lane mountain roads. The rental car's GPS was useless, and his phone hadn't gotten signal since leaving Johannesburg early that morning. He stopped for directions often. This was not only because there were so few road signs in the rural Eastern Cape. It was also because most of the people he asked for directions had never been more than 20 miles from home.

As night fell he listened to African pop music to stay awake. The highway became a series of mesmerizing canyon switchbacks that hugged steep cliffs without so much as a single guardrail. Ten hours after leaving Johannesburg International Airport, he got petrol in Stutterheim, a sleepy little town in the heart of farm country, and went on through the hilly, golden boondocks toward the backwater village of Kei Mouth on the eastern shore.

The last terrestrial radio station fizzled out as he entered the former Transkei, land of the Xhosa tribe. Xhosa children bartered beaded necklaces for candy bars as he waited twenty minutes for a single-car ferry to take him across the Kei River.

Carver entered the village two hours later. There were few services in town, and the few that existed had posted signs saying CLOSED FOR WINTER in English and Afrikaans. Business windows – all of them – were dark. Finally he spotted the sign that read BED AND BREAKFAST that had been included in the intel report. He turned down a spooky-looking street that led to a gray cement building. This was supposed to be the place. It had better be, Carver thought. He had come a very long way from Washington under completely unreasonable time constraints.

He shut off the car engine and opened the car door. A pack of dogs raced out from under the front steps. Skinny, tenacious mutts. All bones and teeth. In the face of a hard drizzle, Carver fended these hounds of hell off with the car door, bonking their bony heads with it as they bit and tugged at his left ankle. He felt the familiar warm trickle of blood dampen his sock. Barking in the distance spared him further bloodshed as the pack suddenly broke away, howling at breakneck speed down the street he had driven in on.

"We're closed!" yelled a woman's voice from the motel office. She spoke from behind a screen. She sounded American. Good. This was definitely the place.

He unfurled himself from the car, smoothed the wrinkles in his gray suit and approached the building with his hands in the air.

"I'll shoot," the voice warned.

"I'd rather you didn't," Carver said as he measured his approach. He stood several feet from the door and could only make out a shadow in the dense screen door. "It's Madge, right?"

More silence. Then the voice said, "I suggest you get back in the car."

"Tell your husband Blake Carver is here to see him."

He heard her step away from the door. She returned moments later and opened it wide for Agent Carver to enter.

He stepped inside. The house smelled of barbecue. Aside from an expensive-looking entertainment console at the living room's far wall, the place was sparsely furnished. There were few books and no pictures on the wall except for a cheap print of DaVinci's *The Last Supper*.

Madge held a sawed-off shotgun. She looked unhappy. She had gained a great deal of weight since she had last been photographed by the CIA. Her long brown locks had been clipped into a short, unflattering cut. Madge was graying around the temples, and judging by the jagged pattern of her bangs, she had done it herself using shearing scissors.

"Nice dogs," Carver said. "Yours?"

Madge didn't smile. "The kitchen." She pointed to the next room.

Carver found Nico Gold sitting at the kitchen table with three kinds of meat on a plate before him. He looked much as he had when Carver and O'Keefe had first met him in the Lee Federal Penitentiary the previous year. The African sun had added little pigment to his pale skin, and the meat-centered African diet had hardly fleshed out his lanky frame. He had, however, dispensed with his eyeglasses and had dyed his hair blonde. The tattoos that had read "EVA" on both forearms were gone, replaced with a simple heart with a ribbon around it that said JESUS. He wore a t-shirt that said OBEY in stylized font.

"Close the door," Nico told him.

Carver sat in the chair where Madge had no doubt been eating across from her husband minutes before. The ex-con's face was full of dread. He had the sweet smell of alcohol on his breath. There was an empty bottle of pinotage on the table and another that was half-full.

"Dreamed the grim reaper was coming for me last night," Nico said. "Couldn't shake the feeling all day. Never had a dream like that before. So bad."

Carver said nothing. He watched Nico's hand shake as he held his wine glass.

"I need to know how you found me," Nico continued. "I don't use credit cards. I've taken nobody into confidence. My only bank accounts in this country are in a town 200 miles away under a different name. They draw their funds from banks abroad that have no idea who I am."

"Don't blame yourself," Carver said. "You were good. The best."

"So how in God's name did you find me?"

"Your eyes gave you away," Carver said, referring to the corrective vision procedure he'd had in Durban earlier that year. "Organ theft is a bit of a problem here. The government requires that doctors document every eye that gets the surgery. The images are uploaded into a national database. Naturally, we have a script running that scans every image of every retina and matches them up with profiles on our list."

Nico pounded the table with his fists, bouncing the dinner plates.

"Everything okay?" Madge yelled from the other room.

"Fine dear," Nico yelled back through the door. He steadied his gaze on Carver and lowered his voice.

Nico reached for the open bottle of pinotage on the table and poured himself a full glass. He offered some to Carver, who politely declined. "I'd forgotten what a teetotaler you are," he said. "Probably made it all the way to Africa without so much as a wink of sleep or a drop of caffeine."

"I'm not here to talk about me."

"I read about O'Keefe," Nico said. "I'm sorry. I could tell you two were close."

Carver got up, pulled a cup from the cupboard and helped himself to some tap water. He drank eight ounces and put the cup down. "I don't discuss Agent O'Keefe with anyone."

Nico finished his glass. "So. I guess Eva sent you?"

"Careful. Nobody calls her by her first name now. Not even me."

"She's going to hand me over to the Saudis, isn't she?"

"She was thinking about it. Then she read Haley Ellis' report detailing the miraculous way that five Ulysses Bradleys disappeared from the South Lawn just in time for the motorcade to come through."

Nico folded his arms across his chest, looking partially validated. "Well, if you're packing a

Presidential pardon, I'd say it's high time you whip it out."

"The way the President sees it, you owe her one more favor."

"I'm retired," he said. "Don't even own a computer. I've spent the last year learning Afrikaans and Xhosa. Madge tends to the guests during fishing season and cooks. I make repairs to the place, read books. We're not hurting anybody."

"I don't have that luxury." Carver pulled two newly issued passports from his jacket pocket. Nico picked them up. They were American passports containing his and Madge's real names and digitally aged photos. "We have an issue that needs tending to. Your services are required."

Then he pulled three South African Airways tickets from his pocket and laid them on the table. The flight was to leave from Johannesburg International Airport and land in Washington some 17 hours later.

"This flight is tomorrow morning!" Nico raved. "We'd have to drive all night to get to Johannesburg in time."

Carver gripped Nico's spindly right arm and pulled him from the table. "Good point. You've got one minute to convince Madge that it's a good idea. I'll give you ten to pack."

Made in the USA
Lexington, KY
24 March 2012